Undead Dread

Blue Moon Sacramento

Alex Gates, Steve Higgs

Contents

Under the Streetlight.
Friday, June 30th.
2347hrs.

A BRANCH CRACKED IN the dead of night, firing like a dry bone snapping clean in half. Then the night fell eerily quiet. The crickets, for only a second, stopped with their stridulations. In the dead of summer, beneath a mostly full moon and a bed of stars, a hot, barely existent breeze whispered across the street—but even that halted for a breath at the breaking noise. The owls ceased to ask their constant, monosyllabic question, though Jackson Armstead thought of it.

Who?

Who was there?

Someone had followed Jackson home from the movie theater. They stayed out of sight, ducking behind trees or bushes, disappearing into shadows whenever Jackson glanced over his shoulder.

At the sharp, sudden fracture, Jackson shifted toward the source of the noise. Like the rest of the night in response to the sound, he held his breath, adding to the heap of eery silence.

A hundred yards ahead stood a low-lit streetlight. Its dying illumination barely touched the cement below it. From where Jackson had come, none of the streetlights shined at all.

The city neglected the houses on Ottobonn Way, saving their budget for upscale neighborhoods. Whenever they found enough time and money (and the excuse) to replace the failed streetlights, they would discover them shattered. Broken, not burned out. Only darkness existed beneath their bulbs.

Behind him, Jackson saw dim, flickering porch lights. He saw a yellow hue emanating from living rooms or kitchen windows. The effect provided a strange, patch-work glow that made the darkness even more prevalent. The old homes stood buried in deep shadows, their properties an ocean of oily gloom. The exterior lights, those that actually chased away the night, shined like dying torches. Moths and mosquitoes buzzed around them, creating a living mist.

Who! Who! The owls broke the silent, paralyzing spell.

The night crashed back into motion and noise.

Crickets chirped. From the distance, the unending traffic of Sacramento buzzed along Highway 50 and through the downtown streets.

Jackson exhaled. He returned his attention forward and continued his trek home.

He lived at the end of Ottobonn Way. Well, he lived on the corner of Ottobonn Way and Lincoln Road. More accurately, as a junior in college, he lived in his parents' house (with his brat sister, River) on the corner of Ottobonn Way and Lincoln Road.

Fortunately for Jackson's parents, their house bore the Lincoln Road address, which represented a safer, more affluent street and helped with the home's overall market value... if they ever sold. They had lived there before Jackson was born. Still, they had the Lincoln Road address, and the city had bothered to install a functional and brightly lit streetlight directly in front of the house.

Jackson often complained about the light, though. Why wouldn't he? The glow cut through his bedroom window all night, every night. He had stuffed a pillow into the transom window. He had hung a sheet. He had tried a sleeping mask. He had stooped to bartering with River to switch rooms. Her walls were pink and her bedroom smaller and nearer to their parents' bedroom, but Jackson no longer cared.

He wanted nothing more than to rid his room of that light.

Except at the moment, walking home alone in the late dark from the movie theater.

Jackson stared at the light from a hundred yards away, like a captain tracks the beam from a lighthouse. He moved toward it, following that conical glow. That bar of bright light existed as his safety base (like when he used to play tag as a kid and there was always a base to find refuge) from the night, from the strange silence and the stranger noise.

From that presence that existed just out of sight and had followed him.

Ninety yards away.

Eighty.

The Armstead's lived less than a mile away from a movie theater and a few restaurants in a niche little area of downtown Sacramento. It wasn't a rowdy night scene, but it boasted of a few solid restaurants and an old cinema recently remodeled to include reclining seats in their three auditoriums.

Jackson had spent the night on a date at one such restaurant—a Mexican place with the best chips and guacamole in all of Sacramento; also, their margaritas were tasty enough to always order at least two.

He and Cecilia had met in their summer British Literature class at a community college. The professor, who wanted to avoid teaching during the summer at almost any cost, had assigned a group project for the class. He had randomly generated groups of two, creating seven total groups. Much to Jackson's delight, he found himself paired with Cecilia Ochoa.

The professor *assigned* each group a gothic novel to read, analyze, and teach to the rest of the class (Mr. Rice preferred his students to teach

each other while he sat back and collected his paychecks). After a few study sessions on their chosen novel, *Frankenstein*, Jackson found the courage to ask Cecilia on a date.

Dinner at his favorite hole-in-the-wall Mexican restaurant and a movie afterward.

The two agreed to forgo seeing the latest blockbuster and purchase tickets to an animated film over three weeks old. Jackson couldn't remember the name of the movie. To be fair, he watched none of it. They made their decision on which film to watch based on two important factors. One, the time matched when they would be at the cinema. Two, very few children went to watch a movie after nine o'clock, and less went to watch a movie over three weeks old after nine o'clock.

Cecilia and Jackson owned the auditorium for the ninety-seven minutes the animation played.

Forty yards away from the streetlight now.

The fear born from the night going silent for a half-second earlier had eased... mostly.

The presence following him from the movie theater seemed to have vanished in that span. It no longer felt like predatory eyes bored into the back of his skull.

Maybe he had been paranoid and his imagination had overtaken his better sense as he walked across the dark, dangerous sidewalk of Ottobonn Way. Maybe now that he had come nearer to the streetlight constantly shining through his bedroom window, rational thought had stapled itself back into place.

With a renewed calm and confidence, his awareness dwindled and his mind shifted back to the movie theater—to the embarrassment at the movie theater.

How would he pass his summer class now? To pass meant he had to do the assignment, and to do the assignment, Jackson had to meet with Cecilia for the group project. Was that still a possibility after the disastrous date?

"Whoever came up with reclining seats in a movie theater... they're a genius," Jackson had said, leaning his chair back and glancing at Cecilia. She looked good, and Jackson wasn't shy to tell her. "You're sexy. You know that?"

Cecilia stood from her chair and climbed atop him. She kissed his neck and his lips.

The animal characters from the animated movie sang the opening song. Their high-pitched, cartoonish voices serenaded the moment.

Cecelia's soft hands snaked down to Jackson's pants. They worked his buttons and zipper with ease.

Jackson fumbled with her bra strap, clumsy and incapable. After a few awkward seconds, Cecelia reared back and sighed impatiently. She bent one arm behind her back and unsnapped the latch. The bra loosened inside her shirt.

Like a ravenous lion introduced to his prey, Jackson dove into her chest—squeezing and groping and biting, his lips and hands frantic and rough.

Their engagement didn't last long after that. In fact, it ended before the characters finished their introductory musical number.

Cecilia returned to the seat beside Jackson. She scrolled through her phone. A bored expression showed on her face from the illuminated screen.

Jackson, whose pants had never come off during their short-lived activity, excused himself and went to the restroom. When he returned to the auditorium, Cecilia had gone.

Ten yards from the streetlight now. Ten yards was as close as he would ever come again to his street corner.

Someone stepped from the hedges surrounding the Armstead property. They stood squarely in the spotlight.

Jackson gasped. His earlier terror returned, doubled and tripled. He backpedaled and tripped over his feet (his athleticism rivaled his prowess with a woman). He fell on his butt hard enough to bite his tongue. Blood filled his mouth. His lips murmured incoherently as his mind processed who—what—stood before him.

Impossible, he thought.

It was impossible.

Yet, despite the insanity and the impossibility, Maria Lopez swayed at the corner of the sidewalk. His dead ex-girlfriend stood directly in front of Jackson's house. If he screamed, his dad would most likely hear and bookmark the latest sermon and run out the front door.

Except, Jackson couldn't scream anymore than he could last longer than a minute with Cecilia's gentle hand. His voice was like trying to scream with his face buried in mud.

Jackson was present when Maria Lopez had tragically died five years ago in a boating accident.

Maria was wakeboarding. Jackson was drinking, and he had been drinking most of the day. He was also driving the boat... without control or regard for Maria's safety.

She fell.

The side of her face smashed into the edge of the board. Maria had died in a second. Less than a second.

Jackson's friends had all been on the boat when the accident occurred. One of them, Ashton Snell—a high school track athlete with a scholarship to college and a strict Mormon—never drank. Fortunately for Jackson, Ashton found it morally acceptable to lie.

When the police asked about what happened, Ashton lied through his Mormon teeth. "I drove the boat. It was an accident."

Six of them attended the boating expedition.

Five of them returned home to their families.

UNDEAD DREAD

One of them had died.

None of them faced legal trouble.

Now, under the streetlight, Maria Lopez had returned from the dead.

She stood spotlighted by the overhead streetlight.

In the accident, her shins had snapped where they bent unnaturally in their boots, and her face was akin to a pumpkin after taking a hit from a baseball bat.

Beneath the light, Jackson could see her pulpy face and the fractures in her shins. He noted the waxy, undead pallor of her face.

Maria dripped water onto the cement beneath her, creating a reflective puddle. She wore the same dark-green bikini from that fateful afternoon. Jackson remembered her body in that bikini—it was a sight difficult to forget.

A sickening thought crossed his mind. *She still looks good wearing it.* That almost made him lose his dinner and three margaritas.

Maria wobbled on her broken legs. Her bones jutted from her skin. After a second, maybe a minute or an hour of staring at each other in horrified silence, she hissed at Jackson. Most of the teeth on the right side of her face no longer existed.

Jackson, still sitting on the asphalt, scrambled back to his feet. He stared at the undead woman. "How?" His voice barely leaked from his mud-filled mouth.

The zombie, for that's what she was—a corpse risen from the dead (he had attended her funeral)—charged toward him in an awkward, unnatural gait. The undead creature moved lightning quick for someone with two broken legs and half a face.

Jackson turned and ran back through the dark street he had come from... or so he intended. His body failed to move. Twice tonight his body had failed him. Where before it had sprinted, though, now it froze.

Fight or flight... or freeze.

Maria Lopez, the woman he had killed in a drunk boating accident, lunged at him. She was small in stature, but vicious, and she wielded an unnatural strength.

The strength of the dead, Jackson thought, his last thought before his head snapped (like a dry bone snapping clean in half) off the cement.

The streetlight's glow dimmed and went dark. After all the complaining he had done, the light finally stopped shining.

The Vampire. Tuesday, July 4th. 0148hrs.

THE VAMPIRE OF SACRAMENTO'S long, taloned fingers broke through the window screen like a cadaverous hand bursting from freshly filled dirt.

For over a month, he had diluted his human supply of blood with that of animal's blood. If he perfectly drained every ounce of blood from his victims, he would collect about a gallon (maybe a gallon-and-a-half). That allowed him around sixteen nights of sustenance, or one cup of blood per night, to continue living. He could extend that time by mixing animal blood into human blood. However, it never worked as well. When rationing human blood by incorporating the animal blood, he always felt bloated, thick, woolly in the head.

The concoction kept him alive, but it provided nothing more.

Only human blood served as the true treatment of his condition. To harvest it proved more than difficult and dangerous, though.

The vampire had started his predatory practices in the slums of society—in the dark corners of the world, where no one cared to look. He preyed on sex workers, runaways, the homeless population. He chose his victims carefully, opting to hunt those tapped out on booze or drugs.

Though society turned their eyes away from what they considered the stains on their community, the forgotten population didn't forget about each other. The homeless looked out for one another, as did the sex workers. They all kept tabs on the transient kids, who searched desperately for a better life in all the wrong places.

His potential victims noticed his menacing presence after five brutal murders. The vampire hadn't any precision at the beginning of his hunting career. He had no technique beyond cutting deep gashes into their necks and bathing in their currents of blood.

They became aware, and they adapted, forcing the vampire to search for new hunting grounds. Otherwise, he would starve to death.

As a vampire, he couldn't cross a threshold unless the owner invited him through. An open or unlocked door—or window—translated to an open invitation.

To break bread. To share wine.

The modern vampire had its advantages with invitations. Businesses, especially night-exclusive businesses such as bars and clubs, posted their invitations in bright, neon letters. They welcomed all.

He graduated from the rats of society to the gerbils—both rodents, though people see one as a pest and the other as a pet. With humans, capitalism owned these people, and its bars and clubs were their cages.

The vampire snickered at the imagery. He thought himself clever, especially considering his analogy. Dracula had power over rats. He could command them to do his bidding, just as Chase would soon command this city to serve and obey him.

The music in the clubs had thumped, beating hard enough to wobble the vampire's eyeballs. Lights flashed and strobed in a brilliance of bright colors, casting the jumping and dancing crowd in hues of pink, green, and orange.

The night of his first meal (according to the police and media), Chase slithered to the back corner of the club. He stood out of reach from the stretching lights, hidden in the darkness. There he watched the crowd. He ogled over their youthful, sweaty bodies. He could smell their sweat, the alcohol and drugs tinging it.

After hours of hiding in the corner and watching, Chase saw her. He instantly knew. He would feast on her. She would serve as the gateway from one hunting ground to the next. She would represent his transformation from primal and savage to ordered and precise.

No one else in the club mattered. The music and the light swallowed them whole. Only that one woman existed, ensconced in a radiant, white glow, like an angel appearing in a vision of Heaven.

She left with three of her friends. They staggered along the downtown sidewalks.

He followed them to their apartment. He watched their home all night, all the next night, and all of that week. He watched and waited.

The vampire had packaged nearly three-quarters of her blood (it was his first attempt at storing his harvest, and he had spilled some). He shelved it in a freezer. Over the two weeks, he consumed one cup every night.

He stuck to the same pattern—frequenting a bar or a club, waiting for his intuition to highlight his prey, to identify the weak from the herd.

The second victim was an old man from a gay bar.

The third was an old woman at a dive bar.

The fourth was another old man from a strip club.

Chase perfected his practice, and he learned to collect the last drop of blood from their bodies. Each night, he mixed animal blood with the blood of his victims.

As the time passed, though, and his supply waned, the media had caught up to him, as had police investigations. Chase returned to the familiar well of the nightlife. Except, he had found the downtown streets flooded with security and law enforcement. They combed the bars and clubs in search of him, of the vampire.

Not caring to risk a confrontation with a police officer, Chase once again migrated to a new hunting locale—residential neighborhoods. These proved more difficult than ever.

Three weeks had passed. No unlocked houses welcomed his presence. How could he enter a home and feast unless they invited him in?

Three weeks.

Over four hundred homes.

Zero prey.

He had nearly exhausted his stash in the freezer. Before, he had mixed a fourth of animal blood with three-quarters human blood. Now that role had reversed. Soon, he would only have animal blood to live on.

Then, as it always had, his persistence paid off.

He found an open window, though it had a screen mesh acting as a barrier. Did that count? No, it didn't.

It was unlocked and open, welcoming the vampire into the home.

Unforced Entry. Tuesday, July 4th. 0150hrs.

THE VAMPIRE STARED INTO the dark room beyond the window. The torn screen flapped in the gentle breeze.

What if multiple people slept inside the house? Who did he harvest?

Chase would do as he had always done—hunt through instinct. If his instinct directed him to slaughter an entire family, he would, without hesitation. If his instinct guided him to carefully and quietly take the life of only one person, he would.

He crawled through the window and landed on a carpeted floor in a bedroom filled with boxes and a spare, stripped bed. Chase stood still for a moment, listening to see if someone had noticed his intrusion.

After a few quiet seconds, he glanced around the spare bedroom. Chase leaned over and pried the flaps open on the box nearest to him, opening it. Paper-wrapped photographs in decorative frames stood in a line like a drawer of old records.

Records like his father played in the living room.

Chase's father would dance with Chase's mother to Elvis Presley. They would spin and laugh beneath the orange fanlight, stealing a quick kiss every so often.

Chase would watch them, at least until his mother grabbed his skinny arm and dragged him to the rug. His father shoved the coffee table off to the side, creating enough room for a three-person dancefloor.

Elvis Presley picked up the pace from *Can't Help Falling in Love* to *Hound Dog*.

They danced until their stamping, sliding feet cut their living rug into shreds, and then they collapsed onto the couch, laughing and wiping away tears.

Chase shivered at the memory—a memory long ago dead and buried.

He reached into the box and removed and unwrapped a picture. He blew off the dust that had settled across the thin glass.

The picture portrayed an elderly couple, maybe in their mid-seventies. They stood before a dazzling Eiffel Tower at night. The two people in the picture mirrored Chase's parents well—so in love, despite the corrosion from time and experience spent together. They held each other tight, and they smiled like two teenagers wildly in love and running from the world.

Chase brought the picture closer to his face and sniffed, as if he could smell what remained of the couple's life through the grainy pixels and the dusty memory.

He dug through the other boxes and found linens, clothing, and books, along with decorative trinkets and knickknacks. Junk. Clutter. Unnecessary materials.

Had the elderly couple recently moved homes? It seemed likely, but Chase didn't think so. People as old as that couple in the picture didn't just move into a new house. They moved into a care facility.

Chase wondered if they had passed away, if he stood in the house of their son or daughter who had inherited their junk.

The vampire felt a temporary moment of... sadness.

His parents had passed away almost two years ago, and their passing had staked him through the heart. Chase hadn't recovered, the wound hadn't even scarred over yet. It continued to bleed and hurt.

He turned over the picture of the couple at the Eiffel Tower, removed it from the frame, folded the photograph in half a few times, and stuffed it in his back pocket. Chase didn't know their names, had never met them, but he missed them all the same. He would grieve for them later that night... as he consumed the blood of their son or their daughter.

The vampire crept into the dark hallway and listened.

The house was a crypt—silent as a tomb.

Chase lived in the darkness, and his eyes had adjusted over the years. To his right was a hallway leading to three doors, most likely bedrooms and a bathroom. To his left, a living room and a kitchen.

Maybe the picture of the elderly couple had softened him and distracted him from his hunger, but curiosity now attracted him to the living room.

He ran his fingers along the wall as he walked, and he studied the hanging photographs. One of them he removed and regarded.

Three people—a man, a woman, and a child—posed at Disneyland. They offered their most forced smiles to the camera. Chase touched the child's face. Mom, father, and child, just like his family, though they had never forced smiles. Happiness came as naturally to them as breathing.

Chase's heartbeat quickened. Could he separate a family? If not, could he slaughter the entire family?

"I have to."

If not, he didn't know when he could find another welcoming home. It had taken him over two hundred attempts to find this unlocked house. Could he survive another three weeks with his measly supply of blood?

Chase didn't think so. He had to harvest.

The vampire settled his mind and returned to his mission. To his starvation. He was a predator, those in the house were his prey. The dead parents didn't matter. The family of three didn't matter. Nothing mattered but survival, but extracting blood.

They had welcomed him into their home, and he would feast.

Chase backtracked through the house. He pushed open the first closed door he came to—a bathroom. He continued down the hallway. It brought him to a fork with two doors on either side of him.

With little thought or reason, he pushed open the door to his left.

It exposed a child's bedroom. Toys and unfolded laundry littered the floor. A sound machine played ocean noise, and a low, red light emanated from the device, diluting the darkness.

A little boy slept in the twin bed. His mother slept beside him, snuggled up tightly.

Chase licked his lips. His heartbeat raced, pattering in his chest like fleeing footsteps.

He and his mom used to sleep like that in his bed. She would read to him and sing to him, and they would fall asleep together. During the night, she would wake and return to her bed with his father. Sometimes, Chase would tag after her, and they would all sleep together.

The kid is too small, Chase thought. *So is the mother.*

Also, if he pounced on the mother, that would wake the child, who might scream and wake the father. A predator always attacked the isolated prey.

Chase backed out of the room, quietly closing the door behind him.

He opened the other door, the one on his right; the one where the father slept alone.

Darkness bled through the master bedroom. A nightlight didn't cut through it, and a sound machine didn't obscure the perfect silence of the night.

The vampire drifted into the bedroom like a phantom. He glided across the carpet without making a sound. When he reached the edge of the bed, he stared at the husband. The man had looked bigger in the pictures, taller and broader. Up that close, the man had an average build—five-feet-ten and a hundred-sixty pounds.

Chase swelled with excitement and confidence as he drooled over his helpless, sleeping prey. He loomed over the man who lightly snored, removing the blood-crusted razor, the leakproof plastic garbage bags, and the rope.

Once ready, the vampire crawled into the bed.

The man stirred. His breath hitched. But he settled, and he didn't wake.

He would never wake again.

Detective Ted Wilson. Tuesday, July 4th. 1057hrs.

Fred Rogers, my oversized assistant, stared blankly across the office and snacked absentmindedly on a bag of popcorn.

I followed his gaze to the window. It overlooked the third floor of the next-door building. I returned my attention to Fred and cocked my head.

He spurred into action, diving to the ground and grabbing the trash-can beside my desk. The rough, heaving sound of vomit splashing against plastic interrupted our slow morning.

He returned to a slouched position, dropping his head against the chair's backrest and staring at the ceiling.

"I've had that garbage can since college," I said. "You ruined it."

"If you've had this since college, someone should've ruined it long ago. You can't convince me I'm the first person to get sick in there."

I cracked a knuckle. "You nervous?"

"What gave it away?" Fred cleared his throat and smirked. "I used to always throw up before games. I played football my entire life. You think I would have gotten used to the nerves and the crowds, but they only got bigger from Friday to Saturday to Sunday, and I only got more and more anxious. Threw up before every single game."

"That's a good thing, right? Doesn't that mean you care?"

"Why does that mean I care?"

"I don't know." I frowned. "I thought I've heard that before from Michael Jordan... or someone like that. Nerves mean you care about what you're doing."

"I've never heard that. I don't think it's true either."

"No?"

"It's not like I care about Vincent all that much. Why am I nervous about officiating his wedding?"

"Because you're afraid of everything," Alina said. She was my sixteen-year-old intern. She leaned against the office's front door frame with her arms crossed. "I once saw you jump and yelp at your own shadow."

"It snuck up on me." Fred chuckled.

"Why aren't you in school?" I asked Alina. "Summer session doesn't let out until 1100hrs, and it's..." I trailed off, glancing at my new watch, "just now 1100hrs."

"Last day of my four-week session was yesterday. I only had to take a test, and it was easy, and I finished early."

"How did you do?" Fred asked.

"Aced it." Alina popped off the doorframe and closed the door behind her. "Also, today is the Fourth of July. It's a national holiday. No school, even if I had school." She plopped into the second client chair set before my desk and wrinkled her nose. "Gross. What smells so bad?"

"My breakfast," Fred said. "And second breakfast. And my snack." He shoved another handful of popcorn into his mouth.

Alina glanced at the trashcan and grimaced. "Ew. What's wrong with you? Did you drink too much last night? You know it was Monday last night? What were you doing drinking? Or are you sick? Freddie—"

"I told you not to call me that."

"If you're sick, why are you at work? You know how I'm a germaphobe. If you sneeze near me—"

Fred reared back and lurched forward with unmatched aggression, sneezing the ultimate dad sneeze, though he faked the entire thing with perfect exaggeration.

Alina jumped to her feet and backed away. "August, send him home."

"He's not sick," I said. "He's officiating Vincent's wedding tonight, and he's scared."

Alina nodded as understanding settled over her. She shuffled back to the empty chair. Before taking her seat, she socked Fred in the shoulder. "You're the worst."

Fred grinned. "Love you, too, Kiddo."

Alina rolled her eyes. "Who has a wedding on a Tuesday night, anyway?"

"That's the question you have about this wedding?" I asked. "That's what shocks you? Not, who marries their dead wife's long-lost twin sister intending to pretend she's his dead wife?"

"Who asks me to officiate a wedding?" Fred's eyes returned to the window overlooking the alley.

"You going to vomit again?" I asked.

"No." He spoke as if gargling on bile, though.

"When you two headed off to do all that wedding stuff?" Alina asked.

"After work." I glanced at my desk, which was currently empty of any work. "The wedding doesn't start until nine. They're hoping to sync their, *you may kiss the bride,* with fireworks."

"That's so gross." Alina stuck out her tongue. "I might vomit. I think I'd rather sit here and bask in Fred's upchuck than watch them kiss to fireworks." The kid snapped her fingers as a stray thought centered in her mind. "Speaking of kissing to fireworks, guess who has a plus one?"

"No way!" Fred's attention wavered from the window and focused on Alina. "You?"

"Why do you sound so surprised?"

"Because you're... well, you're you."

"What's that mean?" Alina asked.

"You know," Fred said.

"I don't know. Elaborate."

"You're, like, I don't know, a know-it-all, and you talk a lot, and you do this thing where you don't let others finish—"

"In other words, I'm obnoxious and rude?"

"Your words, not mine." Fred scratched his head and stared at the trashcan. He cleared his throat and stood. "I should probably take this out, yeah?"

"Probably." Alina scowled at the oversized man, and he no longer seemed so large.

Fred collected the trashcan and hurried out of the office.

"Aren't you too young to date?" I asked with a grin.

"Don't get me started."

"What's his name?" I asked.

"Are you going to be all weird about this?"

"What?"

"You're not my dada, and I'm a big girl."

"I only asked for his name."

"Why do you care who it is? So you can look him up, run his name through your police connections and see what he's all about? Well, he's about drug trafficking and drug running and drug selling and drug using. He's actually a member of a motorcycle club called Sons of Anarchy. He's murdered someone... multiple someones."

"I stopped caring. You don't have to tell me anymore."

"He once punched someone through their chest, ripped out their heart, and ate it while it was still beating right before their dying eyes."

"Does Maya know?" I asked.

"About his tendency for violence and wanton aggression?"

"That you have a date."

"Are you kidding me?" Alina scoffed. "No. Never. She's worse than any overprotective, simple-minded father who can't dare see his little princess in a healthy relationship with another man. So, in an act of rebellion, that little princess dates the prototypical guy she knows her father will hate the most. And tensions flare and arguments intensify. To further prove her father wrong, to prove his chauvinistic, old-school beliefs make no sense and he's a moron, she and her little get-back-at-daddy boyfriend spend a lot of time in the back of his car, and she calls her boyfriend daddy, and she does it all to get back at her daddy for oppressing her and suffocating her and controlling her." Alina stopped her rant to breathe.

I twisted my wrists in a slow circle. "So, Maya doesn't know?"

"You didn't let me finish my story."

Knowing I would hear the end of her story no matter what, I folded and said, "Abridged version, please."

"Girl gets pregnant. Daddy kills the father of the baby. Daddy goes to jail." Alina frowned. "I don't like that. Abridged versions suck because nothing naturally flows. It's too staccato and bare bones, you know?"

"Why won't you tell Maya?"

"She's worse than the dad who killed his baby princess's boyfriend. She's so much worse."

Maya was Alina's aunt. They lived together at the moment. Alina's mom had disappeared into the ether, which apparently she did from time to time when she relapsed into drugs. This time, though, she had been missing for over two months, nearly matching her longest absence. Alina's dad had moved out of state to live with another woman not long before that.

"I told Glacia," Alina said.

Glacia was a previous romantic friend of mine who lived a state away in Oregon.

"What does she think of your plus-one?" I asked.

"She likes him."

"Well, if Glacia approves, so do I."

"Do you have a date?" Alina pulled in her lips, instantly aware of what she had asked and visibly embarrassed.

A little over a month ago, my short-term girlfriend, Cambria Parker, was murdered by a deranged psychopath. I hadn't really thrown myself back into the dating world since then. Instead, I had spent a lot of time with my sister and her husband, with my brother, my parents, and my friends. In fact, I hadn't really accepted any fresh cases during that month off.

I'm a paranormal investigator for the world-renowned company Blue Moon Investigative Agency, established by Tempest Michaels. Normally, I would have accepted as much work as possible, drowning my life with the cases.

After Cambria's death, though, I focused on living, not just existing. I had earned enough money to take a break. I had done just that, rewiring my brain to enjoy life again.

"I'm sorry," Alina said. "I didn't mean to..."

"It's okay." I shared a gentle smile. "I do, actually."

Fred entered the office at that not-so-convenient moment, without a trashcan, of course. I figured he had tossed it in the dumpster outside. "You do what?" he asked, sitting beside Alina in the second client chair.

"Have a plus-one," I said.

"What?" Fred's eyes widened. "You have a plus-one?"

"I do."

"Who? Palmela Handerson?"

"Gross," Alina said. "Why are you like that?"

"Why didn't you tell me?" Fred asked, ignoring Alina.

"Because you would blow it out of proportion and make it weird."

"That sounds nothing like me. Now, who is it?"

"I'm not telling you."

"Glacia?" Alina asked, her face brightening with excitement. She had a strong bond with the woman who lived in Oregon. "Is she coming down?"

"It's not Glacia," I said.

"Who?" Fred demanded.

"If Alina tells me her plus-one, I'll share my plus-one."

"You're such a loser," Alina said. "You know that?"

"I've heard something like that a few times."

"Speaking of losers," Alina glanced at Fred. "How's your *Dungeons and Dragons* campaign going?"

"Okay," Fred said, raising his hands. "Hold on. Wait, wait, wait. Did you call us losers for playing the single most incredible game ever created?"

"Yes," Alina said. "I called you a loser to your face, and I also use that term to describe the two of you behind your backs."

"For playing a game?"

"A nerdy game."

"You're a nerd!"

"Easy with the insults," I said.

Alina stuck her tongue at Fred, and he poked his tongue out at her.

Daphne—Fred's wife—and Fred had wanted to play *Dungeons and Dragons*. They begged me, and since I'm on a self-improvement routine and actively trying to spend quality time with family and friends, I said yes to their request. My sister and her husband had also joined the campaign. Admittedly—though I wouldn't ever say this aloud—those four-to-eight hour sessions at the tabletop were quite fun.

"What do you play?" Alina asked, nodding at me. "Like class and race and all that?"

"A human warlock."

Alina chuckled and shook her head, amused by my character. "You're so predictable. Let me guess. You sold your soul to a demon to gain powers and avenge the cult that murdered your family?"

"No," I said, though unconvincingly. My backstory more or less matched her prediction, but I couldn't admit that to her. "I bet you would like the game."

"Probably would. I'm not denying that."

"Play with us then," Fred said.

"Nope."

"Why?"

"I'm a sixteen-year-old with a life. Why would I sit around with a bunch of old people and pretend to be a wizard when I could hang out with my new boyfriend?"

"Boyfriend?" Fred asked. "You said plus-one."

They broke into a chippy, fast-paced conversation that I lost track of when my phone vibrated. Detective Ted Wilson. I stood from my desk and walked to the coffee bar at the back of the office.

"Watson," I answered.

"Detective Wilson here."

I grabbed a styrofoam cup from the stack and placed it on the table. "Detective Wilson? Did I hear that correctly?"

"You did. They promoted me last week."

I poured the lukewarm coffee into the cup, turned my body, and leaned against the table. I watched Fred and Alina bicker. They grew animated, using their hands to emphasize whatever nonsensical points they made.

"Congratulations," I said.

"You can congratulate me when I solve my first case."

I closed my eyes, knowing why he called.

Around the time Cambria died, Ted Wilson had called me with an offer to contract through the Sacramento Police Department and lend my expertise to help capture the Vampire of Sacramento—a serial killer who had claimed four known victims. I had turned down his offer, knowing if I took the case, it would mentally break me. I had needed a break from the chaos, from the unending work. I had needed a break from always running away from my problems. So, I had turned down the offer to stop and breathe.

"It's been a month," Wilson said. "We're not any closer to finding him than we were when you and I last spoke."

I sipped the stale, lukewarm coffee.

"He killed again late last night. Well, early this morning. That's his fifth victim in as many months that we know of." Wilson coughed.

I held my coffee and my tongue, allowing my old friend to get to his point without interruption.

"Listen, we'll pay your standard rates, as if we're a regular customer. The only difference, you're helping us solve a serial killer case. Also, you'll have to sign some nondisclosure agreements. We're keeping what we know close to our chest right now."

I had meant to call Ted Wilson (Detective Ted Wilson now) at the end of the week, after the wedding, and accept his offer if it still stood.

"What do you know?" I asked. "Can you share any details?"

"Not until you sign the agreement."

I nodded, figuring as much.

"Media has most of it wrong, too," Wilson said. "You can read the articles they've circulated, but it's a crapshoot with who has what details correct."

"It usually is."

"What do you say?"

"Can we meet tomorrow and discuss this investigation in person?"

"Should I bring the paperwork?"

"Just in case."

Detective Wilson sighed. I could almost hear his thoughts choosing which direction to go—end the conversation or ask an old friend how he's doing. I hoped for the former.

"You doing okay?" he asked.

"Better than yesterday." I don't know where I had adopted that slogan, but recently I had worn it out. Between my mom and my sister and Maya constantly barraging me with, "are you okay?" I guess I had coined the phrase. Better than yesterday. Which was true. I strived to do better than yesterday.

That's all anyone could do, right?

"Glad to hear it," Wilson said, most likely understanding the unspoken male agreement—we don't force a conversation about another's feelings, rather we assume everything is status quo.

"What time tomorrow?" I asked.

"Coffee and breakfast at the usual spot?"

That was code for 'McDonald's, and when I start my shift.' He assumed I knew the dayshift hours, which I admittedly did.

"See you then."

To Catch a Serial Killer. Tuesday, July 4th. 1507hrs.

I SEARCHED FOR AND read every existing news article and Reddit forum about the Vampire of Sacramento. I watched every media report and YouTube video.

A few constants strung all the conflicting information together. The vampire exsanguinated all of his victims. However, the manner of exsanguination varied based on who reported the speculative information. One article claimed fang marks on the victims' necks. Another video insisted the vampire had ripped open the jugular like a wolf tearing apart its prey. He not only consumed the blood, but bathed in it.

Wilson had said the department had kept the details of their investigation quiet for now, so that explained the conflicting information bandied about the internet. Still, they all agreed that a vampire had drained its victims of their blood.

The comment sections beneath the videos and articles were breeding grounds for conspiracy theories. Despite the deluge of nonsense, some commenters provided workable leads. They provided possible names of suspects, or details of similar crimes not attached to the five murder victims, or eyewitness descriptions.

I had Alina help with the research. She jotted notes and bookmarked anything that seemed a percentile credible. Once finished with that insurmountable chore, she would filter through each individual lead to further narrow the legitimate claims, if any existed.

We had to begin somewhere, though.

Fred practiced and fretted over his speech for the wedding.

Hours passed. Alina closed her laptop and leaned back in her chair. She rubbed her eyes and groaned. "So many people think he's an actual vampire."

"No such thing," I said.

"You don't know that," Fred said, lending his help for the first time all day.

"I know that because vampires don't exist."

"You can say that with certainty?"

"Yes."

"You think they're real?" Alina asked.

Fred shrugged. "It's possible, right?"

"No," I said.

"UFOs weren't real until the government admitted their existence," Fred said. "I'm just saying, there's a possibility vampires exist. I won't write it off, that's all."

Alina raised her eyebrows. "He has a point, you know? How do we explain the drained blood from every victim?"

I shook my head, refusing to continue exploring the idea of an actual vampire. "I'm sure Detective Wilson will have a theory about the blood loss, and I'm sure it's founded on evidence from the crime scenes."

"Have you ever dealt with a serial killer before, like back when you were a cop?" Alina asked, her tone shifting from amused to curious.

"Never." I had policed in a small, rural town thirty miles outside of Sacramento—the same town where I had grown up and where my family still lived. Apart from the occasional drug-related homicide and meth labs, Galt avoided crime-related news. "This is all new to me."

"So you don't know how to catch a serial killer?"

I removed a stick of cinnamon gum and folded it into my mouth. I hadn't any idea where we should begin our investigation. Without the police having shared any details with the media or with me, we had limited information to build on.

"We have the internet sleuths," I said, nodding at Alina's closed computer. "We continue with anything they say that might seem remotely credible. We also know the victims' names. We can start making a list of all their contacts and cross-referencing them to see if they share any mutual friends."

"You want to continue with this investigation right now, right?" Alina asked.

"Why wouldn't we?"

"There's a wedding in a few hours, remember?"

"I'm the best man, remember?"

"I'm the officiant, remember?" Fred looked sick again. "Why would he ask me? He doesn't know me. Why did I say yes?" He tossed a handful of popcorn into his mouth, but continued to speak despite the obstruction. "The romance of the moment swept me away."

"What romance?" I asked.

"It was beautiful, that moment."

"Shannon had a gun in his mouth, ready to stage his murder to look like a suicide."

"It's kind of romantic," Alina said.

"You don't dare take his side."

"Think about it," she said.

"I prefer not to."

"His wife died, but he fell in love with her long-lost identical twin sister. He actually believes his wife returned from the dead to spend her existence with him. That's lovely."

"What she said." Fred pointed at Alina. "Romantic."

"It's creepy," I said. "He calls Shannon by his dead wife's name. She only claims to love him because he's stupidly rich and she wants his money. It's pathetic all around. From both parties."

Alina rolled her eyes and sighed. "You're so grumpy, Mr. Grump. First off, they're happy. Be happy for them. Oh, wait, you are happy for them, because you're supporting and advocating their marriage, because you're the best man. So, either you're okay with what's happening, or you're a hypocrite."

I ran my hands through my hair. Alina had a not-so-subtle way about her, and she wasn't shy about calling out any discrepancies she noticed.

"I like Vincent," I said, speaking the truth. I hadn't spent a lot of time with him—heck, I barely knew him beyond the case I had worked for him and his bachelor party—but I liked the old dentist. More, though, I enjoyed helping people find happiness. If standing beside Vincent as he married his dead wife's sister, believing her to be his dead wife, made him happy, then it didn't matter how creepy I thought the arrangement was. "Shannon makes him happy."

"Shelly," Fred corrected—well, fake corrected. It was all a confusing mess with the names, and one I was happy to look beyond in the next few hours. Shelly had died, but Fred insisted on referring to his new wife, Shannon, as his late wife, Shelly.

"Shelly makes him happy, and I guess that's romantic in a creepy way."

"That's all you had to say," Alina said, opening her computer. "So, we're working on the case now?"

"You want to work on it?" I asked.

"August," Alina said, "you might not know this, but Maya and I are a lot alike."

"I know."

"What's that mean? Why do you say it like that, all snooty, with your nose pointing at the ceiling?"

"My nose wasn't... it means nothing," I said.

"Nothing?"

"Oh," Fred said, clicking his tongue. "When you say nothing like that, it obviously means something."

"I really don't like the dynamic between you two," I said, pointing at each of them. "It's toxic. You bring out the worst in each other."

"What do you mean by nothing?" Alina asked.

"I can tell you're related to each other. That's it."

"Hand me your shovel, buddy, because you're digging a deep, deep hole."

I glared at Fred.

"That's it? You can tell we're related... how?" Alina asked.

Because they were both know-it-alls who verbalized each thought that popped into their head. They were impulsive and reckless. I refused to admit that to Alina, though, so I took the more mature route.

"Because you're both too smart for your own good."

Also true. Maya and Alina had IQs off the charts. High intelligence doesn't equal great decision making, though, especially when each of their parents modeled terrible life decisions throughout their childhoods.

"I know you mean that as a back-handed compliment," Alina said. "But I'm choosing to accept it as only a compliment. So, thank you. Now, I'm also a lot like Maya because I don't really care to spend hours readying myself. I'll throw on some jeans and a nice shirt a few minutes before we leave."

"Jeans?" I asked. "It's a wedding." I glanced at Fred. "Tell her it's a wedding."

Fred aggressively shook his head back and forth. "I learned long ago not to tell women how to dress or when to dress or anything that has to do with dressing. That's their wheelhouse, not mine."

"I'm not wearing a dress," Alina said. "I hate dresses."

"You're going to wear jeans, though?" I asked.

"You of all people are really going to give me fashion advice? You, the person who owns two jeans, five shirts, and a single pair of shoes? What are you going to wear, Ralph Lauren? You own nothing nicer than your black jeans, and they're not even nice."

"How do you know that?"

"I lived with you, remember? I went through your closet."

"You did what? Alina, that's extremely inappropriate."

"It's inappropriate that a thirty-year-old allowed a sixteen-year-old girl to stay in his apartment for a week. We had only met once. What if you were a pervert or a sexual predator? Turned out, you were just a slob. Guess who fixed you up in that department? Me. Now look at you. Clean-shaven. Nice haircut. Tidy house."

I bit my cheeks for a few seconds. "I bought a pair of slacks."

"Yeah, well, that's my influence on your life," Alina said. "You went out and bought a pair of slacks for this wedding. Pointy shoes, too?"

"Yeah."

"You're fancy, Mr. Fancy. Mr. Marc Jacobs."

"You're annoying."

Alina smirked. "Thank you."

"You can't wear jeans to a wedding."

"You can't tell me what to do. Or what to wear."

I pinched my cheekbones between my thumb and index finger, then ran my hand to my hair and scratched my head. "Let's circle way back. You want to investigate the vampire case right now?"

"Duh."

"Make some lists, then. We have five victims. I want their entire family tree. I want to know their friends, their co-workers, their church family, their rec-league teammates, their sneaky links—"

"Don't say that," Alina said. "You're too old."

"She's right," Fred said. "You shouldn't say sneaky link. It sounds weird coming from you."

"You're the same age as me," I said.

"Fred isn't awkward when he uses current slang, though. Just stick to the basics, August. It's better for everyone."

"I want a list of everyone they knew," I said. "I want a list of the regular places they visited. I want a list of the secret and not-so-regular places they attended. I also want a list of every single stop and phone call and conversation they had on the day they met the vampire. Is that enough to get you started?"

The kid stuck out her tongue, but she reopened her computer and went to work without another word to me.

I stood and headed for the exit.

"Where are you going?" Fred asked.

"Sarah wants my help with a client," I said.

"Is her client's name Richard?"

"No, why?"

"Dick," Alina said behind her laptop screen. "He's asking if her client is Dick. More explicitly, Fred's asking if her client is your—"

"Nope." I opened the office door and closed it before those two clowns could harass me any further.

The Missing Boy.
Tuesday, July 4th.
1521hrs.

I leased office space in downtown Sacramento. The brick-faced building's first floor was a restaurant. I had only eaten there once, and the food had turned out pretty good. Small businesses rented the three floors above the restaurant for office space. I shared the third floor with a defense attorney, Sarah Herling.

Sarah and I had worked a doppelgänger case together. She had defended a woman, Claire Balzan, arrested for theft and homicide. Turned out, the actual murderer had framed Sarah's client—they looked identical, and the woman had a personal vendetta against Claire. Before that case, I had ran into Sarah because we shared the third floor. After that case, though, we seemed to run into each other often.

I didn't mind, either. She was easy to talk to and easier to look at.

As I crossed the hallway separating my office from her office, the elevator at the end of the hall dinged. The doors slid open. A young woman no older than twenty-one marched right past me and toward my office door. She grabbed the handle.

"Excuse me," I said.

The young lady turned to me and frowned. She had what Maya and Alina often cited as R.B.F. (Resting Bitch Face). It's when women had an aggressive, don't-come-near-me look stapled across their resting visage. The young woman's iciness surprised me, and I instinctively stepped back.

"I'm sorry if I startled you," I said. "That door you're about to open... it's mine."

"You're August Watson?"

"I am." My mind tingled as it did now when new clients approached me. Had Daniel Quinn sent them in my direction?

Daniel Quinn, if that was his real name, had placed his fingerprints all over my last few investigations. He believed he and I were a real life iteration of Batman and Joker. His delusional thoughts and actions had set in motion the events that led to Cambria's death. I didn't doubt for a second that if given a chance, he would aim to hurt me or someone close to me again.

I first met Quinn through the Sacramento Police Department. He disguised himself as a detective responding to the case I had worked.

When I later shared his name and a physical description with the department, no one recognized him.

I had approached previous clients who had spoken with him face-to-face, but they had no more information about the man other than his appearance.

All my leads depleted quickly, and I now spent hours every night before bed scrolling through Facebook and Instagram profiles, scrolling through public records of different law enforcement agencies to find a picture resembling the man. I searched for the world's smallest needle in the universe's largest haystack.

In short, Daniel Quinn was another ghost. Except, he was the ghost I couldn't unmask.

With the thought that Quinn could have sent this woman to me, I carefully navigated the interaction. "How did you hear about Blue Moon?"

"An advertisement."

I frowned, unsure if I had paid for any kind of advertising. That was in Fred's wheelhouse, and he also ran the financial side of the business with full autonomy. Had he run an advertisement somewhere? Possibly.

"Where did you see the ad?" I asked.

"On Facebook. I was researching local detectives..." she trailed off, biting her lip. "Paranormal detectives," she said with finality. "I couldn't convince myself to call anyone, though. It's embarrassing. Anyway, I went to Facebook to scroll for a while, and your ad popped into my feed." The woman sighed. "Here I am."

Believable, except I knew nothing about an advertisement. Had Tempest Michaels noticed the decline in clients over the last month? Had he taken out an advertisement to push business in my direction?

"Do you know a man named Daniel Quinn?" I asked.

She narrowed her eyes. "No."

"Did anyone refer you to me?"

"I saw an advertisement." The woman turned her shoulders and faced the elevator doors. "I knew this was a bad idea. Forget I came."

I exhaled. "Wait, wait, wait." I dared not reach out and grab her, but I hoped my tone of voice would prevent her from leaving. "I'm sorry." I cracked a knuckle. "I'm not making this any easier on you. How can I help?"

The young woman glanced around the hallway. "Out here?"

"Of course not. Let's go inside."

I led her back into my office. I sat in the rolling chair behind my desk and gestured for her to sit in the client's chair where Fred had sat earlier.

Speaking of the giant, he peeked his head over the receptionist's counter.

"You run an advertisement on Facebook?" I called across the room.

"Me?" Fred asked. "Yeah. Alina convinced me to do it."

"What?" Alina looked up from her computer.

"The Facebook advertising," Fred said.

"Oh, yeah. August, we had to keep turning away word-of-mouth clients because you wouldn't accept a case."

I raised a hand, waving her into silence, and I faced the young woman sitting before me. "Again, I apologize for the disorder. Things have been hectic. I'm August Watson. How can I help you?"

"I'm Cecilia Ochoa, and..." she trailed off.

A lot of clients often mirrored her behavior—shy, if not embarrassed, to sit across from me, a paranormal investigator. I was a last-ditch, desperate attempt when all other avenues failed.

"Someone abducted my friend."

"Abducted?"

"Someone took him. Kidnapped him."

I knew what abducted meant, but I had hoped she would provide a few more details about the abduction.

"Did you go to the police?" That was always one of my first questions, especially when considering a possible legal matter. I wasn't a cop any longer, and I had no arresting powers beyond that of a citizen. Any reports of crime that fell on my desk had to funnel through the police.

"Yes."

"What did they say?"

"That they're looking into it."

"You don't trust their investigation?"

Her face scrunched. "They suspect I'm involved."

"In the abduction? Why?"

"We are in the same summer session together. The teacher paired us to work on a project. Through our sessions, we developed a mutual attraction, I guess. Jackson—that's his name. Jackson Armstead. He asked me on a date. We had dinner and went to a movie."

"The night he went missing?"

Cecelia nodded, but she stared at her lap, probably too embarrassed to look me in the eye. "Dinner was nice enough. Jackson is sweet."

"Sweet?"

"That means he has little to no redeeming qualities," Alina said from a half-dozen feet away. "Not attractive or funny or intelligent. Probably doesn't have any interesting hobbies. My guess, he's nice enough to convince some girls into bed with him."

"He's sweet," Cecilia said, lifting her gaze enough to glare at Alina. "I liked that specific quality about him. Anyway, we... we fooled around in the theater. That was, it was less than sweet."

Alina coughed, laughing.

"I didn't know what to do after that. I was disappointed and angry. I also felt dumb for accepting the date. So, I snuck away when he went into the bathroom. When I got home, I sat in my car for a while and thought about the night. I felt bad for leaving. Also, we still had that project to finish, so I knew I had to see him again. I went back to apologize. He wasn't there. I thought he might have left, too... gone back home. I drove to his house." Cecilia's body went rigid. Her mouth remained partly open. She didn't blink.

I waited for the story to continue, not sure yet why she had sought my paranormal investigative services.

"I know this sounds crazy," she said. "I feel crazy saying it. I feel crazy believing I actually witnessed it. But I know what I saw."

"What did you see?"

"She stood under the streetlight, or rather it stood under the streetlight."

"It?" I asked.

"A zombie."

Fred rushed to his feet, standing upright and staring in our direction. "Zombie?"

Alina lowered her laptop screen and glued her eyes on us.

"A zombie?" I asked.

Cecilia shook her head. "I don't think so. It was like Frankenstein's monster. That's the book we have to read and analyze. In the novel, Shelley described the monster as a collection of body parts from different corpses."

"The monster is a golem," Alina said. "Golems aren't quite undead like zombies, but constructed through magical means from rock or clay... or human body parts."

Cecilia nodded. "Yeah, exactly. That's what the creature reminded me of. It had mismatched legs with bones jutting from each one."

"Mismatched?" I asked.

"Different widths and lengths. It moved in a strange lurching stride. The arms were the same—mismatching. I only glimpsed the face, but it seemed like a stitched hodgepodge of features, too."

Fred slowly sank back into his chair, disappearing behind the high counter, probably quivering with fear.

"The skin really gave it away," Cecilia said. "It was gray and waxy, like from a corpse, or multiple corpses. I watched from across the street as it stood under the light on its broken legs. It sort of wavered in place. Then, without warning, it stumbled forward and attacked Jackson."

"He was there?" I asked.

"He must have walked home from the theater."

"What happened next?"

"The golem overpowered Jackson, brought him to the ground, and knocked him out. Then it dragged Jackson away." Cecilia shook her head and returned her attention to her lap. "I sat in my car, too confused and terrified to move. I just sat there. I don't know for how long. When the adrenaline finally hit me, I threw open the door and sprinted after them, but they were gone. That's when I called the police."

"You told them what you told me?"

"Yes."

"They didn't believe you?"

She chuckled. "No."

"They suspect you?"

"They haven't outright said that, but it's been four days, and there are no leads. No contact from Jackson. Nothing. They brought me in for questioning earlier today, and it seemed a lot more accusatory. At least it felt that way. I saw your advertisement a couple of days ago. Call me jaded, but I don't trust the cops, and with them likely looking at me, I needed to find someone else to help find him."

I added nothing to the conversation, apart from tapping an unused pen against a blank notepad. Patience and quietness often proved the most essential strategy to gain more information.

"I had nothing to do with his disappearance," Cecilia said. "The golem took him." She laughed, a sound bordering on hysteria. "Does that sound crazy? I feel crazy saying it. I feel like the mayor of Crazy Town."

"It was dark that night?" I asked.

"It stood under a streetlight. Two different but very broken legs. A broken and scarred face. Puffy, corpse-like skin. I've seen a dead body before. The creature was dead, or rather..." she laughed again, shaking her head. "Created from the dead."

"Where did the golem drag him to?"

"Down the street. Once it left the streetlight's glow, it was dark. I saw it drag him down the street until I couldn't see them anymore."

"You understand I'm not the police, right?" I asked, moving toward my least favorite part of the job—a price discussion with someone scared and begging for me to help them. "This is a private business, and my clients pay me a certain rate to perform certain tasks. I can't arrest anyone, but I can provide any incriminating evidence to the police. They do with that as they will."

She tucked her hair behind her ear. "I understand."

I shared my rates with Cecilia. "Does that work?"

"It will have to, right?"

Aggravated Assault. Tuesday, July 4th. 1536hrs.

I WALKED CECILIA BACK to the elevator. She pressed the ground-level button. At the last second, her hand snaked out, preventing the doors from shutting. The young woman looked at me, her eyes wide as they held all her fear.

"It wasn't my family either. They didn't hurt him." Her arm dropped back to her side, and the elevator closed.

I scraped my teeth over my lower lip and watched her disappear behind the door. My question sat heavy on my tongue, weighing it down and preventing me from speaking. Though, I didn't need to ask it, anyway, at least not to her.

Why would I suspect your family? Why say that?

Because the police have not only Cecilia square in their sights, but her family, and for a legitimate reason. I would learn their suspicions soon enough, and Cecilia most likely understood that, which was why she had uttered the last-ditch plea. *It wasn't my family either. They didn't hurt him.* She had approached me because the police wouldn't listen to her. She had approached me because she needed a champion at her side.

"I believe you," I said to the closed elevator doors. I turned around and headed back toward Sarah Herling's office.

Giovanni Mitchell greeted me with a broad, contagious grin. Gio was Sarah's paralegal and receptionist, and acted in a similar capacity as Fred did for me—fielding calls and potential clients, responding to emails, and performing preliminary investigative research. Giovanni and Fred alike were invaluable to Sarah's and my small businesses.

"Good afternoon," Gio said. He stood from his chair behind the counter and circled around to shake my hand. All the while, he wore a bright, broad smile. When I say he wore a smile, I mean he wore it like a mask. It covered his entire face. He grinned with his cheeks, his brow, his eyes.

Despite my natural hesitancy to smile, I couldn't help but mirror his expression. "How's it going?"

"Well, honestly, awesome."

"You're working on a national holiday. How is that awesome?"

Giovanni rolled his eyes. "Sarah had an emergency client meeting, and she asked if I could come in for an hour. Anyway, that's not what's so awesome. I may have finally found love."

I thought of Cambria, and a pang of jealously sparked through my body. I quickly shoved it aside, choosing to hold my smile and show happiness for the young man. My emotions had no bearing on him, and though misery loves company, I refused to force people to my pity party.

"I love hearing that," I said.

"Thank you. I've been wanting to tell your little intern about him, but I haven't seen that mosquito for a few weeks. Where's she been?"

"You mean Alina?"

Giovanni chuckled. "I call her a mosquito because she's constantly buzzing in my ear. Even if I swipe at her, she comes back for more juice, always buzzing. In the best possible way, though."

I nodded and half-laughed. He was dead on in his comparison of Alina to a mosquito. Also, his mention that he not only knew Alina, but also had some kind of relationship with her didn't surprise me. She had a tendency to include herself in everyone's business.

"I wanted to gloat to her about my boyfriend," Giovanni said. "She always said I'm too nerdy to find someone as awesome as me. I wasn't ever sure if that was a compliment, but I wanted to gloat."

"I've learned that with her, if it borders on a compliment, it probably is."

"True, true. I also wanted to thank her."

"I can't imagine for what," I said. "Do you thank a mosquito for sucking your blood and leaving an irksome, itchy rash on your skin?"

"If a mosquito removed rattlesnake venom from my veins, I think I can handle the itchiness."

I cocked my head.

"That was lame." Giovanni snickered and glanced up to the left. "I think it's fitting, though. I quit smoking on her recommendation, which is almost like having her remove venom from me. And believe me, the nicotine withdrawal is itchy."

"Well, I'll let you tell her. I refuse to pass along the information. She's sixteen, Gio, and she's already been right one too many times in her young life. Correctness is not a healthy habit for an overconfident youth."

"Oh, you're so cynical. I love it!"

I hadn't ever carried on a conversation with Giovanni beyond *Hi* and *How are you?* My stamina for bantering had exhausted itself, and I refocused. "Where's Sarah?"

"In her little prison."

I glanced across the waiting area to a closed door, which led into Sarah's personal office.

"She's with Gerry," he said.

I scrunched my face. "Who's Gerry?"

"The homeless man who lives in the alley."

"I thought his name was Gerald."

"I call him Gerry," Giovanni said.

"I think I'll stick to Gerald."

"Alina also calls him Gerry."

I scratched my head, growing more and more confused by this conversation. Was there anyone in my life who Alina didn't know?

"Alina knows him?"

"Oh, yeah. They spend a lot of time together."

I tilted my head and sucked on my teeth for a while, processing that comment. Why was Alina spending a lot of time with a sixty-something-year-old homeless man?

In my time with the Galt Police Department, I hadn't dealt with a huge transient population, but I had my run-ins with the homeless. Maybe my tenure with law enforcement had instilled a cynicism within me, and I now saw the world through a lens of black and white—good and evil, right and wrong. I felt a twinge of guilt and embarrassment, realizing that might be the case and knowing that was a limited and ignorant perspective on life. Nothing was ever just black and white, or good and evil, or right and wrong, but shrouded in vagueness and grays. Yet, my minimal encounters with the homeless population had never resulted in happy memories. They usually ended in a violent or less-than-pleasant manner. Maybe my jaded perspective was ultimately incorrect, but I think it's what helped me become halfway decent at my job.

No matter how I flipped the coin, though, I felt uncomfortable knowing Alina spent time with a homeless man.

"You think that's a good idea?" I asked.

"What's that?"

"Alina spending time with Gerald."

"You've talked to him, right?"

"I've nodded at him and spared him a dollar every now and again, but we haven't spent a lot of time together."

Giovanni smiled and shook his head. "He's a great dude."

"A great dude?"

"Sure. I've chilled with him and Alina before. We sit in the alley and smoke—well, we did. Not recently."

"Alina smokes?"

"No, Gerry and I do… did. Alina sits upwind of us and scolds us for smoking."

That sounded more accurate.

"Anyway," Giovanni said. "Gerry is a great guy."

I narrowed my eyes and furrowed my brow, not quite convinced considering the current circumstance. "Why is he meeting with Sarah, then? You know she's a defense attorney, right? You know that means she defends people charged with crimes."

Giovanni's cheeks ballooned, and he farted out a laugh. "Dude, seriously? Marijuana is still a chargeable crime. Let's avoid discussing crime and its relation to whether a person is good or bad."

"Why's he meeting with Sarah?"

"Aggravated assault against a group of kids while under the influence of drugs."

I crossed my arms and leaned forward. "Gio, I understand what you're saying about good people and crime. That makes sense. Sure. Aggravated assault against kids? You know Alina is a kid, right? What if he had attacked her?"

"August, you know our brand. We only represent clients we believe are innocent. Go into Sarah's office and get the story straight from the source. It's crazy—like Greek mythology kind of crazy. You ever hear of Hercules' madness?"

I had read the story once or twice. "Aggravated assault against a group of kids?"

"He's innocent... ish."

"Ish?"

Giovanni raised his hands in surrender. "I'm done. Go into the office. They're expecting you, anyway."

I turned toward Sarah's door, took three steps, and stopped. "What do you three all talk about?" I immediately regretted the question and spoke before Giovanni could answer. "Never mind. I don't think I want to know." I opened the door and entered Sarah's office.

Giant Chickens.
Tuesday, July 4th.
1549hrs.

Sarah Herling sat on the edge of her desk. Gerald sat in one of her two client chairs. He wore his usual ratty and stained garb. The office stank of sour body odor and something else entirely unidentifiable—almost like wet, musty farts.

"Hey, August." Gerald had a rich and velvety voice, like a radio jockey. In a different life, he could have counted down the top-forty songs of the week. Heck, maybe he could have sung in one of those top-forty songs. Gerald would occasionally position himself near the front of the building and play an old guitar and sing. He played and sang expertly, in my uneducated opinion.

"Gerald." I nodded at him, closed the door, and leaned against the wall, keeping as far from the source of the stench as possible. I glanced at Sarah. She looked as pretty as ever in her professional attire and pulled back hair. "Gio provided me with the bullet points."

"I told him not to say a word." Sarah rolled her eyes. "He's all giddy and overly chatty because he has a date tonight."

"He mentioned he found love."

Gerald snickered. "That man is dramatic as they come."

Not caring to re-explore Giovanni's love life, I shifted gears. "Well, what's happening?"

Sarah stared at Gerald. "Tell him."

The old man swallowed and inhaled. "They arrested me for punching on some kids."

I reached into my pocket and folded a piece of cinnamon gum into my mouth. "Did you punch them?"

"In their faces."

I frowned, completely lost. "Ms. Herling only represents clients falsely accused of crimes."

"That's true," Sarah said.

"I don't understand." I cracked a knuckle.

"You want to tell him, Gerry?"

The old man scratched his hairy neck and cleared his throat. "I was reading in the public library. *The Piano Teacher* by Elfriede Jelinek. It's always been on my list of novels to read, and I finally spied it in the library. It's a beautiful, emotional, haunting story about self-destruction. Anyway, the tale had entranced me when a group of kids entered the library. They were loud."

"Loud?" I asked.

"Disruptive to the sanctity of a library."

I twisted my wrists. Gerald surprised me—he didn't fit into the mental mold I had created for him, for a homeless person. He spoke as if educated, and he spoke with confidence.

"I ignored them, though. They were kids, only hellbent on pushing boundaries to taste independence. Who am I to suppress their growing pains?"

"So you didn't punch them because they were loud?"

Gerald chuckled. "God, no. The library checks out headphones and laptops. I signed out a pair of headphones and a computer, and I returned to my reading spot, drowning out their voices with music."

"At first," Sarah said.

"At first," Gerald repeated. He paused for a few seconds before continuing. "I smelled it."

I looked at the man. He had a thick, bushy gray beard, matted and dirty. His clothes possessed stains and tears all along them. His skin scuffed with grime.

"What did you smell?" I asked, fully aware of what I smelled right then.

"I don't know." Gerald sniffed, as if the action might trigger his olfactory memory. "Nothing. It smelled like nothing."

"How does something smell like nothing?" I asked.

"I can't explain it."

"It doesn't matter," Sarah said. "The point is, he smelled something different before—"

"Before those kids... before they turned."

I tilted my head. "Turned?"

"They changed into giant, fantasy-sized chickens. Wings grew out of their backs." Gerry breathed rapidly through his teeth. "Beaks burst out of their face. You... you wouldn't believe it."

He was right. I didn't.

"They didn't speak English anymore. They clucked. They flapped their wings and shed feathers that were as big as a book. Bigger."

"Gerry has a deep-rooted phobia of chickens," Sarah said. "He experienced a childhood trauma. Anyway, he saw the man-sized chickens and screamed."

"They walked up to me. Surrounded me. Clucking. Pecking at me. I reacted out of fear."

I saw Aaron Brooks in my mind's eye as he pointed his gun at me, and I reacted out of fear.

"I stopped thinking," Gerald said. "My body acted out of fear. It worked outside of my control."

I saw myself drawing the gun from my hip, firing the weapon. The airsoft BB from Aaron Brooks' gun bounced across the asphalt as the teenager slumped to the hot asphalt. I had acted out of fear, outside of my control, allowing my emotions and impulses to dictate my actions.

"I believe you," I whispered.

"I grabbed the book I was reading and used it like a brick against the giant chickens."

"How old were the kids?" I asked.

"Twelve and thirteen," Sarah said.

"What's the extent of their injuries?"

"One has a broken nose. The others are mostly just a little bruised and battered. It doesn't matter. A sixty-three-year-old man attacked a group of four children."

"Chickens," Gerald said.

Sarah hopped off the ledge of her desk and circled around to her chair. She plopped down, leaned back, and stared at the ceiling.

"Do you take drugs?" I asked Gerald.

"Not since my thirties or forties."

"There's security footage from the library, I assume."

"We don't have it yet," Sarah said. "The library isn't cooperating with us. They saw a homeless man scream, then attack four children. They don't really care to assist our defense."

I chewed on my gum. "Gerald, could you excuse Ms. Herling and me for a few minutes?"

"You can wait outside, Gerry," Sarah said.

The man nodded and stood. I opened the door and stepped aside, and he ambled into the waiting room with Giovanni.

I closed the door and wrinkled my nose at the lingering stench. "Why am I here? Do you suspect the paranormal? Or was this an episode of a mentally unstable man having a breakdown?"

"This happened two weeks ago," Sarah said, her attention fixed upward. "I did my homework before inviting you to join this meeting. I didn't want to waste your time."

"Thank you."

"Gerald spent a few days in jail, but with the way bail works in California and his lack of income, well, you know. Anyway, I sent him to a psychiatrist. I had him drug tested. I dotted my *i*'s and crossed my *t*'s. He's homeless, yes. He's mentally healthy, though, and he's sober. His mind didn't snap. He didn't suffer a drug-induced hallucination or an episode of paranoid schizophrenia."

"Yet he believes he saw four giant chickens attacking him." I chewed on my cheek, waiting for Sarah to respond. She didn't. "When the library finally shares the security footage with you, what will we see?"

"A man attacking four teenagers," she said.

"Not attacking giant chickens?"

"Probably not." Sarah licked her lips and settled her gaze on me. "He's not lying. You helped with Claire Balzan. Security footage showed her murdering someone, yet we proved that wrong. We proved her innocent, right? Well, Gerry's not innocent. I'm sure he attacked those children. But, August, he suffered some kind of spell. A spell. That's paranormal. That's why I need you."

"He's homeless, Sarah. The stress of life momentarily broke his mind." I sighed, inhaling the stench soaking into the office. I tasted it on my tongue and nearly gagged.

"I would pay you for your time," Sarah said. "I know you're taking a break from work, so I won't expect much. I just want you to think about it."

"I'm back in the saddle. I just accepted a golem case, and I'm going to help the Sacramento Police Department with the Vampire of Sacramento. I don't think I can allot the time to help with this one. I'm sorry."

Sarah nodded. "Can I ask you one more favor?"

"Of course," I said. "Anything."

"The court highly recommends for Gerry to find a place of residence until his sentencing date. They almost refused to release him because of his homeless status, but I interjected." Sarah pulled on her lips and raised her eyebrows. "I had to."

"Sarah." I knew the favor before she could ask. "There's no way. That's why they created halfway houses and homeless shelters. Resources exist for this exact reason."

"Six weeks at the most."

"No."

"Doesn't your big, fancy new house have two bedrooms?"

"Not happening."

"Two baths."

"Sarah, no. I'm not a public service agency."

She pouted out her lower lip. "For me? Please."

I ran my hand through my hair and cracked a knuckle, angry with my inability to say no to a woman. "I don't understand why you can't explore other options. He doesn't have to be on the street, and he doesn't have to be in my house. There are other avenues available."

Sarah looked at me like a little girl might look at her father—all bright-eyed and gorgeous and manipulative.

I dropped the back of my head against the door, knocking my skull on the wood and sighing.

"Is that a yes?"

"I'm not driving him over there. You can drop him off."

Sarah popped out of her chair, squealing with excitement. She slammed into me, hugging me, and out of nowhere, she kissed me on the mouth. She pulled away, grinning at me. "I love the taste of cinnamon gum."

Moving In.
Tuesday, July 4th.
1731hrs.

I HAD OFFICIALLY MOVED out of my apartment a month ago. The lease expired at the end of July, but I hadn't cared. I paid for it to remain vacant while I lived in Glacia's Nana's old home.

The cost evened out. Glacia had gifted her Nana's house to me. I paid for real estate fees, title costs, and all other accrued charges from the escrow period, plus an added dollar. Technically, I had purchased a twelve hundred square foot, two bedroom, two bathroom house on two acres of land for the cool cost of a dollar. I could afford to continue paying the last month of my apartment's rent, despite no longer living there.

Alina had helped me organize the new house with my limited supply of belongings. I had promised her a bedroom—one only for her and her alone to do whatever in the world she wished—so she had some stake and opinion on how the house appeared.

"An in-room cinema," Alina had said, standing a step inside the bedroom I had given to her. "Surround sound. A projection screen and a projector. I don't want a bed, but a massive couch that I can sleep on and can also act as a table when I want to eat something. It should have a mini fridge built into it. I'll obviously Pinterest some ideas, but it's going to be a cinema-themed bedroom."

"You'll never leave here," I said. "I can't allow that. You have school, and you have work."

"It's my room to do with as I please." She grabbed the side of her door, "Bye now," and slammed it in my face.

That was three weeks ago. Alina had leaned a few framed movie posters against the barren walls. The rest of her furnishings remained unattainable with her current income—zero dollars an hour. I needed to reconsider her intern designation, though.

The company generated enough cash to justify paying her, and she deserved more money than I paid myself or Fred combined. Without her voice and input with our investigations, I'm not sure how many cases we would have solved.

I thought of Alina, her empty bedroom, her lack of income because it was the second bedroom in my house, and Gerald would show up at any minute to live here for six-ish weeks. Earlier I had caught Alina up to speed on the whole Gerald situation, and she had gladly offered her bedroom to the man.

The doorbell rang as I stood in the master bathroom and trimmed my beard. For a quick second, I almost considered ignoring the visitor, but I clicked off my electronic device and padded to the front door.

Sarah greeted me with a warm smile. Gerald stood ten feet behind her. He carried a stuffed black garbage bag over his shoulder and looked like Santa Claus delivering presents door-to-door.

"Thanks," Sarah mouthed to me.

I grinned with only my lips. "Come on in. I'll show you around." I about-faced and led them into the kitchen. "That's the living room." I pointed across the bar, which separated the kitchen from the living room. "If you head through that doorway out of the kitchen and take a right, you'll come across two bedrooms. The one at the very end of the hall with an en-suite bathroom belongs to me. Gerald, yours is the other one."

"I can crash on the couch or the floor," Gerald said.

"Well, lucky for you, the guest bedroom only has a floor to sleep on. Besides, you should have your privacy. Sleeping in the living room strips you of that."

"Thank you," Gerald said.

"I have a wedding to attend this evening, and I won't be back until late. You can make yourself at home. There's not much food in the refrigerator or pantry, but I'm sure you can find something edible around here."

"You know it's almost six o'clock, don't you?" Sarah asked.

"Yeah, why?"

"What time does the wedding start?"

"We're eating around 1900hrs. They're doing the whole thing backwards. After dinner, we'll move to the ceremony. They want to kiss as fireworks begin."

"You have a plus-one?" Gerald asked.

I scrunched my face. "You want an invitation?"

"I love weddings."

"Already have a date, buddy," I said. "Sorry."

"Who?" Sarah asked, angling her body back and crossing her arms.

I smirked. "It's a surprise."

"You can't tell me? I won't even be there."

I shook my head.

"Can you tell me?" Gerald asked.

"I can't tell anyone."

"Ugh, fine," Sarah said. "Have fun at your wedding. Gerry, behave yourself."

"Always," he said.

"Gerald," I said, not quite comfortable with Gerry yet, "I'm following Sarah out the door. Behave yourself."

"Always."

I had held my reservations about leaving Gerald at my house alone, but Sarah and Alina trusted the man, and I trusted their opinions.

"You're going like that?" Sarah asked me as I closed the front door.

"What?" I glanced at my outfit. Jeans. A T-shirt. Sneakers. "Not wedding attire?"

"You're serious?"

"It's sad that you think I'm serious."

"Sad for you. That means I believe you would actually wear something like that."

"I'm the best man."

"I didn't think anyone liked you that much."

"The offer surprised me, too. Anyway, he has the suits at his house. That's where the wedding is. His house."

"Does he have a razor? You forgot to finish trimming half of your face."

I touched the bushy side of my cheek. "Thank you for the reminder."

"It's the least I can do. Thanks for taking in Gerry. He's a great guy. Don't judge him because he's homeless and a little stinky. You'll see."

"You owe me."

Sarah smirked and spun on her heel. She glanced over her shoulder at me. "Call for that favor any time."

Part of me wanted to chase after her, grab her shoulder, turn her toward me, and further explore that kiss from earlier. Instead, I waved goodbye.

She sat in her car and blew me a kiss from the driver's seat. As she backed away, I went into the house and grabbed my trimmer.

Wedding Gifts. Tuesday, July 4th. 1841hrs.

VINCENT DUPREE HAD SPENT his adult years as a happily married man and a successful dentist who owned his practice. He lived on enough acres to justify planting a sprawling olive orchard, pouring cement over a quarter-mile-long curving driveway covered in over-hanging trees, and building a custom mansion. To top it off, like the bright-red cherry on an overdone sundae, Vincent Dupree had commissioned the digging of a personal pond, complete with a dock and a paddleboat.

The pond was where he had (or most likely Shannon) instructed the decorators to focus their wedding attention. A flowering arch stood at the end of the dock. About four dozen fold-out chairs rested on the lawn, as did a catering table, a mobile dance floor, the DJ's equipment booth, and a pop-up bar.

The property looked incredible. The orchard backdropped the small pond, and the plantation-style mansion with the wraparound porch backdropped the attendees. I'm sure the pictures would turn out splendidly.

I stared out the glass door, which overlooked the side of the property from a second-story guest bedroom. Shannon had staked her claim on the master bedroom, leaving the groomsmen and the groom with a view of the orchard and the farms beyond it.

When I say groomsmen, I mean two, plus Fred.

There was me, Vincent's best man for some odd reason. I had known him all of two months, and we had spent time together once outside of the investigation he hired me for. His bachelor party. That hardly counts, though, since we technically lost Vincent and spent the entire trip looking for him. Either way, it would have made way more sense for his co-worker, possibly business partner (I wasn't quite clear on their relationship) to serve as his best man.

Scott Moreno, a short, penguin-shaped man who wore circular, frameless glasses and had never met a comb or a toothbrush—which I thought strange considering his occupation. The man had rancid breath and mustard-colored teeth, and during the bachelor party, he admitted to having forgotten his toothbrush at home. I didn't believe him, though.

There was also Fred, who readied himself with the groomsmen, though he acted as the officiant to the ceremony. Currently, Fred sat on the balcony outside the glass-paneled door I looked out from. He had his eyes closed and head rested on the outdoor table.

"He'll do great." Scott slapped his sweaty hand on my shoulder. I could feel the cold perspiration through my thin dress shirt. "I don't know why he's so worried." His breath wafted over my shoulder like a green, cartoonish cloud.

I swallowed a cough, reached into my pocket, and pried out a stick of gum. "Want a piece?" I folded the cinnamon-flavored gum into my mouth.

"No thanks. I can't stand it. Trashy, or so my mom raised me to believe. Besides..." Scott raised a beer can to his lips and went bottoms-up. After he chugged the beer, he belched without bothering to turn his head. It was like chemical warfare. "Gum doesn't pair well with beer, and we're at a wedding. Beer is mandatory."

I raised my eyebrows and struggled not to vomit, struggled against the devil on my shoulder, instructing me to open the door and walk off the balcony.

"Have you seen the bridesmaids yet?" Scott asked.

I hadn't. Vincent and Shannon had opted out of a rehearsal dinner. "Waste of time and money," Vincent had said to me over the phone about a week ago. "You know how to stand, right?"

"Yeah," I had said.

"And walk with another person?"

"Mostly."

"You can take orders?"

"Questionable."

"Well, what's there to rehearse? Listen to what the wedding coordinator tells you, walk down the aisle, stand beside me while Fred delivers the speech of the century."

"I haven't seen them," I said to Scott—a mistake. I should have listened to the devil and walked off the balcony.

"My man. My man. Check it out." Scott placed his hands on his chest and ballooned them outward, gesturing breast size. "It keeps going, too," he said, stopping when his hands modeled impossibly sized breasts. "I mean, huge. H-U-G-E big. I mean the maid of honor. She's a little thicker, sure, but that's how I like my women, anyway."

I wondered if Fred would try to prevent me from jumping. Would he talk me out of it, or would he allow me to end the misery of continuing that conversation with Scott?

"I don't understand men into skinny women. It's as if they're into little boys. I mean, if you like fit, muscular body types..." Scott shrugged his shoulder up to his ears. He almost looked like a turtle. "That's cool. Do your thing. But quit hiding in the closet, right? Just admit you're attracted to men. Don't package your infatuation up in a female body."

My hand touched the doorknob.

"Anyway, her name is Ruth. It's old school, but I like that, too. Big women with old school names and old school values. Pop out a few brats. Make dinner. Keep the house clean. Lay down and let me have my way, as God intended. That's Biblical, you know? You ever read the Bible? I think that's where we've gone wrong in this world. Too many people reading the news, reading what the media has to say, and listening to celebrities who only care about expanding their influence and fortune. Not enough people reading the Bible, listening to God. Let me tell you something." Scott jammed his finger into my arm. "End of times, the rapture, it's here. We're living through it."

I wavered. The fumes spurted from his constant jabber had me flirting with unconsciousness.

Vincent Dupree saved my life. The groom barged into the guest bedroom, fumbling with three boxes. "My boys!" he exclaimed, glancing around the room. His gaze settled on the dresser where Scott had stored his four empty beer cans. "I see we're getting the party started early. Good. Drink up. Drink up. Enjoy yourselves." Vincent chuckled and exhaled. "We ready for this?"

Scott finished his fifth beer, crushing the can and throwing it on the dresser with the other empty cans. He whooped. "Let's do this!"

"Are you ready?" I asked.

"Am I ready to marry the woman of my dreams?" Vincent scoffed and placed the wrapped boxes on the bed. He crossed the room and embraced me in a full hug. "I can't wait. And, August, I wouldn't have this day without you. You allowed this to happen." Vincent broke away and patted my shoulder.

"Just did my job," I said.

"Well, I didn't know how to thank you for what you've given me."

"You already paid me for doing the job. That's thanks enough. It's what we agreed to."

"No. Nonsense. What you did went beyond a job. What you did was universal. It was fate. It was... was destiny. You brought my wife back from the dead."

"Well, that's not—"

"Not all the money in my bank account could thank you for that."

I frowned, considering how many millions he probably had in his bank account. "I disagree."

"You know how I can thank you?"

"All the money in your bank account," I mumbled.

"Infusing love and life into your world, as you infused love and life back into mine."

Oh, boy, I thought. I didn't like where Vincent steered this scenario. I glanced at the bed, and I saw one box rattling, and I heard a gentle whining. *Oh, boy.*

Vincent backpedaled away from me, never removing his anticipatory eyes from mine. He leaned over and grabbed the moving and whining box. He carried it back over to me. "Go ahead. It's my gift to you. Open it."

"You didn't have to do this." I really meant that, too. He didn't have to do it, and he definitely shouldn't have done it. Yet he had done it. There's no shoving the toothpaste back into the tube once it's out.

I accepted the gift.

Vincent grinned ear-to-ear, chuckled, and rubbed his hands together like a comic book villain. He leaned forward, past me, and knocked on the glass-paneled door. "Fred! Get in here. We're opening presents."

Fred's lowered head tilted upward, and he glanced through the glass. Vincent waved, gesturing for the bear-sized man to come into the room. With a physical sigh—I couldn't hear it through the closed door, but his entire body deflated—Fred stood and lumbered into the room.

"Hey, big guy," I said.

"Hey."

"You okay?"

"I'm going to bomb this. It's going to be a hot disaster. Out of sheer embarrassment, you'll fire me from my unpaid position. Daphne will leave me for a real man. I'll be alone for the rest of my life."

"You're going to drop bombs," Scott said, slapping Fred on the back. "The people won't know what hit them."

"Also, to boost your spirits a little and hype you up," Vincent said, "I bought each of you a gift."

My gift rattled in my arms. It also yelped—a distinct bark.

I glared at the groom. "Vincent."

"Open it." He covered a childlike smile with his hand. "Open it!"

He had wrapped the gift with sequenced paper and a bow. I ripped it off, revealing a box with knife slits sliced into the cardboard.

"Is there an animal in here, and you gift wrapped it?"

"Only right before I entered the room," Vincent said. "I swear. I also cut holes for it to breathe. It's fine. Go on. See what's inside."

I pried open the box, and inside lay a scared, trembling puppy—some over-priced poodle mutt that everyone seemed to own.

"I didn't know if you were allergic to dogs or not, so I bought the goldendoodle. They're hypoallergenic. This one is actually a double doodle. Poodle and labrador for the first generation. That was his mom. Dad was a golden retriever and poodle mix. So, it's poodle, Labrador, and golden retriever."

"Triple doodle," Fred said.

"Well, not really," Vincent said. "Labradoodle and goldendoodle. Double doodle."

My head swam as I processed the gift. They had also said doodle about three too many times. "You bought me a dog?"

"You love him already, don't you? He's a cutie, isn't he?" Vincent reached forward and petted the puppy.

"What am I going to do with a dog?"

"Love him. You're so alone all the time. Whenever I talk to you, you're by yourself. A dog is good company, my friend."

I blinked and stared at the poodle mutt. It had dark-red curly fur and a streak of white over its nose and up its brow—almost like the paint on a horse's face. It also had one foot with a white-furred sock.

"Name him Peter," Fred said, reaching over my shoulder to pet the dog. "He looks like a Peter."

I glanced back at the big man. "Why?"

"Peter Parker. Cambria Parker. It's a nice, not on-the-nose way of remembering Cambria's life through that little guy. Look how sweet he is. And he's scared. Get Peter out of the box and snuggle with him."

"Go on now," Vincent said. "Snuggle with Peter."

I reached into the box and scooped out the dog, and I held him close to my chest. His little body trembled against me, and it buried its face into the crook of my arm. I immediately felt a connection to the dog—like it had chosen me, like it had ducked and avoided everyone else in the room and chosen me.

"Bagley." I scratched the puppy's floppy ears.

"What?" Fred asked.

"His name is Bagley."

"What about Peter? I thought you loved Spider-Man."

"I'm a DC guy," I said. "Batman. Flash. Aquaman."

"Take it back." Fred stepped forward and around me, to look me in the face. "Take it back or I'm telling Alina what you said."

"What did I say?" I asked.

"Aquaman?"

"What's wrong with Aquaman?"

"What's not wrong with Aquaman?"

"He's the most over-hated and underrated superhero ever. Read his comics. He's legit."

"You're joking, right?" Fred coughed an embarrassed laugh. "This is one of those rare moments where you're messing around, yeah?"

"His name is Bagley." I scratched the dog's head and rubbed my nose against his back. He was warm and stank, but like a puppy. An almost pleasant stench, if such a thing exists.

"Where's Bagley come from?" Vincent asked.

"I'm telling Alina," Fred said. "I'm not only telling her about the DC blasphemy—it's not better than Marvel; only mentally unstable people think that—but I'm also telling her what you said about Aquaman."

I turned to Vincent. "A comic artist. When I was a kid, he drew some of my favorite comics, both in Marvel and DC. When Fred said Peter Parker, I instantly thought of Mark Bagley."

"Peter is such a better name," Fred said. "You can call him Pete, or Petie, or Peter-Peter-Pumpkin-Eater, or Peter Pan, or Peter Parker, or—"

"Or Bagley." I glanced at the bed and the two other gifts. "Maybe Vincent bought you a puppy, too. You can name it Peter."

"If I had a dog, I would name it Chewie," Fred said. "Like Chewbacca."

"I have other gifts." Vincent collected the presents and divvied them out to Scott and Fred.

I loved on Bagley, never registering what the other two opened.

Imaginary Date. Tuesday, July 4th. 1921hrs.

THERE WAS A SIMPLISTIC reason I hadn't shared my plus-one with Alina, Fred, or Sarah. Yes, I had a date. But I didn't know who she was. I didn't know what she looked like or what she might be wearing. I had never even learned her name.

Glacia had this "great" (I use great in quotes because she referred to it as great, I referred to it as terrible and flawed) idea to set me up with someone on a blind date. An actual blind date.

"It's a disaster waiting to happen," I had said.

"Why?" Glacia asked.

"It won't ever work."

"Make it work."

"I'm not good at approaching women."

"That's the point. It gets you out of your comfort zone."

"So you want me to live out a nightmare scenario? Small talk with people I don't know."

Glacia chuckled. "If you find her attractive, you'll approach her and talk to her. She doesn't know your name or what you look like either. So, if she finds you attractive, she'll engage in the conversation. It negates any awkward and forced company."

"You're behaving like my mother," I said. "You know she does this to me—sets me up on blind dates."

"Think of it this way: if you find her unattractive or strange or whatever, don't tell her you're looking for a blind date or that you know me. Move on. No one gets hurt because no one is the wiser. Maybe you two just never crossed paths at the wedding."

"It's a terrible idea," I said. "I hope you know that. I've known Maya for a handful of years now, and I've known Fred for my entire life. They're the king and the queen of bad ideas. This, though, this takes the cake. This makes their ideas sound reasonable." I exhaled a forced laugh. "How do you know her?"

"High school."

"Friends?"

"Acquaintances. We ran in different circles. I follow her on social media, though, and she follows me. She posted something the other day about going to a wedding, and I commented, and, well, you know how it goes."

"I can't say I do." I'm not sure I had ever commented on anyone's social media account in my entire life, dating all the way back to high school.

"We got to chatting over Instagram."

"And I came up in conversation?"

"I said I knew someone also attending Dr. Dupree's wedding. She inquired. I mentioned you're a great guy who lives in Sacramento, and you and I had a fling. I jokingly mentioned she and you should get together and talk terribly about me. The rest is history. I hatched my little genius plan."

That was that. I had a blind date with a woman I knew absolutely nothing about. I had to wade through the crowd of fifty-ish people to find her.

I sat at the bridal table for dinner. Vincent and Shannon positioned themselves in the center. Her two bridesmaids fanned out beside her, and me and Scott sat next to Vincent.

Scott hadn't lied about the maid of honor. She was hefty and busty. He kept leaning forward and glancing past me, Vincent, and Shannon, obviously staring at the woman. His creepy tactic must have worked, because she continually glanced back at him and smiled.

I tried my hardest to blind them from my periphery and study the crowd.

At the table nearest to ours, Fred sat beside his wife, Daphne. Along with them were Maya and her new boyfriend Evan, as well as Alina and her plus-one—a handsome kid with a sharp suit and a bright smile.

Vincent didn't have any living family. So the attendees were mostly friends and co-workers, ranging in ages from early twenties to late eighties.

I moved my attention to the second of eight tables, observing the people sitting around it, and so with the next and the next, until I had glanced at all eight tables. I counted three women I found attractive and didn't already know.

At a little after 1930hrs, the caterers delivered our dinner.

I ate my steak and vegetables, dismissed the desert (I never had much of a sweet tooth), and excused myself from the table.

Two empty chairs remained at Fred and Maya's table. I wondered if Glacia had somehow contacted Vincent and asked him to leave the seats open in case my date and I joined my friends later in the night. I took a seat beside Maya's boyfriend, Evan. He was, in the purest sense of the word, handsome. I could have snapped a photograph of him with my outdated phone, sent it into a magazine, and he would have made the front cover. Unfortunately, Evan was also intelligent and charming and all around extremely likeable.

"Evan," I said. "How's it going?"

"Considering I'm sitting at a table with the three most beautiful women at this wedding, apart from the bride, of course," Evan snickered and grinned, "I'm doing incredible. Incredible wedding, right? I love how against the grain it is."

"It's different." I nodded at Alina. "Guess what?"

Her face broke into a wide, beaming smile. "You got a puppy! Are you kidding me? A puppy! Where is he?"

"How did you know?" I asked, deflated that she already knew. I glanced at Fred.

"What? You expected me not to say something? It's a freaking puppy!"

"I like the name Bagley," Alina's date said.

"Oh, shut up!" Alina and Fred simultaneously said.

"Quit being rude," Maya said, elbowing Alina in the ribs. "Are you going to introduce your brown-nosing boyfriend to August?"

"Date," Alina said, glaring at her aunt. "August, meet my date. Myles, August."

"Hey." Myles stood from his seat and reached across the table to shake my hand. "I've heard so much about you."

I shook his hand. "It's a pleasure."

"You really like DC more?" Alina frowned. "Fred told me. He told me everything. He even told me about Aquaman. Aquaman, August! I knew your standards were low with entertainment value, but I didn't think—I couldn't even imagine—they were that low. Nonexistent. Like, like, what?"

"He's an excellent character."

"Please, don't say that around me. It hurts." Alina pressed her palms over her ears and shook her head. "It hurts my head when you say that."

Maya stuck out her tongue and made a gagging noise. "No one cares about superheroes. I want to see Bagley. Why isn't he here? Where is he? How could you leave him alone? Do you have a heart? A soul? Are you a monster?"

"I thought you had a date?" Fred crossed his thick arms over his broad chest. "Some big, secret date. Where is she?"

"She's sitting right there beside him, duh," Alina said, gesturing to the empty chair beside me.

"Oh, I see." Fred tapped the corner of his eye. "Hello, Miss. I'm Fred. What's your name?" Fred looked at me with a stupid smirk. "She's quiet, huh?"

Comments and verbal assaults came from every direction. I couldn't keep up with the whirlwind of words. "Good to meet you, Myles. Evan, pleasure as always. Daphne, you look stunning. The three of you can do far better than the three of them." I stood and evacuated the war zone before another explosion of unwanted remarks crashed into my ears.

The DJ had strict instructions to play casual music during dinner. After dinner, around 2045hrs., the attendees would migrate over to the ceremony, where Fred would officiate and marry off Vincent and Shannon Dupree. The newly married couple would share their first kiss as the first firework exploded—and the photographer had better capture the moment. Only then would the DJ ratchet up his music to something more lively, drawing the energetic crowd onto the dance floor to celebrate new love and the liberation of America. No first dance. No mother or father dance. No speeches or toasts.

Dinner. Ceremony. Party.

That order, though different from the traditional wedding, was inconvenient for me finding my blind date. I had a hard enough time in ideal circumstances talking to women I didn't know. I couldn't just insert myself into a conversation at a random table with one of the three women I found attractive.

So, I veered back toward Vincent's mansion, where I had left Bagley in a crate. Along with the puppy, Vincent had also purchased me a crate, a few toys, food, a leash, and a collar.

As I climbed the three steps onto this wraparound porch, one of the three women I had spotted earlier stepped out of the house.

She gently smiled at me when our eyes met. "Hi." She skittered down the steps right past me, not sparing a second glance.

Was that her? Only one way to know.

"Hi." Warmth fled from my groin, allowing a frigid clamp to pull my testicles into my body. The escaped heat rushed into my face. My cheeks burned and my ears simmered.

The woman glanced over her shoulder at me. She had mousy-brown hair styled in an updo, and she wore a simple black dress and flat sandals. She smiled, and her entire face lit up. "Hello."

I cleared my throat and smiled back. The forced motion from raising the corner of my lips felt awkward, and I remembered what Fred, Alina, and Maya had said about my smile in Santa Cruz. That I looked like a serial killer. So, I stopped smiling, but I wasn't sure what to do with my mouth. Did I frown? Smirk with only my lips. A few terrible quiet seconds passed, and I realized I just stared at the stranger, making weird facial expressions, and saying nothing. I cleared my throat again.

"Can I help you?" she asked, and her smile slightly wavered.

"I'm August."

"Hi, August."

"Hi."

"Okay, then."

"How do you... how do you know the, the bride?"

"I don't."

"Oh." My heart stopped beating, and my chest hurt. I thought, for only a breath, I was having a heart attack.

"I know the groom," she said. "We work together. Well, he's my boss."

"Oh."

"I'm a dental hygienist at his office."

I don't know what tossed the next statement out of my mouth. I don't think I ever would have consciously spoken it, but at that moment, I just spoke words to say something and break the awkward silence. "You ever work on Dr. Moreno's teeth?"

The throwaway comment broke the ice.

The woman flashed a smile that could have melted a glacier, and she laughed—something like fire crackling at the bottom of a warm, inviting campfire. "That's why I recognize you. You sat at the bridal table, right? You're the other groomsman."

"Guilty."

"Well, I haven't cleaned Dr. Moreno's teeth. I don't think anyone, including himself, has cleaned his teeth for years."

"He's a dentist, though."

"Orthopedic surgeon. Still, he believes in some fringe science that preaches about the harmful effects of toothpaste and mouthwash."

"So... what does he do?"

The woman shrugged and giggled. "Ancient techniques. I don't know. But it's raunchy."

"Has he ever burped beside or near... or on you before?"

"What?" she asked, drawing out the vowel in a shocked laugh. "Did that happen to you?"

"Not even an hour ago."

"And you're still here, not on life support at some hospital?"

"I owed it to Vincent to power through the distress. I have this constant pressure in the back of my throat, though. It feels like at any moment, I might vomit." I coughed, a rough hacking noise, and I leaned forward, toward the woman, as if I might lose my dinner all over her cheap sundress.

She squealed and hopped away from me, fully laughing from her stomach, though. "Don't you dare!"

A half-smile (a natural one) rose at the corners of my mouth.

"You're August, right?"

I nodded. "And you are?"

"Lauren."

Did I mention Glacia's name to Lauren? I wanted to. I had this impulsive need to ask, to know if she was my blind date. But I bit my tongue. What if she said no? Where did that leave me? Spending the rest of the night with Lauren, or searching for the woman Glacia had arranged for me to meet? What if she said no, but she was Glacia's friend and she didn't enjoy my company?

Too many concerns. Too many unanswered questions.

"I have a puppy," I said, cheating. Puppies are life's cheat code.

"Do you?"

"Vincent bought him for me as a groomsmen gift. He's in the house. Do you want to see him?"

She hesitated to answer, understandably so. We had met two minutes ago, and I invited her into the home, where she and I would be alone. I instantly regretted the invitation and felt more than embarrassed by it.

"I'm sorry," I said. "That sounds really creepy."

"It does."

"I revoke my invitation. I don't want you anywhere near my new dog."

"That sucks, because I love puppies."

"I'm still going to check on him, and I can't prevent you from inviting yourself to meet him."

Lauren crossed her arms and popped her lips. "August, can I be candid with you?"

"Please."

Lauren hesitated. "I'm here on a date."

"Oh." My heart sank into my stomach. "I see."

"But, and this probably sounds strange, but I—"

"You don't know who he is."

Lauren slowly nodded her head up and down. "How did you know?"

"Funny enough, I'm also here on a date, and I don't know who she is."

"That's a really weird coincidence."

"Seems almost... premeditated," I said.

Lauren broke off another giggle and bit her lower lip. I could have looked at her all night like that—gently swaying in the soft breeze with her hands crossed at her waist and her sundress swishing around her legs, and that smile and those eyes.

"Well, well, well," a familiar and unwanted voice chided from behind me. "Who's this?" Maya bumped her elbow into my arm. "Your imaginary date?"

"I'm Lauren."

"I'm Maya. You here with August?"

"I don't know." Lauren never looked at Maya, only at me, and she bore a quarter-grin the entire time.

"She's with me," I said. "Lauren, Maya. Maya, Lauren."

"How do you two know each other?" Maya crossed her arms and reared back her head in a judgemental stare. "I've never heard about you before."

Maya and I had a complicated relationship. We both had romantic feelings for each other, but the timing had never worked out (she always had a boyfriend or I always chickened out from making a move), and as we grew closer together, I learned we weren't romantically compatible. I didn't want to change her, though, and I know she wouldn't want to change me. So, we co-existed as friends with complicated, tangled feelings for each other.

"We just met," Lauren said.

"Right here? You just met, and you're still hanging around talking to this guy?"

"He's charming."

"Him?" Maya pointed at me with her thumb. "Charming? We're talking about August, right, not that tree?"

"I think he's funny."

Maya turned her full attention to me and narrowed her eyes. "How much did you pay her? Has anyone ever described you as funny before?"

"Maybe funny looking," Fred said. He had snuck up behind me, and the sound of his voice startled me.

"I think he's funny in like a sad way." Alina appeared as if from thin air.

How had I missed the hate mob congregating around Lauren and me? Had I been that infatuated with my blind date?

Alina clicked her tongue. "You know, like you laugh not really with or at him, but for him."

"Why are you all here?" I asked. "Don't you have dates to entertain?"

"I wanted to see Peter," Alina said.

"Bagley," I said. "You're not naming my dog."

"I love the name Bagley," Lauren said.

"Also, Vincent was looking for you," Fred said. "I think we're getting ready."

"You ready?" I asked. "With the speech and all?" I mentioned the speech to shut him up. It was three against one, and I hoped to even the odds a little—though I don't think the odds ever stood in anyone's favor when Maya and Alina stood against them.

My tactic failed, however. Fred showed me his teeth in a predatory grin. "Oh, it's ready."

Maya, who stood about two feet away from me, leaned into my shoulder and whispered in my ear. "I helped encourage him a little, emphasis on the courage. Liquid courage."

"You got him drunk?"

"I'm not drunk," Fred said. But since Maya had showed her hand, I could hear the slight slur and the slow speech pattern.

I cracked a knuckle. "Lauren, that's Fred. He's an idiot because he never learns his lesson and, for some odd and unexplainable reason, continues drinking with Maya."

"You have a beautiful smile," Fred said.

"Thank you," Lauren said, brightening her beautiful smile.

"That's Alina."

Alina waved a finger.

"You've met Maya," I said. "Everyone, meet Lauren."

"Your imaginary date?" Alina asked.

"Yes." I glanced at Lauren. "Right? Date?"

"Yeah," Lauren said.

"My imaginary date," I confirmed.

Wedding Reception. Tuesday, July 4th. 2107hrs.

FRED HAD KNOWN VINCENT Dupree as long as I had. Yet, he somehow strung together a beautiful ceremony by following the two basic rules of speaking. Short and sweet.

While standing on the dock beside Vincent, in front of the rest of the attendees, I had a difficult time keeping my eyes off Lauren. A twinge of guilt knotted in my stomach—a natural feeling I had no more control over than the weather. The guilt rooted in Cambria's death. It came from the idea that Cambria's life had ended, and my life had continued. I felt something toward another woman again, and only two months after the tragic incident. That knowledge didn't sit well with me.

It felt unfair.

At one point, Lauren raised her hand to her shoulder and waved at me, letting me know she had caught me staring at her.

I shifted my eyes like a young boy will glance away after his grade school crush notices him watching her from across the room. I smirked, though, happy that she had caught me in the act.

"I want to finish with this." Fred addressed Vincent and Shannon.

I appreciated that about his delivery. He rarely acknowledged the attendees, but remained focused on the bride and groom, for they deserved all the attention.

"We all know the cliche marital bible verse. Love is kind. Love does not envy. So on and so forth. Before we pray over this marriage and seal the deal with a whopping smacker, I want to provide a simple twist on those verses in First Corinthians." Fred shifted his eyes and stared outward, most likely at Daphne, and he paused. "We all know the verses, but we don't take into consideration the entire chapter. If we read verse eleven, it says that when I was a child, I acted like a child. But when I was a man, I put aside my childish ways. When we were children, we loved in childish ways. We loved impatiently. Enviously. Boastfully. So on and so forth. But love grows up, and we must mature with it. Love matured looks like Jesus. And it's our job to love others, especially our spouses, as Jesus loves us."

I glanced at Maya. She held Evan's hand with both of hers. Alina sat next to them with her head on Myles' shoulder.

I thought of Cambria as I returned my attention to Lauren. Life never makes sense, and I don't think it's our job to make sense of it. Fred, despite his many obscurities, was a reflective person, and he said one thing that resonated deeply within me. It's our job to love others, and to love them like a mature adult.

Fred went through the vows, the rings, the whole nine yards. He smiled first at Vincent, then at Shannon. "It is my honor to present Mr. and Mrs. Vincent Dupree. Now, go on with you nasty selves." He raised a hand into the air, and a second later, a high-pitched whine streaked into the sky. "You may kiss the bride."

Vincent and Shannon kissed. Behind them, fireworks exploded into the shapes of red, white, and blue hearts.

"God bless America!" Fred said. "God bless the Duprees. Let's party!"

The D.J.'s song thundered throughout the yard. *God Bless the USA* by Lee Greenwood.

Vincent and Shannon exited the aisle first and headed straight to the dance floor. Most everyone else crowded in with them, dancing and jumping and singing along to the lyrics.

Even I joined in, shouting as I pumped my fist into the air, "and I'll gladly stand up!"

The D.J. mixed the record and sampled another number over the patriotic one playing, changing the songs with no lag—some hip-hop tune from my high school years. It reminded me of dances in the gymnasium and college parties in the dormitories.

I slipped away from the dance floor when the music changed, not needing to relive my formative years. I padded over to the pop-up bar. The bartender was a tiny woman with tattoos sleeving both of her arms, a shaved head, and piercings along her eyebrows.

"You have a water bottle?" I asked.

The woman leaned forward, nearer to me. "Speak up! I can't hear you."

"Water."

She nodded once, bent over, and grabbed a bottle of water from beneath the counter. "Anything else?"

"No, thank you." I tipped her a few bucks and paced to the empty table where Fred and Maya had enjoyed dinner earlier. Currently, they and their dates, along with Alina and her date, cut up the dance floor.

I sat and watched them with a simple sense of pride.

I enjoyed the moment—the pure, raw excitement of new life and new love. Of everyone dancing and singing and laughing. My mind drifted, as it's apt to do, to Aaron Brooks and Cambria Parker. Whenever a surge of happiness jolted through me, I instinctually thought of them. It was a knee-jerk mentality, something I doubt I would ever rid myself of, but their lost lives didn't cloud my bright evening. That was a win. I thought of them, and with a little effort, I dismissed those thoughts.

As if life rewarded me for actively trying to move on from my past, Lauren appeared from the crowd. She walked to the table and sat beside me, scooted her chair to face the dance floor. A natural, permanent smile covered her face as she watched everyone boogie.

"You're not much of a dancer?" she asked, her voice loud to overcome the music, her gleaming eyes fixed on the dance floor.

"Not usually."

"How do you know Glacia?"

"She gave me her house."

Lauren shifted her attention to me. "She what?"

"Her Nana's house. It was haunted—well, supposedly haunted—and I fished out the ghosts."

"Hold on, hold on, hold on. That's a lot. Her Nana's house was haunted?"

"Yes."

"You fished out the ghosts? What does that even mean?"

"I'm a paranormal investigator."

Lauren no longer found any interest in the dancing occurring on the dance floor. She stared directly at me, lips curved upward into that fixed grin. She exuded a contagious high energy. In her presence, I wanted nothing more than to smile and laugh and... and dance even.

"Really?" Lauren asked. "So you actually hunt ghosts for a living?"

"More or less. Ghosts, believe it or not, don't exist."

"You're kidding?"

I smirked. "People hire me to investigate supernatural occurrences, or occurrences they believe are supernatural. I'm more grounded in logic and evidence than most other people in my field, so I often find rational answers. The ghosts in question haunting Nana's house were none other than Glacia's mom and uncle."

"Really? Why? What's the motivation for something like that?"

"That's the exact question I always ask." I blinked a few times to regather the simple facts of the story. "Glacia lived—still lives—a state away. Her Nana willed her the home, but she didn't want the headache of maintaining it from five-hundred miles away. Her mom and uncle figured if they became a ghostly nuisance, Glacia would wash her hands of the entire ordeal and gift the home to them. They would turn around and sell it for a fortune."

"Wow. I thought my dad loved a good get-rich-quick scheme. That's next level."

I scanned the dance floor until I saw Shannon. *She's the get-rich-quick queen*, I thought. I dismissed my cynicism, though, when I saw Vincent beside her, dancing and laughing like a kid—like someone without a worry in the world.

"But she gave the house to you instead?" Lauren asked.

"What's that?"

"Glacia gifted you the house, not her mom."

"She did." I licked my lips. "We also had a brief romantic affair."

"Really?" Lauren didn't sound jealous or upset about the information, more playful, as if teasing me.

"I really liked her."

"She's really easy to like."

"She didn't think the long-distance would work, and she enjoys where she's at and what she's doing in Oregon." I kept my gaze on the dance floor, but I could feel Lauren's eyes on me.

"Why would you tell me about you and her?"

"I'm big on honesty."

"You're not afraid that'll scare me away?"

I considered how to respond, peeling the layers of her question. In the end, I stopped complicating matters more than necessary. "If it had scared you away, I don't think I would have chased you."

Lauren returned her attention to the dance floor. The song ended, and another began. "Are you working on a case right now?"

"Two of them."

"Can I ask what supernatural flavor they are about?"

"A golem attacked and kidnapped someone."

Lauren grimaced. "A golem? What's that mean?"

"A creature magically formed from the body parts of random corpses."

"Gross."

"Also the Vampire of Sacramento."

"The serial killer?"

"Yeah."

"Is that scary?"

I had never factored fear into my job, at least not until Daniel Quinn appeared, threatened my family, and murdered Cambria. "It can be scary. If someone like a serial killer learns I'm after him, or that I'm close to finding him, they can turn their attention to me and those I care about. That's scary. Knowing my work might hurt someone I love." I paused and cracked a knuckle. "Knowing it has."

"It has?"

I hesitated, but made the hard to decision to tell her about Cambria. Why wouldn't I? If anything blossomed between Lauren and me from this night, she would eventually learn of it. Why not save the time and tell her everything right then, especially if it potentially kept her from danger?

Lauren said nothing for a long time. I thought she was waiting for a window to appear so she could jump through it and leave. "They work for you." Lauren nodded at the busy dance floor, but I knew who she meant.

"Fred's my assistant. Alina is an intern. Maya writes for the *Here & Now*. She and I often help each other out, though—I provide her with an exciting story, and she helps me solve the case. She and Alina are related, and they're both... brilliant. Borderline geniuses. In fact, there's not a single case I could've solved without their help." I grabbed my water and drank. As I placed it back on the table, I realized Lauren didn't have wine or beer. "You don't drink?"

Lauren scratched her cheek and shook her head.

"You care if I ask why not?"

Her illuminating smile faded into a grimace. "I'm not deceitful, but I'm also not as openly honest as you. Is that okay?"

"Yeah."

"I don't want you to hate me. Not tonight. Maybe if we see each other later, I'll tell you then. But tonight, I don't want you to hate me."

Aaron Brooks flashed across my mind. "I understand."

Maya staggered from the assembly, dragging Evan behind her. A tendril of hair stuck to her sweaty forehead, and she breathed hard.

"Hey," Evan said, tugging at her arm and moving toward the bar. "You want a drink? I'm going to grab a beer."

"Red wine," Maya said. She turned to me and smiled. "Hey, you."

"How's the dancing?"

Maya's smile widened, and she giggled.

"What?"

"Come on."

"What?"

"August."

"No," I said. "I'm here with Lauren."

The song changed, slowing to something anyone could dance to, as long as they had a partner to hold. Maya held out her hand. "Will you dance with me?"

"No."

"Do it," Lauren said.

"What?"

"Do it, but only if you promise me the next slow song."

From where I sat to where she stood, I stared up into Maya's dark eyes. God, she was beautiful. The stars twinkled above her like a cape of diamonds—like beads of water holding sunlight. I almost could have reached up and grabbed them, drank them, become drunk on them.

"Please?" Maya asked.

I sighed and grabbed her hand. "Fine."

Lauren clapped in delight.

Maya led me toward the dance floor.

"What's Evan going to think of this?" I asked.

"He won't care."

"You're sure?"

"I'm sure." Maya stopped on the edge of the hardwood laid over the grass, and she pressed her body against mine. Chills sprinted down my spine, and I had to remind myself to breathe. "How did you meet Lauren?"

"A wedding."

"Whose wedding?" Maya placed my hand on her hip. She held my other one in hers.

"Vincent Dupree's," I said.

"You met her here?"

"Glacia set us up on a blind date."

"That's... odd, but okay. Do you like her?"

"I only just met her. "

"Quit being so politically correct all the time. You meet people and you instantly like or dislike them. Do you like her?"

"Yeah."

Maya rested her head on my chest as we slowly swayed to the love song. "It's okay to like other women. You know that, right?"

My hand felt sweaty and heavy on Maya's hip. Did she notice that? I lifted my fingers off her dress and cracked my wrist, releasing tension before returning it.

"I really like Evan, like I like him a lot," Maya said. "And he likes me, too. I know he does. If you're waiting for me, August... don't." That single word crashed into my heart, and it hurt. "Okay? Never wait on anyone. Especially the dead."

My stomach clenched as I thought of Cambria.

"She and I had drunken, sloppy conversations in Santa Cruz," Maya said. "She really liked you. Do you know what that means when someone really likes you? For example, you really like me, don't you?"

"It depends on the moment."

I felt her smile rise on my chest. "What do you want for me?"

I didn't answer her immediately, but waited a second, allowing myself to answer her completely. "Happiness."

"Exactly. Cambria really liked you, which meant she wanted you to be happy. That's what people do for other people they like, right? They make them happy. I know it's tough for you with what happened, but Cambria liked you, August. She wanted you to be happy. I want you to be happy. That's all I wanted to say. You're allowed to be happy."

My eyes filled with tears, and I blinked them away. I laughed to pass the silence between us. "What do you think of Myles?"

"If Alina asks, he's the worst. I can't stand him. Reverse psychology, though. She'll want to rebel and date him because I don't like him. But I love that sexy, little, underaged boy. If I was Alina, oh, man." Maya chuckled and stared up at me. "You look really handsome tonight."

"You look really pretty, yourself."

In the distance, a firework exploded, followed by another.

I'm not sure if the slow dance or the love song or the fireworks or the romance sitting heavily in the air got to me, but I spoke without thinking. "I really want to kiss you."

Maya, still with her head on my chest, stared up at me and sucked in her lips, as if hiding them from mine, as if putting them away so I couldn't kiss her. "Me, too," she said.

The song ended then, and Maya broke away from our embrace. She snickered and skipped back to the table. Evan waited with a glass of red wine. Lauren sat there, too, biting her lip and smiling at me.

Back at Home. Tuesday, July 4th. 2342hrs

THE HEADLIGHTS OF MY Honda Civic hybrid cut through the pervading darkness and shined over Nana's (my) house. I had lived there almost two months now, and I still hadn't become used to referring to the home as mine. If it wasn't Nana's—a woman I never had the pleasure of meeting, though I heard she was quite incredible—than it was Glacia's house. Not mine, though.

I hadn't lived there. I had only stayed there. I had existed within the walls, storing my belongings there and sleeping on a mattress placed directly on the floor.

I glanced to the passenger seat, where my new puppy curled into a furry ball. I reached over and stroked his back.

"Maybe you can help me turn the place into a home," I said. "You and me, and occasionally Alina, with her movie marathons. She has to put her room together, though." I chuckled in the dark silence of the cab. "We'll eventually make it a home. Soon enough, right?"

Bagley continued to sleep.

My mind ran backward, falling and landing at the wedding reception. The D.J. played his last song at 2300hrs. By that time, Lauren had convinced me to dance—not slow dance, either, but to actually dance. Well, in my case, it was more like flopping around randomly, doing my best impersonation of a fish out of water. No one cared, though. They were all drunk, or terrible dancers, or both, and they all just wanted to have fun. My unique movements blended into a crowd of people with little rhythmic skills.

Once the last song concluded, I looped my arm around Lauren's shoulder, and we staggered to the table, laughing all the while.

I held onto that moment for a second—us stumbling off the dance floor, laughing for no other reason than we were drunk on the night, and holding each other.

It's strange to live again after experiencing emotional death. My life had continued, still continues, after I murdered Aaron Brooks. That continuation proved nearly impossible for me, but after a lot of work, I had climbed from that grave and breathed fresh air again.

After Cambria's death, I stood on the edge of the chasm, tempted to leap back into the darkness and lose myself once more. Except, instead of struggling and fighting against those who cared about me as I had before, I allowed them to hold me, to prevent me from losing myself.

I only knew Cambria for a few weeks before her death, but we had made a special connection in that short time, and we had explored a relationship. Still, we hadn't known each other. Not really. I mourned her loss, and I blamed myself for her death. I felt anger and frustration. Most of all, guilt consumed me—guilt that I lived, breathed, danced at weddings, and laughed with new women.

It all meshed and mixed into a confusing concoction.

The most pressing emotion didn't even center on Cambria's death, but on the anger directed at Daniel Quinn for his role in her murder. Anger that his existence now prevented me from bringing new people into my life. My family and friends were in constant danger because they knew me.

That rationale turned into a slippery slope, though. Did I separate myself from everyone I cared for to prevent Quinn from hurting them? If I did that, I returned to my original position—buried in darkness. Living but dead.

You're allowed to be happy, Maya had said as we danced.

"What do you think, Bagley?" I asked.

The puppy turned his block head upward and yawned.

"I'm overthinking things? You're right. Lauren is a big girl. I'll sit down with her and lay everything out, allow her to make her own choice in the matter. If you think that's best, so do I. I should call you Yoda, for you're a wise little puppy."

I scooped Bagley up with one hand and turned off the car with the other. The headlights dimmed, entrenching the property in darkness once more.

I padded up the front porch steps, unlocked the front door, and made my way into the kitchen.

Gerald lay on his back in the living room, feet propped up on the wall, and he held a book up in the air. A guitar lay beside him. The man was buck naked. Everything that God and man had given him lay out for the world (me) to see.

Without words able to form off my lips, I cleared my throat.

Gerald held the book in one hand. With his free hand, he showed me the universal finger for 'wait a second.' After thirty seconds had passed, the man closed the book and said, "How goes it?"

"Not well," I said.

"What happened? Lady trouble? Did your plus-one not show?"

"Man trouble."

"Oh, I'm sorry. I assumed your plus-one was a female. I'm an idiot. I asked Sarah about that, too... your sexual orientation. Not that I care. I don't. It's just Gio... he's, well, you know." Gerald lowered his voice and whispered, "Gay," as if uttering a bad word. "I asked Sarah why you and Gio never went on a date."

"My man troubles are lying on my living room floor. Naked and far too exposed."

Gerald's eyes widened. "Oh, August. I'm sorry if I gave you any kind of impression, but I'm not into men. And if I were, I don't think you would be my type. You're a very sweet and attractive man, but you're just not my flavor. Your vanilla, and I like a swirl. You know?"

I shook my head, not having a clue what he meant. "Why are you naked, Gerald?"

His lips formed a circle. "I see the confusion now. You're confused by my naked body."

"Very much so."

"You thought I was trying to seduce you?"

"Didn't think that."

"I'm not."

"Why are you naked?"

"I took a bath," Gerald said, as if that simple statement explained the entire situation.

"Okay."

"Cleaned my body." He rolled over and sat his hairy butt on the hardwood floor—bare skin to the ground. The man stroked his unkempt beard.

"That doesn't answer my question. Why are you naked?"

"Well, after I cleaned myself up, I realized something. I only had my old clothes. They're dirty and stinky. I shuddered at the idea of slipping back into those stiff, ripped pants and old shirt. Also, I didn't want to go through your closet and steal your clothes."

"So you're naked?"

"Yeah."

"Why not a towel?"

"I didn't think about that."

Gerald was a few inches shorter than me, but probably weighed a few extra pounds. We most likely wore different-sized jeans, but I thought he could fit into a pair of my old sweatpants and a T-shirt.

"Wait here." I slipped out of the kitchen and grabbed Gerald some spare clothes I hadn't worn in years. I handed them to him. "You can wear these tonight. Tomorrow, I'll take you shopping for some clean clothes that fit you."

Gerald stepped into the sweatpants and reached into the shirt, pulling it over his head.

I had a few foldout chairs placed around the living room, but no other furniture. I sat on the ground, though, and set Bagley beside me. "What are you reading?"

"Dracula. I hope you don't mind, but I found it in an opened box. I didn't go through anything else. I swear."

"You ever read it before?"

"I have," Gerald said. "A few times."

"Really?"

Behind his gray beard, his light blue eyes boasted of an unexpected youth. "You think because I'm homeless, I can't read?"

"No," I said.

"That I'm lazy?"

"No."

"Dumb?"

"It has nothing to do with your lifestyle. Most people haven't read Bram Stoker. My family and friend group won't read anything, let alone classic literature."

"Frankenstein is my favorite," Gerald said. "Few people realize Victor Frankenstein was the monster, and his creation was the victim. God abandoning humankind." Gerald laughed. "It's a tragedy, that story."

Bagley sniffed the floor, paused, and made a puddle on the ground. He stomped through it, tracking pee-paw marks across the floor. I stood and ambled into the kitchen, collected some cleaning spray and a hand towel, and wiped up the mess and the dog's feet.

"New dog?" Gerald asked.

"Bagley," I said. "A wedding gift."

"To you?"

"Yup."

"You care if I pet him?"

"Go for it."

Gerald palmed the puppy and held him in his lap, scratching the dog's ear. "A poodle-golem?"

I cocked my head, surprised by the timely reference, considering my active case. "Yeah."

"How was the wedding?"

I thought about Fred's speech and dancing and meeting Lauren—of her smile and her laugh and the way her sundress fit her body. "It was good."

"I noticed you didn't bring your plus-one home."

"It's not that kind of relationship," I said.

"You're not that into him?"

I rolled my eyes. "Her. I'm into women, and I was very much into her. But there's a lot of complications involved. I'm not sure what to do."

"Old Gerry doesn't have a lot to offer, but he always has an ear to lend."

I half-smiled.

"You don't trust the advice of a homeless man? I used to teach, you know? High school English in a county program. To succeed in that kind of classroom, I had to learn how to listen to the students. They don't care about what you have to say until you care about what they have to say."

I eyed the man sitting in the living room, wearing my clothes, petting my dog. "What happened?"

"You mean why am I now homeless?"

I nodded.

"Call me a bleeding heart, but the education system is as backward as the criminal justice system. I made a choice, and I chose not to be a part of the cog. Politicians and bureaucrats don't care about the kids. They don't care about those rotting in prison. They don't care about equality between genders or races or whatever. They care about influence, power, and money, and they will say or promise whatever they need to say or promise to earn their influence, power, and money." Gerald cleared his throat. "I refused to act like a pawn in their game. So, I quit teaching, and I quit the capitalistic, oppressive society. I chose, and I continue to choose, homelessness."

I clicked my tongue, instantly thinking of about a thousand other options Gerald could have pursued. But who was I to inundate him with my opinions? Opinions were, after all, subject to perspective and personal experience. To criticize his belief was akin to insulting him and what he had gone through. Besides, his intentions seemed noble enough, and he seemed aloofly happy.

"Do you find it all rewarding?" I asked.

"I find it enlightening," Gerald said. "I can view society from an angle you couldn't imagine seeing it from."

"Does that angle flatter us?"

"Not usually. If I sat on one side of the alley, and a starving dog sat on the other, most people with a helping bone in their body would go to the dog before attending to me, another human. If they care enough to approach me, it's never met with eye contact. They drop a few dollars into a hat, and they move on with their day. I'm invisible because people choose not to see me."

I thought of what Gio had shared with me—he and Alina often went to the alley to smoke with Gerald.

"What about Alina?"

The man looked at me with his gentle blue eyes. "That young woman is special. She could save the entire world, like a real-life superhero."

I lowered my gaze into my lap.

"And she sees you as her hero," Gerald said. "Do you know what kind of power you hold over her? You're the hero to a hero. Don't you dare ever forget that."

"I won't." I already had too many emotional conversations that night, and I had grown weary of them. I shifted gears. "Tomorrow morning, I have a meeting. You can come with me, and I'll buy you a McGriddle.

When I'm done, we'll head to a store and get you some clothes. Not only that, how does a haircut sound?"

"What about this little cutie?" Gerald nodded at Bagley, reminding me I now owned a puppy, and I had to attend to its needs.

"I'll drop him off at the office before we hit the shops. I'm sure he'll find enough friends to keep him company there." I stood and retrieved my dog from Gerald. "Thanks for chatting. I'm off to bed, though." Not that I would get much sleep, but maybe I could make some progress in my investigations.

"Thanks for opening your house."

I regarded Gerald for a second, debating whether I should ask what popped into my head. "Did you do it?"

"Beat up those kids?"

"Yeah."

Gerald slowly nodded. "I truly, in my mind, believed they had trans-formed into giant chickens. I know how that sounds, but it's the truth. I attacked them to defend myself—at least that's how it played in my head. I wouldn't knowingly hurt anyone, let alone a kid."

I looked into his soft-blue eyes, and I watched his face as he answered me. When Gerald finished speaking, I believed him.

The Bloody Affair. Wednesday, July 5th. 0653hrs.

I HAD FIRST MET Ted Wilson in Sacramento State during a criminal justice class. We never really hit it off in college, and when we attended the police academy together, we remained acquaintances rather than friends.

Wilson was the cop's cop—big and broad and loud, bearing the confidence of a lion. During the academy, he excelled in every simulated situation, hand-to-hand combat, and firearm accuracy. After training ended for the day, he always led a group of cadets to the bar, where he always bought the first round and out drank anyone who wished to keep up with him.

Detective Wilson now sat across from me in the McDonald's booth. He was big, but different from Fred's gargantuan size. Fred physically towered over Wilson at six-feet-six and well over two-hundred-fifty pounds, and he didn't possess the physical stature of a professional athlete like Fred. Ted Wilson, though, ballooned his size with confidence—or rather, arrogance. If he and Fred walked into a room together, eyes would naturally settle on the imposing nature of Wilson, and Fred might appear small next to the smaller man.

I scanned a one-page brief written on the Vampire of Sacramento. It didn't provide me with any new information from what I had already gleaned from forums and media sites, but it filtered out the nonsense, magnified the rare bits of truth that had leaked to the public.

A man, probably in his late twenties or early thirties, had brutally murdered five people over seven months. He drained their bodies of blood through a precise gash to their carotid artery. Though some of the blood splashed onto the crime scene, most of it vanished with the vampire.

Did he consume straight from their body, or did he store it and transfer it back to his house? I leaned toward the latter.

No credible witnesses had come forward, though the latest murder—the one from two nights ago—had happened in a residential home while the wife and child slept. The wife apparently crawled back into bed with her husband, finding him cold and stiff beside her.

I dropped the brief on the table, cracked a knuckle, and drank some coffee. "No legitimate leads?"

"I have one person—the woman who found the second body—claiming she saw a bat hanging from a rafter. It was watching her. She's called after every other murder to remind me that vampires turn into bats. That's our most legitimate lead."

"You think he's an actual vampire?"

Wilson boomed with laughter. "No. No, no, no. I don't. I think he's a psychotic, unstable individual who needs to be put down like a rabid dog."

I tugged at my earlobe. "I'm not here to help you put someone down like a sick dog. You know that, right?"

Wilson smirked and nodded as he bit into his egg sandwich.

"Also, you're asking for my help, which means you're asking for help from a paranormal investigator."

"Oh, come on, man. Not even you believe any of that nonsense. Every one of your cases winds up as something normal. What's Sherlock Holmes say? The simplest explanation or answer is always better than the impossible. Something like that. You know what I mean?"

"If you eliminate the impossible, whatever remains, however improbable, must be the truth."

Wilson snapped and pointed at me. "That's it. You do all that reading stuff?"

"Now and again."

"Good for you. It puts me to sleep. I prefer talking to people. If they don't talk, I prefer punching people." Wilson flashed a playful smile, but I thought he might be serious. "Anyway, impossible is impossible. Vampires are impossible. So, what does that leave us with?" He reached over to the empty chair and placed a folder on the table. He slid it over to me. "NDA."

"Can I share the information with my team?"

"Whoever you share this information with has to sign a contract."

I grabbed the manila folder and opened it. I signed without reading. Wilson was boisterous and impulsive, but he wasn't looking to take advantage of me. I trusted his contract without having to waste time reading it.

"Let's get down to business, huh?" he asked.

"That's why we're here."

Wilson reached over and produced another folder. He exchanged the contract with the case file, sliding it to me.

I opened it and saw pictures and reports from each of the five crime scenes. In the middle—the vampire's third kill—was Patricia Huffman, the woman I had danced with at the dive bar. I fixed my attention on her picture. She was naked, lying in a cornfield, shriveled and impossibly pale.

I remembered her asking me to dance, and we had danced to a country song. She had two-stepped her way around me, full of life, infusing me with life.

"You alright? Need a bucket?" Wilson asked. "You look green."

I ignored him and skimmed the file. A laceration to her carotid artery. At one point, the killer had propped her upside down to encourage the blood to continue to flow from the wound. She, as were all the victims, had been alive as the vampire drained them of their life source. He gagged and bound them—ligature bruises showed on the victims' wrists and ankles. After removing all their blood, the vampire cut out their hearts. He removed the gags and binds from the corpses, cleaned up the scene, and disappeared into the night.

"Five victims?" I asked.

"Completely random, too," Wilson said. "He murdered a middle-aged father from a couple of nights ago, an older woman, and two elderly men. The first victim was—"

"The young woman." I flipped back to the first page where it showed the young lady's body.

"My best theory is that the vampire drains the blood and stores it somewhere. He drinks it until he runs low on the supply, and then he has to replenish by killing again. What do I know about vampires, though? That's why I need your help."

I closed the file, no longer caring to see the pictures of the bodies. "Five victims?"

"You can ask that as many times as you want, but the answer remains constant. Five victims."

"I don't know."

"Don't know what?"

"I mean, why drain blood now? Why not a year ago, or ten years ago? What changed in this man's life? Or was he already consuming blood, maybe just animal blood? Maybe he worked for a blood bank and pilfered his supply before getting caught. Desperate times call for desperate measures, and without the constant supply of blood, he had to resort to murder. Is it a sex thing? Does he get off on it? Is it a psychological thing?"

"I think we can answer yes on that one. He's definitely deranged."

"If psychological, what mental disorders drive people to drink blood? Have similar crimes occurred elsewhere? Has he killed before... maybe practice kills—kills that won't match his current style, but helped perfect his methods. Maybe he's new in Sacramento, but he's an established murderer in Los Angeles or Austin or New York City."

Wilson furiously scribbled on a notepad to keep up with my questioning. I wasn't always the greatest at speaking, especially about myself, but I had a knack for asking questions and listening to what others had to say.

"Anything else?" Wilson asked

I drank some more coffee and thought for a few seconds. "Have you created a timeline for the days leading up to the victims' deaths? What did they do? Where did they go? Who did they speak with? Did they or anyone else notice someone following them? Serial killers see themselves as predators, right? They often stalk their victims. They're not like mass murderers, who rampage and take as many people as quickly as possible. Serial killers are deliberate and thoughtful with what they do. They're purposeful. Did the neighbors notice anyone strange? Co-workers? The victims' families? Have you talked to any of them?"

Wilson's cocksure smile waned. "I've made a list of people to call, most being those you named. I inherited this case from Madden, and he left me with very little. We haven't uncovered a single thing. Not one witness testimony. Not a shred of evidence. Nothing. Nada. Zilch."

"I need contracts for three other people to sign. If you want to have a shot at solving this case, you need my team involved."

"Three contracts? You only have two people on staff."

"Three. That's nonnegotiable."

"Okay. I'll make it happen."

"Once they sign the NDAs, I'll give them the case files and assign them some legwork. I'm not sure if we'll find anything you couldn't, especially considering we don't have the resources you have access to."

"You're not wearing a badge," Wilson said. "Folks talk differently to you. You can walk through doors that don't even open for me. We both have things the other doesn't. So, why not share our toys?"

"Speaking of sharing," I said. "What do you know about Jackson Armstead?"

"Don't know the name."

"Could you look him up for me, let me know if you have anything on him?"

"Another case?"

"Another case where I have little to nothing to work from. If you can provide me with something... well, sharing and all that, right?"

"Right." Wilson jotted down the name. "Jackson Armstead."

"Yup."

"I'll get back to you later with what I find, and with some contracts for your team." Wilson slid out of the booth and stood, stretching his arms above his head. "You good, man?"

I knew what he meant—good with Cambria and what had happened in Santa Cruz. "I'll be okay."

"Just last time... last time something like this happened, we lost you for a while."

"It's different this time." I thought of Maya, Fred, and Alina, of my sister and brother and parents. I had them there before, with Aaron, but I had pushed them away. I didn't believe in myself enough to accept their support. I thought I should drown, so I had drowned myself in booze. Now, after Cambria's death, I swam to each one of them, hoping they could keep my head above water. So far, it had worked.

"I hope so," Wilson said. "You're a damn good detective. If you ever want a consistent salary with strong benefits, we could use someone like you on our team." He thew up the peace sign. "I'm out of here. Talk soon."

The Golem. Wednesday, July 5th. 0837hrs.

FRED CALLED IN SICK for work about the same time I purchased Gerald jeans and enough shirts to last him through a week, along with a new pair of shoes.

"You don't have to buy all that," Gerald said. "I don't need a full wardrobe living on the streets. I'm off the grid, remember? And by choice."

"If you're going to stay with me, you're going to wear clean clothes—operative word, wear. No more naked lounging." My phone buzzed in my pocket. "When you leave, you can leave the outfits you don't want to carry around in the linen closet, in case you ever need them." I removed my phone and checked the screen. Fred. "Did you forget the office keys again? Alina's already there, hanging out with Bagley. Call her and have her let you inside the building."

"I've come down with something serious." He faked a pathetic cough directly into the line. "I've been stuck to the toilet all night long. All morning, too. It's coming out on both ends, man. Front and back. Top and bottom. I don't think I can make it into work today."

The cashier rattled off the total cost for Gerald's clothes.

"That's too much," Gerald said. "And it's unnecessary."

"You're going to wear clothes in the house," I said.

"What?" Fred asked, his voice suddenly chirpy.

"Not you." I glanced at Gerald. "You can pay me back, but you're getting these clothes." I peeled a credit card from my wallet and handed it to the cashier. "Fred, you there?"

Another weak cough. "Barely."

"You're hungover."

"August, you don't understand how sick I am. I can't even think about food right now, let alone eat it. Food doesn't sound good to me. I might be dying."

The woman behind the counter returned my credit card to me and bagged the outfits. Gerald accepted the purchase, and we headed to the car.

"You don't get a sick day for hangovers. You're coming into work if that means temporarily converting our bathroom into your office space. We have too much at stake for you to ice your poor decisions from last night."

"I get sick leave, and you can't question it. It's illegal."

"You don't get sick leave because I don't pay you. You're not contracted through me." I realized too late the mistake of my admission.

"So I volunteer my time. Good point. I'm not volunteering today."

"Fred, I expect you at your desk when I'm back. We're working on a serial killer investigation, which means we're working despite how lousy we feel. It's not my fault you drank gallons of beer last night, but the maniac vampire won't take a day off because you drank with Maya again."

"She's such a bad influence. Why do we hang out with her?"

"I don't know."

"It's because you're in love with her."

"Get dressed, showered, pilled up, and to work, now."

"Who has a wedding on a Tuesday night? How does that make sense?"

"Fred. Work. Now."

"I hate it went you speak in fragmented sentences to me. One more thing, though."

"What?"

"Will you bring me a late breakfast, early lunch kind of meal?"

"Brunch?"

"Exactly."

"I thought food made you sick right now?" I asked.

"I'm usually pre-breakfast, breakfast, and post-breakfast by now, thinking about pre-lunch. I haven't had any of those today. So, I'm three meals short. I need to eat. I'm starving."

An hour later, I entered the office with Gerald in tow. He carried the shopping bags filled with his new clothes, and I had my hands full with Fred's hangover cure.

Fred sat behind the reception counter. He held an ice-bag to his head.

As I approached him, I craned my head over the partition and shouted. "Hey!"

Fred grimaced.

"Quit yelling," Alina called from the back of the room.

I glanced over my shoulder. She sat on the floor and dragged a thin rope back and forth. Bagley jumped after it. Gerald crossed my line of sight to drop the shopping bags on the client's chair. He joined Alina on the ground.

I returned my attention to Fred. "I'm glad you made it to work, though I'm not sure how you managed the feat. How are you feeling?"

"Like someone fixed my face to a railroad track, and a train rolled right over my skull. Like I died and came back to life as something no longer human. Undead. A zombie. And I have this terrible hunger for blood... brains. I'm so hungry."

I've watched soap operas containing less drama than Frederick Rogers. "Well, hunger is a good sign." I dropped the plastic takeout bag over the counter and on Fred's desk. "Tri-tip sandwich with extra mayonnaise and pickles, a bag of barbecue chips, and a chocolate-chunk cookie, all from your favorite little boutique sandwich shop." With my other hand, I set a large styrofoam cup on his desk. "A coffee-chip milkshake, extra whipped cream. That should help with your calorie deficit."

"You're like an angel." Fred snatched the milkshake and shoved the straw into his mouth. "If I wasn't married, I would grab you by your sweet face and shove my tongue down your throat."

"I'm not sure that's the compliment you think it is."

"He likes women," Gerald called from across the room. "Shocked me, too."

"What?" Fred narrowed his eyes and raised his brows. "What's he talking about?"

"It's a long story. Anyway, you're welcome. Feel better and get to work. I want a list of the vampire victims from you by the end of the day. Names. Family members. A friends list. I want to know the place they were last seen alive. Was it somewhere public, like a bar? If so, I want a list of all the employees on staff the day of the homicide."

"Aye, aye, Captain." Fred saluted me by removing his icepack from his forehead.

I tapped the counter and made my way to Alina. She watched Bagley near the table where we kept our coffee, so I helped myself to a hot cup.

"How's he doing?"

Alina glanced up at me. "Pooped twice, peed thrice. Don't worry, I'm saving the mess for Fred to clean."

I sipped some steaming hot coffee.

"Don't give me that dismissive look," Alina said. "I'm joking, of course. I already cleaned it up."

My knees cracked and snapped as I squatted beside Alina and my dog. "We didn't really have time to talk much last night."

"By design. I avoid you when possible."

"I wanted to talk with Myles a little, as well. Get to know him."

"Ew. Gross. Why would you do that?"

"No reason."

"It's not like that, you weirdo. I brought him along to make Maya uncomfortable. She hates the idea that I'm sixteen now and boys find me interesting." Alina handed the dog toy to Gerald and scooted to a seated position, her back against the wall and her knees hugged into her chest.

"How did you meet him?" I asked.

"You realize I'm in a public high school. A lot of boys go there."

"You met him at school?"

"Duh."

"Why haven't we heard about Myles before?"

"Because most dudes are boring, so I don't talk to them, lest I get dumber by association. Boys are simpleminded and disgusting, and all they think about is sex. That's it. Naked women and sex. In those rare instances where they're not fantasizing about some girl, they're talking about sports. Sports are nothing more than games, and they discuss those games like they're the secret to life." Alina poked out her tongue and gagged.

"Football is life!" Fred said from across the office.

Alina gestured to him and widened her eyes. "Case in point. If they're not into sports, they're into chess or tabletop games or cards. Games, though. There's no nuance to a high school boy. Sex. Games. That's it. The ones that are nice and pretend like they don't care about sex or games, they're the worst. Manipulative and secretive."

"Hey," I said, snapping my fingers a few times in quick succession. "Stay on track and answer my question. Why the sudden interest in Myles?"

"We attended the same summer school class."

"What's he doing in summer school?"

Alina scoffed. "Vice principal suspended him, and he missed class for a week or two, fell behind on the assignments, failed a couple of tests. The teacher who advocated for his suspension wouldn't help Myles catch up enough to pass the class. He failed by her design."

"The teacher sounds like a piece of work." I glanced at Gerald to see if the ex-educator had tuned into our conversation, wondering if he cared to lend his opinion on the topic. He made no sign of it.

"You wouldn't believe why she suspended him, either," Alina said.

"Why's that?"

"A fight."

"That's pretty serious."

"Like everything in life, there's depth and perspective to this story. See, there's this kid named Carlos who's mildly autistic—enough to be strange, but not enough to prevent moronic Neanderthals from picking on him. Anyway, he gets bullied by this one kid all the time. Bradley. Nonstop, too. Classic bullying. Bradley will punk Carlos out of his lunch, or pants him in front of the class, or, I don't know... all kinds of cruel stuff. Anyway, Myles grew sick of watching it happen.

One morning, Bradley was bullying Carlos, pushing him around a little, and Myles stepped in. That's it."

"Did Bradley get suspended, too?"

Alina snickered. "God, no. He's the son of the teacher who failed Myles, so there's that bit of nepotism going on."

"How badly did Myles beat him up?" I asked.

"Broke his jaw."

I pondered that. "Now I really wish I could have talked to him last night."

Alina shrugged.

"What game does Myles play?"

"Video games."

"And you like him? Do you think he's cute?"

"Ew. You're so weird. No. No to all of that."

"Hey, hey, hey!" Fred called from across the office. "Hurry your be-hinds over here and check out this fine slice of information."

I marched to the receptionist counter and stood behind Fred's desk. He had a video pulled up on his computer. The headline beneath the clip read, ZOMBIE TERRORIZES GAS STATION.

"What do you have?" I asked.

"I was on YouTube looking for reported Vampire of Sacramento clips," Fred said, turning his head to look at me. "Or to hear the crazies theorize about him. I wanted a public understanding of what we're dealing with. The media opinion is often skewed for ratings, but I—"

"No one cares about your opinions or methods," Alina said. She stood on the other side of Fred's chair. "Play the video."

Fred tapped the spacebar on the keyboard, and the paused image went into motion. The clip showed grainy black and white CCTV footage of a naked female figure breaking into a gas station convenience store after hours. The creature appeared, from what I could discern, to be a woman—slender build, long hair, and female genitalia, including breasts. However, the body was a mess of scars and stitches and mismatched limbs.

What had Cecilia said yesterday about the golem she had witnessed beneath the streetlight? Bones stuck out both its legs. They were obviously and gruesomely broken. The skin really gave it away—gray and waxy.

The shambling creature on video had gray, waxy skin, but it didn't have the bones breaking out from the legs. Had Cecilia witnessed another golem? If so, how many existed and rambled around Sacramento?

"Is that the golem our client saw?" Alina asked.

"What if it's not a golem, but a zombie?" Fred asked. He wheeled back his chair a foot from the computer. "I'm not prepared for a zombie outbreak. No bunker. No cache of weapons. I can't keep food sitting around my house longer than three days, let alone for years." He ran his hands over his head. "Guys, I can't handle something like this. Daphne always wants to go out and buy a gun, and I shut her down. I'm too nervous to own one. Now I look like an idiot."

"Don't be too hard on yourself." Alina patted Fred on the shoulder. "You've always looked like an idiot. That's not a singular and present look."

Fred must not have heard the teenager. He continued rambling, speaking more to himself than to us. "If I had only caved and bought a gun, I could defend Daphne and myself from the zombies. Now... now I'm just a big hunk of tasty, dark meat. The zombies are going to have a Thanksgiving feast of my body."

"Fred, calm down," I said. "The creature on video isn't a zombie, it's a golem. They're different. Also, it's not even a golem. It's a human."

Fred stared at me with wide, terrified eyes. His hands snaked out and grabbed my wrists with vice-like strength. "August, I can't die. I have a deep-rooted fear of getting eaten alive, or of being eaten at all, by anything. I can't even hardly picture worms and maggots picking at my corpse. But a zombie. Come on, August, this is too much."

"That's a golem." I pointed at the computer screen. "We're not dealing with a zombie outbreak."

"One zombie. That's all you need. That one zombie will infect someone else, and those two infect two other people, and those four infect four other people a piece, and those eight—"

"We can all do basic math," Alina said.

I watched as the golem terrorized the snack aisle. She thrashed the liquor off the shelf and capsized the donut display. When satisfied with the destruction, the golem lumbered out of the store, disappearing from the video.

"When did this happen?" I asked.

Fred scratched his head and pointed at the time stamped on the top right of the video. "Late last night."

Daniel Quinn crossed my mind. The unidentified man had already created a Changeling and a Doppelgänger. He had also created a ghost to appear on a highway in Santa Cruz—a trick I hadn't figured out yet. The psychopath enjoyed challenging me, though. Was the golem another one of his games?

"I'm going to reach out to Jackson Armstead's family," I said. "He's our only connection to the golem at the moment."

"Cecelia, too," Alina said. "I think we revisit her after we collect a little more information about Jackson."

"What about the vampire?" Fred asked, his voice soft and shaky—still dealing with the effects of his fright. "You asked me to look into the vampire."

I rubbed my eyes, feeling the weight of the two cases already pressing against me. The eight weeks I had taken off felt distant, like something from another life. The stress of work crashed all around me again, burying me deep amongst its rumble. I inhaled slowly and deeply, parsing through my investigations.

The Vampire of Sacramento.

The golem.

The giant chickens Gerald had witnessed and attacked.

Daniel Quinn.

I strongly suspected that if I solved the Daniel Quinn dilemma, most of my other problems would disappear. Yet, I couldn't allot my immediate time looking into him.

The Vampire of Sacramento would kill again. I had to identify and capture the serial killer before he claimed another victim.

The golem had already created harm and destruction. I had to solve that case to prevent anything more from occurring.

And the giant chickens. I still didn't know what to think or do about them. Gerald seemed honest enough, but he had lived on the streets for at least as long as I had owned the company—seven months—and probably much longer than that. If I had to guess, he had lived out in that alley for years. Could I dismiss the idea of a temporary mental breakdown?

"We don't have any leads on the vampire," I said after a second. "Detectives have reached out to any potential witnesses, but no one has provided any reliable information. Fred, keep building on that list of potential contacts. You're going to break open the door on the vampire case for us."

"What about us?" Alina asked.

"We're going to get our hands dirty and pursue the one clue we have access to. Jackson Armstead."

"Right now?"

"You up for a field trip across town?"

"What are we going to do with Bagley?"

I nodded at Gerald. "He'll hang out with him."

A Little Convincing. Wednesday, July 5th. 1304hrs.

ALINA KNOCKED ON THE Armstead's front door with three forceful raps.

A weatherworn scarecrow sat in a rocking chair on the Armstead front porch. Cobwebs covered the Halloween display, and not the decorative type. A string of Christmas lights went across the roofline. I respected their decision to leave up the holiday decor, at least from the standpoint of dedicated laziness.

I lingered a few feet behind Alina, a stride off the single step leading to the porch. Alina preferred to exercise her jaw in these situations, and I preferred to rest my tongue to observe and listen. We had come to an unspoken agreement that she, as long as she remained professional and reserved, spearheaded interviews. I would listen and butt in when needed.

I glanced around the property as we continued to wait for someone to answer the door. The Armstead's lived in a two-story house on the corner of two intersecting streets—Ottobonn Way and Lincoln Avenue.

One street boasted of middle-class living—nice cars parked in washed driveways, manicured yards, and clean sidewalks. The other street offered a dirty, smeared reflection. Cars on blocks, without doors or windows, seemingly untouched for years. Dead or dying yards. Trash along the walkways. Abandoned homes, or homes that appeared abandoned.

I wondered how two streets in such proximity could co-exist. My cynical nature offered an answer. People minded their business. They left their neighbors alone, and they hoped to be left alone. They had fences separating them, locked doors to hide them, baseball bats or shotguns standing in the hall closet, neglected but not forgotten, to defend them. Don't tread on me or mine. No trespassing. Beware of dog. The nearer the neighbor, the more lost people became in their own world. It was a strange paradox to think about. It seemed country folk had the strongest ties to their neighbors, where apartment dwellers might not even know the first name of those living across the hall from them.

I couldn't recall the name of the tenant who had lived across the hall from my apartment. What a strange existence humans often lead.

The Armstead's house seemed to transition the polarized streets from low-income homes to white picket fence, two-and-a-half kids, two-story houses. They had a lawn, though it appeared as if they hadn't upped their watering practices during the summer months. The tan stucco, along with the asphalt shingles on the roof, had faded tremendously. I'm not much of a contractor or a designer, but even my unpracticed eye discerned the house required some aesthetic maintenance. However, despite its visual faults, a nice Acura rested in the driveway. The fence appeared new—it smelled new, too. That fresh lumber, sap-infused scent permeated the immediate area.

Alina knocked again.

My eyes settled on the streetlight standing at the corner. It had to be the light Cecilia had referenced, the one that had beamed over the golem. I stood about fifteen feet away from it, but in broad daylight, I had a decent vantage of the area.

No blood stained the gray asphalt beneath the pole. Nothing evidenced an assault or an attack of any kind.

The front door's deadbolt unlatched, and the hinges creaked. A middle-aged woman with ratty hair and no makeup stood framed in the doorway. She wore sweatpants and an old shirt that looked as if it might have belonged to her husband.

She waved her phone before her haggard face. "I don't know who you are or what you want, but if you're not off my property in the next thirty seconds, I'm calling the police."

"Mrs. Armstead, I'm Alina Moore. That man behind me is August Watson. We're private investigators." She said private instead of paranormal investigators.

"I don't care who you are, what you want, or why you're here. You can leave. I've spoken to the police, to the media, and I'm tired, and I'm done talking."

"Please, we're here to help," Alina said, lowering her voice to a calming tone. "We're investigating the disappearance of your son."

"Who hired you?"

"I'm sorry, but that's confidential."

"Cecilia Ochoa?" Mrs. Armstead asked.

"I can't disclose that information."

"Well, I can't allow you to remain on my property."

A young woman appeared beside Mrs. Armstead—a replica, though thirty years younger, of the exhausted lady framed in the doorway. She wore sweats and a T-shirt, and she hadn't yet bothered with readying herself for the day.

"Did Cecilia tell you about the zombie?" the new girl asked.

"I'm sorry, but I can't share any client information."

Mrs. Armstead spared a disbelieving chortle, and she glanced at who I believed was her daughter. "Don't tell me you believe that nonsense."

"They're private investigators looking into Jackson's disappearance. Who do you think hired them? It was Cecilia. She's the one who mentioned the zombie theory."

"A zombie didn't get my son! I don't need Cecilia wasting my time, the police's time, or Jackson's time with stories about zombies."

The younger woman squeezed by Mrs. Armstead and sighed. She looked at Alina. "I'm sorry. We've had a stressful and confusing week. I'm Lindsey, Jackson's sister."

"I'm Alina. That's August." She nodded back at me. "Though I can't reveal who hired us, I can say that we're investigating the possibility that a golem had something to do with Jackson's disappearance."

Mrs. Armstead shook her head. "This is ridiculous."

"We're part of the Blue Moon Investigative Agency," Alina said. "Have you ever heard of it?"

"On Facebook," Lindsey said. "One of my friends knew the Verdin family through a friend of a friend, or something like that. Anyway, they posted about the case and mentioned your company."

"That was one of many strange cases we have solved. We specialize in unexplainable incidents, usually where the paranormal is involved, and we come up with a grounded, logical conclusion that doesn't involve the supernatural." Alina paused for a breath. "We don't believe a golem took Jackson any more than you do, Mrs. Armstead. However, we believe Cecilia's story to an extent. She saw someone posing as a golem and dragging Jackson away from that streetlight." Alina pointed over her shoulder at me. "We have a perfect success rate with our investigations so far. Please, allow us a moment of your time, and we can help find your son."

A swelling of pride filled my soul. Despite Mrs. Armstead's initial reaction to our presence, Alina had remained poised and professional. I knew that was hard for her, too, as she often shared whatever thoughts raced through her head.

Her hands, positioned behind her back, flexed in and out of fists.

Mrs. Jackson sighed in defeat. "I'm Lorrie. Come in. Remove your shoes, though."

The Boating Accident. Wednesday, July 5th. 1311hrs.

I SAT ON A comfortable leather couch beside Alina. Lorrie and Lindsey sat across the coffee table in high-backed chairs. Even inside the house, the Armstead's had remained consistent with their hodgepodge of holiday decor—a nativity scene on the entryway table, pumpkins tumbling across some shelves, a fake plant with pastel-colored styrofoam eggs on the kitchen counter.

Once we all settled into our seats and a stretch of silence filled the room, Alina took control. "What do you think happened to Jackson?"

Lorrie gnawed on her lower lip for a couple of seconds. "I don't think a zombie, or... what did you call it?"

"A golem."

"Sure. I don't think that kidnapped him."

"Neither do we, but that's our only lead."

"From that Ochoa girl, I'm sure. Well, I think that the Ochoa girl hurt Jackson—her or her family."

"Can you elaborate?" Alina asked.

"Speculation, but I think something happened, and she panicked. She construed this ridiculous story to hide her tracks." Lorrie pinched her shoulder blades together and sat straighter. "That's what the cops think, too. They told me she's their number one suspect. Last to see him alive and all that. You're wasting your time with the golem."

I fished into my pocket and removed a stick of gum. The practice of chewing on something helped me think, and I had a lot to consider. Lorrie's (and the cops') theory made perfect sense.

Jackson and Cecilia had gone on a date hours before he disappeared. Had he misinterpreted her idea of the date? Had he gone too far, despite her protests? Had she lashed out to protect herself? Had she told someone in her family what Jackson had done or attempted to do? If so, who, and had that person retaliated?

Cecilia fit into the mold as a person of interest. Except I didn't believe it. She had sought my help, meaning the police had ignored her story—which also made sense, considering they suspected her. Still, she had sought me out.

If Jackson had acted inappropriately toward her, I assumed Cecilia would've shared that information with me. She hadn't, though. In fact, she had said the opposite. She said they had engaged in consensual sexual activity, albeit disappointing activity.

Cecilia had left Jackson after his poor performance, but she had returned to apologize for her abrupt exit. Again, maybe that was window dressing to a darker story, but I didn't get the impression Cecilia lied to me. Besides, why would she fabricate a story about a golem as her alibi? It was too farfetched.

"What do you think about all of this?" Alina asked Lindsey.

Jackson's sister couldn't have been much older than Alina, nineteen at the most. "I don't know what to think. I don't know why Cecilia would lie and make up such a crazy story, but I don't know why the cops would suspect her unless she played a role. I'm mostly confused and scared about everything."

I cleared my throat, speaking for the first time since arriving at the Armstead home. "I want to clarify the timeline for everyone here. Jackson and Cecilia went to dinner and the movie. According to Cecilia's statement, while in the theater, she and Jackson fooled around."

Lorrie glanced off to the left and pinched her lips tightly together. I don't think she cared to hear about her son's sexual activities.

We needed to get on the same page, though, so I pushed forward. "Cecilia felt angry and disappointed after the experience. When Jackson went to the bathroom, Cecilia left. She felt bad about walking out, so she came back to apologize. However, Jackson was no longer at the theater. Cecilia drove to your house. That's when she saw the golem. That's where she saw Jackson get attacked."

Lorrie didn't respond, but kept her attention focused off to the side.

"Does all that align with the story you're familiar with?" I asked.

"Yes," Lindsey said.

"Well, from that sliver of information, we can deduce three things." I poked out my index finger. "Cecilia saw what she saw." My middle finger counted the second scenario. "Cecilia made up a story to protect herself." My ring finger joined the other two. "Cecilia made up a story to protect someone else who attacked Jackson."

"Option two or three," Lorrie muttered, still unable to meet my gaze.

"To consider options two or three, we would most likely have to entertain the idea that Jackson harmed Cecilia, and that's why she left and later returned—for retribution."

"What are you saying?" Lorrie asked.

"The timeline clearly presents to us that Jackson and Cecilia engaged in sexual intercourse," Alina said. "If Cecilia returned to cause harm to Jackson, that was for a reason."

"You're saying he raped her?" Lorrie asked. "Jackson wouldn't do anything like that."

"I'm saying if Cecilia attacked your son, or if she had someone attack your son, she would only do so under the influence of extreme emotion."

"No. Jackson wouldn't do that. What if he broke up with her, and that made her angry, and so she killed him? Crazier things have happened."

"We're at this crossroad," I said. "Jackson somehow hurt Cecilia—physically or emotionally—enough for her to lash out. Maybe he raped her. Maybe he broke up with her. Maybe she found out he was talking to another woman. I don't know. Whatever the scenario, she felt hurt, and she retaliated."

"Or?" Lindsey asked.

"Cecilia is telling the truth about what she saw," Alina said.

"The police have already dedicated their attention to Cecilia lashing out and harming your son, as you've mentioned," I said. "I'm going to explore the alternate route—that Cecilia provided us with the truth, and a golem attacked your son."

No one in the room spoke for an uncomfortable ten, fifteen seconds. I considered that a sign we all read along together on the same page.

Alina must have drawn the same conclusion. She once again broke the silence and continued with her questioning. "Does your son have any friends?"

"What do you mean?" Lorrie asked, her voice icy and brittle. Our presence and offering to help find her son hadn't warmed her in the least. "Of course he has friends."

"Who would you say are his closest friends?"

"I don't know." Lorrie scratched her head, mussing her already messy hair. "What do you think, Linds?"

Lindsey shook her head. "Since college, he hasn't made new friends, and he doesn't talk to his high school buddies anymore, at least not since the accident. How long ago was that, Mom? Four years ago now?"

"It was the summer after his junior year of high school. He would've been, what, seventeen? So, yeah, four years ago."

"What accident?" Alina leaned forward, staking her elbows on her thighs and resting her chin on a fist.

"A boating accident," Lorrie said.

"Can you tell us exactly what happened?"

Lorrie chewed on her lip for a minute. "I don't know how it's relevant." She fiddled with her wedding ring.

I wondered about her husband. Where was he and what might he contribute to this conversation?

"Everything matters," Alina said.

"I just don't—"

"They borrowed a friend's boat and went out on the water," Lyndsey said. "I was fifteen then, and I wanted so badly to join them, but Jackson said I was too young. In reality, I don't think he enjoyed the idea of his idiot friends staring at me in a bikini."

"Who were his idiot friends?" Alina had her phone in her hands, ready to jot down the names.

"Ashton Snell," Lindsey said. "He was driving the boat when it happened. Connor Pellerin. Leon Lambert." The young woman counted her fingers. "Maria Lopez. Jackson. Was that it?" She looked at her mother.

Lorrie shrugged, obviously unwilling to revisit the story.

Lindsey continued without her mother's help. "Maybe Timothy Porter. Timmy is what we called him. They were Jackson's high school buddies."

"They don't talk anymore?" I asked.

"I'm not sure if they text or not, but none of them come by anymore," Lindsey said. "They all went off to college, and I haven't seen one of them since."

"Leon went missing in high school," Lorrie said.

"Excuse me?" I asked.

"That's right!" Lindsey shook her head and lowered her gaze. "Leon Lambert, he went missing his senior year. They found his remains not long after."

Alina typed the information on her phone. I'm not sure why she didn't record the conversation, but I trusted her process.

"What do you know about Maria Lopez?" Alina asked.

Lorrie barked a sharp laugh. "Why does it matter?"

"She was Jackson's girlfriend," Lindsey said.

"What happened on the boat?"

"Maria died," Lindsey said.

"It was an accident," Lorrie said. "That's it. An accident."

"She was wakeboarding, fell, hit her head on the board and went unconscious. I'm not sure if she drowned, or if she died from the trauma to her head, but she died." Lindsey grabbed her mom's hand in both of hers. "Since then, Jackson has mostly kept to himself."

Lorrie jumped on the brief silence and blurted, "Her family is in a gang."

"Maria's family?" Alina asked.

"You didn't consider that option, did you? A gang. That's what the cops told me. Jackson probably went out with her, and her family didn't like a white boy taking out their sister or their daughter. So, they waited for him after the date and that's what happened. Not a zombie or golem attack. Cecilia is protecting her family. If you want to help find Jackson, go to them. They know what happened." Lorrie stood. "I think it's time you leave."

Without argument, Alina and I obliged.

Lindsey escorted Alina and me to the front door, opening it for us. When we stepped onto the porch, she beckoned for our attention. "I called Ashton Snell about a year ago. He and I... we liked each other, but we never acted on our feelings because of Jackson. Anyway, we would always talk. After the accident, he stopped texting me. Last year, I reached out to him on an impulse. I wanted to see how he was doing. He never responded. I called, and his number wasn't in service. I looked him up on Facebook and Instagram and Snapchat, but he didn't have any active accounts on any platform. Desperate and a little nervous, I Googled him." Lindsey blinked hard a few times.

I cracked a knuckle, anticipating what she would say. Two—Leon and Jackson—is a coincidence. Three, though, that's a pattern.

"The article said a farmer found the body parts belonging to the missing Brigham Young University freshman."

My heart hammered in my chest. "Did they belong to Ashton?"

Lindsey nodded and wiped the blade of her hand across her eyes. "I think Jackson is in real trouble. Can you help him?"

"We'll do our best," Alina said.

Maria Lopez 4.0. Wednesday, July 5th. 1333hrs.

JACKSON LAY FLAT ON a steel table. Leather straps bound his ankles, his wrists, his waist, his skull to the slab. His mouth had dried, and his throat hurt—mostly from screaming it raw, but also from the lack of water since his imprisonment.

He didn't know how much time had passed since the night of his capture. It was hard to keep track of something like minutes, hours, days when nothing existed but one low-burning light in a cold, empty room without windows.

That's where he had first awoken from his unconsciousness.

Jackson had blinked through a disorienting, bright-burning headache. His body vibrated with shivers. The air felt icy and damp. When his vision adjusted to the dimness of the room, he stared upward at a stone ceiling. The stone walls around him glowed a campfire orange, absorbing the glow of the single dangling bulb in the center of the room. A dirt-covered floor held his blood-soaked cot. Another blood-stained cot rested across the way, another body beneath threadbare blankets atop of it.

Before risking engagement with the mass of human-shaped sheets, though, Jackson opted to study his prison further. Four stone walls without windows. A stone ceiling with wooden beams and a single dangling light bulb. A dirt floor. A bucket at the foot of his cot, one at the end of the other cot. At the sight of the buckets, as if his vision connected to his olfactory sense, a stench formed. It stank like rotted blood and old feces and decay.

Like corruption and rot.

Like death.

Jackson closed his eyes. A brightness throbbed behind his forehead, exploding a brilliant white with each pulse. The pain blinded him from forming coherent thought, but fragmented memories flashed across his mind. Maria Lopez, undead, swaying in the streetlight's glow.

If he wanted answers, he had to confront whoever lay in the bed across the room from him.

"Hello." Jackson's timid voice echoed off the stone walls. "Who are you?"

The body, which was completely hidden with tattered blankets, shifted and turned. The covers slid off her face—her pale, waxen, corpse-like face.

Maria Lopez stared back at Jackson like something straight from the Devil's imagination.

He gasped and scampered to the back of his bed, placing himself against the cool stone wall. A flood of adrenaline momentarily softened the edge of his headache.

The radius of the single light illuminated the entire chamber, but only to a dim extent. Shadows enshrouded Maria's face, but Jackson knew it belonged to her.

"What do you want?" he asked. "What do you want from me?"

Maria moved her waxen limbs and planted her bare feet on the dirt. The shin bones split outward from her legs, and dried blood caked the surrounding skin. She stood. The blankets fell away from her, revealing her naked body—scarred and stitched together like some horrible iteration of Frankenstein's monster.

"Why are you doing this?"

Maria's cracked voice carried across the ten feet separating them. "It's me."

Not a woman's voice, and definitely not Maria's voice—at least not the voice Jackson remembered, though it rang familiar.

"It's Ashton," Maria said.

That two-syllable name stole Jackson's breath like a stunning blow to the stomach.

"I'm... Ashton Snell."

Finally, words—broken and soft as they were—bubbled from Jackson's lips. "I don't understand."

"She's practicing." The corpse of Maria (Ashton) rose off the bed and crossed the ten feet of space. She (he) reached Jackson's cot and sat on the edge, breathing with a raspy whine that came from within her (his) chest. The undead corpse stank of festered wounds, much like the buckets.

Something wiggled near Maria's shoulder blade, catching Jackson's attention. A maggot feasted on a gooey, open wound on the living corpse's back.

A wave of heat overwhelmed Jackson, followed by a gushing of saliva into and through his mouth. He dove for the bucket and vomited until his balls shriveled and ached and his throat went raw. When he had nothing left to offer the rusted, stained bucket, he hopped from his bed and sat on the cool ground, hugging the blood-encrusted bucket to his chest.

He screamed as loud as his burning throat would allow. "Help! Somebody help me! Help!" He screamed until he no longer had a voice to scream with, and then he cried.

"No one is coming for you," Maria said. Though, after the initial shock had dulled, Jackson realized it really wasn't Maria's voice at all.

They had dated near the end of Jackson's junior year, and they spent every waking moment together. He had known the sound of her voice as well as he knew the sound of the voice that constantly spoke in his mind. He knew her inflections and nuances. The voice coming from the undead creature sitting on his bed didn't belong to Maria.

That's death's toll, he thought. *The maggots destroyed her vocal cords.*

The image nearly drove him mad—nearly whipped him to his feet and spurred him to pound on the heavy oak door until his fists were nothing more than pulpy sludges of blood.

"I don't understand," he said.

"She captured Leon first," Maria said in a cracked voice that didn't belong to Maria. "Leon told her everything."

"Told who everything?"

"It's not obvious? Maria's mother, of course."

"Clara?"

Maria's mom was young for a mom. At least Jackson had always thought so—thirty-three with a seventeen-year-old daughter. Clara had always warned Maria and Jackson not to make the same mistake she had made.

"I'm a mistake," Maria would say, laughter in her eyes, though she attempted to keep a straight face.

"You know what I mean."

Clara, despite the obstacle of raising a child at sixteen, had overcome the adversity. Her young boyfriend had stuck around, and they married. Not only that, Armando's parents were near and Clara's parents were near, and both sets of parents forced their children to graduate high school as they cared for little Maria. Clara went on to college, then to medical school. She became a cosmetic surgeon. Despite her success story under the circumstances, she didn't wish for her daughter to walk in her exact footprints, for her daughter to get knocked up while in high school.

To respect Clara, Jackson and Maria had abstained from sex, though they had explored a few of the bases.

"After Leon," Maria (Ashton) said in a weak, hissing voice, "she had Connor. Then Timmy. She learned the entire story, and... and she practiced."

"Practiced what?" Jackson asked, though he wasn't entirely sure he wanted to know the answer.

Ashton pointed at himself. "To recreate Maria."

In the dull orange light, Jackson could see sweat on Ashton's brackish brow. The living corpse had dark hair, though it lightened into something nearly blonde at the roots—the same sandy blonde hair that Ashton had always possessed.

Jackson swallowed a surge of bile, and he scooted forward for a closer inspection.

Ashton bore scars on his shoulders and hips where the arms and the legs would connect to the torso. He had fake breasts and scars around his removed genitalia.

"Recreate her," Jackson said, seeing first-hand what Ashton meant. Absolute terror sprinted down his spine. Had Clara captured Jackson to transform him into her daughter, too?

Jackson dropped his head in the bucket again, coughing and spitting into it. Would he ever not feel sick again? When the last long strand of saliva broke off his lips, he lifted his head and wiped his mouth with the back of his hand.

"What happened to the others?"

Ashton stared at the floor. "I don't know."

"You weren't with them, like I'm with you?"

"Timmy captured me. He appeared one night on campus, though he… he was Maria, as I now am. More crude, though, if you can imagine it. Clara used us to perfect her practice. Anyway, Timmy captured me, as I captured you."

"Why wouldn't you say no? Why go through with this?"

Ashton tapped the back of his skull. "An implant."

"An implant? Like something for a movie?"

"Yes." Turning his head away from Jackson, Ashton coughed into his fist. He inspected the spray of blood across his hand. "If I refuse to do what she commands, she'll kill me."

"Death has to be better than..." Jackson trailed off, realizing he had spoken his thought aloud—his thought that advocated for his friend to choose to die.

"It's not death that worries me. Clara threatened to go after my family. To turn them into Maria if I refused to accept the role."

Jackson's lips parted, and he meant to ask why, but he didn't have the breath to speak. So, he stared at Ashton with wide, unbelieving eyes, his why painted across his face.

Ashton heard the unspoken question. "She wished to have her daughter again. She wanted to bring Maria back from the dead."

Days, weeks, months went by (time had become an anomaly), and Jackson lay strapped to the steel surgical table. He stared into the bleak darkness, uncomfortable from the static position. His face also itched, but he had no means to scratch it.

Hours ago, for the first time since his capture, Clara had visited his cell. She arrived after he finished a meal, one which had made him groggy.

"I sedated you," she said. "I didn't want you having any ambitious ideas." To emphasize her point, Clara kissed the barrel of a gun to Jackson's temple and instructed him to stand.

The hallways lurched and spun as he walked. Clara's voice and the pressure of the gun directed him into another room. She stripped off his clothing, helped him onto the cold slab, and tightened the leather straps across his body. She sat on a stool, scooted it beside the operating table, and spoke inches from his ear.

"I know everything about that day, Jack. You were drunk, and you drove foolishly with her—with my daughter—behind the boat. You killed her. You murdered my baby. Your greatest sin, you lied about it."

Jackson wanted to plead with her, to beg her forgiveness, to scream. Instead, he cried.

"You took her from me. Now you will give her back to me... with your body. Do you understand? You will sacrifice your body to become Maria."

"No."

"You don't have a choice."

"Please." Snot trailed over his lips. Tears slipped down to the table.

"Before we begin any surgical procedures, I will have to insert this little device into your skull." Clara held up a capsule the size of a grain of rice. "Don't worry, dear, it's nothing like you would imagine. It's not a bomb that will detonate in your head. You should think of it as a shock collar that helps me control you. There are four settings—a simple, uncomfortable shock, a more painful jolt, a debilitating current, and a pulse that causes a tiny detonation. You would essentially suffer an aneurysm if I activated the fourth setting." A second of terrible silence passed. "Do you understand the procedure?"

"Yes."

"Good. If I ever detonate the Level Four charge, that doesn't mean I'm through with you. Your family will step into your role, and they will sacrifice their bodies to become Maria. Are we clear, Jack?"

It was just as Ashton had told him.

"Yes."

"The implantation won't take longer than an hour. Afterward, I'll suture your scalp together. You'll have a quick recovery time of a week or two. Once I confirm there's no infection or other complication from the surgery, and once you have fully healed, we will proceed with the transformation. Are we understood?"

Jackson squeezed his eyes and aggressively nodded, confirming that he understood.

"Very well. Let's begin."

Reconvening. Wednesday, July 5th. 1959hrs.

My parents lent me one of their folding tables shortly after I moved into the house. They often hosted events at their property, so they had a collection of tables and chairs stored in their shop. Each table was circular and big enough to seat eight people comfortably.

My dad had dropped it off after learning I ate most of my meals on the island. Along with the table, he had also lent me eight folding chairs.

"I don't even have eight friends," I said.

"Well, you have eight family members, and I'm including Fred, Daphne, Maya, and Alina."

Currently, seven of the eight chairs had occupancy. Fred, Daphne, Maya, Evan, Alina, Gerald, and me. I had only invited Fred and Alina over to discuss the investigations—and Gerald, because he was like my shadow for the time being. Always around.

Fred insisted on a big, hearty dinner. He called his wife and asked if she had time for a last-minute meal at my house. "You're the chef, too," he had said on the phone.

Daphne, an incredible and passionate cook, had readily agreed. She arrived at my place before anyone else and used her key to enter (Alina had stolen my house key and made ten copies of it; she passed them out to the regulars without my permission or knowledge). When Gerald, Fred, and I entered the house, the heavenly aroma of bacon filled the halls.

About an hour later, Alina arrived. She was sixteen, but she didn't have a driver's license, and she lived with Maya. When she asked for a ride to my place, Maya invited herself over, along with her boyfriend, Evan.

Daphne made sure we all ate well. Even the puppy ate to his little heart's content. Bagley scampered around our feet, vacuuming anything that fell or that someone handed to him.

"If he gets sick from the food," I said, glaring at Alina, who was the primary culprit for feeding my dog, "you're cleaning up the mess."

"No human and definitely not any dog has ever gotten sick of my cooking," Daphne said.

"Her cooking cures sickness," Fred said.

"Amen to that." Gerald leaned back and held his potbelly with both hands. "I feel a little guilty after eating that meal. Spoiled. But Daphne, I don't think I would refuse dessert if you brought it out."

"Well, it's your lucky day, then." Daphne removed her napkin from her lap and placed it on the table. She stood and marched into the kitchen. A second later, she returned.

Dessert, homemade of course, rivaled dinner.

"Daphne." Evan paused and stared at Fred's wife with a half-smirk pitched across his face. He dabbed a napkin over his lips.

"Yes, Evan."

"You strike me as a capable person."

"Here we go." Fred slapped the table with his palms. "If this is some comment about how Daphne is so much better than Fred, we've all heard it already, buddy. There's no need to beat a dead horse."

Evan's half-smirk worked itself into a full, excited grin. He always wore a smile or tasted some iteration of a laugh. Joy oozed from the man's aura. "No, no, no. Nothing like that. I mean, Fred, you're a catch. I'm sure Daphne is quite lucky to have you. However, in the spirit of complete honesty, you are quite luckier to have her."

"There it is!" Fred threw up his arms.

Evan chuckled. "What I wanted to say, though... Daphne, your artistry in the kitchen is... it's da Vinci. It's Shakespearean. It's Michael Jordan."

"Thank you," Daphne said.

"Can you imagine da Vinci not painting? Shakespeare not writing? Michael Jordan not balling? No. The world is a much brighter place because of their contributions."

"Get on with it, honey," Maya said. "Make your point."

"The world needs Daphne Rogers' incredible cuisine. It transcends art."

"You say the weirdest stuff," Alina said. "Does that just pop into your head, or is it all rehearsed?"

"Alina," Evan said.

"Yeah?"

"We all have a purpose."

"Hopefully yours is to stop talking soon."

"We're all called to contribute to something far greater than ourselves. That purpose, that calling, always revolves around one simple truth." Evan paused, probably allowing Alina an opportunity to interrupt him again and make a snarky comment.

Much to my surprise, Alina tilted her head and sealed her lips.

"Humans help one another," Evan said. He shifted his intent on Daphne. "Your food makes the world a better place. It helps others." Evan smiled. "That's all I have to say, but I feel it had to be said."

Daphne shyly glanced away, her cheeks darkening. "That's kind of you, Evan, but it's not possible."

"Why?" Maya asked. "How could it possibly not be possible?"

"If I pursued cooking, I wouldn't want to cook for anyone but myself."

"And me," Fred said. "You'll have to cook for me."

"No, not like that. I mean, I would have to create my business, not work for someone else's kitchen. I would want to open a restaurant."

"You've never mentioned this to me," Fred said.

"Because it's an impossibility. It costs a lot of time and money, and... and I have an amazing job right now. A job I really enjoy. It pays me an absurd amount of money. It provides ridiculous benefits. It allows me to support Fred while he chases vampires."

"He doesn't do much chasing," Alina said. "Mostly sitting in the office and eating."

"No strings attached," Gerald said, and all eyes turned to the homeless man living in my house.

"What?" Maya asked.

"Hypothetically, if there was no risk involved, if Daphne could do one thing for the rest of her life..." he stared directly at Fred's wife. "Would you cook, or would you do whatever it is you do now?"

Daphne curled in her lips.

"You don't have to answer that now. I don't want to put you on the spot. But think about it that way. No risk involved. What would you do?"

A silence settled over the table. Daphne stared at her empty dessert plate.

I crossed my fork over my plate and set my napkin on the table. "Daphne, you're an incredible talent in the kitchen. Thank you for dinner tonight." I stood. "However, we have work to discuss. Don't feel obligated to wash the dishes. I can do them later tonight. You've already put in enough tonight." I caught Alina's and Fred's attention. "We're going to head to the back patio to talk shop."

"Me, too?" Maya asked.

"You care to sign an NDR? That means everything we discuss is always off the record. No writing or uttering a single word to anyone about anything related to the vampire case."

Maya clicked her tongue for a second. "I'm down." She snapped her fingers. "August, I forgot to mention that I published the Doppelgänger story."

"I saw that."

Maya scrunched her face. "You saw that? You read Here & Now?"

"Just what you write."

Maya frowned, but proudly, as if touched by my statement. "Thank you. So, you saw I plugged your company?"

"I saw."

"I hope that's okay. Considering your time off and all that, I almost asked you, but then I thought you would say no, so I decided forgiveness is always better than permission."

"I think I might have said no. But I'm glad you did it. Thank you."

We migrated to the back patio as the stragglers insisted on cleaning the dishes. Glacia's Nana had outdoor furniture which no one had claimed after her death, so it had remained on the back patio overlooking the overgrown pasture. The sun set to our right, a display of golden red and fierce pink and deep purple fiery clouds.

"Alina, what did you learn about the boating accident?" I asked once we had all settled into our seats.

"Six kids were involved, just like Lindsey mentioned. Apparently, according to a police report I could read, all but one kid had alcohol in their system. Ashton Snell. The Mormon who went off to Brigham Young University, and had his body parts discovered. Both arms, both legs, his genitalia, and all his teeth. That's how they confirmed the identity beyond fingerprints and DNA. Dental records."

Maya scrunched her face in disgust. "What happened to the rest of him?"

Alina shrugged. "Does it matter?"

"Any arrests in connection to the crime?" I asked.

"Nope." Alina popped her lips. "Nada. Not even a suspect. Good kid. Good grades. The whole shebang. Went missing for about a year before the farmer discovered all that carnage."

"Where?" I asked.

"Were his body parts discovered?"

"Yeah."

"Here."

"Here?" Maya asked.

"Sacramento," Alina said.

"Not BYU?" I asked.

"Nope."

"He went missing from BYU, though?"

"Yup."

I scratched the back of my neck and cracked a knuckle. "We need to get in contact with his family to learn if he planned a trip home. We need access to his phone records, his email accounts, and all his social media. I want to know why he came back to Sacramento. Who did he see?"

"That's not all," Alina said.

"What do you mean?"

"A kid coming home from middle school happened on Leon Lambert's body here in Sacramento. Get this. He had his head and torso attached to someone else's limbs."

"Wait. What?" Fred asked. "Say that again."

"Frankenstein stuff," Alina said. "Leon had female limbs on his body, and he had vaginoplasty."

"Same as Fred," Maya said.

"Come on," Fred said. "It's not the time for something like that."

"Breast implants," Alina said. "Someone had tried to transform him into a woman."

"Who did the limbs belong to?"

Alina shook her head. "No definitive identification. Both legs came from different people, as did the arms. At least five different people's parts made up one body."

I watched the sunset and wondered how something like that could happen. "Are we dealing with more missing people? Did other people vanish around the same time as Ashton and Leon? I mean, is our mad scientist kidnapping multiple people and fusing them together?"

"I know that Connor Pellerin and Timothy Porter are both classified as missing persons. They were the other two friends on the boat with Maria Lopez, Ashton Snell, Leon Lambert, and, of course, Jackson Armstead."

My heart raced. Alina had uncovered a lot of information to the investigation, and she spoke slowly, deliberately, as if building up to the climax.

"What else?" I asked.

Alina grinned, proud of herself. "Maria Lopez was the girl who died in that boating accident."

Lindsey had shared that with us, so we already knew it. "Yeah."

"Maria's mom, Clara Lopez, was a pretty renowned cosmetic surgeon. She went missing around the time Leon Lambert went missing, who, according to records, was the first of the boating crew to vanish."

"No," Maya said, chuckling and shaking her head. "No way. That's too much."

"What?" Fred looked from Alina, to Maya, to me. "What am I missing?"

"Where's the dad?" I asked.

"At the house Maria grew up in," Alina said.

"What do the cops suspect?"

The kid shrugged. "I spoke with the lead detective on the case. He doesn't have a clue what's going on, but I don't think he believes Clara abducted the boys responsible for her daughter's death. He had his sights on the father, Armando. He thinks Armando murdered Clara—maybe he blamed her because she allowed Maria to go on the trip. I don't know. Either way, all the boys are missing and Clara is missing, and Armando sits alone at home."

"A cosmetic surgeon?" I chewed on my cheeks.

A farmer had discovered Ashton's body parts, but not his body. A kid had stumbled on Leon's body and attached to it were the limbs of someone else—female limbs. I thought of the zombie—female in appearance and covered in stitches and scars.

"Jeffrey Dahmer tried to turn his victims into zombies." My voice was distant. "Do you think we're dealing with something like that?"

"You think Mrs. Lopez is kidnapping these kids, performing cosmetic surgery on them, and altering them into zombies?" Maya asked.

"Golems," Alina said. "She would have to kidnap the boating crew, as well as young women, cut them all up and string them all together."

Maya snorted in laughter. "That's a little farfetched, even for us, don't you think?"

"We need to speak with the father," I said.

Alina grinned at me with a bright, knowing look. "I already set up a meeting for tomorrow when he's off work. Four o'clock."

I watched the sun sink a littler further; the darkness deepened and rose. After a minute, I looked at Fred. "The Vampire of Sacramento. Any breakthrough information like Alina had?"

"Nothing like that," Fred said. "But I may have found a lead or two. The first four victims were last seen alive at nightclubs and bars."

I thought of Patricia Huffman dancing at the dive bar with me.

"I pinpointed which clubs." Fred paused and coughed into his shoulder. "Excuse me. I contacted the managers, and I received a list of names of the staff working the nights of the murders. I called them already, and I asked basic questions. They all complied, and some even remembered the victims."

I sat on the edge of my seat.

"The first victim, a young woman named Alana Pearson, was at a club downtown. She left with a few friends. The bouncer saw them. He said it was hard not to notice them—a group of women looking like that. Not even ten seconds later, according to the bouncer, a creep exited the club and followed the women."

"Description?" I asked.

Fred opened his phone. "I have it here. Skinny. Average height. Ill-fitting clothes. Dirty and stinky. The bouncer said he smelled him before he saw him."

"Facial description?"

Fred shook his head. "Wore a hood, which dowsed most details of his face."

"Did the bouncer relay the information to the police?" I asked.

Fred nodded. "It's not in your files?"

"No," I said. "No description of a suspect."

"Strange. I called the club the second victim was last seen at. Nothing from the bouncer, but a bartender offered corroborating information. Dirty, skinny, pale man who stank like the bowels of Hell."

My stomach fluttered. I had to call Wilson and share what we had learned. I also had to ask why he hadn't learned it himself.

"There's more," Fred said. "Well, kind of. The clubs erase their CCTV footage after ninety days at most. Some erase it after a few days. Anyway, the strip club where the fourth victim was last seen has records dating far enough back. They offered to let us see the recording from that night without a warrant or anything."

"You set a date?" I asked.

"Tomorrow morning. Any time."

"Anything else?"

"There's this man who keeps calling the office line. He claims he knows Tempest Michaels and has helped him with a few cases before, including a vampire. He wants to speak to you."

"What's his name?"

"Vermont Wensdale."

Ringing off the Hook Thursday, July 6th. 0708hrs.

My phone vibrated as I stepped through the front door of my office building. I backpedaled outside and leaned against the restaurant's brick siding, watching the business traffic pass in slow, angry fits.

"Detective Wilson," I said, tilting my head to wedge my phone between it and my shoulder. "I was just thinking about you."

"Hopefully you're not alone and in a dark room."

The light turned green at the intersection, and a half-second later, the car horns came alive. Pedestrians, moving parallel with the traffic across the crosswalk, passed by like a powerful current.

"My team made some phone calls yesterday," I said, not bothering to hide the annoyance and hint of anger swirling within me like a summer wind carrying a spark hot enough to burn half of California.

"Did they learn anything?"

"A surprising amount, and only from basic detective work."

"What's that mean?"

"We contacted establishments where the victims were last seen. We spoke to the staff who worked the nights the victims went missing. Simple, standard investigative work. Did you miss that day in school, Detective Wilson?"

Wilson remained silent, but his breathing revved like a kicking bull preparing to charge.

"You there, Detective?"

"I'm here."

"Did you not call the clubs or bars after the murders?"

"No."

My blood ran cold.

Wilson had a reputation as a Han Solo type on the force. Shoot first, ask questions later. Even in the police academy, he had tended toward the more newsworthy brand of law enforcement. Brash. Rude. Violent. He had, from my knowledge, never resorted to wanton violence, though he would often display an aggressive posture, a loud voice, and berating remarks when dealing with suspects.

Despite his impulsivity, Wilson wasn't dumb. I considered him a good cop, too. He was like a soldier—he did what he thought best to protect those who couldn't protect themselves. Sure, his methods appeared violent and unnecessary, but it all came from a place of service.

Wilson lost his father in a gang-related drive-by shooting as a kid. He now donned the badge and blue uniform to prevent violent criminals from hurting innocent civilians. He balanced a thin line, though, and like Maya, he always erred to the side of asking for forgiveness.

His tactics had made him a highly decorated beat cop, which I'm sure helped land him the promotion. Unlike patrol officers, though, detectives had to practice more patience and discretion, two skills which often eluded Wilson.

That all directed me to one glaring question. Had Wilson's eagerness blinded him to fundamental, methodical investigative work which resulted in further unnecessary deaths?

"How did you miss it?" I asked with a tight, barely controlled voice. "We received a physical description of the vampire. Ted, had you followed through, you could've released a description to the public. People might be alive right now."

Wilson released a mouthful of colorful language. "Don't put that on me, August. Don't you dare."

"You're the lead detective on this case."

"Only as of days ago. Do your basic detective work before pointing fingers."

I cracked my neck and held my tongue. I usually practiced a slow-to-anger approach, but a person can't always harness their emotions. Mine had frayed. They had become sensitive after what happened to Cambria.

"I only inherited this case a couple of days before I brought you on. You want to chew someone out for ineptitude, chew out the last guy. Not me. I'm swimming in his inefficiency."

I remained quiet, my eyes wide and staring at the busy street.

"Detective Madden circled his retirement date on his Hooters calendar, and he spent what time remained on his time clock doing the absolute least amount of work as humanly possible. I didn't just inherit the vampire case from him, either. There are other open homicide cases sitting at my desk without a dent in the investigations. That's why I called you. You don't get that? I couldn't do this alone. I needed your help, not your critique."

I scraped my teeth over lip and cracked a knuckle. "I didn't know."

"It's good, August. You couldn't have known."

"I'm sorry."

"Just don't come at me like I'm not doing my job. Policing is my life, and I police with my life. Don't come at me like I'm not doing a damn thing."

"You're right. I was angry, and I let my anger get the better of me."

"You have a description of the monster?"

I shared the physical description of the vampire with Wilson, emphasizing the grungy appearance and the foul stench.

"I'll get a forensic artist to the witnesses," Wilson said. "We'll see if they can't create a loose sketch of the vampire."

"Well, we might have more than a sketch," I said. "I'm headed to the strip club this morning."

"Bad call," Wilson said. "I went to a morning performance once, and it's not pretty. They don't even have the C-list girls out there. It Z-list. Bottom of the barrel."

"The club has security footage from that night of a murder. Management offered to show it to us. You up for a field trip at 1000hrs?"

"I'll be there," Wilson said.

"Now that we have an idea what he looks like, we might spot him on camera and have a real image of the man. That's huge."

Wilson sighed. "Madden could have had all this, if not more, months ago. I should knock on his front door and ask him how retirement is treating him."

"Forget about him. Let's keep pushing forward with what we have. Alright?"

Wilson cleared his throat. "Hey, I called you, though, remember? And not to get lectured."

"What's up?"

"You need to know something." He sounded serious, like a doctor about to share terminal news. "It's about Eddie Denier."

Eddie Denier was Maya's ex-boyfriend. He had murdered his ex-girlfriend, Stacey Stokes, making the crime appear like a suicide. He had premeditated the homicide by planting voodoo dolls in the homes of people who had died random deaths, trying to make everything connect and appear part of an elaborate curse.

"What about Eddie?" From across the street, I noticed a tall, muscular man with blond hair. He wore black leather and leaned against the siding of a coffee shop, arms crossed, and the man stared directly at me.

"Recently," Wilson said, "Eddie has suffered severe mental breakdowns."

"Breakdowns?"

"I don't know. Hallucinations and paranoia... that kind of thing. Anyway, mental health decided he should transfer to a crisis bed."

My stomach somersaulted. A phone call about transferring a dangerous prisoner who had a vendetta against me. That meant one thing.

"August, he never made it to the facility."

A public transportation bus drove across the street. When it passed, the man in black had vanished.

Wilson continued speaking. "He wasn't the only prisoner inside the transfer vehicle who suffered from similar mental breakdown. Understand, I only learned of this news just before calling you, though the incident occurred late last night."

"What happened?"

"Vanessa Snow and Trisha Berry were on the same bus."

Vanessa Snow was the Changeling. Trisha Berry was the Doppelgänger.

"They were all on one bus, getting transferred to the same mental health facility?" I asked. "That didn't seem odd to anyone? Who approved that transfer?"

"The bus never made its destination," Wilson said. "A CHP unit found it early this morning on the side of Highway 50. The two officers conducting the transfer were dead. The prisoners gone."

I stared up at the bright, warm sky, unsure of how to handle the news. I had to call Maya before I did anything else. She needed to know Eddie had escaped. I also had to let Zachary and Miette Verdin know that Vanessa Snow had escaped. I had to update Claire Balzan that Trisha Berry had escaped.

I ran my fingers through my hair and stared at the cafe across the street. "We don't have any idea what happened?"

"Nothing yet. I'll keep you in the loop, though."

My phone beeped, implying an incoming call. I pulled it from my ear and glanced at the caller. Lloyd Henderson. My parents' pastor. He had helped care for Randall Fincher, an unstable thirty-year-old man who lost his mother in the Voodoo case.

"Let me know when you learn more," I said. "I have to take this other call, but I'll see you in a couple of hours."

"Bring singles," Wilson said.

I inhaled and switched to the other line. "Lloyd."

"August, hey."

"This about Randall?"

"You heard?"

I shook my head back and forth, but didn't speak. I thought of the prison bus being found empty, apart from the two murdered officers.

"We moved Randall Fincher back into his home a couple of weeks ago. The church still sends volunteers to check on him throughout the day. One of our volunteers will stop by every morning before her pilates class at eight o'clock. She lost her son years ago, and she and Randall have—"

"Lloyd, what happened?"

"Sorry. Sorry. Marge called me a few minutes ago. Randall isn't home. We tried his phone, but it's turned off. I don't know where he would have gone, but that's not like him to leave. Doctors recently diagnosed him with agoraphobia. He won't go outside alone, if at all."

Eddie Denier. Vanessa Snow. Trisha Berry. Randall Fincher. All of them connected to me and my cases. All of them had gone missing.

I thought of David Shaye, the man who had hypnotized Cambria, ultimately resulting in her death. Did he still sit in a Santa Cruz jail cell, or had he mysteriously disappeared, too? What about Glacia's mother and uncle? Have they upped and vanished? What about...

"I have to go," I said. "Keep me updated on anything you learn."

Without waiting for a response, I hung up the phone and called Vincent Dupree. His phone went straight to voicemail. I called Scott Moreno, Vincent's other groomsman.

"Hello?" Scott answered.

"Scott," I said.

"This is he."

"Are you at work?"

"Who is this?"

"It's August."

"Who?"

"Vincent's best man. August Watson."

"Oh, sorry. I deleted your number. I didn't think we would ever talk again after the wedding. What's going on?"

"Are you at work?"

"I am."

"Is Vincent there?"

"He's not."

"Why?"

"Don't know. Probably recovering from the wedding night after breaking in that marital bed." He snickered. I hated the grating sound. "You sound stressed. You okay?"

"If you hear from Vincent, have him call me."

"Sure thing, boss."

I hung up and mentally tallied who I needed to call to warn about the escapees. Before I was two names into my count, my phone rang again. I didn't recognize the number.

My thoughts immediately jumped to Daniel Quinn. I knew that the psychotic maniac orchestrated all this chaos. I don't know how he managed any of it, but I knew he pulled the strings.

"Hello," I answered, my voice sharp and ready to stab.

"August Watson." The voice didn't belong to Daniel Quinn. It was deeper, with a more violent rather than playful hue.

"Yes."

"I've recently learned you've illegally employed my daughter, Alina Moore, at your company, and you've endangered her life on multiple occasions." The man spoke as if reading from a script. "Is this true?"

My anger, which had sparked from Detective Madden's incompetence and laziness, ignited as the added fear and frustration of the past few minutes provided perfect kindling. Stephen Moore poured gasoline on the blazing inferno.

"Don't talk to me about endangering your daughter—you, the deadbeat, sorry excuse for a husband, father, and man, who abandoned his teenage daughter to chase some woman?"

Stephen spoke, sputtering off his script, but I cut him off, not caring to hear what he had to say. He had already uttered about twenty words too many.

"I don't like you calling me. I don't like what it implies—that you're back in town with a sudden, regretful mindset. You want Alina back, but that will not happen. Do you understand? You're like dog crap on the bottom of her shoe. You stink. You stick around though no one wants you, and you're better off tossed in the trash."

Stephen spoke softly now. "I left Alina with Wanda."

I chuckled, but no humor touched even the edges of that laugh. "You left your sixteen-year-old daughter with a known criminal and drug addict who has a history of abandonment herself. Awesome discretion. You knew, or you at least suspected, that Wanda would also leave. Guess what? She left. Your absence spooked her back into drugs. I don't know why you're calling me. I don't know what you have to say to me. But leave well enough alone. That's my advice to you."

"I'm currently sitting in front of Maya's house and waiting for her or my daughter to come outside. When they do, I'm taking my Alina to Ohio with me. I thought I would give you the courtesy of a phone call. If you interfere with me bringing my daughter home, I will pursue legal action against you and your company. Do you understand? I didn't have to call you, but I provided you that courtesy, mostly because I don't want you contacting me after today. Alina comes with me. End of story. I don't care what route you take, the court will always side with her father over a strange man. I'm sober. I'm employed. I have a stable home. She's my daughter. Do you understand?"

I hung up on him. I couldn't speak. Anger incinerated any chance of uttering a single syllable. Anger like a wild fire moving through my body, burning away thought and reason, burning me from the inside-out.

After a minute of forcing myself to calm down and breathe, I marched to my car and called Maya.

A Broken Taillight. Thursday, July 6th. 0816hrs.

I SKIDDED TO A stop in front of Maya's driveway and threw open the door without bothering to turn off the engine.

A rusted-red Toyota exhaled smoke from its exhaust in the driveway. Evan drove a Tesla. Maya drove a Volkswagen, which mostly remained tucked away in her garage as she preferred to Uber around town. Nobody I knew drove a rusted-red Toyota truck.

Without a second's hesitation, I marched straight to it.

Stephen's meaty hand dangled from the driver's window. He wore a thick ring on each of his fingers. I couldn't see his other hand. My police training and experience taught me to proceed with caution in circumstances like this—a scorned father looking to reclaim his lost daughter, his lost property, in his opinion. He could act desperately, impulsively, violently, which meant I had to remain cool and in charge.

I alerted him of my presence by tapping on the bed of his truck. The last thing I wanted to do was surprise him.

From within the vehicle, a popular country tune spilled through the open window. I caught a few lyrics, but I didn't recognize the song. I mostly avoided country music, though Alina and Fred played it nonstop in the office.

I remained a foot behind the driver's door, but within obvious view of his side mirror. From the reflection, I saw Alina's dad. Stephen had shaved his head bald to showcase the tattoos wrapping around his skull, and he had striking blue eyes. They were so blue, they almost looked fake.

He smirked at me. A second later, the uptempo song ceased. "August Watson," he said, eyeing me from the side mirror. "You called Maya. I wish you hadn't complicated this."

A statement, not a question. I had called Maya as I raced to her house, and I warned her about Stephen waiting for Alina, waiting to take her across the country back to his new home.

"I'm not leaving until I have my daughter. You realize that, right?"

"I will not let that happen."

Stephen laughed, genuinely amused. "No? What will you do to prevent it?"

"I'll advise Maya to have the cops remove you for trespassing on her property."

"She rents, so not her property. Besides," Stephen shrugged and smiled, "that's fine. I'll back up my truck, park across the street, and wait there. I'll wait there as long as I need to, but I'm getting my daughter back. Here's the thing: you and Maya have no right to keep her from me. That's kidnapping. So, if you call the cops, it only makes this difficult for you and my sister-in-law. I'll comply with everything they say. I'll tell God's honest truth. You think they won't take my side? I'm her father."

I cracked a knuckle and chewed on my cheek, knowing Stephen had a point. I was a grown man with no familial relationship to Alina. Stephen was her father.

My ignorance on family law didn't help the situation, either. If Stephen up and left his family three months ago, did he have free rein to return and uproot his daughter, completely disrupting her entire life?

I removed my phone from my pocket and called Maya.

"Hey," she answered.

"I'm here."

"Is he going to leave?"

"No."

"Can you put me on speaker?"

I tapped the speaker icon. "Stephen, Maya wants to say something to you."

"That's all she ever wants to do. Say something, as if she has something worth listening to. You hear me, Maya? I know you. You're nothing but a common whore."

I nearly reached into the truck, grasped the back of his head, and slammed his face into the steering wheel. Luckily, I had more restraint, and I prevented myself from making the situation far more complicated than it already was.

"I missed this, Stephen," Maya said, unphased. "I missed our banter. You degrade me, just like you degraded Wanda and Alina, and I fantasize about cutting your tiny—yes, I know it's tiny because Wanda told me—little cock off and forcing you to eat it."

"I want my daughter."

"Honestly, Stephen, what you want sits at the very bottom of my list of things I care about," Maya said. "In fact, I opened a custody claim. A sixteen-year-old girl's father abandoned her, and shortly thereafter, her mother also left. So, I thought, in my, as you would put it, scummy little brain, 'Man, I would hate for those degenerates to come back into her life and make it miserable again.' So, you know what? I reported you two to child protective services, and I opened a custody claim, requesting... drumroll please... that I become Alina's legal guardian."

Stephen's jaw clenched, but before he could spew the word vomit from his mouth, Maya continued.

"You forget one thing, Stevie. Though I'm just a weak, pathetic, stupid woman, and you're a big, strong, imposing man... I'm so, so, so much smarter than you."

"You can't just keep her," Stephen said.

"You can't just return from the dead and demand her. Now, we can do this in a few ways."

"Let me speak to her," Stephen said. "You have no right to disallow her from speaking to me. Put her on the phone."

"Oh, she's sitting right here beside me. You're on speaker, but she doesn't want to say a thing to you. What could she say, other than you're worse than what she flushes down the toilet?"

"Alina," Stephen gasped, leaning forward in his seat and gripping the steering wheel in both hands. "I'm so sorry. I am. Please, Alina. Say something to me."

"Stephen, that's pathetic. Don't grovel," Maya said. "If you really want your daughter back, and you want her to want you back, listen to what I have to say. Back out of my driveway and return to whatever hole you crawled out from. You can call the cops and claim kidnapping or, I don't know, whatever you think I'm doing wrong here. I'll gladly share with them your shining history as the father of the year, and we'll see who they side with. Also, I'm not sure if you're aware, but Alina is sixteen now. She's old enough to have a voice. I know that's scary for you, thinking women can express their opinions, but she can and she often does. What if we go to court, and what if a judge asks Alina, 'Who do you want to live with?' And what if Alina says, 'Maya?' Now before you turn all Palaeolithic on me, keep one other important thing in mind. At sixteen, she can request emancipation. So, Mr. Moore, consider how you wish to proceed."

Stephen wrinkled his nose and sniffled. He sucked on his teeth, and he tapped his thick rings against the dashboard. "Let me talk to her."

"Alina," Maya said, "would you like to speak to your father?"

A second of rustling, followed by pure, pregnant silence. "Dad," Alina said, her voice more scared than I ever heard it before.

"Baby." Stephen nearly lurched out the driver's window to wrestle the phone from my hand. "I've come back for you, to take you home with me. Will you come home with me?"

"You left us," Alina whispered.

"For you. I left for you."

"You left for you."

"No, please, understand. Your mom and I drove each other crazy. I was like a rubber band, stretched to my limit, about to snap. I had to leave. I had no choice. You get that, right?"

Alina didn't speak, though I knew what she wanted to say. I knew she wanted to agree with him. Yes, I get that. I understand. I forgive you. I'll go home with you. It's all she wanted—a family and a sense of belonging, of loving and being loved. That's all anyone ever wanted, especially kids. They craved love.

"Mylene," Stephen said, calling Alina by her middle name. "Baby. It's your dad. It's me. You know I wouldn't do anything to hurt you. Never."

"For months, every single day for months, you hurt me." A chilly quiet filled the summer morning. "I slept in a hundred different beds, in a thousand different rooms, looking out a million different windows, wondering when you would come back. I woke up every morning without you there, every day for months. You left me. You abandoned me without so much as a goodbye. So, don't lie to me and say you wouldn't hurt me. You destroyed me, and then you destroyed me over and over, again and again, day after day." A second of silence passed. "The worst pain you caused, though, was that you destroyed Mom. You destroyed our family so you could get laid."

"Mylene," he said, his voice now thick with emotion. Through the side mirror, I saw tears on his face catching the dying light. "You're upset, and you don't know what you're saying. I'm going to get you back. You should live with your family, with your father."

"I already live with my family," Alina said.

A few breaths later, Maya returned to the line. "Well, there you have it, Stephen. Please see yourself back to wherever you ran off to and never come back. You're not wanted."

"This isn't over."

"It is."

"No, it's not. I'll have my daughter back, Maya. I'll get a lawyer, and I'll have my daughter back. Do you understand me?"

"You can't afford a lawyer."

"You don't know what I'm capable of."

"I know you can explode a family and destroy the innocence of a beautiful little girl." Maya's front door opened, and she stood in the doorframe holding her phone in one hand, holding her middle finger up with the other.

Stephen snickered. "I'm employed. I'm renting a home. I'm sober and I'm attending a support group twice a week. If something unfortunate happened to you, Maya, where do you think the court would assign my daughter to live?"

"Are you threatening me?"

"Only asking a question."

"Stephen, if you ever get the wild idea in your cock-sized brain to show up in my driveway again, I will make sure you don't leave. That's a fact, and it's also a threat. I will shoot you in your big, ugly, bald face. Next time we meet, make sure it's in court." The line went dead, and Maya slammed the front door.

I returned the phone to my pocket and watched Stephen through the reflection of the driver's side mirror. He stared at the lowered garage door, eyes wide and unblinking. After a second, they shifted and settled on me.

"Why did you call me?" I asked.

"What?"

"You called me, not Maya or Alina. You heard I employed your daughter at my company. Who told you that? Who gave you my contact information?"

"An anonymous tip."

"Was the man's name Daniel Quinn?"

"The person never shared a name. They sent me an email asking if I wanted to know about Alina, and if so, I had to follow a couple of steps. When I agreed, the sender responded with your name, business address, cell phone number, and pictures of you and my daughter."

"Do you remember the name of the email address?"

Stephen clicked his tongue. "I'm getting my daughter back. Stay out of my way."

I sighed and stared at Maya's house. "Stephen, the number you called me on earlier, that's your number?"

He glared at me and shifted his truck into reverse.

"I'll speak with Alina," I said. "I'll share your number with her—if she doesn't already have it."

The truck stopped moving backward. Stephen and I no longer needed the side mirror to look at each other. We were eye to eye.

"She's sixteen, not a little girl. But that doesn't change the fact that you're her father. I'll give your number to her, and she can make the choice to contact you or not. How about if you two start there?" I cracked a knuckle. "Let her come to you."

"Brooks0718@gmail.com," Stephen said, releasing the brake and rolling out of the driveway. He turned onto the main road and stopped at the sign. He had a broken left taillight, and he didn't bother with a blinker before turning right.

Brooks0718. Aaron Brooks. I had shot and killed him on July 18th, almost six years ago now. That revelation staggered me. Six years since I shot Aaron Brooks. He would turn twenty-five in August. My heart tightened to think of that, to think that I had stolen a son from his parents.

Is that why I felt a semblance of sympathy toward Stephen, why I offered to help him? Did I believe I could atone for my sin of destroying a family by bringing one back together?

Fingers intertwined with mine. I came back to the present, still staring at the stop sign down the street.

Maya stood beside me.

"You really opened a custody case?" I asked.

"When she first moved in with me. I needed to put it on record, in case something like this happened."

"What if Alina wants to try it again with her dad?"

"He's not a good man, August."

"None of us are truly good, and we all change. A broken taillight is only broken until it's fixed, right?"

"I'm not sure what that means, but Stephen is beyond fixing. He's a master manipulator and a conman. He was like that before marrying Wanda. He was like that during their marriage. He's like that now. He only wants what's best for him. My bet, he gets some government money for every kid he has under the age of eighteen, and that's why he's back. He only ever wants a quick buck, and a quick fu—"

"What do we do then?" I asked.

Maya sighed. "Alina decides what we do next."

The Security Footage. Thursday, July 6th. 0959hrs.

Maya worked as a writer for the *Here & Now*, a tabloid covering paranormal events in the Sacramento region. She spent most of her time at home, writing articles remotely. Occasionally, she went into the field with me, hoping to steal my cases as potential topics.

After the incident with her father, Alina refused to remain cooped inside. Besides, it was summer break. She really only had two options in the matter—stay inside and watch movies or join me for work.

Normally, I wouldn't have hesitated to have her tag along, but I had a scheduled meeting at a strip club. I wasn't too fond of waltzing a sixteen-year-old girl through that establishment.

"Maya has nothing planned today," Alina said. "Do you care if she and I visit Ashton Snell's parents to see if we can't find one of them at home?"

"Sure," I said.

"If not, we'll try to get in touch with Leon Lambert's, Timothy Porter's, or Connor Pellerin's family. I'm not sure they can provide anything new to what we know, but it's worth a shot. Also, it gets me out of the house until four."

"Four?" I asked. "What's at four?"

"Your meeting with Armando Lopez, Maria's father, remember?"

"I remember now," I said.

"You know you have a calendar on your phone to remind you of these things."

"That's what you're for," I said with a grin. It quickly faded. "Hey."

"Hey."

"Speaking of phones." I tapped through my recent calls and shared Stephen's number with his daughter. "You might already have it, but that's your dad's cell phone number."

Alina stared at her phone, at the number. "I didn't have this."

"Well, don't tell Maya I shared it with you. I'm a little scared of her and how she might react."

"Why did you share this with me?" Alina looked at me with wide, wet eyes.

"You should make these decisions, not Maya or me or your dad. You. If you think you should contact him, and speak to him without the interference of Maya, now you can. I trust your judgement."

After our exchange, Alina jumped into Maya's Volkswagen, and they headed toward the address of Ashton Snell's parents.

I drove to the strip club.

Ted Wilson waited in the parking lot. When I pulled up, he stepped out of his vehicle. He was all limbs—long legs and arms, but broad and muscular. Not as tall or as big as Fred, but his wide smile and aura of arrogance made him seem twice his actual size, a giant compared to Fred.

"August Watson," he said, slapping my shoulder with enough force to send me staggering forward. "You look good. Healthy."

"Health is wealth," I said.

"Ain't that the gospel truth?" He glanced over his shoulder at the club's entrance. "You bring your one-dollar bills?"

In the morning light, the strip club looked faded and dreary and dirty. It felt sad.

"Do they take credit?" I asked.

Wilson chuckled. "Money is money is money."

We entered the dimly lit club, which hadn't yet opened, and wouldn't open for another thirty minutes. No music played. No women paraded from table to table or danced on the stages. No one made drinks or shouted above the thumping speakers. It was relatively bright, quiet, and empty within the club. It felt like strange—wrong, almost—to be inside of there.

A man in a dark-blue security uniform approached us. He wore a black utility belt with the likes of handcuffs, pepper spray, and a gun clipped to it. He had thick forearms and no neck. His chin just sat on his chest. "Can I help you?"

"I'm August Watson with Blue Moon, and this is—"

"Ted Wilson, homicide detective with Sacramento Police Department." He flashed his badge. "We were told to meet here around this time to watch some security footage. Can you help us with that?"

The man grunted and padded away, entering an office behind the bar and closing the door.

Wilson exhaled, vibrating his lips. "Strange, isn't it? It's like... like walking into a church on Tuesday morning. It's not the same."

I glanced at the detective and scowled. "I'm not sure anyone has ever compared a strip club to a church before."

The security guard emerged from the office and waved us over. We crossed the sticky floors. My shoes squelched, almost like crossing through a row at a movie theater... except at a strip club. I'm sure, like at other bars, the stickiness derived from spilled drinks and poor custodial work—or so I convinced myself—but the context of sticky floor in a strip club had me feeling like I needed a long, scalding-hot shower.

Inside the manager's office, a pimply faced man who sort of morphed into his chair, as if they had become one entity, greeted us. He drank soda from a gas-station sized cup—the Big Gulp. His desk was a disruption of papers and folders and trash. Four monitors mounted to the wall in front of him, two sat amongst the chaos on his desk. A tablet rested on his lap, playing a hardcore porno video with the volume turned up loud.

Wilson leaned forward to ogle the tablet.

The man flicked the screen to black and looked at a computer on his desk. "You're here for the security tape?"

"We are," I said.

"You have a warrant?"

"I wasn't under the impression we needed one," I said

"There's a cop here. Of course you need one. Unless you can convince me otherwise." The blubbery man rubbed his thumb and index finger together, universally signaling his need for cash.

"How about this, big boy?" Wilson reached into his back pocket and removed a wad of greenbacks. "A band." He tossed the thousand dollars—which equaled a band—at the man's feet. "You never saw me here, did you?"

The manager leaned over and collected the cash. He licked his fingers and counted the bills. After confirming his count, he glanced at me. "You're a private detective?"

"Private investigator."

"There's not a difference."

"There is," I said, biting my lip. "It doesn't matter, though."

"I'll talk to you, because I don't talk to police."

"What's your name?" I asked.

"Liam."

"You spoke with my assistant, Fred Rogers."

"Name sounds familiar."

"You mentioned to him that your security system holds records for longer than ninety days?"

"I back it up onto a personal hard drive. I have records dated back to the night my employment began here. What girl do you want to see? I'll pull her up. If you give me another band, I'll send a copy home with you."

"I don't want you to pull up any girl. I want you to pull up a specific night."

Wilson shared the exact date with me, and I relayed it to Liam since he didn't respond to officers of the law. The manager went to his saved files and scrolled through his records, pulling up the date in question and starting the video from the time the club opened.

"What are we looking for?" Liam asked.

Skinny. Average height. Ill-fitting clothes. Dirty and stinky. That was Fred's description, which was taken from the bouncer who worked at the club. The bartender working at the second club had corroborated the description. *Dirty, skinny, pale man.*

I shared the description with Liam, and we dove into the film. The recording split into eight smaller screens. Customers came into the establishment as rays of light still cut through the door jams. The women danced on stage, and they led men off into private rooms, and they served drinks.

Liam ran the recording on a slow fast forward—fast enough to expedite the process, slow enough to not blur the patronage.

"There." Wilson pointed at the screen. "That's the victim—Herb Nowak."

"Slow the video to real time," I said.

Liam complied. The video crawled at a normal pace. I scanned the eight boxes, searching the separate areas of the club for a man fitting the vampire's description. Skinny. Dirty. Pale. A corpse buried six feet under, not having experienced sunlight or hygiene for months or years. That seemed easy enough.

Except, he never appeared on screen.

The old man, Herb, stood and exited. He walked to his truck, climbed inside, and drove away. We rewound the tape, rewatched it, saw no one and nothing that caught our attention.

"Is this about the Vampire of Sacramento?" Liam asked. "I saw that old man on the victim list. Unmistakable face." It was true. Herb had an unmistakable bulldog face. Heavy, drooping jowls, a wrinkled forehead, and a punched up nose, all accessorizing a large, very round dome. "Also, Herb Nowak is a regular here. He shows like twice a week. You think the vampire was here, in this club?" Liam chuckled. "Man, that's wild to think about. Could have been me, you know? Anyway, probably couldn't locate him in the film because of the reflection issue. Vampires don't have a reflection."

"That's in a mirror," I said.

"It's a reflection. A photograph is just another kind of reflection, right? It's their lack of a soul. There's nothing to reflect or capture in a photograph or on film. If we're dealing with the vampire here, that's why you can't see him."

"He has a point," Wilson said, smirking. "Did you even think about that? Why would you suggest coming out here and wasting our time if you hadn't, Mr. Paranormal Detective?"

"Investigator, and vampires don't exist." I grabbed a stick of gum and popped it into my mouth.

No one had followed Herb out of the club, or had tailed him when he drove away. Liam played the video from Herb's departure, fast forwarding through three hours of the parking lot. No one matching the vampire's description exited or entered the club at any point.

"Hey, guys, I love this detective work," Liam said after another twenty minutes, "especially the way it pays, but we have girls on the stage and customers in chairs already. I have work to do."

I reached into my pocket and removed one of the business cards Tempest Michaels had ordered for me. I was terrible at remembering I had them, and even worse at passing them around. Yet, I kept a small bundle in my back pocket just in case I remembered they existed. "If you think of anything, or if you see anyone, call me."

"Paranormal investigator? You're like a real life Van Helsing hunting a vampire, huh?"

"You'll call?" I asked.

"I'll call."

Wilson and I thanked Liam for his time, and we exited his office and the club, returning to our cars. The parking lot had filled with a few more vehicles since our arrival.

"What do you think?" Wilson asked.

"I have another stop to make. You want to join me?"

"Doing what?"

The Secret. Thursday, July 6th. 1142hrs.

"TAKE A RIGHT." ALINA pointed out the windshield, then out the passenger window as they passed their turn. "Never mind. Go straight, I guess."

"We're not going to the Snells' house," Maya said.

"We're not?"

"No."

"Where are we going?"

Maya licked her lips, itchy to open her mouth and spill all of her secrets. They burned a hole through her tongue, and they weighed heavily on her mind, but she hadn't uttered a word to anyone, not even

Evan. Not even August. Maya hated secrets, too. They were nothing more than an iteration of a lie, and she liked nothing less than lying.

Maya strove for truth, always for honesty. That's what propelled her to drop out of medical school, despite a promising future, and pursue investigative journalism. The investigative journalism she currently worked within didn't entirely scream ideal. She wrote about supposed UFO landings and ghost sightings, and she always bummed August's cases for material to write about. However, she kept her conscience clean by convincing herself that although she wrote about paranormal mysteries, she always provided an honest conclusion. The chupacabra sighting, well, that was nothing more than a shaved, rabid dog.

Jonah, her boss, preferred she keep the illusion of the supernatural alive at the end of her articles, but Maya refused. Any audience always preferred truth. The sad part was, audiences often believed their own truth, and they sought media that aligned with those truths. The audience, like the customer, was never wrong. Only media outlets, especially those pandering to their audience, were wrong.

Maya refused to fall into that trap and deliberately lie to her audience, telling them what they wanted to hear because they wanted to hear it.

Except she had kept a secret from Alina for two months, and it chipped at her soul day by day.

"Maya," Alina said, now staring at her. "Where are we going? Are we running away? Please tell me we're running away like Thelma and Louise. How awesome would that be? We're on the run from, not the law, but from my father." Alina chuckled, but nothing about her laugh held humor. It was a sad, lonely chuckle, the kind produced late at night, sitting alone in a dark room.

"I knew this day would come," Maya said. "So, I made preparations."

"Why are you sounding so ominous? Preparations? You're talking like my dad is the apocalypse, and you're driving me to an underground bunker filled with paperback books and awful food."

"You're sixteen. It's your choice to make, not mine."

"What choice is that?"

"Before I share anything with you, I have to know something. If your dad returns to my door with a subpoena summoning me to court in a custody battle for you..." Maya trailed off and licked her lips. Her mouth felt too dry. "That takes a lot of time and money, and if you want to live with him, I won't stand in your way. You're intelligent and capable, and I believe you know what's best for you. No one knows what's best for you, but you."

Alina slouched in the passenger seat and crossed her arms. Maya wished she could read her niece's thoughts, but the silence stretched between them. Not even the radio interrupted their company. Only the muffled traffic from outside the car.

"Before you answer, I think you should know everything."

Alina turned to Maya and squinted at her. "What do you mean, everything?"

Maya scratched her arm. "When your mom was your age—I think she may have been pregnant with you at the time—and I was a little younger, she disappeared for a few days."

"That's a shock."

"Our mom obviously noticed, but she worked three jobs to keep the lights on. I don't think our dad ever noticed anything about anyone but himself. He never lifted a finger to search for his missing daughter. Anyway, I snuck out one night. Well, I left out the front door and no one realized it." Maya pulled the car to the shoulder and parked. Tears blurred her vision, and she blinked them away, but she didn't think it was the wisest idea to remain on the road while crying.

"You found her?" Alina asked.

"That night, yes. I think I always knew where she was. It wasn't fair between us—between your mother and me. I escaped from the house by going to college and creating a life for myself. Your mom didn't have that luxury, so she escaped in other ways." Maya didn't have to say what those other ways were, but they both knew. Drugs, alcohol, sex, and temporary stays in juvenile hall and later jail.

"No, that's not what I mean," Alina said. "You found her? Now. That's where we're going, isn't it?"

Maya blinked rapidly.

"You found her as a kid and you found her now... and you never told me?"

"Alina."

"How long have you known and not told me?"

"Two months."

"You knew where my mom was for two months, and you allowed me to worry every single day about her safety?" Alina chuckled again, and again nothing humorous shined through.

"She asked me not to tell anyone." Maya's voice barely escaped off her lips. It was so weak and ill-formed.

"And if she asked you to put a bullet through her head, would you have done that?"

"That's a little extreme."

"You not telling me you found my mom is a little extreme, don't you think?" Alina stared out the passenger window and fogged the glass. "Where is she now?"

"A treatment center. It detoxifies their patients from any drugs and alcohol. They provide medical and psychiatric help. They clean up their patients physically, mentally, and spiritually. When ready, they connect their patients with job opportunities and potential places to live. The facility doesn't allow visitors for the first thirty days. Also, their patients can choose to leave. It's a volunteer program. Your mom chose and continues to choose to be there. She's trying to get better."

Alina sniffled as she stared out the window. "That's where you're taking me now?"

"Yes."

"What if I don't want to see her?"

"Do you?"

A second passed. "Yes."

Maya nodded and grabbed her phone off the seat from between her legs. She pressed the screen a few times and placed it to her ear. "Can I speak to Wanda Moore? This is Maya Adler." Maya glanced at Alina and spared a broken smile.

"Can you put it on speakerphone?" Alina turned away from the window and looked at Maya with determination and longing behind her eyes.

Maya shook her head in the negative and looked away from her niece. "Hey, Wandi Bear. It's time. Are you ready?"

"Does she know?" Wanda asked.

"Yes."

"Stephen showed up then?"

"Yes."

"How did he seem?"

"Okay," Maya said.

"He wanted her back?"

"Yeah."

"Is she with you now?"

"Yes."

"Okay. I'll be ready then."

Maya ended the call and sighed, keeping her attention fixed out the driver-side window. "I kept a secret from you, Alina, and I'm sorry for lying. I knew your dad would eventually come back. I remember how I always wanted to escape from my father, so I created exits for you to use in case you wanted to escape yours, too. I opened the custody case, claiming he abandoned you. I doubt it will hold up in court. Judges rule in favor of the parents. That's why I went after your mom. If she's clean and sober, if she has a place to live and a job, she might win a custody battle. It'll be tough, but we have a better shot at it with her in the picture. You're old enough to make that decision yourself, though. You can emancipate, but we'll need August to step in and pay you a salary with benefits for that to have any chance. You can go off with your dad. Or you can stay here with your mom. It's ultimately your choice."

"I watched this horror movie last night," Alina said.

Maya chuckled, because, of course, Alina referenced a horror movie. She faced her niece, watched as the teenager wiped a tear from her face.

"It started off showing the lives of normal kids in an ordinary home. A happy home with parents who loved each other and their children. They ate dinner together. They watched a family movie. Stereotypical stuff, you know? They didn't know their entire lives would change when a murderous monster appeared and butchered everyone they knew. I feel like my entire life has been nothing but running away, trying to survive the murderer. That's all I've known. I never had the ordinary experience of family. Only running and trying to survive."

"I know what you mean," Maya said, and she meant it. She still felt like she was running away and trying to survive her childhood, despite having her dream career, an incredible boyfriend, and an amazing group of friends she called her family.

"I'm ready to see my mom."

Maya shifted into drive and pulled back onto the road. She drove to the treatment center to reunite Alina and her mother.

Stuckey's Bar. Thursday, July 6th. 1223hrs.

WILSON AND I ENTERED Stuckey's bar, the dive Maya had taken Alina and me to a couple months back—the place I had danced with Patty Huffman, the vampire's third victim.

Nick, the bearded bartender, stood behind the counter. He wore an undersized black T-shirt, which emphasized eight of the reasons Maya befriended him for a while. The rest of the establishment was mostly empty, occupied only by a few men in cowboy boots and dirty jeans who ate nachos and drank a draft beer for lunch.

I sat on a stool and nodded at Nick.

He shuffled over to us. "Afternoon."

"Nick, right?" I asked.

"I know you?"

"We met once, a couple months back. I'm Maya's friend, August."

He lifted his head and scratched his chin. "I remember. How's she doing? We haven't talked too much recently."

"She's good." I didn't care, and it wasn't my place to go into the specifics of Maya's life.

"How can I help you?" Nick asked.

Wilson slapped a photograph of Patricia Huffman on the counter. "You recognize this woman?"

Nick eyed Wilson. "This is about the vampire?"

"What do you know about her?" Wilson asked, tapping the image.

"That's Patty. She came here near every night and danced. She loved 90s country when drinking beer, but if she shot whiskey or tequila, Lynyrd Skynyrd rocked this joint. I found her, you know?"

"You found her body?" I hadn't known that tidbit of information.

"Unlocked the place that morning, took out the trash, saw her naked body shoved in the dumpster."

"What do you remember from the night prior?" Wilson asked. "Did you notice anyone in the bar who seemed out of place?"

"I shared everything with the police already. Detective Madden. I remember his name because I'm a fan of those Madden football games."

"Pretend Madden's save file accidentally got deleted, and you had to start the game from scratch." Wilson leaned forward. "Who did you see?"

Nick blinked hard. "I hadn't seen him in here before. He stuck out, too, despite trying to hide in the corner and in the shadows. He wore a black outfit, and he had painted black fingernails. People in here aren't usually too kind to those different from them. So, I had a few customers complaining about the stranger, especially because of his smell. He stank something fierce."

"Do you have security footage?" I asked.

Nick frowned. "It's written over every seven days."

"You never saw him before that night, or since that night?"

"Not once."

"Was he talking to Patty?"

Nick chewed his cheeks for a moment. "I don't think so. He sulked in the shadows and cupped his beer. He never even drank it. After he left, I went over there to collect his glass, and it was full to the brim."

"Did anyone confront him?" I asked.

"They avoided him," Nick said. "They complained to me, and to Snail—that's our bouncer. I don't know why we call him Snail, but we always have."

"Did Snail talk to him?" I asked.

"Doubtful. We can't kick someone out of here because they're dressed funny or they smell weird. He wasn't bothering anyone beyond his stench. He sat alone, quietly hugging his beer."

Detective Madden hadn't cared to document his last investigation. Not only that, but the witnesses fizzled out after a general description, and viable security footage hadn't lent results. Wilson and I had come to the end of the line, faced with the barrier that no investigator wants to come against. We needed another body to dig up more evidence, to find more connections, hoping that time the vampire made a mistake.

"I noticed one thing when he ordered his drink," Nick said. "I don't know why, but it has stuck with me ever since."

"What was it?" Wilson asked.

"Blood covered his hands, almost like a glove it was so thick. He must have caught me looking, because he said he was a butcher. He said it was just pig's blood and that it's hard to wash off. I'd seen other men come in here with blood on their hands and their clothes, but they never creeped me out like he had. He had this soft-voice, and he spoke so fast I barely understood him."

"Did you see his face?"

"You don't have the description?"

"Assume we know nothing," Wilson said.

Nick stared over our shoulders. His eyes went distant. "He had a face like a corpse, like it had rotted away. That's why I noticed his hands. I couldn't look at his face. As bad as that sounds, I couldn't look at it." Nick ran his hands through his long, wavy hair.

Bloody hands did little for us. We could visit every butcher in the area, and we probably would, but I suspected that route would lead to another dead end.

As I sat there, debating what to say, my phone rang.

Glacia.

I excused myself from the bar and stepped into the sunny afternoon. I needed the change of scenery and a mental shift, anyway.

"Hey," I said.

"Hey yourself. How's it going?"

"Same as always. Running in circles."

"The Vampire of Sacramento?"

"Alina told you?"

"Yup."

"Yeah."

"She also told me about the Frankenstein golem case. That sounds creepy."

"It's pretty creepy."

Glacia sighed. "So, how did it go with Lauren?"

"Who?"

"Stop it."

I chuckled. "It went well, but I'm guessing you already know that."

"I spoke to her earlier this morning. She also had fun with you, and I had the impression she would like to have more fun with you, maybe over dinner."

I cracked a knuckle. "I'm not sure I'm ready for a relationship. Not after Cambria, and not after..." You, I meant to say but didn't. "I'm not there yet." I didn't think I would be ready until I found Daniel Quinn and ended his reign of terror. I couldn't risk putting anyone else in danger because of his infatuation with me.

"Well, don't be mad at me then," Glacia said.

"That's never a good way to introduce something."

"I may have shared your number with her. And I also may have told her you wouldn't reach out first, and she would have to reach out to you. So, with that being said, Lauren will probably contact you in the next one to two business days."

I cracked my neck, and I mentally went over my checklist one more time.

Find the Vampire of Sacramento.

Find Jackson Armstead.

Help Sarah figure out why Gerald had temporarily lost his mind.

Figure out a way to prevent Alina from having to go with her father.

Take care of a puppy.

Finish moving into and continue keeping up with a new house.

Find Daniel Quinn.

Figure out why all the people I had arrested escaped from custody.

Spend time with family and friends.

Going on a date, having a girlfriend, despite the fun time I had with Lauren at the wedding, didn't fit in my schedule. I had, mostly, eliminated sleep to make time for everything in my life. How would a girlfriend fit into the equation?

"It won't work," I said. "I'm sorry."

"Well, I'm sorry, because you'll have to tell her yourself when she calls."

I rubbed my temples, wondering why everyone wanted to get involved in my romantic life. *Because they care*, I had to remind myself. Still, it was frustrating.

"Thank you for the warning," I said, staring across the street at a florist shop. Standing off the side of the front door, leaning against the tinted windows, was the tall, blond man I had noticed earlier.

"How's the house? You moved in?"

"Technically, yes." I watched the man who watched me. "Everything I own is in the house, which takes up about a quarter of the space."

Glacia snickered, the sound of the conversation fizzling out.

"I have to go." The man walked toward the corner and turned left, away from me. "Work, you know?"

"Good luck. Oh, and, August."

"Yeah."

"Can you let Lauren down easy? She's one of the good ones, and I hate knowing I set her up for a little hurt."

"You're trying to make me feel guilty, aren't you?"

"Use those people skills to find the bad guys. Talk to you later." Glacia hung up.

I remained outside Stuckey's bar, staring at the corner where the black-clad man had walked around. Should I chase after him and ask why he followed me? I remained cemented to the sidewalk. My thoughts ran rampant through my mind. Vampires and zombies and Quinn and giant chickens and puppies and girlfriends and custody battles and escaped prisoners and strange men in black outfits.

"One thing at a time." I practiced a breathing technique that's supposed to calm the body. "One thing at a time."

Reunited. Thursday, July 6th. 1232hrs.

MAYA AND ALINA SAT side-by-side at a cement picnic table placed in the back of the treatment center. It was a tranquil location. A koi pond trickled with a peaceful water feature just to their right, and to their left, tall, broad trees protected them from the summer sun—a sun which heated the Sacramento region close to a hundred degrees that day.

Sweat glued Maya's shirt to her skin. An occasional breeze cut through the heat, but it offered little comfort.

Alina constantly shifted and fiddled with her hair or her clothes or her fingers, tapped her feet on the grass, popped her lips. Alina hadn't spoken to her mom in almost three full months.

Maya wondered what emotions streaked through Alina's mind? Relief that Wanda was safe and getting better? Anger that Wanda had left her? Fear? Joy? Had they all combined into maddening confusion?

"When will she be here?" Alina asked, staring over her shoulder at the walkway leading outward from the facility.

"Soon," Maya said. "I think they're bringing us lunch, too. We're probably waiting for that."

"Am I allowed to hug her?"

"It's not prison."

"How does she look?"

Wanda had refused visitors. Maya guessed her sister felt embarrassed to be in there, that she wanted to finish the program to provide evidence that she had changed. Often, Maya knew, people thought others saw them as they saw themselves... but that proved far from the truth more often than not. A mirror is the ugliest version of one's self. Who had said that? Maya couldn't remember, but she understood how it could be true.

From behind Alina, an orderly carried a tray with three plates. Walking beside her, carrying a few cups and a plastic pitcher of water, was Wanda. Maya hadn't seen her sister in months, maybe over a year.

"How does she look?" Alina asked again.

"Beautiful. Like a warrior queen. Strong and regal and... and imposing. Like if she wished, she could take over the entire world." Maya spoke honestly, too. Her older sister, from fifteen yards away, walked on air.

She had never seen Wanda with so much confidence. The woman usually carried herself with her head down, shoulders slumped, feet dragging, waiting for the earth to reach out and trip her. That's how she used to look, like she expected to get tripped and fall flat on her face.

"She looks like she can fly."

Alina must have realized Maya described what she noticed in real time. The kid glanced over her shoulder and blundered out of her seat, nearly falling onto the grass. She caught her balance, and without a second of hesitation, Alina charged toward her mother. She slammed into her and hugged her.

Maya moved a lot more carefully than Alina had, standing and ambling toward her older sister. She stopped a few feet away and watched as mother and daughter reunited after months of separation.

"I'm so sorry." Wanda muttered it like a mantra. "I'm so sorry. I'm so sorry."

After a minute, Alina pulled away and wiped her wet face with the blade of her hand. She stood about three inches taller than Wanda, inheriting her father's height. "When Maya told me... I wanted to hate you. I wanted to yell at you and tell you all kinds of terrible things." Alina's face scrunched, and she ran her hand across her nose. "I'm so happy you're here, though. And I'm so happy you're okay. I'm so happy, Mom." Alina dove back into her mother.

The orderly placed the dishes on the picnic table and regarded Maya. "It's protocol that I remain with any patient when they're outside. I'll allow you some space, though."

"Thank you," Maya said.

The orderly—a squat woman in her late fifties with short hair—stepped away and headed toward the far end of the koi pond.

Alina and Wanda broke their embrace.

Wanda set the cups and the pitcher on the table, and then she hugged Maya. Once all the tears and bubbling laughter had run their course, they all sat at the table and picked at their food, discussing the facility.

Was the food okay? Was the staff nice? Did they have suitable entertainment? Good books or movies?

It felt like dipping her toes in the water before diving into the cold depths—exploring Wanda's three-month long absence and discussing Stephen's sudden arrival. If August were with them, he would have grown bored with idle conversation, and he would have switched topics. Unfortunately, Maya never minded hearing her own voice speak about absolutely nothing for far too long, and Alina enjoyed talking even more. Wanda received an earful about Maya's new career, about Alina's internship, about how the two jobs often intersected and the aunt and niece worked in tandem.

"Did you tell her about Myles?" Maya winked at Alina.

"Who's Myles?" Wanda asked.

"No one."

"No one?" Maya asked, pressing her hand to her chest and gasping. "The boy you brought to a wedding is no one?"

"You brought a boy to a wedding?" Wanda asked. "Who is he?"

"He's no one," Alina said.

"Everyone is someone," Wanda said.

"A kid from my summer school class."

"You're in summer school?"

"I was in summer school. I passed."

"Why didn't you pass during the school year?"

"Oh, like you're one to talk about passing high school classes?" Alina asked.

Wanda hadn't graduated high school, though she had earned her GED during one of her stints in jail.

After Alina asked, she exhaled, deflated, probably disappointed in herself. "I'm sorry," she said. "This isn't easy for me, and the longer this goes on, the... the more the shine wears off, you know?" Alina tapped her fork against the table. "Why did you do it? Why did you leave me? Dad already left, and you knew if you left, you left me alone. Why?"

Wanda never skipped a beat, which shocked Maya. No time to think of a lie or an excuse. She shared an honest to God answer with her daughter. "I was weak. Scared. Selfish mostly. Your father left, and I lost everything."

"You didn't lose me," Alina said.

"No, I didn't, but I didn't know that. My entire identity, since before you were even born, revolved around your father. When he left, actually left, it stole everything from me, including who I thought I was. I'm so sorry, Alina. For everything we've ever put you through. For everything I've ever put you through."

"Here's the deal," Maya said, interjecting. Before Alina allowed her emotions to shine, Maya had to present the scenario. "Wanda, how much longer do you have until you finish this program?"

"Tomorrow."

"Really?"

"Yes."

"Okay, well, Stephen mentioned he's sober, has a job, and a place to live. It's a long shot with him living out of state, but if you're not well and able to care for Alina, it's possible he can take her with him. We need proof of your sobriety. We need evidence that you're applying for jobs, or that you have one. You need a stable place to live to support Alina. Finishing this program will look awesome to a judge, especially if you had good behavior and the supervisors can testify on your behalf."

"They can," Wanda said.

"Great," Maya said. "That's great." She looked at Alina. "That means you have to step up, girl. This is your decision to make, and I'm sure the judge will reiterate that. You're old enough to choose, as long as your mom meets the criteria which will allow you to choose."

"Do you have a job?" Alina asked.

"There's a waitressing opportunity I'm going to take,." Wanda pushed the remaining food around her plate. "It starts Saturday morning."

"A place to live?"

Wanda shook her head.

"Yes," Maya said. "She does. I'm going to offer my house. It's a three-bedroom home. I'll move my office into my room and give the vacated space to Wanda. Alina, we've already lived together for a couple of months, and with your mom there, I think the judge will like that."

"You don't have to do that," Wanda said.

"I want to," Maya said. "Besides, it's the best way to keep Alina with us... if that's what she wants." Maya looked at her niece. "Which brings us back to the question, what do you want?"

Lil Adler. Thursday, July 6th. 1602hrs.

MAYA AND I MET up at the office at 1545hrs, and we drove to Armondo Lopez's house. He lived north of Sacramento, nearly fifteen minutes away from the downtown area.

Maya had long ago connected her phone to my Honda's Bluetooth, and she controlled the music from her playlist—a middle school collection of hip-hop songs. She rapped every word from every song. I recognized most of them, could probably duet a few of the verses, but I remained focused on our task, thoughtful and quiet during the drive.

After parking along the curb before Mr. Lopez's driveway, I turned off the car, killing the music.

Maya, unwarned, continued to rap the second verse to Stand Up, by Ludacris. She let the words possess her, like a preacher enraptured with the Holy Spirit, as she shouted the lyrics at me.

"The more drinks in your system, the harder the fight!" Maya dropped an imaginary microphone and mean-mugged me.

"You missed your calling," I said after the car fell into a heavy silence.

"I was this close to making a career of rapping." Maya held her thumb and index finger so close together, the skin nearly touched. "But you know how I am. I suck with titles, and I couldn't come up with a marketable name. Lil Adler didn't quite have crowd appeal."

Fred would have jumped on this pointless conversational train. He and Maya would have bantered hypothetical rap names until they couldn't breathe. I lacked the creativity for such a feat.

"Do you think Alina will be okay?" I asked, focusing my energy on where I thought it mattered.

Maya simultaneously nodded and shook her head, moving it in a circular pattern.

"Is that a yes or no?"

"She's tough." Maya bit at the fingernail on her index finger. "She did okay when her parents abandoned her, so I imagine she'll fare better now that they've returned."

"You think so?"

Maya shrugged. "It's just confusing, you know?"

I twisted my wrists and nodded.

"She had settled into her new life. She was happy, or at least... content. She had a routine. Now both her parents have returned. They've disrupted her regularly scheduled programming. You know what I mean?"

"I think so."

"As a kid—a younger kid than she is now—Alina bounced around from grandparent to grandparent to aunt to uncle to foster home to her dad to her mom. As Johnny Cash once said, she's been everywhere, man. She had finally rooted herself and found her place in this world, and now her parents want to uproot her." Maya pulled the nail with her teeth and blew sharp air through her lips, forcing the remnant onto the floor of my car. "What did you ask again?"

"Is Alina okay?"

"Oh, yeah. She's confused, but she'll get through it. That girl is tough as an overcooked steak. Don't you eat your steak well-done, like a psychotic toddler? It's like chewing rubber. How do you eat that? People actually make reservations at a nice, fancy steakhouse. They circle a date on the calendar, dress up, and save some money for an expensive meal. All of that to order their steak well-done. What's the point? Go to Applebees. Get a steak from Chili's."

"I order my steak medium-rare."

"Really?" Maya narrowed her eyes. "You don't seem like that guy."

"Are you okay?"

"Me?" She pointed at herself.

"You."

"Dandy."

"You're sure?"

"Why wouldn't I be okay?"

"I'm just wondering."

"Are you okay?" Maya asked.

"I don't know."

While finishing our stint at Stuckey's bar, Wilson had asked me the same question. I guess my natural charm and cheery demeanor seemed more dreary than usual. Wilson and I had sat at the bar. I drank water; he drank a beer.

"You okay?" Wilson asked in that same, concerned tone Maya asked.

This happened minutes after my call with Glacia had ended, after I mentally went through the checklist of dilemmas and uncertainties presented in my life, after seeing the tall, blond man for the second time in only a few hours. So much danger loomed on my horizon, like a dark storm rolling in after a bright, warm day.

"August, you okay?" Wilson repeated.

I sipped the iced water. It tasted like chlorine. "A lot on my mind."

I glanced at Maya, debating which of my problems I should share with her, and how much of the burden I should carry alone. "A lot on my mind," I said, providing her with the same utterance I had provided Wilson.

Maya carried a beat across her knees for a couple of seconds. "I am capable of plenty, you know? I verge on synonymous with a superhero, but unfortunately, I don't actually have powers, and I definitely can't read minds. So, do you care to expand?"

I clicked my tongue and sighed. She would press me until the juice squeezed from my pores. Why not save the pain from the process? "I've never really worried much before. My mom always did that, and I think her practice forced me not to worry. I hated how she went about life, always so afraid of everything." I cracked a knuckle and looked out the driver's window. "I'm worried now."

"About what?"

"That I'll never capture the vampire. That I won't be able to save Jackson. I'm worried..." I trailed off, contemplating and ultimately deciding to share the full weight of my concerns with Maya. That's why she had asked. She genuinely cared, and she wanted to help me. Not only that, I had an obligation to tell her that Eddie escaped from jail. "I'm worried Daniel Quinn has something big up his sleeve."

"What do you mean?"

I rotated and faced Maya. Behind her, light poured through the passenger window, enveloping her. She looked radiant with her hair in a mess, wearing tattered, old clothes, not having bothered with any makeup that morning.

"Every person I put in prison through this paranormal investigative business, they've recently escaped."

Maya cocked her head to the side. "Come again?"

"Trisha Berry, the Doppelgänger. Vanessa Snow, the Changeling. Randal Fincher went missing. I haven't heard from Santa Cruz, but I would bet David Shaye has also disappeared."

"What about Eddie?" Maya asked, her tone icy.

I shook my head. "Gone."

"How long have you known this?"

"Only this morning."

"Why didn't you tell me sooner?"

I opened my mouth to provide a lame excuse, but Maya cut me off.

"August, Alina is alone at my house right now. What if Eddie goes straight there? What if she's in danger?" Maya fumbled with her phone, securely gripped it, tapped the screen a few times, and placed it to her ear.

"Maya," I said. "The thing with Stephen happened, and after that I rushed to my meeting with the manager at the strip club—"

She glared fiercely at me. "Oh, don't even bring up the strip club right now. You know I love strip clubs, and I didn't even get an invitation."

"It all slipped my mind until I had a second to breathe."

"Alina," Maya said, her body melting into the seat with relief. "Are you okay? Listen to me. Lock all the doors. Stop asking questions and listen for once in your life. I have a gun. Yes. Yes, of course. Why wouldn't I have a gun? It's in the safe in my closet."

"Maya, you can't give her a gun," I said.

"The code is 012921. It's a Glock. The rounds are in a box on the top shelf. Do you know how to load the gun? You do? How do you know? Mice? What? He's never regaining custody of you... though that sounds like a lot of fun. Anyway, load it. Lock all the doors. I'll explain—well, August will explain everything later. Alright. Peace out."

"Peace out?" I asked. "You just told her to load a gun, and you say peace out?"

"She's safe, not thanks to you, so get over yourself." Maya placed her hand on the door handle. "We doing this? I have an incredibly sexy date tonight. It's with Evan, in case you were wondering. He's my incredibly sexy date. Oh, speaking of sexy dates, how did it go with that chick from the wedding? You two ever, you know?" Maya pounded her fists together.

"That's my cue." I opened the driver's door and circled the car, heading toward Armando's house.

Maya hopped out of the passenger seat. "She wasn't that into you, huh?"

"It's not that."

"Was it your brooding personality that turned her off? Or was it your incredibly muscular physique? Not all girls enjoy that look. It can make men look like they're insecure about the way they look, and women prefer confidence over muscles, believe it or not."

"I believe it."

"On the flip side of that coin, some women are insecure about the way they look, and they don't want their man busting their butts at the gym, making them feel even more insecure."

"That makes sense, too."

"I can't say I relate, because, well..." Maya swept her hands down her body, presenting herself. "I'm perfect the way I am. Some girls find over-muscular men a major turnoff. Maybe your sexy wedding date—"

"Lauren," I said.

"Sure, maybe she didn't like how jacked you are. For me, it depends on the motivation. I know you workout because you're neurotic, right? It's a compulsive behavior for you, some untreated mental disorder. I don't mind that. Besides, I like a little crazy."

"Exercise helps me sleep. That's not crazy."

"You can't sleep because you're..." Maya circled a finger around her ear. "Cuckoo. Anyway, we're all cuckoo, so your reasoning for having such a chiseled, god-like body doesn't bother me. However, if you did it for vanity, that's annoying. I would rather date a giant, steaming pile of crap that smelled like death than a prissy, unconfident, egocentric, doucher."

"Is doucher a word?"

"I'm pretty sure it is. It's, like, someone who douches. Anyway, she didn't like you, huh?"

"I guess I was too buff." I raised a fist and knocked on Armando's front door.

Footsteps approached from inside the house. The deadbolt twisted, and the front door cracked open. A single eye and a shadowed face peered through the splinter. "Can I help you?"

"Mr. Lopez," I said. "My name is August Watson, and I'm with Blue Moon Investigative Agency. You spoke with my colleague, Alina Moore, yesterday afternoon. She confirmed we could speak with you today about your wife, Clara."

The front door opened the rest of the way. A short, stocky man with cuts and bruises along his arms stood before us. "Come inside."

Armando Lopez. Thursday, July 6th. 1611hrs.

THE THREE OF US sat around his kitchen table—a mess of opened and unopened mail, two plates, four cups of various sizes, and a closed laptop littered the surface. Beyond the disorganized table, the rest of the house appeared pristine.

"I'm sorry for the mess," Armando said, collecting the dishes. "I forgot about you swinging by. I was just going through the mail. The bills never seem to stop coming." He chuckled, a nervous sound, as he turned into the kitchen. Plates and cups clattered into the sink. Armando returned a moment later. "Sorry, also, if I smell bad. I just came home from work thirty minutes ago. Construction, and it's hot outside. I sweat all day in the dirt."

"I like the smell of a dirty man," Maya said. "No need to apologize to me."

I mentally shook my head, wondering why I had allowed Maya to tag along?

Armando sat and placed his hands on the table. "How can I help you?"

"You're married to Clara Lopez, correct?" I asked.

"Yes."

"You reported her missing, though?"

"About four years ago, shortly after Maria's... accident."

"You've had no contact with Clara since then?"

Armando pinched his wedding ring and spun it in circles around his finger. "None."

"What were the circumstances around her disappearance? Did she vanish? Was it something you expected? Did she say she was going to leave?"

Armando cleared his throat and excused himself from the table. He moseyed back into the kitchen and opened a cupboard. "Would you like water?"

"No, thank you," Maya and I both said.

Armando returned with his glass of water. He sat, placed the full glass on the table, and stared beyond me. I had surveyed the immediate area when I first walked into the nook. Over my shoulder, directly behind where I sat, a picture hung on the wall—Armando and two beautiful women, who I assume were Maria and Clara.

"A boy came by a month or two after Maria's death," Armando said, never removing his gaze from the picture. "Ashton Snell. It's hard to forget certain things surrounding such a tragedy."

The BB from Aaron Brooks' airsoft gun bouncing across the hot summer asphalt.

"It's also hard to remember anything at all from tragedy."

Apart from still images that played like a slideshow through my head, I struggled to recollect the hours leading up to Aaron's death, details from the incident, and the months after the killing.

"The mind is strange," Armando said. "Anyway, I can remember each of those boys in perfect detail, but I remember Ashton standing at our front door like looking at a picture hung in my head. He looked cried out and was on the verge of breaking down. His body trembled, and he murmured incoherently. I think he was praying. He's a devout Mormon, you know?"

"I heard," I said.

"Anyway, Ashton said he had to confess his dishonesty to clear his conscience."

"What did he say?" Maya asked.

"Originally, he told the police he drove the boat that day, because he was the only one sober. At my front door, though, the broken young man confessed he hadn't been behind the wheel at the time of the accident. Jackson, Maria's boyfriend, steered the vessel. Drunk, too."

"Did you report his confession to the police?" I asked.

Armando grimaced and shook his head. "I thought of it, of course. I wanted to. Clara convinced me otherwise. She said the boys had suffered enough with their guilt, and their families had suffered enough. Why seek revenge when we had already forgiven them?" Armando scratched the skin between his lips and nose. "It nearly broke our marriage, but I agreed. A month later, she disappeared."

"Do you know where to?" I asked.

"No."

"Do you know why she left?"

"No."

"Did she leave of her own free will?"

"I don't know."

"You reported her disappearance to the police, but you never shared what Ashton told you with anyone else?"

"I swore to my wife I wouldn't report those kids. I'm a man of my word, if I'm anything at all."

"Yet you told me," I said.

"You're not the police. You can't charge those kids with a crime." He shrugged. "Sure. You can pass on what I told you, but it won't matter. I'll deny it. I offered you that information since you're a private investigator searching for Clara. All information helps, right?"

"Right," I said.

"Do you have any leads?"

I nodded, biting my tongue. "Someone discovered the remains of Ashton Snell."

"What do you mean?" His gaze never wavered from the picture behind me.

"Forensics identified detached limbs and a collection of teeth as those belonging to Ashton Snell. Not only that, someone also happened upon the remains of Leon Lambert. The other kids, Connor Pellerin, Timothy Porter, and Jackson Armstead, are all currently missing."

Armando sucked on his teeth, and his face twitched, but he remained mostly unmoving. "You think Clara perpetrated whatever happened to them?"

"Do you think that's possible?" I asked.

"I never thought it possible for my baby to die the way she did."

"Clara had a career in cosmetic surgery, correct?"

"Yes."

I sighed. "Did you and Clara have a vacation home, or a cabin, or do you own any other property?"

"No."

"Do you know if Clara's family has unused property or vacation homes?"

"I don't think so."

"If she voluntarily disappeared, Mr. Lopez, do you have any idea where she might have gone to?"

Armando remained quiet, holding his breath. I watched him carefully, searching for signs of a lie—a flippant glance upward, fiddling with something, tapping his foot, shielding himself by placing his shoulder between him and me. He portrayed nothing obvious. He had also revealed secretive information, information I never would have learned of otherwise. I had no reason to doubt him, even during this moment of hesitancy.

"No," he finally said. "I can't think of anywhere she would have gone. At least anywhere she would have gone where I haven't already looked."

I rapped the table with my knuckles and nodded. "Well, I have no more questions. Maya?"

She shook her head. "Nope."

"Mr. Lopez, thank you so much for your time. If we learn anything about your wife, we'll call you immediately. If you learn anything or think of something," I snapped my business card on the kitchen table, "call us."

"Of course." Armando stood and walked us to his front door.

When Maya and I sat alone in my car again, she turned to me with a half-smirk, half-frown.

"What?" I asked.

"I don't like him."

"Why?"

"He's too short. I don't trust short men."

I started the car and chuckled.

"The house was too clean," Maya said. "What man cleans his house like that?"

"Maya, do you have thoughts not prejudiced against height or gender? Men can keep clean homes. My dad does, because my mom is a slob. Short men can also tell the truth, which he did."

"Oh, I forget. You're a superhero, and you can read thoughts, can't you? No wonder why you always think I can read your thoughts, because you can read everyone else's thoughts, and you read his thoughts, and know for sure he told the truth, so help him God."

"I preferred it when you rapped."

"Say no more." Maya connected her phone and turned up the music.

The Next Two Weeks.

In short, over the next two weeks, nothing significant happened.

I exhausted every viable lead related to the Vampire of Sacramento. Wilson and I spoke with all five of the victims' families, friends, co-workers. We returned to every bar and club the victims were last seen, and we spoke to the staff on duty the nights of the murders. We watched and rewatched any available CCTV from the area of the last home invasion and murder. We combed through local butcher shops, asking the managers if they ever or currently employed a man fitting the description we had. We even contacted blood banks to see if they recognized the man.

Nothing. Nada. Zilch.

The investigation into Clara Lopez and Jackson Armstead was more of the same. We, Alina mostly, contacted the parents of each boy from the boating accident. We contacted their colleges, jobs, girlfriends, anyone who had a connection with them. When did they go missing?

Where were they last seen? Who were they last seen with? We asked their parents for phone records, and some complied, and we learned nothing.

Nada.

Zilch.

Alina's mom finished her treatment program. She moved into Maya's home, worked a part-time job at a diner, and attended support classes almost every evening.

Alina's dad didn't go away, either.

Wanda, according to Stephen, was a junkie and whore. Though she seemed alright at the moment, she had a history of failing her stints of sobriety.

He had little ground to stand on himself, other than the argument that after he left Wanda, Wanda abandoned Alina. I had a hard time believing a judge wouldn't side with Wanda and Maya keeping Alina.

Still, they all seemed a little unsettled without a definitive answer.

The escaped prisoners seemed to have vanished without a trace. So far, none of them had attempted to contact and threaten me. Not even Daniel Quinn called to explain himself. The authorities didn't know what happened, either—not a single lead.

To complicate matters concerning my past cases, I had failed to reach Vincent and Shannon Dupree since the night of their wedding.

Also, the Santa Cruz Police Department (Detective Todd Philipps had contacted me) informed me that David Shaye had slipped out of their custody. They hadn't yet tracked his whereabouts.

Sarah Herling had postponed Gerald's court date for another two weeks.

"That's a win. The extended time allows me to come up with a better argument."

What she really meant to say—I saw the truth behind her eyes—was that she needed me to find evidence proving Gerald's innocence.

Frankly, I had done little to no investigation into Gerald. The other problems posed a much greater concern to me.

Gerald and Bagley kept each other company throughout the days, though Bagley slept in my bed at night. I enjoyed (and needed) the puppy snuggles.

Lauren hadn't reached out to me, though Glacia had shared my contact with her. Honestly, I felt relieved about that. I had enough to juggle without having to include a girlfriend on the list.

That's how the intermittent two weeks passed—uneventful, uninspiring, and transitional.

Then July 19th came around, and my world, once again, changed.

The Assignment. Wednesday, July 19th. OO23hrs.

Jackson sat in the back of the car, blindfolded and restrained. Since his initial abduction, Clara had retrieved and laid him on the steel surgical table two times. Once to insert the rice-sized chip into the back of his neck, and once to perform a cosmetic surgery to soften his square, angular chin.

After the second procedure, Clara assigned Jackson to bedrest for two weeks. Ashton had remained in the stonework prison cell the entire time. They chatted when Jackson had the strength and the energy to do so. Ashton admitted he confessed everything to Clara. She accepted the truth and decided not to press charges.

"I thought little of it," Ashton said. He spoke in his voice, though from a face that mirrored Maria's to the last detail. "She thanked me for my honesty and sent me on my way. Senior year came and went. We headed off to college." Ashton swept his dark brown hair from his face. "The summer after my freshmen year, Timothy grabbed me. Same as I grabbed you. He looked identical to Maria." Ashton broke down and cried, sobbing beside Jackson as Jackson's chin ached from the surgery and his head pounded.

"It's okay," Jackson said.

"She made me do it. I didn't want to. But she made me. She made me do it."

"Do what?" Jackson asked.

"Kill her."

Jackson's heart settled into his stomach, and his testicles shriveled into his groin, settling like hot pebbles. "Who?"

"'Kill her, so I can bring her back to life.' That's what Clara said." Snot slimed down Ashton's lips. He didn't bother to wipe it away as he continued to speak. "She threatened to go after my family if I didn't do it. 'I'll use them. I'll have them kill her.'"

"Who?" Jackson asked.

Ashton shook his head and rubbed his arms—the arms that resembled Maria's arms. "I don't know, but she looked like Maria." He stopped rubbing his arms and stared at Jackson with wide, horrified eyes. "These were her arms. I did it. I killed her."

Jackson didn't know how to respond as Ashton wept beside him on the bed. His best friend, who now looked exactly like his ex-girlfriend, had murdered a woman, and Clara had used that woman's arms to attach to Ashton's body.

"Clara had the woman strapped to a chair," Ashton said after a few minutes. "I didn't know what to do, or how to kill her." He sucked in air, nearly hyperventilating. "I didn't want to touch her. I couldn't kill her with my own hands. So, I kicked a leg off the chair. She fell sideways." Ashton stared at a spot on the floor in their cell. It was dark and stained with blood. No one had bothered to clean up the mess.

Ashton couldn't finish the story, but he hadn't needed to. Jackson pieced it together.

Ashton bludgeoned a defenseless young woman to death with the chair's leg. The story carried a terrible meaning, though. Clara forced the boys to murder the women used to transform them into her daughter.

Jackson would have to kill someone, and that someone would provide him with her arms or her legs or hair.

The car came to a stop. The driver's door opened, followed by the rear door. Hands grabbed Jackson's shoulders and dragged him out of the vehicle, ripped the blindfold from his face.

He stood in the darkness of late night, early morning. The witching hour. Jackson didn't know the exact time, but the world was dead quiet. He guessed after midnight.

They had parked in a residential neighborhood.

"Alright, Ashton."

Jackson turned to the voice that he would recognize anywhere. It was the same voice that amusingly threatened Jackson the first time he picked Maria up from her house. The same voice that shouted at the television when the 49ers or the Golden State Warriors played poorly. The same voice that had said, *have her home by ten, Jack. We have church in the morning, and it's our turn to show up early to greet.*

Of course, Jackson didn't get her home by ten. He didn't get her home at all that night.

"You will sneak into the house." Mr. Lopez pointed at a house behind Jackson. "Steal the batteries from their television's remote control."

"What?" Jackson asked.

"Do you not understand the assignment?"

"Why would we do that?"

"Because I said so."

"What does it accomplish?"

"You're not in a position to ask me questions," Mr. Lopez said. "Now, break into the house and steal batteries from the remote control."

"No," Jackson said.

"Hey, Jack." Ashton grabbed his arm. "Let's just do it."

"Listen to your friend, Jack."

"No," Jackson said again. "I'm not doing anything until you tell me the point of stealing the batteries?"

Mr. Lopez reached into this back pocket and removed a small control—something that resembled a television remote, but with fewer buttons. In the dim glow cast by the street lamps and the exterior lights of the houses, Jackson counted four buttons on the control.

What had Clara said about the rice-sized implant? *A simple, uncomfortable shock, a more painful jolt, a debilitating current, and a pulse that causes a tiny detonation.* Four different settings. Four buttons on the control.

Mr. Lopez's thick thumb covered the first button. "You'll do it because I said to do it."

"Why?" Jackson asked, struggling not to show fear or hesitancy, despite the man holding a trigger that could explode his head.

"Because I said so, that's why. If you say another word, I'll shut you up. We clear?"

Jackson, rebellious by nature, almost said, No, just to see if Mr. Lopez would shock him. Instead, he bit down on his flippant tongue, drawing a rush of blood, and he didn't say a word.

"Good dog," Mr. Lopez said after a second. "Now, break into the house and steal the remote control batteries."

Again, Jackson almost opposed the command, begging for Mr. Lopez to prove the electrical charge actually worked. What if it was a bluff?

Could something like that, like a shock collar inserted into his body, exist?

Instead, Jackson followed Ashton up the driveway to the designated house.

It was dark. No exterior lights illuminated the walkways. They passed by an overhang that covered an old fishing boat. Jackson paused and stared at the rusted machine. It looked like it hadn't seen water in over a decade. He hadn't been on a boat since his junior year of high school. Four years. Standing within five feet of one, his chest hurt, tightening, and his stomach flipped.

Ashton grabbed Jackson's arm again. "Let's keep moving."

"How many times have you done something like this?" Jackson kept his voice low. They padded around the side yard and stopped at the gate.

"About once or twice a month," Ashton said. "It's usually something random. Last time, about two weeks ago—right after they brought you in, actually—Armando told me to break into a convenience store and ransack the place. That was it."

"You did it?"

"We don't really have a choice. I belong to them now. So do you. The sooner you understand that, the easier this will be."

"We don't belong to them."

Ashton nodded. "We do. If we refuse—"

"Have they ever shocked you?"

"I never gave them reason to. But that's not the point. They'll go after my family. I can't allow them to hurt my family."

"If they haven't shocked you, they could be bluffing. If they're bluffing about the shock, they're probably bluffing about going after our families. That's too much potential risk for them. Why would they risk everything?"

"Because they have nothing to lose. We took everything from them. Besides, even if they are bluffing about the shock, I don't think they're bluffing about our families. I'm sure they wouldn't hesitate to hurt our families if we allowed them the chance."

"So, what? You're their slave now?" Jackson asked.

"We have to get into the house."

"How?"

Despite having legs that didn't belong to him, Ashton climbed the gate and dropped to the other side. He unlatched the gate and opened it. Jackson hesitated a second, but he stepped into the backyard.

"What about dogs?" Jackson asked.

"They scout before sending us on assignment. If there was a dog, they would've picked another house. No reason to put us in unnecessary harm."

"This is ridiculous."

"What is? Clara turning us into her dead daughter, or us committing random acts of crime as an obedience exercise?"

"All of it."

After scouring the backyard and not happening on a spare key, Jackson picked up a rock to throw through a window. It weighed about as much as a small cardboard box, and it was hollow. Something rattled inside it. After a second of fiddling with the stone, Jackson popped it open and found the spare key.

They went through the front door, as the key didn't open the side or back doors. Once inside the house, Ashton shambled forward—always moving in that strange, unnatural gait. He ventured through the dark house until he found the living room. The remote control rested on an end table beside the couch, beneath the shade of a lamp.

Jackson slid off the back of the control and popped out the double-A batteries.

Ashton headed back toward the front door. Jackson didn't move.

"What are you doing? We have to go?" Ashton hissed, keeping his voice low.

"What if I wake up the home owner right now and tell them everything? What if I screamed as loud as I could?"

"You can't."

"Why not?"

"Mr. Lopez will kill you."

"Good. I don't want to live like..." he meant to say, *you*, like Ashton, like a living corpse in the image of their dead daughter. "Like a slave to them. I would rather die."

"They'll kill your family."

"Not if I tell the homeowner everything." Jackson stood beside the end table where he had found the remote control. "I can wake him up, have him call the police. They'll arrest Clara and Armando. We'll be free. You understand that? Free."

Ashton's eyes widened, and he sucked on his lip. "Free?"

"Yes. Free."

"It's too dangerous." Ashton stepped toward Jackson, away from the front door. "What if the homeowner doesn't believe us? What if they think we're robbing them?"

Jackson's head swam with excitement. He could taste their victory. All he had to do was convince Ashton. "Why would they think we were robbing them if we're waking them up on purpose?"

Ashton stepped within two feet of Jackson. "You're sure we can get away with it?"

"Yes," Jackson said. "We can get away with it. We can get away from this, from them." He pointed at the front door, which symbolized their captivity, and Clara and Armando. "We can win."

Jackson never expected the blow. Ashton's excitement and cooperation blinded him. He only saw freedom. He missed Ashton grab the lamp off the end table.

The bulky metal smacked heavily against Jackson's skull with a pulpy crunch.

Jackson backpedaled a step and wavered. Blood leaked from his ear and down his neck. The room spun around him.

Ashton darted forward, drawing a syringe from his pocket. He jabbed the needle into Jackson's neck, and he whispered as Jackson slumped and flirted with unconsciousness, "I can't ever leave them. I'm too far gone now."

Open Invitation. Wednesday, July 19th. 0214hrs.

A HUMAN HAD ABOUT one-and-half gallons of blood inside of their body. The vampire did his best to drain every drop. The more he killed, the more efficient he became with the exsanguination. Still, the most he had ever extracted came from his latest victim, the husband. He had extracted under a gallon of blood from the man.

Every night, to keep his heart from shrinking and withering, the vampire consumed one cup of human blood.

He mixed a little animal plasma into his concoction, mostly to stretch out the duration of the gallon of blood before having to hunt again. The animal's blood diluted his medicine, though, making it less potent and beneficial.

To keep his heart active, to keep it from shrinking and quitting, the vampire couldn't continue to adulterate the human blood. He had to create a stockpile. A reserve.

He needed more than only one victim.

The vampire had lost count of the houses he had tried to enter when he came across a garage door opened a foot off the cement. He regarded the narrow slit like staring at an invitation to attend a party.

Chase was an inch under six feet, but he weighed well under a hundred-fifty pounds. Whip thin, his dad had always called him.

The concrete smelled like dust as he lay atop it, and it felt cold and scratchy against his clean-shaven face. The texture changed as he wriggled into the garage, sliding himself sideways and scraping his back against the bottom of the garage door. It went from rough to sticky, from smelling like dirt to smelling like spilled booze.

Chase stood in the glow of the LED lights strung throughout the garage. A table rested in the center of the space. Flies crawled on the wet surface, hopping across puddles and into toppled red plastic cups. Hopefully, the scene proved a messenger for the state of the inhabitants—drunk and weakened.

The vampire rather enjoyed this part of the hunt. The calm and isolation, the waiting before the kill.

The inky shadows of night moved through him, and he moved with the shadows across the expanse of the sticky garage to the door leading into the home. He grabbed the handle and twisted, and it turned. The latch clicked.

The door creaked and opened.

The vampire crept into the home. It stank of body odor, sex, and alcohol.

The entry led into the kitchen, which boasted of another party-induced disaster. Garbage bins overflowed with beer cans. An empty pizza box lay open on a table covered in wet playing cards.

The vampire stepped into the living room. Two video game controllers rested on the coffee table, as did three empty red cups, a cheap bottle of whiskey, three shot glasses, a can of chewing tobacco, a bowl of condoms, and a few joints in an ashtray.

Chase bypassed it all, moving as silently as a phantom into the dark hallway.

He opened the first door that presented itself, and he smiled with predatory anticipation and gluttonous glee. Three naked bodies tangled up in the sheets, deep asleep, temporarily lost to the living world.

He entered the room, closing and locking the door behind him.

Two women and a man in their early twenties sprawled out on the queen-sized mattress. The vampire stood at the foot of the bed, staring at his potential victims with rampant hunger. Saliva watered his mouth, and fought against the urge to allow the caged animal within him to escape—to revert to his primal, brutal tendencies when he preyed recklessly on the rodents of society.

The three specimens before him were strong, weakened only through self-poisoning. They were young and primed to provide three rich gallons of blood. Who to steal from first, though?

Chase couldn't kill the three of them and chance their blood going stale and bad. He could only operate on one victim at a time, and the process took over an hour to complete. The vampire couldn't risk the male waking while he worked.

The young man was twice the size of either woman and chiseled with hard muscle. That's who the vampire had to extract from first.

Carefully, he removed his tools—the rope, the razors, the bags. He bound the man's hands to the bedposts, his feet to the legs at the end of the bed. The procedure took over ten minutes as he moved with incredible precision, careful not to stir anyone in the room. No one so much as snored.

The vampire readied the razor and dug the blade deep into the man's carotid artery, quickly sealing a plastic bag around the open wound with tape. He turned the man on his side, allowing the blood to work downhill. Once the source ran dry, the vampire untied the victim's feet and lifted them, attaching them to the ceiling fan, forcing whatever blood remained to creep out of the wound. As a last resort, he slashed the razor across the man's femoral artery and attached a second bag to the gaping incision, collecting the remnants that had stubbornly remained.

He tied the two blood bags and hauled them to the refrigerator to keep them cool while he operated on the remaining two victims.

When the vampire returned to the room, he went to work on the first of the two women. They were both attractive, naked, and unconscious, but Chase never extracted blood to satisfy a sexual urge. It was purely for survival. He needed the blood to live.

As he worked the rope around the first woman, the other one stirred, rolled over, eyes opened wide.

The vampire reached for his razor.

She inhaled to scream, but he lashed out, slicing a deep gash through her neck. Blood poured over her naked torso like a painted-on shirt. Somehow, she stood, gurgling on her life's fuel, and staggered across the room to the door. Her hands grabbed the handle, twisted, but the vampire had locked the door. The woman slumped, falling hard to her knees, tilting sideways, and crashing lifelessly onto the floor where her precious blood spilled and soaked into the carpet.

Dark fury and evil hunger broke through its cage at the act of impulsive violence, at the stench of fresh blood filling the room. The beast locked within the vampire burst free and overcame the vampire's better sense, his rationality.

Whatever traces of humanity existed inside of Chase vanished as the monster reared its vicious, ugly face.

What's Dead Never Dies. Wednesday, July 19th. O912hrs.

I HAD NEVER VISITED Aaron Brooks' gravesite. The idea of standing over him as he rested six feet below made me feel like the one covered in dirt and worms.

Three months ago, with a lot of encouragement from my friends, I mustered the courage to knock on Raymond and Tammy Brooks' front door. I half-expected Aaron's parents to verbally or physically assault me, to call the cops and have me arrested for trespassing and harassing them.

Instead, they invited me into their home.

We broke bread together, and they shared stories of their son with me—the son I had taken from them. We laughed and cried. They held my hands and looked me square in the eyes and said with intention, *We forgive you.*

Those three words held so much power, and they removed an immense weight from my soul, a weight I thought was too heavy to remove. Those three words allowed me to forgive myself.

In doing so, I finally had the courage to visit Aaron Brooks' gravesite on the sixth anniversary of his death.

I had, of course, phoned the Brooks' (they had prompted me to contact them whenever I needed to). I asked if I could visit their son. They not only said yes, but they encouraged me to visit.

"What should I bring?" I asked.

"He loved poetry," Tammy said.

"He wanted to rap as a way of making money," Raymond said. "His idols, or so he said, all drew inspiration from poetry. He read collection after collection, and he loved them."

I hiccuped a single, throaty laugh. People are so dynamic. I love when I'm reminded of that truth. Poetry. Who would have thought a nineteen-year-old kid hellbent on a life of crime loved to read poetry?

"Anything in particular?" I asked.

"Anything at all."

I settled into the grass where he rested and placed the collection of poems atop the simple lawn-level slab of stone bearing his name and his lifespan and a short epitaph.

AARON WALTER BROOKS.

JANUARY 3, 1998 - JULY 19, 2017.

BECAUSE I COULD NOT STOP FOR DEATH,

HE KINDLY STOPPED FOR ME;

THE CARRIAGE HELD BUT JUST OURSELVES,

AND IMMORTALITY.

A vase of vibrant flowers rested on the corner of the headstone, and a framed photograph stood on the other corner—an image of Aaron with his parents, standing between them, smiling against the sun so their eyes squinted and their faces scrunched. A shadow stretched toward Aaron and touched his feet. It most likely belonged to the photographer, who stood directly in front of the setting sun, but I saw that shadow as me.

I was the darkness that had touched the Brooks family, that had stolen their light and their smiles.

I closed my eyes and placed myself back on the blacktop that hot summer day six years ago.

I had arrived at the park, hellbent on avenging a fallen officer from the night before, afraid I might be the next headline on the news. My blood pulsed in my head. My fingers were numb and sweaty, and they gripped the butt of my gun before I even knew the full extent of the threat. My body vibrated, as if operating on a different frequency than normal.

Aaron looked like any other nineteen-year-old kid—full of bravado and angst. He wore ill-fitting clothes that were too baggy, like those worn by kids who wished to hide something. He bore garage-issued tattoos. He held a gun, and he raised it, pointed it at me as I approached.

I don't remember the report of my sidearm firing. Above that, above all the other noises, I heard, like a percussive instrument, the BB from his airsoft gun bouncing, tip-tapping, across the asphalt.

I don't know how he fell, but I remember his form lying in a spreading pool of blood on the gray asphalt.

That image fixed in my mind like a tableau.

For three years, I passed through life in a drunken haze, only able to remember the puddle of blood and the bouncing BB. Only the blood and the BB and the stench of over-irrigated land in the dead of summer.

I exhaled and opened my eyes.

Six years later, the weather hadn't changed. It was a scorching morning. Six years prior, it was a scorching afternoon. Sweat gripped my clothing. My blood pounded in my head, and my hands were sweaty and mostly numb.

I swallowed, picked a piece a gum from my pocket, and popped it into my mouth. I cracked a knuckle. Another.

My phone buzzed in my pocket, but I ignored it. Nothing else mattered.

My entire purpose and motivation for creating PARANORMALIZE (my business name before Blue Moon absorbed me) was to find proof of the supernatural. If I found conclusive evidence that the supernatural world existed, maybe I could discover a manner in which to reach out to Aaron and apologize.

Cambria, who also rested in this same cemetery, showed me the path to speaking to him. *You're in the supernatural business to find proof of the afterlife so you can apologize to Aaron. Well, do what you can control. Apologize to his parents.*

I had apologized to Raymond and Tammy, and they had forgiven me, and that knowledge was supernatural. But I had one more step in my recovery.

Whether Aaron heard me or whether I spoke to a headstone didn't matter. It was a ritual at this point. I had never needed to apologize to Aaron, as Cambria knew. To heal, I had needed to apologize to those who kept Aaron's memory alive.

I ran my fingers over the carving of his name.

AARON WALTER BROOKS.

"I..." I trailed off. I hadn't rehearsed what to say, but hoped the moment would strike inspiration. My thoughts seemed buried in the depths of a dark, stormy sea, though. "I promise, on all that I am and all that I love, I'll take care of your mom and dad. No matter what. I don't know what that means to you, but I will. I'll take care of them. Hopefully, you can rest a little more peacefully knowing that."

I paused for a deep breath, trying to say sorry, but the words couldn't quite roll off my tongue. They felt cheap, worthless.

My dad, a man of few words, always preached that apologies and promises are nothing more than spent air. Actions prove an apology. Actions keep a promise. Actions took time and thought, and we had nothing in this life but our time and our original thoughts.

If you take action, you give everything.

I spoke from my heart. "I used to work at this used bookstore. Maya got me fired. She thought she quit for me, but she really just got me fired. It's okay, though. I don't really have time to work there anymore. I'll still go inside every couple of weeks to purchase books to support Tom. He's a good man, despite not really liking me anymore." I chuckled and wiped my running nose. "Anyway, I swung by there last night after chatting with your mom and dad—great people, by the way. They said you loved poetry. So, I bought you a book of poems. I'm going to, over time, go cover to cover and read through every poem with you. When it's finished, I'll get you a new collection. How's a poem club sound?"

I laughed—a genuine, life-providing laugh. I'm not sure why. Nothing seemed quite funny at the moment.

I'm not a believer in the supernatural. My profession had yet to lend definitive proof the paranormal existed. However, in that moment and to this day, I believe with my entire core, Aaron laughed through me. His spirit infused me with his amusement at my promise and attempt at an apology.

I wiped a tear away and opened the book of poems. I read to him for an hour, taking my time with each poem, rereading them, thinking about them, discussing them with Aaron. We read them as poems should be read—the same as excellent wine should be consumed. Slowly, with purpose and awareness.

After an hour, only making it through three poems, I closed the book.

"See you in a month."

I stood and ambled through the cemetery, not to my car, but to Cambria Leigh Parker's gravesite. Since the burial, I hadn't returned to visit her.

When I reached her marker, I squatted before it.

My sinuses hadn't stopped running after my allergy attack at Aaron's gravesite. I wiped my nose and rubbed my eyes. A headache throbbed between my temples. I felt like I could lie down beside Cambria's stone and fall asleep beside her. Was that a grim thought? I didn't know. It felt comforting to know I could just lay down beside her. Upon reflection, away from my emotions and the scene, it felt strange to think I wanted nothing more than to lie beside a corpse. The mind is a funny, funny creature.

I didn't have a collection of poems to read to her, or anything like that.

"I'm not visiting long today, but I wanted to say hi while I was here, and make you a promise. I'm going to come back, and I'm going to give you Daniel Quinn's head." I didn't literally mean I would decapitate the man, but I meant it figuratively. I would find and stop Daniel Quinn, and I would lay that knowledge at Cambria's gravesite. "He will pay for what he did. If it kills me, he will pay." I kissed my fingers and touched the stone bearing her name. "Until then."

My phone buzzed once more in my pocket. I turned away from Cambria and headed toward my car, grabbing my cellphone and answering the unknown number.

"August Watson."

Shivers sprinted down my spine. I stopped moving as if the cement pathway had swallowed me up to my waist. I hadn't spoken to Quinn since the day Cambria died, and now, as I visited her, he called me.

I glanced over my shoulder, scanning the cemetery. A few people visited their loved ones, laying flowers, drinking a beer, reading a book. A couple of little kids wearing T-shirts that said, *Daddy's My Hero*, ran around the green lawn beside a grave marker adorned in American flags.

Any of those people, apart from the toddlers, could have been Quinn in some sick, twisted disguise.

"What do you want?" I asked.

"To meet you. To speak with you face-to-face."

"When? Where?"

He tsked, clicking his tongue. "Not so fast, Mr. Watson. Not so fast. Though I very much desire to meet with you, you must earn a meeting with me."

"Earn?"

"There's a process involved. Solve your two pending cases—the vampire and the golem before the end of the month. If you have identified the vampire and have located Jackson Armstead before July 31st at midnight, I'll contact you, and we'll set up a meeting." Quinn laughed. "Can I share some advice with you?"

I squeezed my phone so tight, I'm surprised it didn't crush like a can. I wanted to hang up on the man, but I refused. The last time I had allowed my pride and emotions to disconnect a call with Quinn, he had offered me information to find the dream demon. I hung up on him without hearing him out, and as a result, Cambria had died.

"I'll take your prolonged silence as confirmation." Quinn cleared his throat. "Aaron Brooks. Cambria Parker."

"Don't speak her name."

Quinn laughed again. "They're not dead. I mean, yes, they're physically dead. But their spirit, which is only memory, lives. It lives because we live. No one truly dies until everyone who knew their name also dies.

Aaron and Cambria live in you, in their family." Quinn chuckled. I hated the sound of his laugh—like steel grating across cement. "What's dead, August, never truly dies. Keep that tidbit safe in your mind and draw on it for comfort. You keep them alive, and they keep you alive."

"What did you do with the prisoners?" I asked.

The line died. Quinn ended the call.

Why Not? Wednesday, July 19th. 1107hrs.

I HAD LESS THAN twelve days to figure out the cases, at least if I wanted to earn a date with Daniel Quinn. I wanted to earn a date with Daniel Quinn.

I hurried to my car, climbed into the driver's seat, turned on the ignition, and cranked the air conditioner. From habit, I fished into my pocket, grabbed my cell phone, and motioned to drop it in the cupholder where it tagged along on most drives. The screen came to life, though, and I glanced at a notification.

A missed call from my mom.

She must have called while I visited with Aaron. She had left a voicemail, though. "Hi, Gussy. It's Mom."

(As if I didn't know.)

"I was just calling to invite you to family dinner this Friday night. No occasion. Just dinner. Jake has volunteered to grill burgers. Rachel will whip up some guacamole. I told her not to make it as spicy as usual, though. I know you like it spicier, but your dad had terrible heartburn last time. Anyway, bring what you want, or nothing at all. And I don't mean to sound insensitive, but..."

(Always a great way to introduce something—don't mean to, but...)

"I think you should put yourself out there again. I think it's good for you when you're trying to... you know?"

(I knew she couldn't bring herself to say, keep it together.)

"I feel so guilty because I introduced you to Cambria. I'm hesitant to... to match make again. But—"

I pulled the phone from my ear and checked the timer. She was only halfway through her voicemail, meaning she would continue to ramble and stumble over her words for another thirty seconds.

I ended the message and dialed her back.

"Gussy!"

"Hey, Mom."

"How are you?"

"I'm leaving the cemetery. I visited Aaron Brooks and Cambria."

Two months ago, I never would have dreamed about sharing that information with my mother. Since Cambria's death, as if to honor her memory, I had worked at building a healthy relationship with my family.

"Gussy." Her voice dropped an octave.

"It was good for me. It really was."

"I'm so happy for you. And proud."

"Thanks."

She sighed, a transitional noise. "Did you get my voicemail?"

"Most of it. I would like to make dinner, but I'm not sure if I can. Work is…" I trailed off, debating whether I should continue to practice honesty in the light of my investigations and Daniel Quinn. The thing about pure honesty, it's not conditional. I had to speak the easy and the hard truths. "Work has become messy and dangerous. I'm chasing a terrible person, and I have spent every minute I have looking for him."

"Stop it, stop it, stop it!" My mom shouted into the receiver. "I appreciate you sharing your life with us more and more, but I don't want to know everything. Sometimes ignorance is bliss. Lie to me. Tell me you're going on a date, or Fred is taking you golfing and you can't make it to dinner."

"Please, whatever you do, don't put golfing into Fred's head. He's obsessive about new things. You know how he gets. Do you remember the pact we all made? Don't introduce Fred to new hobbies."

My mom took a second too long to respond, and I could picture her face—wide-eyed and lips pulled inward, as if caught with her hand in the cookie jar.

"Mom."

"It was your father, brother, and brother-in-law. Not me."

"Mom."

"Your brother is always home, doing nothing but sitting around and playing video games. I told him he had to get out of the house. Jake went golfing one day, invited Adam and your dad and Fred. Now Fred is asking them to go to the range about every day. I think he's looking into a membership."

"When did this happen?" I asked.

"About two weeks ago."

It was only a matter of time before Fred came to me with a proposition to golf. "Don't tell him anything about anything, Mom. I can't have him knowing about you-know-what."

Again, she held her tongue a second too long.

"Did you already tell him?"

"Gussy, he and Daphne came over last weekend."

"What? Why would that warrant you telling him? Also, why wasn't I invited?"

"It was a triple date. If it makes you feel any better, we kicked Adam out of the house for the night."

"It doesn't. Why didn't he call me?"

"I don't know."

"Who did you triple date with?"

"Jake and Rachel. Dad and me. Fred and Daphne. We do it once a month, sometimes more if our schedules allow. It's charcuterie and games. You would hate it. Besides... well, you know."

"I don't have a date."

"I didn't say that, but Fred insists you would make the worst seventh wheel."

I cracked every knuckle on my left hand and stared out the window at the headstones rising from the ground like gray, jagged teeth.

"Glacia said she introduced you to someone."

"You and Glacia talk now?" I ran my fingers through my hair. "I didn't even know you knew each other."

"Alina told me about her."

"You and Alina talk now?" I asked.

"Occasionally. She doesn't—well, she didn't—have her mom around, and I don't trust Maya as a responsible woman. I would check on Alina to make sure she was attending summer school, doing her homework, and to see how her day was. She's attended church with us the past few Sundays."

Now I took a moment to remain silent for far too long. I didn't know what to say. My mom had a habit of poaching all my friends, hanging out with them, and not inviting me to their hangouts. Fred and Daphne for date night. Alina for church.

"Anyway," she said, "Fred and Alina told me so much about Glacia. I'm sorry it didn't work out between you two."

"It's fine," I said.

"Well, they also informed me of the mysterious woman at the wedding, of how pretty and funny she was."

"I still don't understand why you're contacting Glacia."

"Gussy, she gifted you the house you now live in. The house you still haven't invited us over to."

"She did," I said, still not sure why mom needed to speak with her.

"I asked if you made her pay for the job after she gave you a house. You charged her. Gussy, she gave you a house."

"The money was for the business. The house was for me. Two separate things. You and dad own a business. You know how it works."

"Still. You didn't have to charge, especially if you're getting a house. Anyway, that's none of my business."

Finally, she said something I agreed with.

"Glacia said she set you up with someone," my mom said. "Fred and Alina confirmed. What happened?"

"That's not your business, either."

"It's my future daughter-in-law and grandchildren on the line. It is my business."

"I met the woman once. Future daughter-in-law?"

"There's a possibility."

I reflexively thought of Maya. Whenever I considered the future with a woman—of weddings and babies and getting old—I thought of Maya.

"I don't think so," I said.

"Why not? What was wrong with this girl? She had funny toes?"

"What? No. What?"

"Don't what, no, what me. You provided that lame excuse in high school when you broke up with Callie. Do you remember her? Sweet. Christ-centered. Beautiful. You said she had funny toes."

I remembered her as not so much Christ-centered as centered on me. "Lauren didn't have funny toes."

"What was wrong with her, then?"

"Nothing."

"Why haven't you called her?"

"How do you know that?"

"Fred told me."

"How would he know?"

"Alina also told me."

"How would she know?"

My mom said nothing, but I could visualize her face—chin down, frowning, eyes wide. It was a look that begged the obvious truth. Alina knew everything about everything.

I sighed and twisted the steering wheel in my palms. "Work doesn't allow me to... to have much time for myself right now. Once I settle this investigation, maybe I'll call her."

"It might be too late by then."

"That's fine. I'm not sure I'm ready to date, anyway. When I was with Lauren that night, I felt... guilty all night. I don't want to jump into something with that kind of baggage looming over the relationship. I'm not ready to share those feelings with a stranger yet." I cracked a knuckle. "How did we get on this topic, anyway?"

"I don't remember," she said in a tone that signaled she remembered but didn't want to circle back.

"Fred and Alina told you about Lauren, because Alina goes to church with you now, and Fred and Daphne went to date night." I closed my eyes, visualizing the conversation. "You told me they came over because I said not to tell him, and you said, 'They came over for date night.'" My eyes bolted open. "You told him already!"

"Gussy, I thought he knew. You've known him since you were in diapers. I thought he knew."

As a child, my parents had a membership in a country club. I golfed often, and I received lessons from one of the best trainers in the area. I hate golfing, though. It felt like an old man's sport. So, I told none of my friends that I golfed. As I grew, I played team sports. Golf fell to the side, and I never took it back up.

"I told him you would be more than happy to play a round of golf."

I lowered my head against the steering wheel and wondered why he hadn't booked our tee time yet. Fred probably wanted to wait until we moved beyond the vampire and golem case, knowing I would decline his invitation. So, not only did I have a meeting with Quinn to look forward to if I solved the cases by the end of the month, but a round of golf.

"Also," my mom said.

"Not an also, Mom. I can't handle it."

"I may have acted impulsively. I'm sorry, but you know how I get, and I only want what's best for you."

"What is it?"

"A blind date."

I shook my forehead against the leather wheel. "No. I can't. Mom, I can't. You can't keep setting me up on blind dates."

"It was a group effort. Not just me."

"What does that mean?"

"Will you do it?"

"I can't."

"If you go, I'll tell Fred he can't ask you to golf. I'll tell him he has to wait for you to approach him. He'll listen to me. How does that sound?"

I sighed.

"A date only takes an hour or two," she said. "You can't always work. You'll need to eat, eventually. Why not do it with a pretty lady? Besides, you owe me."

"I don't owe you."

"You're ditching dinner this Friday night."

"You literally told me about it five minutes ago."

"Still, you owe me."

I leaned back in the driver's seat and chuckled. "Fine."

Maybe a change of scenery would jump-start my mind. My first date with Cambria had helped me notice a case in a new perspective, and it ultimately led to me breaking it wide open. Cambria would have wanted me to get out of my comfort zone, to challenge myself. It was all part of the healing and growing.

If someone ever reads this story, and they're looking for a lesson to take home with them, take this lesson and this one alone. Moms *always* know what's best for their children.

"Okay. Why not? When and where?"

The Vampire Hunter.
Wednesday, July 19th. 1121hrs.

I HUNG UP WITH my mom and rested my head on the steering wheel, staring down at the floorboard covered in debris and gum wrappers. For the thousandth time that morning, I reiterated my to-do list, mumbling the tasks beneath my breath.

"Catch a vampire.

"Catch a golem.

"Help Sarah and Gerald.

"Help Alina.

"Find the missing prisoners.

"Find Daniel Quinn.

"Go on another blind date."

I'm sure I had missed something. Alina mentioned organizing my schedule through my phone, and I had to look into that if I cared to keep track of all that I juggled.

As I ran through my list a second time, just to make sure I included everything, a sharp rap sounded on my window—a heavy knuckle berating the glass.

I startled, whipping up and back against the headrest, wheeling my head to the side, half-expecting to see Daniel Quinn and the dark, single eye of a gun. Instead, the tall, blond man who I had noticed a couple times throughout the day two weeks back leaned beside the car. His rockstar hair fell across his face in greasy tendrils.

I rolled the window down an inch and waited for him to speak.

"August? August Watson?" He spoke with a thick southern drawl.

"You are?"

"Vermont Wendsdale."

I pursed my lips and slowly shook my head. "Am I supposed to know your name?"

"If you were worth your salt, you should have come across my name."

"Well, forgive my ignorance."

"I've worked in tandem with Tempest Michaels. Together, we slew a vampire."

"Slew?" I asked, scratching my chin and wondering if he meant slayed. I wasn't sure. Add that to my list of things to solve.

"I hunt supernatural creatures, Mr. Watson. I hunt and kill them. I have traveled the world doing so for many years. I'm experienced, tenacious, and I know my enemy. I have a team who supports me, and I'm protected by the holiness of God." It all sounded rehearsed.

I raised my eyebrows, feigning that his spiel impressed me. I was more disturbed. He had traveled the world hunting monsters, and he had slew (slayed?) at least one vampire with Tempest Michaels. If monsters didn't exist, what—or who—had Wendsdale killed?

"Are you?" he asked.

"Am I what?"

"Protected by God."

"And the Holy Spirit," I said. "Jesus, too, for good measure."

"This isn't a joke, Mr. Watson. You have fixed yourself directly in my path."

"What path is that?"

"I'm hunting the Vampire of Sacramento."

"I see." I didn't know how much more I could handle of this guy.

"He's an aggressive creature, and from what I've observed, you don't have the ability or nerve to defeat him."

"I'm going out on a limb and guessing you have the ability and the nerve?"

Wendsdale swept his hair out of his face. "And the experience."

"That's what makes me nervous."

"I've slain over a hundred vampires on four separate continents."

"Slayed," I said, testing the alternate version aloud. I couldn't figure it out. More disturbing, though, I couldn't figure out if I needed to call Wilson and have him look into Wendsdale in connection to over a hundred murders on four continents.

"I've come to this God-forsaken city to kill the monster and save innocent lives, seeing that you're incapable of doing so."

For the sake of education, I decided on a whim to entertain Wendsdale. "What have you learned about the vampire?"

His eye twitched. "I'm not at liberty to share what I've collected."

So nothing, I thought. He had followed me around and approached me to glean what information I had gained. The Vampire of Sacramento not only eluded the police, but a bona fide monster hunter. A leeching, self-proclaimed hunter who further complicated my life. When did the rain cease for the sun to break through the cold, dark clouds?

My phone buzzed in the cupholder—a welcome savior to this encounter. I glanced at the screen, saw Alina's name, and raised a finger to Mr. Wendsdale. "I have to take this. Excuse me." I answered. "Hello."

"You busy?"

I glanced at the man dressed in black on a summer day topping a hundred degrees. "Not at the moment."

"I found something on the golem case."

"What?" I leaned forward in my seat.

"It's a video. I just sent it to your phone." As she said that, my phone vibrated against my cheek. "Watch it when you can. I'm not sure yet how it connects, but I know it does. I'll keep digging."

"I'll watch it now."

"Let me know what you think."

"I will."

"How did it go with Aaron?"

"Good," I said. "I read him poetry."

"That's... cool, I guess?"

"He thought so."

"Alright, well, watch the video."

The second she hung up the phone, another call came through. Ted Wilson. I turned to Wendsdale. "Sorry, buddy. I have another call. I guess I'm a pretty popular guy these days." I accepted the incoming line. "Detective Wilson."

"August, are you busy?"

"Not particularly."

"He attacked again."

I stiffened in my seat and stared out the windshield, careful not to look at the vampire hunter and clue him into what Wilson had shared.

"I've secured you clearance onto the scene," Wilson said.

"How?"

"Let's just say you owe me."

"Sure, yeah. Anything."

"I wanted you to walk through the crime scene. It might be more beneficial than reading a report. I'm pulling a lot of strings getting you here. Keep your lackeys at home. Do you understand? The VIP pass is for you alone."

I exhaled as we ended the call, and I turned to Wendsdale with a forced grin splashed across my face. "Duty calls."

He narrowed his eyes. "Have you learned something about the vampire? If so, you must tell me, otherwise you risk placing this entire community in danger."

"It was about my old pal Varney." I swelled with pride at the comment, feeling like Alina must feel most of the time. Even if the reference went over Wendsdale's head, it filled me with a sense of minor accomplishment.

I shared a two-finger salute and shifted my car into drive.

House of Horrors. Wednesday, July 19th. 1211hrs.

THE CONFLUX OF EMERGENCY vehicles and news station vans created a roadblock on the residential street. Yellow emergency lights strobed throughout the early afternoon. The first responders in the varying uniforms busied in and out of the home like ants from the colony. Some clustered in groups, smiles plastered across their faces, laughter bubbling into the air, as if they hadn't responded to a multiple homicide.

Stay-at-home parents gathered on the sidewalk across the street, and their children—home for the summer—stood beside them or lingered further back in their yards.

I parked a block away and strolled toward the house. I wasn't in a hurry to witness the crime. As I walked, my phone rang. Alina again.

"Hey," I said.

"Did you watch the video yet? I haven't heard from you."

"I... forgot," I said.

"How could you forget?"

"Wilson invited me to inspect the latest vampire homicide right after you sent that text, and it slipped my mind."

"The vampire killed again?"

"Yeah."

"Jesus. Okay, well, when you're finished, watch the video. It's of a golem—a different one from what we saw ransacking the convenience store—kidnapping a young woman who looks awfully like Maria Lopez."

That information froze me mid-stride. "Have you identified the woman?"

"Yeah. Gladas Vasquez. She went missing three years ago. Not long after, they found her body. She had no legs, and someone had shaved off her hair."

"Sacramento?"

"Reno."

I licked my teeth and contemplated the information. Thoughts of the vampire crowded my head, though. I had to complete one thing at a time, starting with the recent homicide.

"Keep scouring the internet for any other connections to this golem case." I massaged my temples. Fred worked on locating the missing people related to my past cases. I worked on the vampire investigation. We were doing all we could with what we had. "Alina."

"Yessir?"

"One more thing. We need to schedule a quarterly review of your job performance. The higher-ups believe you've earned yourself a raise."

Alina chuckled. "You're serious?"

"Stay focused on the golem right now. Later, we'll discuss a promotion and what that means regarding your schedule, especially considering school begins in a few weeks."

Placing Alina on the payroll was something I had considered for a while. I wouldn't have solved half my cases without her input. Also, Maya had informed me that if Alina ever wished to emancipate, she needed a source of income. With her home life in a constant state of flux, I wanted her to have all options available.

We ended our call as I neared the emergency scene. I stopped at the edge of the driveway on the cusp of the yellow tape, and I studied the property. A dirty old car with gray and nearly bald tires was on the far side of the driveway. Beside it was a glimmering car with the blackout treatment and tinted windows. The yard had a green but overgrown lawn filled with weeds. Watered but not maintained. The rose bushes beneath the front window had gone too long without trimming. Three steps led up to a front door. The garage was to the left, forward of the house. It was partially open, maybe about a foot or two.

"August." Wilson jogged across the street, punching through a crowd of reporters and a gaggle of police officers. "Thanks for coming."

"It's been a while since I've attended an actual crime scene."

"Yeah, well, this one doesn't hold back either. I've seen nothing like it. Doubt many people have."

I cracked my knuckles. "I know you want me to see everything with fresh eyes, but I have to know, Ted... are there children in that house?"

"No."

A massive weight lifted off my chest. I wasn't sure if I could walk into the home and see the fresh corpses of children. I would have, if it meant capturing the vampire and preventing him from another atrocity, but it would have destroyed a part of me.

"It's bad, though?"

"It's a house of horrors," Wilson said. "Come on." He lifted the yellow caution tape over our heads, led me around the cars, up the steps, and to the blue front door. "You see that kid over there?" Wilson pointed across the street where he had come from.

A young man about twenty-three spoke with a few other officers. He wore a casual outfit and a backward fitting hat. He rubbed his face, ran his hands through his hair, scratched the back of his neck, and looked up at the sky.

"Jared," Wilson said. "He lives here, but he stayed with his girlfriend. She corroborated his alibi, along with her two roommates. Anyway, the kid came back to change and get ready for work around ten this morning." Wilson cleared his throat. "He found the front door locked, and he thought that was strange."

"Why?"

"He said they usually lock the door at night, but they keep it unlocked throughout the day as they come and go. Only if everyone is out, or if they're all asleep, do they lock it, and not even all the time." Wilson pushed the door open.

"How did the vampire get into the house if they locked the front door? Did he have a key?" My body buzzed with a potential lead. Had the victims known the vampire?

"The door leading from the kitchen into the garage was unlocked."

"And the garage door was open a foot."

"Yeah," Wilson said. "It's hot in July. The young men cracked the garage door to prevent it from turning into an oven. It must have slipped their minds to shut it before bed."

"No forced entry with the fifth victim, either," I said, recalling the vampire's last homicide.

Wilson shook his head. "The creep crawled through an open window."

"Vampires can't pass through a threshold unless they have an invitation."

"Sure."

"I wonder if this guy actually believes he's a vampire. Maybe he interprets an open window or door as an invitation. Maybe that's how he's deciding who to attack. It's all random. He goes from house to house, trying doors and windows, until something gives."

Wilson shrugged. "Maybe, or maybe he doesn't want to set off a security alarm, so he focuses on homes already open to him."

It wasn't a point worth exploring at the moment, but an interesting pattern.

Wilson stepped to the side and gestured for me to enter the home.

"You're not coming?" I asked.

"I've seen it once, and I bet I'll continue to see it in perfect, horrific detail for the rest of my life."

I nodded and took a deep breath, centering my mind and my intentions to remain calm and collected. I reminded myself I did this to save lives, to stop a monster from preying on innocent people. I convinced myself I could handle whatever waited within the bowels of the house, and I wouldn't only handle the gruesome stimuli, I would filter through it to discern something that could help me locate the psychotic killer.

"You good?" Wilson asked.

Without a word of confirmation, I stepped inside.

It stank like a frat house—spilled beer and body odor and sex—mixed with blood and decay.

The front door led straight into the living room. Gaming controllers rested on a coffee table littered with chewing tobacco debris, spit cups, shot glasses, a bottle of whiskey, snuffed cigarettes and joints, and a bowl of condoms. No pictures of family hung on the walls, only movie posters and pinups of naked women.

I ventured toward the kitchen. The dining room table had toppled beer cans spilling their contents across the surface. Playing cards lay in a messy, sticky stack, along with a scattering of coins and open pizza boxes. Flies engorged themselves on the remnants.

Empty beer cases tumbled out of the trashcan, which stood beside a door. I opened it.

The garage was where the partying happened. They strung LEDs like Christmas lights along the length of the ceiling, moving down the corners of the wall, and running along the baseboards. A beer pong table took up the center of the garage. Solo cup and orange ping-pong balls sprawled over it. A big screen television mounted to the wall above the washer and dryer.

It was Wednesday, yet the house appeared as if the occupants had partied all of Tuesday night. I guess that's how I had approached college—like one big, constant, never-ending party.

A trail of bloody footprints exiting the house headed toward the narrow opening of the garage door. I kneeled on the cement floor and cocked my head, staring at the opening. I doubted I could have squeezed through the space, but a skinny enough person might have done so.

I stood and followed the path of bloody prints. They exited from the kitchen, the living room, the hallway before, originating behind door number one.

I stopped. In the hallway, the blood trail crisscrossed in a flurry, as if the vampire had frantically paced. The prints moved from one door to the next, passing over each other, turning from clear indentations to thick smudges of blood.

What had happened?

I exhaled and placed my hand on the door handle, not really wanting to answer that question.

I had a job to do, though. I pushed the door open.

Three bodies lay in the room. A young man lay on the bed, covered in blood-soaked sheets. His body was the only one not marred beyond human recognition. A second body hung half on and half off the bed, shredded as if mauled by a wild, vicious animal. The third victim rested directly at my feet, as if she had attempted to escape from an unspeakable evil.

I swallowed a current of bile and looked up to avert my gaze.

Blood spattered the ceiling. The walls. I couldn't look anywhere without seeing blood.

Once I regained my bearings, I returned to the bodies. The man on the bed appeared whole, intact. He was pallid and waxen, drained of all the blood in his body. He resembled the other vampire victims.

The victim half off the bed and the one beside the door broke the vampire's pattern. I'm not sure why he had deviated, especially if it meant wasting so much blood.

My memory tickled, as if I had heard of a similar brutal murder before. Where? I mentally noted it and continued to study the scene.

I'll spare a description, because it's unnecessary, but the two women no longer resembled anything like humans. They looked like props in an especially gruesome horror movie.

"If she tried to escape," I muttered aloud, "she could've fought back."

I squatted and inspected her hands and fingernails for signs of a struggle. Maybe she scratched the vampire. Also, to do what he did to her, the vampire would have to touch her. Did he wear gloves? Or could we find fingerprints?

I backed out of the bedroom, into the hallway, and I treaded deeper into the house, toward another closed door. I braced myself before opening it.

When the door swung wide, it revealed another bloody, deranged scene. Once again, blood covered the entire room. Floor to ceiling, wall to wall.

Unable to remain in the house, I exited the front door to breathe fresh air.

Recalibration. Wednesday, July 19th. 1548hrs.

I ENTERED THE OFFICE physically and emotionally exhausted. After forcing myself to endure that house of horrors, to swallow back disgust and shock, to compartmentalize the experience as I debriefed with Wilson, I barely had the energy to hold my head up. I went straight for the coffee counter and poured myself a cup.

Alina sat on the ground beside the bookshelf, where she usually set up her camp. Fred sat in a client chair beside her with his legs kicked up on the windowsill. He had his laptop balancing on his thighs. In his left hand, he held a half-eaten corn dog.

I grabbed my rolling chair, dragged it over to them, and plopped into it. The coffee tasted burned and lukewarm, but I didn't care. My chair creaked as I leaned, rolling my head over the backrest. I closed my eyes, but the images of the dead crawled back to life in my mind, so I reopened them and exhaled.

"Fred. Alina." With my free hand, I massaged temples. "I need some good news."

"Good news is subjective," Alina said. "Some people might think a well-executed genocide is good news, while others consider it an atrocity."

I sighed, knowing, based on her answer and initial silence when I entered the office, she and Fred had learned something, but they were hesitant to share.

"What did you find out?" I asked.

"I'll go first," Fred said, grinning. He had some corn dog stuck in his teeth. "I need to get this off my chest." He adjusted his posture, dropping his feet to the floor, straightening his back, and setting his laptop off to the side. He tore off a bite of his corn dog. "Are you sitting down for this?"

"No," I said, as I sat two feet away from him.

Fred finished chewing his bite, swallowed, and spoke. "Remember, don't hate the messenger, hate the game."

"Don't hate the player, hate the game," Alina said. "Don't shoot the messenger. You're mixing—"

"Hush, little girl," Fred said, waggling his corn dog at Alina. "This is hard enough as it is." He cleared his throat and faced me again. "So,

I looked into the missing criminals connected to our investigations. Except, a little bell jingled in the back of my head, trying to remind me of something I couldn't quite pinpoint... until it crashed into me like a... like a flying cow."

I crinkled my face, half-wishing Fred would forgo the groundwork and just tell me what he discovered. But I let him ease his way into it. His procrastination to avoid telling me what he learned amused me; it helped lighten the darkness clouding my mind. Or the coffee had kicked in. I would credit Fred, though.

"Flying cow," he said again, raising his palms.

"Yeah," I said, more confused than ever. "I don't understand."

"The voodoo case. We investigated a flying cow, remember? That's how Gilbert Tonyan met his final destination."

"I see what you did there." Alina pointed at Fred. "Great wordplay." She looked at me. "He related Tonyan's untimely death to the horror franchise, Final Destination. Have you ever seen it?"

"No."

"It's great. I mean, not great like good, but great like fun. You know what I mean?"

"Not really."

"You'll have to take my word. They're fun. Great, memorable kill scenes, too. Terrible characters. Horrible writing. Fun, though. And when we boil movies down to a single factor that determines whether they work, isn't it always entertainment? Don't we measure them by their enjoyment factor first? So, that's why they're great, like fun, but not great, like good."

"Okay," I said, still not any closer to knowing what Fred and Alina had learned while I was away.

"Speaking of movies," Alina said. "*Martin*, by George Romero, the director who created *The Night of Living Dead*, is a low-budget movie about a kid who thinks he's a vampire. It's a great, wildly underrated movie. Great in the sense of good, not fun. Though, if you're like me—someone who has fun watching well-made movies—then also fun. You should also watch *The Skin I Live In*, starring the impossibly attractive Antonio Banderas in his prime. Wow, that man is a snack."

"Hey," Fred said. "You're hijacking my turn."

"You brought it up," Alina said.

"Brought what up?"

"The movies?"

"No I didn't."

"*Final Destination.*"

"I made a reference. You're right, by the way—"

"Duh," Alina said. "Always."

"Great, but in a fun way."

"Right?"

"Guys," I said, cutting them off. "As much as I love your pointless banter, we need to dial it in and focus. Fred, you mentioned Gilbert Tonyan."

Fred clicked his tongue and glanced upward, as if searching his mind for his train of thought. "Gilbert Tonyan had not only a wife but a lover. Wife, Greta Tonyan. Lover, Christopher Steele. Oh, wait. You distracted me." Fred stared directly at me, not Alina, when he said that.

"I distracted you?" I asked.

"Yeah, you threw me off my groove. The little bell in my head, ringing. It was trying to remind me that Randall Fincher had gone missing."

A pattern emerged, and I now noticed it. "Greta and Christoper are missing, too?" I asked.

"Why do you have to steal my thunder?" Fred asked.

"You can't blame him," Alina said. "It took you too long to get here."

"I had this great reveal planned." He bit on the corn dog, dragging the last bite off the stick with his teeth. "Do you remember James Connors?"

The client who had hallucinated a Sasquatch.

"Yeah."

"Gone. Claire Balzan?"

The woman falsely arrested for the crimes committed by Trisha Berry, her doppelgänger.

"Gone. Miette Verdin?"

The woman taken as a child and replaced with Vanessa Snow, the Changeling.

"Gone. Her brother, Zachary Verdin? Gone. Johnny Lantz?"

The survivor from the dream demon attacks.

"Missing. Not only that, during my lunch hour, I spared the time to swing by Vincent Dupree's house, since he's been dodging my calls."

My torso turned into a blender and turned all my insides into gravy.

"Car in the garage, as is Shannon's," Fred said. "They're both missing, though. I called their work offices, neither have come in for weeks. Apparently they reported Vincent and Shannon as missing, but there's no record with Sacramento Sheriff's Department, Sacramento Police Department, or California Highway Patrol. So, I don't know who intercepted the calls. Well, I do. We all do. But I don't know how."

"You're telling me every individual directly associated with my prior cases has vanished?" I asked. I fumbled digging my phone out of my pocket, secured it, and scrolled to Glacia's number. I had just spoken with her... when?

Her phone rang once.

Two weeks ago.

"Alina," I said, lowering the phone from my mouth. "When's the last time you spoke with—"

"Hello?"

My voice caught in my throat. The floor fell out from beneath me, and I dropped, cascading into a perpetual darkness.

"Two days ago," Alina said, her voice muffled as if she had shoved a pillow over her mouth.

"August, you there?" Daniel Quinn asked, speaking into Glacia's phone. "Cat got your tongue?" He laughed like ice cracking and splitting.

I had no words. Daniel Quinn had already taken Cambria from me. Now he held Glacia's phone to his ear, speaking into it. Where did that leave Glacia? Had she fallen as the latest victim in his self-assigned game against me?

"It's disappointing how long I've waited with this phone, waiting for you to contact me," Quinn said. "You're usually so intuitive and observant. I guess the Vampire of Sacramento has really grabbed you by the face and forced your attention on him. Or is it the golem? Tick. Tock. Tick. Tock."

"Where's Glacia?" I asked.

"August, earning a meeting with me means so much more than you're aware. We agreed for two weeks, right? Well, I feel that's too generous. How about a week from today? From right this second. You solve both your cases, you'll earn yourself a date with yours truly. I'll take you to all the missing people. If you cannot solve your investigations within the week... well, you don't deserve a date with me, and you'll never see Glacia again."

The line died.

Two hours prior, I had combed through a home soaked in blood and guts, had investigated the corpses of five young adults. My nerves had frayed. My emotions shot. When Daniel Quinn disconnected the call, I screamed and threw my mug of coffee at the wall. The cup shattered, and the coffee splashed across the paint like dark blood streaking and dripping to the floor.

I breathed heavily through my mouth and stared out the window at the brick building across the alley. "Alina."

"Yeah?"

"What did you learn about Jackson Armstead?"

"Jake, your brother-in-law—"

"I know who Jake is," I said, the words venomous on my tongue. Heat rose to my face in a wave of guilt. Alina didn't deserve my fear, or my insecurity, or my wrath. Quinn deserved it, but not her. "I'm sorry."

Alina licked her lips and nodded. "He's in the police academy, right? Well, he has a few contacts already on the force. I reached out to him and asked if he could secure me a background check on Armando Lopez. I know you said he's a broken man who lost his wife and daughter, and you believed he told the truth. Maya didn't like him, though. She said as much. And his daughter died, and his wife disappeared, and... I don't know. I revisited him."

"What did you find?"

"He worked construction, past tense. Three years ago, he stopped showing at the job. The background check provided me with his employment history, and I reached out to his employer. Armando lied about working. He doesn't have a job, at least not a legal one or one on the record."

"Any theories?" I asked.

Alina nodded. "He's the mask—the sad, relatable mask of a man going through unimaginable Hell. He still attends service every Sunday. He shows up at community events. People flock to him and shower him with platitudes and compassion. He's the mask, though, hiding what lies beneath."

"Which is?"

"Specifically, that which lies beneath his house," Alina said.

"What do you mean?"

"The county possesses approved blueprints of Armando's house. I worked my charm and got a copy."

"You did all this today?" I asked.

"No. No, no, no," Alina said, chuckling. "I'm flattered you think I can do that, but unfortunately, not even my wicked allure can bypass all the bureaucratic tape. I've been working on this for, I don't know, a week now. Maybe longer. Like I said, Maya never really trusted Armando. So, I went about collecting more information on him."

"Why didn't you tell me this sooner?"

Alina smirked and shook her head. "Well, today I made a few calls to expedite the process. Both the county and my police contact had my information, but they hadn't yet shared it with me. Apparently, they preferred for me to follow up with them."

"You're a little genius," I said.

"I know." Alina showed her teeth. "Anyway, I compared the original blueprints to a recent Google Earth overhead image, and the home has changed. Renovation and add-ons not permitted by the county. No record. So, we don't know what's actually changed beyond some exterior modifications. If I had to guess, they expanded the basement and turned it into some kind of dungeon-slash-operating room. You ever heard of Josef Fritzl?"

"No," I said.

"Most sadistic individual I've ever had the displeasure of learning about. Held his own daughter captive for twenty-four years. Had seven babies with her. Anyway, he expanded his basement and turned it into a prison cell. I think we have something similar with the Lopez's."

I crossed my arms and clicked my tongue. "You're sure about this?"

"No," Alina said. "But that's my theory."

I cracked a knuckle. The court wouldn't issue a warrant to me, a private investigator, and breaking into Armando's house could lead to our arrest. We couldn't legally enter and search the house unless Armando allowed us to. We needed a way in and an excuse to explore the home without him realizing anything was wrong.

In the prolonged silence, a grating imitation of music cut through the office. I cringed as the bleating noise burrowed into my ears.

Fred had a harmonica to his lips. "How did that sound?" he asked.

"Like a cat dying," Alina said.

"That's improvement then, I think. Daphne said it sounds like the tormented souls of the Underworld."

"She probably said it sounds like something used to torment souls in the Underworld," Alina said. "Why do you have that?"

"I'm learning."

"Why?"

"A new hobby. Daphne is always telling me all I do is work and sit on the couch. I've been golfing a little, but I can't always do that because it takes a lot of time. Harmonica, though, it fits in my pocket and I can play it anywhere. Except at home. Daphne said I couldn't play at home anymore."

"You can't play here, either," Alina said. "I forbid it."

"You forbid it? Okay. I forbid you from humming anymore."

"What?"

"You heard me."

"My humming is at least good, and on key."

"It bugs me."

"Does it really?" Alina frowned at him.

"No." Fred frowned. "You sound like a dang song bird. It's beautiful. I actually wish you would hum more often."

"Fred," I said. "No more harmonica. I need to think, and that sounds like a train derailing."

"Rude."

"True," Alina said.

"Okay," I said. "Fred, Alina."

"Yes," they both said.

"Armando knows me and Maya. He doesn't know either of you. You two need to come up with a plan to get into his house with his permission. Once inside, one of you will have to distract him, while the other accidentally," I put accidentally in air quotes, "stumbles into the basement."

"You're sure about that?" Fred asked. "I mean, Alina said it was only a theory. If something goes wrong, we could put the entire company in jeopardy. Not just us, either, but Tempest Michaels. The Blue Moon name. We're not vigilantes."

I thought of Glacia held captive somewhere by Quinn, and I thought of all the other people he had taken and hidden away. I had to solve both my cases within a week to secure their safety. I had to bend some rules to speed this investigation along.

My attention drifted to the coffee stain on the wall. I wasn't sure about anything anymore, apart from knowing I had to solve these cases, save Glacia, and stop Quinn.

"Alina," I said.

"Yeah?"

"You said this is only a theory?" I asked.

"Yeah."

"How confident in the theory are you?"

Out for a Drink. Wednesday, July 19th. 2042hrs.

I SAT AT STUCKEY'S bar alone. Old, sad country songs played over the speaker system, the music nearly muted by the collections of patrons drinking, talking, and shouting as they threw darts or shot pool.

Nick, the burly bartender, chatted with an attractive woman wearing tight jeans, cowboy boots, and a crop top stressing her best physical features.

After Alina and Fred clocked out of the office, I was alone with my thoughts. Dangerous company, considering the times. The longest day ever had started at the cemetery, moved to the house of horrors, and concluded at the office. The glue between each event was Quinn, his voice, his ultimatum—solve your cases in two weeks, in one week, and you can meet with me. To meet with him meant the chance at saving Glacia and Vincent and everyone else Quinn had abducted.

I finally watched the grainy video Alina sent me. A golem—one with the face of Maria, though the body of a young man—attacked a woman in her early twenties. Authorities later identified the woman as Gladas Vasquez. Shortly after her abduction, a citizen discovered the remains of her body in Reno. Gladas Vasquez had no connection to Clara or Maria Lopez, or to any of the boys present on the boat the day Maria died. She was a random girl who met a terrible fate.

We had nothing more on the vampire, other than bodies barely recognizable as human. The corpses, the blood, the brutality, the amused voice of Quinn, the headstones of Cambria and Aaron all swirled together into a dark, oily shadow that tormented me as I sat alone in my office. Laughing from sidelines, mocking me, stood the blind date my mother had set up for me, stood Gerald and his giant chickens, stood Bagley, stood Alina and her parents.

I cracked my knuckles. I folded a stick of gum into my mouth.

Nothing quieted the madness.

So, I did the one sane thing I could think of—I walked toward the only light I could see in that moment. I called Maya.

We agreed to meet at Stuckey's at 2030hrs. As usual, she was late. Twelve minutes late, which, to her credit, was almost early for her.

She entered Stuckey's like a whirlwind. Every eye fixed on her. She plopped on the stool beside me. "What are you drinking tonight?"

"Coffee." I said, cupping the warm mug.

"Going with the hard stuff, huh? You okay?"

"I don't know."

Maya raised a hand and snapped her fingers. "Nicholas, if you don't make me a drink, I'm going to tell that lovely young lady why you have all those muscles. It's because he has such a little—"

"Maya," Nick said, turning away from the woman who had kept his attention for the past five minutes, "how may I help you?"

"I was going to say little ego." She snickered and waved at the woman across the bar. "He has a little ego, and what I mean is that he's selfless in all the right ways. Giving and charitable." Maya winked. "If you know what I mean. If you don't, I'm talking about in the bedroom."

"Okay." Nick pushed himself off the counter and approached Maya. "Hello. Hi. It's great to see you after two months of getting ghosted."

"Pun intended." Maya elbowed my arm and chuckled. "Because August is a ghost doctor and what not?"

"I'm not a ghost doctor," I said.

"Detective. Doctor. Investigator. They're all the same thing, right? Identify the disease and remove it. Bada bing, bada boom."

"Can I get you a drink?" Nick asked, crossing his arms.

"A shot of tequila," Maya said. "August never would have invited me to a bar, let alone this bar, unless he's feeling rather... well, unless he's feeling his feelings. So tequila to get me on his level, because tequila makes me feel my feelings. I don't know why, but it does." Maya grinned. "Thank you, Nicky."

The bartender grunted, grabbed a shot glass, reached for the tequila on the bottom-most shelf, and poured it. "Enjoy," he said, sliding the clear liquid to Maya.

"You sound mad at me." Maya pinched her shot glass between thumb and index finger, tapped it against the counter, and threw it back.

"I am mad at you."

"What did I do?"

"You ghosted me."

"Nick, we were bedroom buddies. I don't even know your last name."

"Tate."

"Well, there you have it." Maya threw up her arms. "Mr. Tate. I don't really like that last name. So, all is well and all that, right? We never would have worked out, anyway. Maya Tate? It sounds so forced."

Nick stood there and listened to her, and I'm not exactly sure why he didn't about-face and return to the woman waiting for him.

"Maya Richards, though," Maya said, nodding her chin up and down, "that's the name of a bigwig scientist who pushes the boundaries to create life-saving serums. Maya Richards. That's powerful. Maya Tate? Nick, with a last name like that, you should've known we never stood a chance."

"Maya Richards?" I asked.

Evan's last name was Richards.

"I always think about that. I've thought about Maya Watson, too. It sounds like a literary character who's noble and brave and always does the correct, boring thing. It doesn't work, does it?"

"Not for you."

"I thought that, too. Not for me. I like the kick ass scientist, though. I feel like Maya Richards is a superhero waiting to grant herself superpowers through accidental means."

"What about Maya Rogers?" Rogers was Fred's last name.

"No. First, he's married to the baddest woman alive. I can't even think like that. Besides, hearing you say it aloud, Maya Rogers... ew. It sounds like a housewife. Gross." She faced me, smiling with her lips, but her eyes showed her true feelings. She was nervous. It probably stemmed from me inviting her to a bar.

"I don't plan on drinking," I said. "I have no temptation to drink."

"Why this bar?"

"You brought me here to celebrate a couple months back. I danced with Patricia Huffman. She ended up becoming the vampire's third victim."

"Why call me?"

"I can talk to you."

"You can't talk to anyone else?"

"Not like I can talk to you."

"Are you flirting with me, Mr. Watson?"

"I'm being honest with you."

"So... yes, you are flirting with me."

"Don't make this harder than it already is."

Maya chuckled. "Do you care if I have another shot?"

"Have as many as you like, but I'm not paying for them."

"That's fair." Maya stood, leaned halfway across the bar, and collected the tequila bottle from the other side. "Barkeep!" She held the bottle above her head, waving it around. "Thirty bucks for this dime-store bottle? That sound fair? Or do I still get free booze?"

"Fifty bucks," Nick said, once again having a conversation with the other woman. "You also have to promise not to bother me anymore tonight."

"Fifty dollars!" Maya leaned back on her stool. "What happened to the free booze?"

Nick eyed her with a look that begged for Maya to continue the argument. My money said he wanted a reason to kick her out of the establishment.

"Right," Maya said, settling into her seat and pouring another shot into her glass. "I guess I lost that perk. How about twenty-five dollars?"

"How about seventy-five?" Nick asked.

"You drive a hard bargain, Sir." Maya looked away and rocked back and forth, clicking her tongue as she considered his offer. "Fifty it is."

"And don't bother me again."

"Do you have a tip jar anywhere around here?" Maya asked, scanning the countertop. "I need to offer you a few customer service tips."

Nick shook his head and returned his attention to the blonde.

Maya drained the shot she had poured for herself.

"How's Wanda doing?" I asked.

"Great. She has a job. She's sober. She makes time for her and Alina, which is the most shocking development."

"And Alina?"

Maya scowled. "You should probably talk to her about how she's doing. I'd rather not speak on her behalf."

"That's fair. How's Stephen?"

"Relentless. But with Wanda trending in the right direction, Alina sixteen and able to decide for herself, and me being a steady fixture in Alina's life, it doesn't seem likely Stephen will win the case."

"That's good."

"He's still a headache and unnecessary stress, especially in Alina's case. She's gone through enough in her life. I don't know why Stephen has her going through all of this." Maya poured another shot, but she tempered herself, keeping the liquid in the small glass. "You're not here for any of that, though. Not saying you don't care, but that's not why we're here."

"It's Glacia," I said.

"Listen, I told her not to talk to your mom. I know you get weird about that kind of thing. She wouldn't listen."

"She's missing."

"Wait. What? What does that mean?"

"Daniel Quinn has her."

Maya's eyes narrowed, and her brow furrowed. "That makes no sense."

"Daniel Quinn, over the past few weeks, has captured every person directly related to any of my cases—perpetrator or victim."

"And done what with them? That's a good number of people to take and stash somewhere."

"I don't know what he's done with them, but he somehow orchestrated the prisoners to escape. He has Vincent and Shannon. He has Glacia and most likely her uncle and mom, too."

"Why?"

I shook my head. "If I solve the golem and vampire case in the next week, he'll arrange a meeting with me."

"If you don't?"

"I don't know."

"How many people does he have?"

I mentally counted the victims and perpetrators from my past cases, beginning with the Living Gargoyle case, moving to Rabid Sasquatch, Voodoo Doll Killer, Nana's Haunted House, Doppelgänger, Changeling, vengeful spirit tormenting her husband, and the dream demon. "Almost twenty, maybe more, depending on how Quinn defined connected to my cases."

"That's a decent amount of people to vanish."

"I know."

"How does someone orchestrate a prison escape?"

"I don't know. That's not the point right now."

"I guess not."

"Quinn has Glacia and Vincent. If we want to save them, we have to solve the golem and vampire cases. End of story. And I'm lost, Maya. We might have a lead on the golem case, but I don't know. Maybe we're grasping at straws."

"The vampire?"

"I have nothing." I paused and drank my coffee and stared at the mirror-backed shelf holding all the alcohol. "Wilson allowed me to walk through the crime scene today."

"And?"

"Five kids, all college-aged. Maya, it was like something made up for a horror movie to shock the audience. One body fit the vampire's MO—neatly drained, body intact. The other four, though…" I trailed off, unwilling to paint the picture for her. She would have to take my word for it.

Maya chewed on her knuckle and stared across the bar at Nick, who flirted with the woman. She raised the shot glass to her lips and sipped the tequila. "What do you know about vampires?"

"The killer isn't a vampire."

"What if he thinks he is? What if that's how we catch him?"

"What do you mean?"

"Entertain me. What do you know about vampires? They're allergic to the sun, right?"

"Sure."

"Garlic? Crosses? No reflection in a mirror? They need blood to live. Come on. You're in the paranormal business. You know more than the basics."

I considered her question. "They can't enter a dwelling without invitation."

"Okay."

"Wilson told me the vampire went through an open window with the first residential murder. Last night, he slid beneath the garage door. It was partially open. So, he might consider unlocked or open doors as invitations."

"He hunted at bars and clubs before, right?"

"Yeah."

"Public establishments. Open to all. Invitation always extended to everyone and anyone." Maya's face lit up like a Christmas tree, but she said nothing.

"What?"

"You're desperate to catch this guy?"

"Yeah."

Maya finished her shot and gagged on the burn. "Have you ever heard of the saying when the predator becomes the prey?"

"I've heard when the hunter becomes the hunted."

"Same thing. You get the point."

I realized as soon as Maya opened her mouth to explain what she meant. I shook my head, cutting her off. "No. Not happening, Maya. I'm not that desperate. It's not even a discussion."

Of course, when Maya has an idea and she convinced herself of it, she never took no for an answer.

"I'm doing it," she said. "I just have to figure how to do it." Maya poured another shot. "Luckily, tequila is my muse."

A Silly Mistake. Thursday, July 20th. O953hrs.

Liam, the strip club manager, had contacted the office. Fred had answered, and he forwarded the call to my cell phone.

"I made a silly mistake," Liam said before I finished saying hello. "Same time? Same place?"

I agreed and immediately phoned Detective Wilson. He answered on the fourth ring, right before I almost hung up and shot him a text message. His voice carried the same hoarseness as someone battling a severe cold over the past week.

"August Watson. You better be calling me with good news. After yesterday's slaughter, the higher-ups are on my ass. They sat me down and explained the rules of the game. If I don't win, I lose, you know?

I'm no longer a detective, barely a police officer. This case defines my career."

"Did you tell them about Madden's fiasco?" I asked.

"They don't care about my excuses. They care about me getting you on the scene, originally convincing them to contract your services. You see what I'm saying? Madden is moot because I have you assisting, and the reporters captured your involvement yesterday afternoon."

A pit hollowed my stomach. My name and business now had ties to the Vampire of Sacramento. If we failed to solve this case before the vampire killed again, I could lose my entire livelihood.

"The bigwigs want the case solved before there's another murder," Wilson said. "Five brutally murdered kids don't sit well. My leash is short. I'm on thin ice. All the sayings. All the things."

His gravelly voice made more sense now. "You didn't sleep last night, did you? Brass got under your skin?"

"Under my skin, in my head, whatever you want to call it. I didn't sleep. No. I stayed up and read and reread and re-reread every report we have on the vampire, along with any report that might relate to him."

"Find anything?"

"Yeah."

I held my breath. "What?"

"That at a certain point in the night, after reading for hours, after staring at ink and paper for hours, my eyes do this funky thing where everything just kind of... melds together into a giant, blurry blob."

"That happens to me, too. I splash cold water over my face, bust out a hundred push-ups, brew a pot of coffee. On really terrible nights, I take a walk. It wipes away the fuzz every time."

"I never knew the life of a detective was so nocturnal."

"Neurotic."

We shared a tired laugh.

"Hey," I said when we sputtered out the last of our joy. "You ever hear of a Vermont Wendsdale?"

"He a cartoon character?"

"No."

"Sounds like it, with a name like that."

"He's a self-proclaimed monster hunter. He tracked me down to get information on the vampire. I think he wants to kill him."

"Good. Let him."

"Wilson," I said.

"I'm just saying, with the vampire dead, I might get some sleep."

"Can you look into the name for me?" I debated whether to share that Wendsdale had maybe murdered over a hundred people, believing them to be some shade of a monster. I kept that information for the moment, preferring to hear what Wilson's results told us before revealing anything more.

"Liam called," I said.

"Who?"

"Strip club manager."

"He learn something?"

Twenty minutes later, Wilson and I met in the strip club's parking lot.

The day's temperature already flirted with ninety degrees, and the forecast showed the weather would rise well above a hundred by 1500hrs. Heat and exhaustion, in my experience, never paired well. The hotter the day, the more exhausted the mind, the slower in thought and reflex.

Inside the strip club, the air conditioning blasted. Chills immediately cut down my spine as I shivered from the drastic change in climate. Without waiting for a security guard to escort us to Liam's office, Wilson and I went straight for the closed door.

The detective raised a fist and knocked hard three times.

"I'll do the talking," I said. "Remember, he's not a fan of cops."

"Yeah, yeah, yeah. I'll eat my tongue. Lucky for you, I haven't had breakfast yet."

The door slivered open, and a pair of monocled eyes peered outward. "Ah," Liam said. "Good. It's you." The office door fully opened, and Liam, still in his rolling chair, slid away from us and toward his messy desk. Without a word, he went straight to a monitor mounted on the wall and maximized a security video to fill the entire screen. "Here's what happened," Liam said, his voice more nasally than I remembered. "I took a vacation about a year ago. I don't really ever do that, but my Dungeons & Dragons group wanted to do a getaway to finish our five-year-long campaign. A marathon. Craziest, most fun gaming experience I've ever done. I can't even explain it."

"I'd rather you didn't, anyway," Wilson said, not chewing his tongue.

Liam frowned. "Well, when I came back to work and resumed saving the security footage..." He sighed and cleared his throat. "You should know how my system works. Naturally, the file erases to clear space for a new recording every three days. It's my personal crusade, and private crusade, to download the footage onto hard drives."

I didn't care to ask Liam why he saved the footage, though I had a few guesses.

Liam paused all the same, as if expecting either Wilson or me to question his practice. After a few seconds of quiet, he continued. "When I returned from my long weekend, I had to catch up on downloading the surveillance. I left for four days, so I lost a day in my recordings. I didn't realize it until months later, and by then I couldn't go back and dig up the lost date. It had erased. A terrible tragedy, one which hurts my heart a little."

I thought of Aaron Brooks, of Cambria Parker, of the vampire's many victims, of Maria Lopez and all those connected to her death. Tragedy paraded through my mind. Liam, comparing his private porn stash of illegal security footage, ignited a rage-fueled fire within me.

"What happened?" I asked, my voice tight and barely containing my anger.

"I always save the footage and write the corresponding date. When I missed that one day, I never went back to correct it. I'm always, technically, a day behind."

"We watched the wrong footage," I said. Despite the blasting air conditioning and the air cranking for the fan on a filing cabinet, heat boiled within my body and simmered off my skin. "We wasted two weeks on this investigation because you can't record dates properly?"

"Easy, August," Wilson said. "He's sharing what he has. He made a mistake. It's okay."

Liam gulped. "You watched footage from the day before the date you asked to see." He looked up at the screen mounted on the wall above his desk. It glowed a brilliant blue in the dim room. "This is the actual footage from the night of the murder."

"Play it." I stepped forward to see the video in its entirety.

Liam pressed the spacebar. He must have already watched the footage. He didn't have to fast forward to the correct time. Instead, the old man—the victim, Herb Nowak—sat squarely in the frame. He sat in a leather chair before the stage, smoking a cigar and drinking what appeared to be a whiskey as he watched a naked woman dance.

"Okay," Liam said. "That's your boy, right?"

"Yeah," Wilson said. "That's Herb."

"Now..." Liam moved the cursor across the screen, tapped a few buttons, and moved to a different camera angle. He grunted as he half-stood and pointed at the monitor. "There. Right there."

I squinted and leaned forward.

The vampire was tall, though I couldn't determine exactly how tall—a few inches over six-feet though. He wasn't just skinny, but sickly. Emaciated. A skinny that requires a double take. A skinny where the elbow joint is wider than the forearm and biceps, and the knee is wider than the calf and thigh. A skinny where his face sinks into his skull. The vampire wore a hat, and he wore a hood over the hat. The combination completely obscured his face.

"Take screenshots," I said.

"Already did." Liam dug through the debris scattered across his desk, found a manila folder, and handed it to me. "Printed screenshots of every angle I could get on the guy."

"You're sure he's the one?" Wilson asked. "We need proof other than he looks like the killer."

"You tell me." Liam navigated to the footage, fast-forwarding to Herb standing from his chair and hobbling out of the club. Liam switched over to the parking lot camera.

Herb stepped into his truck. As he did, another figure entered the screen. The supposed vampire lurked out from the club, ambled across the parking lot, and climbed into an old, white, windowless van.

Herb's truck left, and the van followed.

Liam sucked on his upper lip for a second before swiveling around and facing us. "Screenshots of the van are also in that folder." He reached out a meaty, pale hand.

"We already paid," Wilson said.

"For what I knew then. I now know something new."

"And if something pops into your head tomorrow, what then?" Wilson asked.

"Well, I don't work for free," Liam said.

"How about this?" I asked, cutting between Liam and Wilson. "You tell us everything you know right now. No more games. We'll pay appropriately for your information. If, however, you do remember something else tomorrow or any other time in the future, and you insist we pay you, Detective Wilson will make this process a lot more difficult for you. He'll request a warrant. He'll have this place buzzing with police officers. He'll monitor the club every single day, just in case the vampire returns. Do you want that kind of heat? Do you want the police breathing down your neck every day of the week, every week of the month?"

"I want another thousand dollars," Liam said.

"Wilson, do you have money?"

"Yeah, I have money, and I'll keep having it until this overstuffed worm shares every drop of juicy intel he knows."

"I confronted him that night," Liam said. "The man. The vampire."

I could have slapped the manager across the face, but I didn't.

Wilson, on the other hand, had stayed awake all night, worried about his job security. He lunged forward, grabbed Liam by the collar, and ripped him from his chair. The shirt tore, and the hefty manager slipped from Wilson's grasp and stumbled to the ground. Wilson was on him, though. He rolled Liam onto his stomach, bent an arm behind his back, and lowered to his ear.

"You confronted him, and you didn't think to mention that to us?" Wilson growled. "Did you read or see the news today? The vampire murdered again last night. Five college-aged kids. Butchered them. Five. That's on you. Their blood and their lives, that's all on you. You spoke to him? You confronted the vampire?"

Liam nodded his face up and down against the floor, and he muffled some words.

Wilson lifted the manager's head off the ground. "What did you say?"

"Nothing."

"You just said you confronted him. You did it that night?"

"Yes."

"You didn't tell us?"

"It's not important."

"Every detail is important. How did the conversation go, word for word?"

Tears and snot streaked down Liam's face. He knew Wilson wasn't posturing. The detective would hurt Liam if he didn't cooperate. He would hurt him, and he would get away with it, especially if it led to Wilson solving the case and finding the vampire.

"Wilson," I said, interjecting before it went that far. "Ease up. You made your point. Liam, you'll talk, yeah?"

"Yes."

"You hear that, buddy? He'll talk to us. Let him up."

Wilson grunted and pushed on Liam's back to stand. He cracked his neck and backed up to the door. "If I even think he's lying or withholding the truth, I'm not going so easy on him. You hear that, fat boy? That was me going easy."

Liam rolled onto his side and sat, though he remained on the floor. He stared into his lap.

"You also lost your extra band," Wilson said.

"We made a deal with him," I said, growing a little irritated by the detective's behavior. "He agreed to share everything he knows, and we agreed to pay him. He's not losing his compensation for cooperation."

"Cooperation, my ass."

"Enough, Wilson," I said, snapping at him. "Enough. Let him talk."

Wilson crossed his arms.

"Liam, go ahead."

"It wasn't anything, really," the manager said. "A few of my girls noticed him, felt uncomfortable, and reported it to me. If that happens, I discreetly approach the guest and explain to them they need to stop whatever they're doing, otherwise they'll have to leave. If they refuse or make a scene, that's when security gets involved. Our number one priority is to protect these girls." Liam looked at the paused security footage.

I wondered how stealing security footage for his personal reasons protected the women in his employment.

"The woman who notified me said the man had done nothing wrong, other than he creeped out her and some of the other girls." Liam looked at me, though he avoided glancing at Wilson. "I can't ask someone to leave unless there's cause, but I like to have the women's back. I don't want them to feel unsafe or vulnerable. So, I approached the man to see if I couldn't find an excuse to ask him to leave."

"What time was this?" I asked.

"About the time Herb was getting ready to up and leave."

"What happened?"

Liam returned his attention to the floor. "He stank. My dad used to work as a butcher, and he'd come home smelling like blood. It has such a distinct smell. That's what the man stank like. Old blood. It wafted from his pores like a gas."

"Did you see his face?" I asked.

Liam nodded. "Up that close, yeah. I saw his face. I don't mean to sound insensitive, because we all deal with our insecurities and flaws, but that man... he didn't have a face."

I narrowed my eyes. "What do you mean?"

"Not a human face, at least. He almost looked like a burn victim—boils and scars covered everything. No eyelids, though he had bushy eyebrows, and no lips, which made his teeth always visible." Liam shivered. "I see why people call him the vampire. He looked like Nosferatu, except maybe uglier."

"Did you get a name?" I asked.

Liam shook his head. "I couldn't speak. I know how that sounds, but his appearance shocked me to silence. I mean, I didn't know what to say. I couldn't ask him to leave because of the way he looked. Or because he smelled bad. I could get sued for something like that."

"What happened?"

"His eyes never really saw me. They were always looking past me. After watching the security footage, I realized he was watching Herb. Once the old man left, the vampire followed. I never said a word to him. I approached, and he walked away. All that happened in seconds. That was it."

I glanced at Wilson, who glared at Liam with fire in his eyes. "Pay the man in full, and let's get out of here."

Tug of War. Thursday, July 20th. 1242hrs.

ALINA AND I SAT inside a local sandwich shop. I dropped lunch off for Fred, picking up Alina and driving her a half-mile to one of my favorite delis. We could have walked, but the heat proved too much to bear, especially when my car offered the comfort of air conditioning.

While waiting for our food to arrive, I stared out the fogged window at the small parking lot. Alina had opened her bag of chips and slowly picked away at them. I hadn't asked her how she was handling all the recent developments in her life.

I had a lot of distractions on my mind, though that excuse made me feel guilty. Despite my problems, I should have made time to listen to Alina's worries. Now that I had, I didn't know what to say. Conversation has never really proved my strength.

"I've been watching vampire movies and golem movies."

"Have you?" I asked.

"Yeah." Alina drank her lemonade. "The oldest mention of a golem comes from Judaism. Did you know that?"

"I didn't."

"Well, think about it. God created Adam from clay right. Technically, he's a golem. The traditional golem is created from mud through means of divinity. The golem we're chasing was created through the other human body parts through the practice of a deranged doctor. Frankenstein's monster is essentially a golem—a flesh golem."

"That sounds perverted."

"It is," Alina said. "In every story I read, and movie I watched, golems serve their masters. The term is also used as a metaphor to portray an entity that serves its master under controlled conditions."

"Controlled conditions?"

"It won't hesitate to harm its master if it believes it can retaliate."

"Interesting," I said. "Does this help us, though?"

"I think so."

"How?"

"The video from the convenience store of the golem tearing through the racks." Alina shrugged. "That's it. The zombie broke in, ransacked the place, and bounced out. No theft. Nothing."

"Yeah?"

"What if it was a loyalty test?"

"What do you mean?"

"What if Clara wants to control her golems? Maybe she doesn't want them to only look like Maria, but behave like her, too, so Clara needs to command their minds."

"How would she do that?"

"Conditioning. Forcing them to do crazy, erratic things, like breaking into convenience stores and thrashing the place."

I cracked a knuckle. "That's a pretty wild theory. You watch too many horror movies."

Alina snickered. "Probably."

"Hey, I wanted to ask you... how are you doing?"

"Fine."

"I mean, you know, with all that's going on. Your dad, your mom. I can't imagine how you might feel, but I'm sure it's not top-notch."

"It feels like I'm a rope."

"A rope?"

"A rope. My mom has one end of me, and my dad has the other end, and they're pulling me like a game of tug-of-war. That's how I feel.

Like I'm nothing more than a game to them. Do you know what happens in tug-of-war once someone wins? They roll up the rope and throw it in a closet until they're ready to play again."

I sucked on my teeth, searching for the right question to ask, or the right words to say. Luckily, our food arrived. The waiter dropped it off, asked if we needed anything else, and walked away.

"I called my dad the other night," Alina said, snatching the speared pickle off my plate.

"You did?" I asked.

She bit off the end. "I don't know why I tried. I don't know what I expected from him, but whatever I expected, that's not what I received."

"What did you tell him?"

"That I loved him, because I do. He's my dad." Alina crinkled her face.

"Of course."

"I'll always love him. I told him I forgave him, too." She rolled her eyes.

"What did he say?"

"'Forgive me for what?'" Alina broke off another bite of the pickle. "That annoyed me, so I told him how happy I am right now, in this specific season of my life, with Maya and you and school and the agency. I told him I was happy, genuinely, for the first time, probably ever."

"I'm sure he didn't like that."

"He liked it less when I asked him to drop the custody battle. I told him I would visit him, that he could visit me, that we would stay in touch." Alina bit her upper lip and shook her head. "'No. I can't.' That's what he said. He wouldn't drop it. He didn't give a reason, but I know why. He's too prideful, and he can't allow anyone to beat him, especially not my mom. He doesn't care how much it hurts me, either. I'm not the prize, you see. Winning against my mom is the prize."

"And once he's won, he'll roll the rope up and throw it in the closet," I said.

"Exactly." Alina sniffled and bit into her sandwich.

We ate for a few minutes, chipping away at our lunches.

"What about your mom?" I asked. "She's doing better, right?"

"I don't know. She's done better in the past, too. She's been sober and employed and checked all the right boxes before. She'll do better now, too, at least as long as she's tugging on her side of the rope. She doesn't want to lose to him, and she'll do anything to win. In all my life, they've never cared about me. They only consider me when they're thinking of themselves. Nothing has changed now. Except, I was happy for a second, and now I'm lost and confused again. I'm stretched tight, and all I want to do is snap."

I cleared my throat and stole another bite of sandwich.

"I'm going to emancipate, if I can. I'm sixteen. You're paying me now, but I want to go on independent study at school and work for you full-time. It'll look better in court, I think. I have a full-time job, and I'm attending school still, working for my diploma. Not only that, the full-time income will justify any expenses I would need outside of my parents."

"Will a court allow that?"

Alina took a bite of her sandwich. "I don't know. I've looked into it a little, and that seems the clearest path to emancipation. Maya could testify on my behalf, as could you and Fred. Glacia, too…" Alina trailed off, probably thinking what I thought.

Hopefully Glacia, too.

"It also benefits me," Alina continued, "that both my parents abandoned me for three months." She laughed and shook her head. "If you can call that benefiting me. What a silly thing to think about. Anyway, their neglect, both their histories of abandonment and criminality will help with my emancipation." Alina glanced out the window. "You know, normal sixteen-year-old stuff."

We finished our meal and remained seated.

"Are you okay?" Alina asked.

"I feel like someone buried me alive, or is burying me alive. Shovelful after shovelful of dirt is landing on me, weighing me down more and more, and I can't escape." I looked the kid straight in her eyes and chuckled. "That's why I have you, though, right? You and Maya and Fred, my family. You'll dig me back up."

"So long as my hands don't get dirty. I hate the feel of mud."

"Have you and Fred come up with a plan?" I asked.

"With the Lopez family and their zombie children?"

"Yeah."

"Not yet. He's like working with a giant toddler. He's afraid of everything. Every single idea I come up with, he shoots it down, saying this or that can go wrong. How have you worked with him for so long? Does that man not believe in risk? Also, I thought NFL players were supposed to be tough."

"Don't bring that up with him. He hates that stereotype. 'NFL players have emotions, and they're sensitive, too.' That's what he'll tell you, and that's the tip of the iceberg. He'll dive into an Alina-styled rant."

"Alina-styled rant. What does that mean?"

"One of those rants where you just talk to hear your voice."

"I never talk to hear my voice. I only speak to prove a point, and sometimes my point is too complicated for simple minds like yours to fully understand. So I have to break it down for you to follow, process, and comprehend. Otherwise, I lose you in the dust."

"So no plan?"

"We're working on it."

"Will you keep me posted?"

"Sure thing, boss."

I wanted to assure her that everything would work out, and we would survive the tangled mess we found ourselves in, but I didn't know how it would all turn out. I also hate lying. In the end, assurance would have been nothing but a lie.

Steak and Eggs. Thursday, July 20th. 1931hrs.

Jackson Armstead sat on the cot, his back against the stone wall and his knees hugged into his chest. Across the room, seated on his cot, Ashton echoed Jackson's pose. He also echoed Maria's appearance with eery similarity. Despite having seen Ashton every day for weeks, Jackson couldn't overcome his friend's resemblance to his dead girlfriend.

They stared at each other. One watchful, acting as the warden. One perceptive, acting as the antsy prisoner, hatching a plan to escape.

Armando never issued a shock the night Jackson failed the assignment. Only Ashton delivered punishment, striking him across the skull with the lamp. When Jackson returned to his senses, Ashton was dragging him out of the stranger's house.

Jackson opened his mouth to scream, but only managed a weak grunt. Ashton must have heard him. He dropped Jackson's legs, stepped forward, and kicked him squarely in the ear.

No electrical shock, though. Only blunt force trauma.

"They don't control you," Jackson said. His voice bounced off the stone walls. "You're not a slave to them."

"I am what I am," Ashton said.

"What's that mean?"

"I took part in the accidental murder of their daughter. Do you not see that?"

"Key word, accidental," Jackson said.

"You were drunk. I lied about it. I protected you at the cost of my soul."

"Now, what? You're atoning for that by submitting to these people?"

"I already atoned by confessing my sin to them. They've threatened my family, and I won't be the reason anyone else dies."

Jackson couldn't help but keel over and spill laughter across the room. "What a ridiculous thing to say. You murdered an innocent woman for her—what did you say?—her arms and hair. Well, your legs once belonged to someone else, too. Did you murder the woman who gave them to you?"

"Enough," Ashton said.

"What about me?" Jackson asked.

"They won't kill you."

"How do you know that?"

"You're the last operation. Clara perfected her technique with me, and she will apply all she learned to you. You will become Maria."

"But I'll need new legs, right? New arms? Hair? So, I'll have to murder someone for Clara."

"Yes," Ashton said.

Jackson spit out laughter. "You're a hypocrite. Your entire purpose for Clara is for other people to die. Don't hide behind that sheer veil."

"You will kill the next woman. Not me."

"We could've escaped, but you prevented that. You could have refused to murder, refused to capture me, but you didn't. You knew what this would cause, yet you went about it. Do you remember what you said before you knocked me out with a lamp?"

"I remember."

"I'm too far gone."

"I remember."

"You don't care if people die on your behalf. You care about your reputation. If you escape, no one will accept you in the real world. You're a murderer."

"No one will accept me back because I look like this!" Ashton roared.

"Well, I won't let it get to that point."

"What do you mean?"

"I'm not murdering for Clara."

"They will make you," Ashton said, speaking through a mouth identical to Maria's.

"Na," Jackson said. "They won't."

"What about your family?"

"Clara won't put a finger on my family. Armando threatened activating the shock-chip, but he never did it." Jackson snickered. "We don't have such a thing in our heads. It's all a manipulation. I'm calling their bluff."

"It's not a bluff."

"Believe what you will, that's fine. Sit here and do their bidding like an obedient servant. But don't force me into this nightmare. You can save my life. Maybe I won't die, but they're trying to kill Jackson Armstead all the same. They're going to kill me to revive Maria. You said you don't want anyone else to die on your behalf, well they'll use me to kill other women, and they'll ultimately kill me. So help me live. Help me escape from here."

"They'll go after my family," Ashton said.

"God." Jackson fell into a fit of angry cursing. Tears streamed down his face, dripped off his cosmetically altered chin. "Just help me!" He gasped for a few seconds, regaining control, and he lowered his voice. "Help me, please."

A knock sounded on the door. The heavy thuds reverberated through the room like thunder shaking the world. A second later, a doggy door opened and two trays of food slid through.

"Eat up, Jackson," Armando said. "You'll need all your strength for tomorrow night."

Jackson didn't ask what they had planned tomorrow night. He didn't need to. They intended a cosmetic surgery, or vaginoplasty, or limb transplants.

Hopefully not limb transplants, he thought. That meant he would have to make good on his claim and not kill whoever they threw in front of him. When push came to shove, would he kill to preserve the possibility of excruciating pain or his death? He didn't know, and he didn't want to find out.

Ashton crawled off the bed and shuffled to the door, bent over, and collected the trays. He dragged his left foot when he walked, pulling it along with his right leg. Jackson wondered if the transplant hadn't gone as smoothly as planned.

You're the last operation. Clara perfected her technique with me, and she will apply all she learned to you. You will become Maria.

As Ashton hobbled nearer, Jackson noticed something about his legs. He probably noticed it before, but in his state of absolute shock and confusion, he hadn't registered the difference.

"You no longer have your shin bones sticking from your legs."

Ashton handed Jackson a tray. "Can I sit here?" he motioned to the edge of the bed.

"Sure." Jackson scooted forward and dropped his legs onto the floor.

They sat together at the edge of the bed, eating potatoes, steak, eggs, and toast for dinner—with their hands, though. Clara never provided utensils.

"The broken bones were cosmetic," Ashton said. "Clara attached them and dressed them up to mimic my... Maria's corpse."

Had he almost said my corpse, Jackson thought.

Ashton swallowed a mouthful of food. "She wanted to scare you."

"Well, she succeeded. The entire bit scared me. It still scares me."

"Me, too," Ashton said. "I don't want to die."

You're already dead, Jackson thought. He glanced at his friend—at the undead version of his dead girlfriend. "We're going to escape. Or I'll escape, and I'll come back for you."

"I'm sorry about the other night," Ashton said. He gnawed off a bite of steak and chewed. "I panicked. It's not just... I don't know." He stared across the room at his cot and chewed on another bite. "It's not just fear they'll hurt my family if I disobey. It's fear they're my family now."

"What do you mean?"

Ashton scratched the back of his neck. "I have four new limbs. I have a new face. I have new genitalia—female genitalia. I have breasts. Not even my mother would recognize me. What if I escape with you and return to my family, and once they see what I've become, they shun me? What if they reject me? What if they refuse to acknowledge me? What if they claim their son died... how long has it been?"

"Three years," Jackson said.

"Three years is a long time, and for me to return looking like this. It's too much."

"They would take you back. Imagine if someone you loved went through everything you went through, and they returned three years later. Would you reject them? Would you turn your back on them?"

Ashton shook his head. "No."

"There's no way they do that to you either."

The man who resembled Maria placed his tray on the floor and stared across the room at the stone wall. "Between the operating room and their house, there are eight doors. They're all locked with padlocks.

Each padlock requires a different key. No two are ever the same. Escape isn't a possibility. It's a dream."

"And what are dreams but lights guiding us through the darkness?" Jackson asked, quoting something his mother said to him every night before tucking him into bed.

Jackson finished his meal. Armando was right. He would need his strength—every ounce. If he couldn't escape from this madhouse, he would die trying, for he truly believed death was more fitting than what they had in store for him.

Banana Pancakes.
Friday, July 21st.
1917hrs.

I SPLASHED COLD WATER over my face and stared into the tooth-paste-stained mirror. My face was a window into my heart. It showed the stress I harbored, the exhaustion I courted. Black bags dragged down my eyes, and red splotches mixed into my pallid coloring. My body hadn't drifted away from me, though. Despite the emotional fatigue and pressing nature of the cases, compounded with Daniel Quinn, I still made time for the gym each day—usually late each night. I had to, otherwise I would lose my sanity.

Once shaved, hair styled, and dressed, I walked into the living room.

Gerald strummed on a battered ukulele and hummed a Jack Johnson song. He sounded pleasant, like I could curl onto the couch (if I had a couch to curl onto), close my eyes, and fall into his music.

Bagley felt the same. My puppy, who had grown like a weed over the past couple of weeks, curled into a tight ball and slept beside Gerald. The pair had grown inseparable, and I felt a little jealous. Bagley was my dog, though the animal responded to Gerald more lovingly and with more affection. I guess quality time means more than I give it credit for.

"You look good," Gerald said, resting the ukulele in his lap and petting Bagley's head.

"I have a date," I said.

"Exciting. With Sarah?" He meant Herling, his attorney, my work neighbor.

"No."

"Alina has mentioned you're in love with her aunt. Maya, I think she said her name was? Is it her?"

"Nope."

Why did everyone feel the need to interject in my romantic life? I should have applied for a reality show the way people showed interest in who I dated. My annoyance must have shown.

"I'm sorry," Gerald said. "It's not my business."

"You're fine. My mom likes to play matchmaker, and she thinks it's fun to set me up on blind dates. I try to avoid them altogether. Maybe it's me, but I've never been too good at saying no to my mom."

"I'm not sure anyone is, unless they're teenagers." Gerald chuckled—a rich, chocolaty sound like Santa guffawing.

I smirked. "Well, I should be home before midnight. Definitely before midnight." I hoped before 2200hrs—show up at the restaurant at 2000hrs, make awkward small talk, eat, and go our separate ways.

"Do you know her name?"

"My mom doesn't enjoy telling me those things. I'm an investigator, and she thinks if I know a name, I'll investigate the woman and form an impression before meeting her."

"Would you?"

"Probably."

"Do you know what she looks like?"

"Another secret my mom likes to keep from me."

"How do you find her?"

"I tell the host I'm half the party to a reservation for Watson. They lead me to a table. My blind date mentions Watson when she arrives, and she's led to the same table."

"What if she's... not your type?"

"Like not a man?" I asked, breaking off a genuine smile.

Gerald enjoyed my joke. "I'm sorry about that. I really thought you preferred men."

I smirked and glanced at my watch, not sure how to respond.

"Well," Gerald said, leaning back and strumming the ukulele strings, "anyway... What if they're not your type? I don't mean physically, as in subjectively ugly. What if there's no chemistry? What if she's dull, and you don't share any interests? What if she lacks humor, or she's too crass? You see what I'm saying?"

"Yeah."

I thought of Maya, who attracted me in a physical sense, but also in all the intangible ways I couldn't quite understand. On paper, we seemed like a match made in Hell. When I was with her, though... I saw the world differently, through a brighter lense. I felt lighter and stronger and filled with energy.

"What do you do then?" Gerald asked.

I shrugged. "It's happened a few times. I usually buy her dinner, a few drinks if she wants them, dessert, too. We make the best of the night before we go our separate ways. That's it."

"Well, good luck tonight. I hope she's incredible."

"Thanks, Gerry."

"Gerry?" he asked, running his fingers over the ukelele strings. "You've never called me that before."

"I heard your friends call you that. I figure we're good as friends now, right?"

Gerald paused his strumming. "I'd like to think that."

"Me, too." I smiled with my eyes. "Have you had any more hallucinations?"

"No."

"Violent thoughts?"

He shook his head and picked his instrument up off the floor, strumming it for real now. "I keep going back to the odor that didn't quite smell like anything. It hit me right before I saw the giant chickens."

"It wasn't the smell of books or a dusty library?" I asked.

"Maybe." Gerald played a calming melody for a few seconds. "Sarah thinks we can make a plea deal. I don't have a criminal record, which bodes well for me and any potential time I might spend in jail. If I confess to the crime, the prosecutor will settle."

"What would the punishment be?"

"I volunteer to stay in a mental facility until they deem me no longer dangerous to myself or the public. After that, probation and community service. Also, I would need a place to live where I have professional support during my parole—most likely a halfway house."

I closed my eyes, wanting to help him, but knowing I couldn't. Other than the odor that smelled like nothing (whatever that meant) we had nothing to investigate, not until the library released the security footage of the incident.

"Will you take the plea deal?" I asked.

"Sarah said she would speak with you before advising me."

There it was. Gerald was probing my thoughts. Did I believe we could prove him innocent? Did I believe he was innocent?

"To be honest with you, Gerry, I bowed out of your investigation. I have two other cases, and they're burying me."

"You care if I ask what those cases entail?"

I considered his question for a second, reflexively wanting to deny his curiosity. "The Vampire of Sacramento and—"

Gerald cut me off. "You're investigating the Vampire of Sacramento?"

"I am."

He stopped playing the ukelele. "Living on the streets has put me in contact with a lot of different people. Do you have a description of the suspect? I could help identify him."

A flash of weightlessness overtook me. For a second, I thought I might lose my balance and topple over. It passed, leaving my insides in a state of zero gravity.

"You might recognize him?" I asked.

"I've spent a lot of time on the streets of Sacramento, and I've come across a lot of different individuals. It's dangerous living as a homeless person in this world. We're prey more often than not because society won't miss us. We're easy targets. To survive, we ally together. It can be tribal, which is something I love about the lifestyle. We look out for each other, because we're all we have."

I glanced at my watch. I had to leave soon, otherwise risk being late. "Hold on," I said, disappearing into my bedroom, opening my backpack, removing the manila folder filled with the security footage screenshots. I returned to the living room.

Gerald had resumed his humming, playing Jack Johnson's *Banana Pancakes*.

I interrupted him and handed over the folder.

He placed his ukulele back in his lap and rifled through the images. He paused on one, removed it, and held it in the light.

"There's not a clear shot of his face," I said, "but witnesses have consistently described him the same."

"Does he stink like rotten blood?"

Chase Richards.
Friday, July 21st.
2015hrs.

As I DROVE FROM my house to the restaurant, already fifteen minutes late to the dinner, I dialed Wilson.

"Talk to me, Honey-Bear," he said.

"Chase Richards."

"What?"

"That's his name. That's the vampire's name. Chase Richards."

"You identified him?"

"It's a long story," I said. "Instead of listening to it, use the time to break down his door."

"I need a warrant to break down a door. What do you have for me?"

"I showed an informant the stills from the strip club's security footage. He immediately identified the man as Chase Richards."

"Those images don't provide a clear shot of the face. That's not a legitimate identification. It won't garner a warrant from any judge."

I sighed. "You can trail Richards, right? Find his address, park in front of his house, and trail him until you have cause to pull him over?"

"I'm in it thick, man. I can't risk you being wrong about this. I can't risk accepting an identification from those images. I'm sorry. Even if you're right, it's not enough to tail him."

I thought about Gerald. Did I trust what he said? Did I trust his word? I thought about what Gerald said about homeless people having to look out for each other, like members of a tribe.

"I'm sure about the name, Wilson. Chase Richards. He's our guy. He cut his teeth by preying on the transient population. That's how he started. Look up murders from a year or two ago involving sex workers or the homeless. Those homicides will match the grisly nature of the five-count homicides the other night."

Wilson sighed.

I spoke before he could turn down my circumstantial evidence. "The transient community banded together and fought back against the vampire. They drove him to a new hunting ground. That's when he turned to the clubs and the bars."

"You're sure about this?"

Gerald had seemed sure. So, did I believe him? Did I believe the man who saw giant chickens and attacked them?

"Look up the name. Pay him a visit. Do your job. This doesn't have to be an arrest."

Wilson clicked his tongue. "I don't know. I'm already on a fragile limb in the middle of a windstorm after bringing you into this case. I can't afford a false lead, especially if it results in harassing an innocent man. Besides, even if you're right about this, we can't blindly rush in. What if we spook him by showing our hand too soon? What if, after we leave, he skips town? When we approach him, we arrest him. That's how it has to be."

"Wilson," I said, not sure what to say next. I needed the detective to do his job and knock on Chase's door. I had to solve this case to meet with Quinn and save Glacia.

"What if he leaves the state?" Wilson asked. "We can't follow him outside city limits. The sheriff can't follow him beyond the county. Highway patrol can only follow him to the border. So then what? I can't let him escape. I'd rather gather evidence and then arrest him when he can't run. I'm not allowing him to see me until I can pull the trigger."

I slammed the steering wheel and screamed a profanity. "Wilson, sure, do that. But search for his name in your database. Find an address. Ask a judge for a warrant to kick down his door. If you get one, you'll have your evidence. I guarantee it. If you don't get one, at least you have his information. You can tag him and tail him, wait in the shadows. Hunt the hunter. Do you get it?"

"I get what you're suggesting, yes."

"Then do it."

Without waiting for a response, I hung up the phone, too angry to continue convincing him otherwise. I understood his trepidation and caution about showing our hand too early, but we couldn't fold either.

We had to do something.

Distracted. Friday, July 21st. 2021hrs.

I ENTERED THE RESTAURANT, feeling flustered. The hostess greeted me, and I said Watson, party of two, and she smiled and led me to the table my mom had reserved.

Lauren, the same Lauren from Vincent's wedding, sat at the table. She wore a black tank-top and white denim pants, and shined in the dimly lit restaurant. She also glared at me, impatience and frustration emanating from her eyes.

"You're twenty minutes late," she said.

"I'm sorry." I scrunched my face and stood beside the table. "Do you care if I sit, or should I leave?"

"Would you prefer to leave?"

Yes, I thought. My stomach rumbled, though. "I mean, I am hungry. Why not eat while I'm here?" I tried on a coy smile, but it didn't fit quite right on my face, so I erased it.

"Sure. Sit. Why not?"

I sat across from her. A candle flickered between us, doing little to melt away her iciness. I guess that left me to tackle that task.

"First, I'm sorry for being late. No excuses, other than I'm a complete moron."

"You're preaching to the choir."

"I'm also sorry for this date. My mom thinks that I'm incapable of finding a woman, so she meddles, though I've asked her more times than I care to count to stop."

"Yet, you continue to say yes."

"It's hard to say no to her."

"You're playing the victim?" Lauren asked, her voice sour—completely opposite of the sweet, carefree tone she had exhibited the night of the wedding.

"I'm a victim of wanting to please my mother. Going on a few bad dates is the least I can do for her, after all she's done for me."

"What does that mean?"

"Most of these dates are disasters." I remembered what Gerald questioned about me not having chemistry with the person across the table. "There's no connection."

"Do you try for a connection?"

"I didn't have to try a few weeks ago with you."

Lauren leaned back in her chair and whistled. "You think we had a connection?"

"Do you disagree?"

"Why didn't you call me, then?"

I snickered and shook my head, not sure how to answer that.

"What's so funny?"

"Glacia gave you my number. Why didn't you call me?"

"I gave you my number. Why would I call you when you not so much as sent me a text message?"

"You prefer brutal honesty or a throwaway response?"

Lauren crossed her arms. The date, to my mental calculations, was going tremendously.

I grabbed the perspiring glass of water and drank. "There's a thousand reasons I didn't contact you, and I'm not sure where to begin. You should understand it's better that I didn't call. Didn't Glacia not tell you I'm a wreck?"

"Glacia told me nothing other than you have an old-fashioned charm and you're sweet. She also said you're impossibly attractive."

"She said that about me?" I jutted out my lower lip, feeling quite proud of myself.

"I don't see it," Lauren said, shattering the momentary boost of confidence. "You're an average sort of attractive. Jensen Ackles, you know?"

"I don't know who that is."

"From *Supernatural.*"

I shook my head. "Not much of a movie person."

"It's a television show."

I shrugged.

"Let's begin with the first thing that pops into your head."

"What?" I asked, confused.

"The excuses for why you failed to call. You said there's a thousand reasons, and you don't know where to begin. Start with the first one that comes to your head."

I cracked a knuckle and thought of the best, most simple explanation.

"No thinking. On the count of three, just speak. One. Two. Three."

"I'm scared."

Lauren spread out her arms and grinned at me. "Was that so hard?"

"Extremely."

"Scared of what?"

"That's even more difficult."

"We have to talk about something."

"Whatever happened to amicable silence?"

"Would you rather discuss these sweltering temperatures, or maybe stutter our way around current politics? We can, as you kindly recommended, sit here in amicable silence, eat dinner, and waste the night and each other's time. Or, novel idea, we could give this date an actual shot. If it doesn't work, at least we tried."

My mom had perfected her blind date filtering process. I had gone through a lot of riffraff over the past few years, but Cambria had been a home run. Lauren seemed more than promising, too. Sharp, quirky—when she wasn't angry at me—and intelligent. That scared me more than anything. Could I bring her into the chaotic orbit of my life?

"Did my mom tell you anything about me?" I asked.

"I know nothing of you, other than what I learned at the wedding."

"I'm a private investigator who looks into mysterious, seemingly supernatural cases."

"You mentioned that at the wedding. You're a paranormal investigator, like Tempest Michaels. Now he's impossibly attractive."

"He's technically my boss," I said. "He bought my business and franchised Blue Moon. I operate his Sacramento branch."

"That's super cool. Wait. Wait. I knew your name sounded familiar. You're the dude who caught the Voodoo Killer, right? And you solved the Doppelgänger murders?"

"With a lot of help. Without my team, I'm not much of a detective."

"Hmm." Lauren tapped the edge of her mouth. "I don't think that's true. Without a leader, a team doesn't know where or even how to proceed. You provide direction, which is the most important part of any journey."

"You're like a bag of fortune cookies, aren't you?"

Lauren giggled—the melted slosh drooling off her icy demeanor. "My dad was a philosophy professor at a community college before he retired and moved into a little cabin in Tahoe with my mom. He smokes a pipe and reads books with titles I can't even pronounce. He's also a vegetarian who grows his own food."

"Old-fashioned charm," I said.

Lauren's giggle expanded into bubbling, overflowing laughter. "Don't give yourself too much credit, Mister. I'm not ready to compare you to the likes of my father." She reached for her glass of water and drank. "Anyway, you're a paranormal investigator."

"My cases are often dangerous."

"Like the vampire and golem cases?"

The waiter appeared at the side of our table. "Hello," he said. "I'm Marcus. Can I get you started with drinks and appetizers?"

I glanced at Lauren. "Whatever you want. It's my treat."

She stuck with water and ordered onion rings for an appetizer. After the waiter left, she turned to me. "You don't drink, do you?"

"No, but it wouldn't bother me if you wanted a drink."

"I'm not much of a drinker, especially not by myself." Lauren rested her chin on a fist and smiled at me. The candlelight danced in her eyes. "You're scared if we get too close, something bad will happen to me, and you'll blame yourself."

My voice caught as I thought of Cambria. I nodded. Had I told her about Cambria at the wedding? I couldn't remember, but I might have.

"I'm thirty as of a week ago," Lauren said.

"I'm sorry I missed your birthday."

"I had an awesome party, too. You would've loved it. Clown themed."

"Well, happy late birthday, and that's terrifying."

"I'm actually excited for thirty. Most people fret over it, but I see it as the next chapter in this book titled Lauren Marie Gomes. Maybe it'll prove more exciting than my twenties. Hopefully Lauren learned from her youthful mistakes, too, and she's grown wise. Which is a perfect transition—you're not my protector."

"What do you mean?"

"I've lived my own life, one chock-full of mistakes and experiences. I've hopefully learned from them and matured enough to not make those same mistakes. I've had the training to protect my own feelings. You don't get to decide what's best for me. That's infuriating and degrading. I can look out for myself without you having to worry."

I swallowed a mouthful of embarrassment. "I'm worried about getting myself hurt again. I've learned from my mistakes—mistakes that have cost lives. I don't want to experience that again. That's what I'm afraid of. That's why I never called."

"So, what? You're going to live your life afraid and miserable? You won't take a chance with someone who wants to take a chance with you?"

"Is that what you want?"

"I'm speaking and asking about you in a general sense."

I thought of Daniel Quinn and the danger he constantly posed. I couldn't responsibly get into a relationship with Lauren or any other woman, as long as Quinn remained in the picture.

"How about that weather today? It's hot, huh?" I asked.

"Stop it," Lauren said, chuckling. "Don't dodge the question."

"It's too complicated to dive into."

"You don't think my tiny, woman-sized brain could comprehend it?"

"Not what I said. I don't want to get into it right now. Can we keep things simple?" The conversation had grown intense, and my body had become white hot. While handling the grilling, though, I hadn't thought of the vampire once. Maybe that was a sort of victory—a mental distraction was probably in my best interest. "What do you do for a living?"

"I'm an actress."

I hadn't expected that answer. "Seriously?"

"I'm not Jennifer Lawrence, and you wouldn't find me in any movies. I have a credit for a cable television show, though. I played a dead girl."

"Did you crush the role?"

"I have limited experience with being dead, so I couldn't really draw on my previous experiences for inspiration. I had to wing the acting, but the directors thought I did an okay job. You can almost see my entire face as the forensic team zips up the bag."

"Impressive."

"I'm also in a commercial that never aired, and a music video that got scrapped."

"I'm surprised I've never heard of you."

Lauren chuckled, and her eyes glowed. "I make an okay living, believe it or not, from my performances—mostly through theater. I'm not charting my yacht and filling it with bikini-clad models, but I make enough to pay rent... sometimes, though that mostly comes from my barista job at Starbucks."

"What plays have you performed in?"

"Oomph, let's see." Lauren exhaled and vibrated her lips.

She really looked beautiful. Had I told her that? If not, should I mention it, or had too much time passed?

"*Book of Mormon*, *Wicked*, *The Lion King*... I mean, you name it, I've probably performed some role in it at your local theater."

"Do you sing?" I asked.

"I do. I'm like a circus act. I sing, dance, yodel, and balance on my head."

"Can you juggle?"

"Not with three or more items."

"But you can stand on your head?" I asked.

Lauren shied her eyes and giggled. "No, and I can't ride a horse, though that's also in my resume. But I can yodel. Want to hear it?"

I shook my head. "Not right now."

So the night went. We talked about our lives, our interests, our hobbies, we talked about nothing and everything all at once. It was like being at the wedding again, feeling that ease of conversation and the simplicity of just being with Lauren. Everything felt comfortable, as all the right edges fit together seamlessly.

The restaurant closed at 2300hrs. We stayed until they kicked us out, and then we walked around Old Town Sacramento. We found a place to sit that overlooked the river, and we watched moonlight dance on the rippling water.

After midnight, I walked her to her car.

"You'll call me tomorrow?" Lauren asked.

"I'll call you tomorrow," I said.

"You promise, because I had a lot of fun with you at the wedding, and I had a great time tonight. I would really enjoy a call."

"I promise."

Lauren leaned forward and kissed my cheek. Her lips were warm, but my skin quickly grew cold as she pulled away, as if it had lost all life in her absence.

"Goodnight, August Watson."

"Goodnight, Lauren Gomes."

The Vampire. Saturday, July 22nd. O543hrs.

Chase Richards sat on a torn cloth chair and watched the initial hint of the sunrise from his patio. The dark sky lightened to a neon purple, and the pale moon and glimmering stars dimmed against the ascending sunlight.

He held a goblet filled with blood—the last of the blood he had salvaged from the disastrous hunt a few nights ago. Mixed with animal plasma, Chase might stretch his intake another two days, at most.

He had to hunt again, though it was far too soon after his last attack. Chase preferred a cooldown period, if possible.

Earlier in his murderous career, when he had preyed on the homeless population and sex workers, he attacked with no forethought, drinking as much of their blood as he desired.

When he finished quenching his appetite, he abandoned them, wasting so much as their blood soaked into the asphalt, absorbed into the dirt, rotted beneath the treacherous sun.

In his recklessness, his crimes had nearly caught up to him.

His victims learned to recognize him—not his face; Chase always covered his face. They recognized his lean, writhe physique, and his wild stench. They reported what little they suspected to the police. Law enforcement cared little for the blisters of society, and they mostly ignored the pleas for help.

Still, Chase had outgrown his hunting grounds. He abandoned them, switching his territory to the clubs and bars. They also grew a familiarity with Chase; they developed an instinctual sense of the predator who hunted them.

Now Chase had migrated his hunting path into the residential neighborhoods, and it had proven disastrous. A learning curve always existed, of course, but three nights after the kill, his supply waned.

Without the fresh blood, his body would turn against him. His heart would shrivel and shrink, and it would produce blood poisonous to him.

It would slowly and excruciatingly kill him.

The media had dubbed Chase the Vampire of Sacramento. Their label wasn't too far from the truth. Chase suffered an extreme and violent allergy to sunlight. The ultraviolet rays poisoned his body. The sunlight eroded and ulcered his skin, scarred his corneas, discolored his teeth, burned away some of his facial features.

Chase's parents always dressed him in long sleeves when he was a child. He wore hoodies and hats, and when outside, they kept him under an umbrella at all times.

The weight of Gunther's Disease ultimately led to his parents divorcing. He remained with his mother, and she sought comfort through sleep, as if she could dream herself into another life.

In his father's complete absence, Chase, as a child, dealt with the disease alone. It broke him, shattered his mind.

He spent most of his teenage years in a mental health facility. That's where he first learned about the benefits of animal blood.

One patient had a therapy dog. Chase stole the animal, brought it back to his room—only for comfort, at first. Then a wild impulse (a stray thought) instructed him to consume the blood of the animal, to supplement his toxic blood for the pure blood.

It had worked, too. At least for a time. He felt more energetic, more positive, and stronger. At least until he didn't.

Chase needed more blood. His body demanded it. To satisfy his urges, Chase set traps outside his window to catch birds. He would drain them of their blood, satiating his appetite, keeping himself alive and well.

So, the media had it right. Chase was a man who required fresh blood to live; a man whose skin scarred whenever sunlight touched his body.

"A stake through my heart would kill him," Chase said, chuckling as he sipped the thick concoction. He knew the means by which to kill a vampire—a stake through the heart, decapitation, getting burned alive. They would all result in his death, too.

Did that make him a vampire?

"Yes."

And to continue living, he would have to collect more blood. He couldn't allow his carnal, primal instincts to take over. Not again. He had to control the beast within him.

The sky was no longer a deep purple, but bursting with orange and pink and blue.

Chase stood from his chair and shuffled into the house—his mom's house. The woman who never woke.

Dark red painted the walls of the house. Cow and horse and pig blood covered every square inch, every piece of furniture and countertop. Chase had smeared it across the mirrors.

"I don't have a reflection, either." He cackled.

Blood lathered the floor and dyed the bedsheets.

Chase snuck into his mother's room. She, as always, slept in her bed. Her hair had grayed and frizzed, and the lack of sunlight had paled her skin—not that she cared. She only cared to sleep.

He leaned over and kissed her cold cheek before ambling into his bedroom. Chase crawled into bed.

"I should buy myself a coffin to sleep in," he said to the blood-drenched emptiness.

Instead of a coffin, he had blackout curtains draped over his windows, and a thick canopy over his bed. His room was dark as a crypt.

He would sleep until the sun set and the moon stood sentinel in the sky with its army of stars. Under their watch, Chase would hunt again.

The Plan.
Saturday, July 22nd. 1249hrs.

WANDA STOOD AT THE front door with her purse in hand, and she looked back at Maya with an excited grin. The woman had gained a few healthy pounds, and when she turned her head, the sun caught her through the entry windows. She looked beautiful.

Young again, Maya thought.

Not beautiful because of her youthful appearance, though. Wanda had a short-lived window of prime beauty. Hard drugs and hard living at a young age had quickly aged her.

Standing in the crossing light at the front door, Wanda appeared young in the manner of innocence. She had the carefree demeanor of a teenage girl about to leave the house and grab ice cream with her friends.

"Why are you looking at me like that?" Wanda asked.

"You look incredible." Maya smiled at her older sister, proud of her. "I really enjoy seeing you so happy."

"I enjoy feeling this happy. It's a welcome change to how I usually feel, which is crummy."

"You'll be okay tonight?" Maya asked.

Wanda frowned, but she nodded her head. "I think so. You said she's doing okay, right?"

"She's doing okay, I guess. She would really like to see you."

"Do you think so?"

"That's what she told me."

Wanda coughed out a gruff laugh.

"What are you going to do?" Maya asked.

"I think we're going to watch a movie, like we used to do before everything turned sour with us. Mom used to love *The Princess Bride*. I always pretended to hate it just to make her mad, but I think I remember liking it. It's been so long."

"Is that what you're going to watch?"

Wanda bit her lip. "Do you think she'll like that? Should we watch something else?"

"She'll love it," Maya said, crossing her arms and shedding a slight smirk.

"You think it's okay I stay the night there?"

"Do you think it's okay?"

Wanda readjusted her purse from one shoulder to the other, and she switched her stance, bearing her weight on her right leg rather than her left. "I'm sure she'll bite into me." Wanda scraped out a reluctant laugh. "You know, share a few of her unwanted opinions about my weight or my decisions. That's who she is, I guess, and she's not changing now."

It was a sentiment Maya had crammed into Wanda's head since she moved into the house. She's your mom. She's old and sick, and she's slowly losing her mind, but she's your mom. You can't change her. You can only love her.

"That's right," Maya said.

"How bad is it? Will she know who I am?"

Maya bit her cheeks, blinked hard, and nodded. "She'll know, at the very least, who you were. Her little girl. She might bring up some stuff from middle school and high school, stuff you don't remember, but topics her failing mind somehow conjured. There's no need to correct her. It will confuse her more. I think the movie is a great idea, though. I really do."

"And she won't get scared in the morning when she sees me at her house? She'll remember me?"

Maya considered the question, not wanting to lie to Wanda. "She's not that bad yet. She'll remember, and she'll be glad you're there. I've talked to her, and she's beyond excited to see you." Maya blinked fast, pushing back tears.

It was difficult to watch her mother fade away, essentially to lose herself while living. It was terrifying to think dementia was hereditary. Maya had always relied on her mind and intelligence. It had defined her. What if she lost that one day?

Wanda blew Maya a kiss. "See you tomorrow morning," she said, walking out the front door.

Alina had disappeared to work hours ago. Something about saving someone from becoming a golem—Maya hadn't paid too much attention to her niece, as she poured her attention into the vampire case. A write-up on the Vampire of Sacramento could launch her journalistic career, vault her beyond the *Here & Now* and into something more credible where she could make a difference.

"Once I save Jackson," Alina said, milk spilling down her chin as she scarfed down a bowl of cereal, "I'll have to wade through the police rigamarole. After that, I'm heading to August's house. He bought something for my room. I'm kicking out Gerry for the night. August isn't sneaky, and he sucks at surprises. I know he bought me a television as a signing bonus, and I'm watching horror movies all night long. Zombie movies. *28 Days Later. Shaun of the Dead.* And my personal favorite, *Train to Busan*. Ah! But there's *Night of the Living Dead. Dawn of the Dead. Zombieland.*"

"Enough," Maya said, dropping her spoon in the empty bowl. It clattered loud enough to silence Alina momentarily. "Zombie movies suck. They're the worst flavor of horror movies."

"Take that back," Alina said, pointing her spoon at Maya—milk dripped from the end onto the tabletop.

"Name a worse subgenre. I dare you to."

"Found footage."

Maya inhaled her lips and shook her head back and forth. "Zombie is worse."

"Torture porn."

Maya bit her lip, not able to refute that answer.

"Gore for the sake of gore sucks," Alina said, a victorious sneer stapled across her face. She went in for another mouthful of Cheerios. "Gore isn't creative, nor is it symbolic. It's not anything but lazy, and it sucks. Zombies at least have a rich history and deep metaphorical nuance. They can symbolize so many aspects of society, and they're always unique in the hands of a strong storyteller."

"You're annoying." Maya stood and walked into the kitchen, setting her bowl in the sink.

"You're mad because I'm right."

It was true, but she wasn't mad when Alina left the house, leaving Maya alone. Blessedly alone.

Maya poured another cup of coffee, grabbed her laptop, and snuggled onto the couch with a cozy blanket. "What heat wave?" she asked, settling into her spot.

She shifted all her attention to the Vampire of Sacramento. Alina had shared his name. Chase Richards. Maya typed it into Google, filtering the results through location. *Chase Richards Sacramento.* He didn't have any social media platforms.

Throughout her life, she had dated a variety of men who worked in a variety of professions, and she was naturally inquisitive. Maya never knew what skill would come in handy while investigating a particular story to write, so she absorbed as much knowledge from them as possible. With the help of a savvy ex-boyfriend from a few years back, Maya had learned how to access police databases through a backdoor. She typed in Chase Richards' name into their search engine.

Nothing.

"Great," she said, speaking to the empty room.

Maya searched his name against property records, against employment records. As she dug, her phone rang.

"Hello," she answered.

"Hi," Evan said, his voice sporting the smile he always wore. "You busy?"

"Always."

"I had a quick break and couldn't stop thinking about you."

"Oh, yeah?"

"Yeah."

"In the obsessive serial killer way?"

"More of you being scantily dressed."

"Bikini?"

"Not at work," Evan said, half-laughing.

"You brought it up," Maya said.

"How's your morning?"

"Frustrating. We learned the Vampire of Sacramento's name—and no, I can't share it with you; I shouldn't have shared that we learned his name—but I can't find him anywhere. It's almost like he's a ghost."

"He's a vampire," Evan said.

"Hilarious. I've searched criminal records, property records, educational records, employment databases."

"Do you have a degree in background checks?"

"Something like that," Maya said.

"I'm surprised you can't get into his medical records." Evan chuckled.

A wave of furious energy poured into Maya. She sat up, throwing her blanket off her shoulders and setting her coffee on the end table. "What did you say?"

"I'm surprised that after everything else you checked, you can't look into his medical records." Evan spoke slowly, as if confused by what he was saying.

"You're a sexy genius, my little cheetah."

"Little cheetah? What's that mean? Are you okay?"

"Whatever image you had of me in your head, keep it there—better yet, relay it to me through message. Let's turn that fantasy into a reality. You earned it."

"Is the cheetah comment about the other night? We talked about that, and—"

"Don't forget to text me the look." Maya hung up the phone and returned to her computer. Her hands trembled from excitement, and she mistyped about eighteen times before hacking into medical records.

She found something extremely interesting.

"Hello," August answered.

"Hey, Big Boy. What are you up to?"

"Walking through this plan with Alina and Fred. What's up?"

"Playing Maya the Vampire Hunter, starring Maya Mylene Moore, and she's a bad bi—"

"Maya, you're doing that thing where you make no sense at all. What happened?"

"I found something."

August responded by saying nothing.

"We have an honest to God vampire hunting in our city."

"What do you mean?" August asked.

"Vampires are allergic to sunlight, right? Well, Mr. Chase Richards is also allergic to sunlight. I hacked into his medical records. Don't ask me how or if it's legal, because I'm pretty sure it's not, but you can ask Fred if his little tech-savvy butt could do something like that? He'll say no, which makes him disposable to you. Me, though? I'm indispensable, and you don't even pay me."

"I don't pay Fred, either."

"You talking about me?" Fred's voice boomed through the phone's receiver.

"Maya, you learned of private information through illegal means?" August asked, his tone turning self-righteous. "We can't use that against him because of one important fact. You learned it through illegal means."

"No one will have to know."

"Maya."

"Listen, buckeroo, I can help you catch this vampire. Do you want my help or not? You can at least do yourself the favor of hearing me out."

Again, he responded with that fun trait where he says absolutely nothing.

"He's allergic to the sun. The condition is called Gunther's Disease, or more medically appropriate and annoying to say, congenital erythropoietic porphyria. I probably butchered the enunciation, but that's beside the point. Richards spent time in a cuckoo home."

"Mental facility?" August asked.

"Tomato, tomato. Anyway, his mom signed him into Arkham Asylum when he was underage. To do so, she had to provide a contact number and an address in case they needed to reach her."

Once more, August said nothing. Maya thought he might show a little more excitement about the development in his case.

"Did you hear me?" she asked.

"I heard you."

"Why aren't you jumping up and down and screaming how much you love me, and how amazing I am, and that I'm the smartest, sexiest woman you've ever had the pleasure of knowing?"

"I already have his address, and through legal means."

"Alina never told me that!" Maya growled. "Alina! Am I on speakerphone? Alina, can you hear me? I could have saved so much time."

"Why do you need his address?" August asked, his voice level and probing.

"Uh, to share with you." Maya was terrible at lying, and that one didn't come out clean.

"You're not planning to visit him, are you?"

"The police already have his address?" Maya scratched her head, wondering why she hadn't found his address when she used the police database to search his name. "How?"

"We have a picture of his license plate."

Maya clicked her tongue and shook her head, disappointed in her failure. How had she not thought to hack into the DMV?

"Well, I guess I am disposable, aren't I? Are they on their way to arrest him?"

"Wilson hasn't decided what to do."

"What do you mean? What other option is there? Let the vampire roam around freely and kill again?"

"There's no direct evidence Richards is our killer," August said.

"Oh, come on. You're rolling with that? Please. He literally has a vampire disease."

"Circumstantial proof won't hold up in court. We need concrete evidence. Besides, the informant who shared Richards' name isn't the most reliable witness. Wilson isn't likely to get a warrant based on the testimony we have. He doesn't want to knock either, not out of the blue. He doesn't want to tip Richards that we know who he is. So Ted's in a precarious situation."

"Hmm."

"Maya," August said. "I don't like when you don't say words. You're speaking nonstop, and silence means you're thinking. You don't need to be thinking right now."

"They have someone at his house?"

"Maya."

"Do they?"

August sighed. "I believe so."

"You believe so, or you know so?"

"Maya, what are you thinking?"

"August, it's none of your business. Does Wilson have a unit outside of the house?"

"Wilson said he would get someone to tail Richards. If they bust him in the act, that's all they need for a legitimate arrest."

"That's what I figured," Maya said. "I'll call you later. Good luck with the golem."

Sidelined. Saturday, July 22nd. 1443hrs.

I SAT ALONE IN the eerily quiet office, feeling useless, and I couldn't have hated anything more.

I poured a cup of coffee, chugged the lukewarm, bitter elixir, and poured another. I paced the small office, murmuring to myself, wondering how the trajectories of my cases intersected here, at a place where I could do nothing but sit back and watch. It tore my mind apart.

Glacia's life, Vincent's life, all the lives of the escaped prisoners and captured victims hinged on this moment, and I had to sit on the sidelines, cheering for my team to succeed.

Alina and Fred had deployed to Armando's house. They planned to stumble into the basement and find Jackson—if that's where the Lopez's held him. We had no direct proof, only our suspicions, desperation, and a lot of hope. If they went to Armando's, learned he had nothing to do with the golems, then we fell to square one with nothing to build on.

Time would expire.

I pressed my palms against my face and exhaled.

The Vampire of Sacramento had also fallen out of my control. Sacramento Police Department had a name, and the name had produced an address. I no longer had any voice in their investigation.

Did that count as solving it before the deadline Quinn had imposed upon me? Or did an arrest need to occur for Quinn to consider the case solved? I didn't know, and there was nothing I could do but wait.

Wait.

Do nothing.

Sit back.

My heart hammered, antsy to move, to act, to perform. My mind revved, but it remained parked. Still. Planted.

I sat down at my desk and turned on the computer, opened the web browser, stared at the Google homepage. I stood again, paced the office, poured myself a cup of coffee, slammed my open palm against the wall and shoved my fist into my mouth to stifle a scream.

I exhaled and removed my phone. I stared at the screen, waiting for Alina or Fred or Maya or Wilson or someone, anyone, to call and ease my mind. A wild thought burst into my head—something that might help settle me.

I scrolled through my phone and dialed her number.

To my surprise, Lauren answered. "You called," she said.

Yeah, I thought, but didn't say. I said nothing at all.

"August, you there? Is this a butt-dial? If this is a butt-dial—"

"It's not a butt-dial," I said, though quietly.

"Booty call?" Lauren asked.

"What?"

"It's like a butt-dial, but more fun... sometimes. Actually, butt-dials might be better."

Again, I remained silent, standing and sweating in the middle of my office.

"August, are you okay?"

"No," I said.

Her voice softened. "What's wrong?"

I swallowed, and tears stung my eyes, but I answered with the first thought that entered my head. "I'm so scared. My team... I can't do anything to help, and I just... I don't know what to do."

Lauren hesitated for a few seconds. "You're the leader, remember? You led your team to whatever moment you're now in. Trust yourself and your work. Trust that you prepared them for this moment. Trust them to execute and succeed."

I calmed my breathing. My mind cleared. The root of my fears appeared—Cambria Parker. With the dream demon case, I had left her alone, and she had died. I was terrified something might happen to Fred and Alina.

"Thank you," I said.

"Will you call me later about what happened?"

"Yeah," I said, nodding my head.

"Cool."

We disconnected, and I exhaled, feeling loads lighter. I returned to my desk and stared out the window, nervous still, but no longer frantic. There, I held my phone, and I waited.

The Lion's Den. Saturday, July 22nd. 1457hrs.

MAYA PARKED AT THE curb at the end of the uneven driveway. She glanced at her phone and checked the address, compared it to the one painted white on the sidewalk and stenciled on the mailbox. They matched. She licked her lips and wiped her sweaty palms against her jeans.

Showtime, she thought.

Maya surveyed the street, searching for the undercover police tail. She saw a litany of vehicles parked along the street's curb, but she didn't see an officer.

"That's the point, though," she said. "Remain invisible."

She shot August a quick text message. *Tail is good. Kudos to Wilson.* An instinctual feeling, one based on self-preservation more than anything, convinced her to share her location with August, as well.

Detective Wilson most likely shared the vampire's address with August, but in case he hadn't, for some procedural reason, Maya would feel safer knowing August had her location.

She typed in the address and sent that as well.

She also typed a third message, for good measure. *Make sure you let Wilson know I'm here, in case his tail has fallen asleep and missed my grand entrance.*

Maya reached into the backseat and grabbed her handy-dandy stun gun. Did electric shocks deter vampires?

Maya snickered. "I'll find out."

She glanced around the neighborhood one more time. It had a pale-gray street cutting through the center. An empty lot covered in dead weeds sat beside Richards' house—which was also a mess of weeds and neglect. His fence leaned at a forty-five degree angle, and the weeds grew two, three feet high. They encroached on his house, a single-story home with boarded windows.

A desperate urge to turn on her car, drive home, and pour a glass of wine overcame Maya.

Why interfere with the police investigation? They had a plan, right? August had a plan, right? Maya trusted they did, but she didn't trust the expediency of their plan.

What if Chase slipped away from them and killed someone else?

Her interference had a more foundational impact than timing, though. A serial exposé could skyrocket her journalist career. If she not only broke the story, but exposed the serial killer, she could leapfrog her way out of *Here & Now*. Serial killers didn't fall in just anyone's lap, especially for a journalist. This was a career-defining moment, and she wouldn't allow the opportunity to slip away.

Maya stepped out of the car and marched up the driveway. She paused beside a white, dust-covered van parked in front of the garage. She cupped her hands over the window and peered inside. Nothing out of the ordinary, at least from her cursory inspection. She tried the door handle. It was locked.

Maya gave up on the van and continued to the front door, where she activated the voice recorder on her phone. She rang the doorbell and followed that up with a quick succession of knocks.

Fifteen seconds ticked away.

Thirty.

Maya rang the doorbell again. Knocked again. "Hello! Is someone home? My car ran out of gas." She leaned to the boarded entry window and banged on the plywood. "Hello!"

Maya predicted the vampire might sleep during the day, especially with his sun allergy. She got the address through the information Richards' mom shared with the mental health facility. Even if the vampire slept, his mother would open the door.

Right?

The idea that Chase no longer lived with his mother also crossed her mind. Maya preferred that scenario. She could speak with Mrs. Richards about her son, and learn about the vampire through indirect means. However, Maya had a deep-rooted suspicion Chase lived with his mother still.

If his mother still lives at all, Maya thought, and a sharp chill cut down her spine.

She rang the bell three more times. "I see your van in the driveway! I know you're home!" Maya pounded on the weathered door with her fist. She stepped off the patio, into the overgrown flowerbed, and peeked through the spaces in the boarded windows. "Hello!"

"I'm coming!" A man's voice called from the bowels of the house.

Maya's breath caught in her throat, and her heart dropped into her pelvis. For a moment, she stood frozen. She shook off her shock, refocused, and climbed onto the patio.

An eternity later, or so it seemed, the door split open, revealing nothing but darkness and the silhouette of the vampire.

"Who are you?" he asked, his voice predatory.

Maya licked her lips. "Mylene," she said, providing her middle name.

"Do I know you?"

Maya couldn't see him, but she could smell him through the open door—like the assault of a rotted corpse when opening a coffin after years buried beneath the ground.

She shoved her hand into her pocket and touched her phone as reassurance.

"Do I know you?" he asked again, perturbed by her presence.

"I'm lost." She faked a laugh. "My phone isn't working. It's been on the fritz for a while, but I think it finally went out. Do you mind if I use your phone to make a call? I'm sorry if I'm intruding, but I could use your help." Maya held her breath.

The man behind the door exhaled. The door swung fully open.

Maya stepped inside the lion's den.

How Does She Die? Saturday, July 22nd. 1458hrs.

Clara escorted Jackson from his cell to the operating room—a square space equal in size to half a tennis court. Four doors stood around the room, one on each wall, teasing escape. He could eliminate the door he had entered through to the operating room, but Jackson didn't know which of the remaining three led to sweet, elusive freedom.

The metallic slab table must have come equipped with wheels. Someone had shoved it to the edge of the expansive room. In its place, in the center of the floor, spotlighted by the overhead surgical light, kneeled a young woman.

She had wide, dark eyes that pleaded and begged him to help her. A gag filled her mouth. Sweat beaded her forehead, gripping tendrils of wet, black hair. She was naked.

A wave of sensations and feeling crashed into Jackson when he saw her. First lust for the woman's body, followed by guilt—guilt that his body noticed and responded to the helpless, naked woman before him. Dread came next, as the pieces puzzled together. His time arrived. He would have to murder her. Anger arrived, hot and furious and untamed.

Clara hadn't bothered to drug Jackson, though had bound his hands behind his back. She also held the four-button remote. The chip in Jackson's skull didn't frighten him, though. He didn't believe it existed, but that Clara had fabricated the bluff as a control tactic.

Jackson sidestepped, turning his body so the naked, terrified woman kneeled to his left, and Clara stood to his right. He faced his captor, fire blazing in his eyes.

"I won't do it," he said.

Clara smirked at him, amused. She said nothing, though she raised the hand holding the remote face high, and she hovered her thumb over the bottom-most button.

"Do it," Jackson said. "Prove it. Fry my brain. I'd rather that than what you have planned for me."

Clara's arrogant sneer twitched and wavered, and her eyes narrowed, but only for a split second. She tossed back her head and cackled at the ceiling. Her screeching laughter pierced Jackson's ears, cut into his head like a serrated saw. After a few exaggerated guffaws, she leveled her steely eyes on her prisoner and inhaled.

"Jackson," she said, stepping away from him, circling the kneeling woman, walking toward a stand hosting a variety of surgical instruments. Clara, like a cartoonish villain, lifted a tool resembling pliers. She inspected it for a second, but ultimately returned it to the station, along with the remote. She clapped her hands together and faced her prisoners. "What do you think I have planned for you?"

"You'll have me..." he trailed off, not wanting to frighten the captured woman more than she already appeared.

"Have you what?"

"You'll turn me into Maria. I'm not Maria. Ashton isn't Maria. Don't you see? No one is Maria but Maria, and she's gone. You can't bring her back from the dead. You can't recreate her. "

Clara raised her chin and stared down her nose at Jackson, but she said not a word.

Jackson's heart assaulted his chest, and his internal heat rose to such an extreme temperature, it burned his cheeks. He glanced at the woman kneeling before him.

She didn't shed tears, but she breathed too fast, on the verge of hyperventilating.

"You can't make me do anything," Jackson said. "I'm not your daughter, and I'll die before you turn me into her. Before you use me to hurt anyone."

Clara ambled to the door nearest to her—it stood opposite from where Jackson had entered the operating room. That narrowed his odds of escape to two possibilities: the door to his left or right. Clara fiddled with her keyring, unlocked the door, and opened it.

Much like Jackson's cell occupied a space at the end of a hallway, Clara opened to a hall with another door at the end. She drifted over, opened it, and stepped aside.

Maria Lopez, or rather, a poor recreation of Maria Lopez, shuffled from the room. Clara handed the creature her keys and muttered a few unheard words. The Maria golem trundled into the operating room, took a left (Jackson's right) and opened the door standing on that wall.

Jackson glanced to the remaining door left of him. *My escape*, he thought. *That's the way to freedom.*

A handful of seconds passed, and the Maria golem returned with a cruder rendition of Maria. The newer Maria pushed the surgical table nearer to the kneeling woman. The older version of Maria kicked the young woman in the back, knocking her flat on her face. She (*he*, Jackson thought; *it's Timothy or Connor*) grabbed the imprisoned woman by her hair and pulled, lifting her head and exposing her throat.

Clara secured a scalpel and went down on one knee. She rubbed the flat of the blade against the prisoner's smooth, sweaty face. At the end of her sweep, she twisted the knife, drawing a line of blood.

The prisoner hissed.

Clara turned to Jackson. "She will die today, no matter what. Her arms will become your arms no matter what. That's not a question for consideration."

Jackson remained stiff and silent. His eyes snuck glances at the closed fourth door.

Clara stood and stepped toward Jackson. "If you refuse to kill her, I'll have one of my daughters do the honors." She meant one of her Maria creations. "They have an ear for screaming, and an appetite for torture. They'll drag out her death. They'll make it painful and excruciatingly long. This young woman will beg for us to kill her. She'll look at you with disgust, knowing you could've killed her quickly and mercifully, yet you chose for her to endure so much unnecessary pain because you shouldered a fruitless crusade."

Jackson blinked hard, forcing back his tears of terror.

"Kill her, Jackson, and make it quick, otherwise she'll know unimaginable pain. Either way, she dies today, and you wear her arms tomorrow."

Footsteps echoed in the hallway behind him. Instinctively, Jackson glanced over his shoulder. Ashton, the purest of the three Maria creations, approached.

"Will you let me use the scalpel?" Jackson asked. He had no intention of killing the nameless woman with the surgical instrument, but of attacking Clara as soon as his fingers touched it.

"No weapons."

"How do I kill her quickly without a weapon?"

"Know your fists will kill her far sooner than our methods."

Jackson closed his eyes, squeezed them shut, forcing back the stinging tears. After a second, he opened his eyes. "You tied my hands behind my back. I can't use my fists."

"Maria," Clara said, nodding at Ashton. "Unbind him."

Ashton's cold, dead fingers—fingers belonging to a random woman he had murdered—brushed Jackson's skin as he worked the rope. When the restraint dropped to the floor, Ashton circled around and stood beside the surgical table.

Jackson's hands dangled at his hips, numb and heavy. How would he lift them to throw a punch, let alone enough strikes to kill someone?

He looked at the woman who lay on her stomach. A Maria pressed a knee into her back, held her face high off the ground.

I could step on her, Jackson thought, disgusted with himself. *I could stomp on her and end it fast.*

The young man saw no other way, nothing as fast and efficient. He moved toward her, paused, wavered, turned his head, and lost his breakfast across the stone floor.

School Project. Saturday, July 22nd. 1459hrs.

"In short," Alina said, hissing at Fred, "I do the talking. We clear?"

"He won't believe it." Fred glanced down the road, staring at their Uber as it drove away. "Why would a sixteen-year-old girl carry a conversation instead of her father? That makes little to no sense."

"Your face makes little to no sense," Alina said. She stood on the sidewalk at the end of Armando's driveway, looking at his house. "Now stop arguing with me and worry about what you're going to do if a golem attacks us."

"August assured us there aren't any such things as golems. I'm not worried about it."

Alina turned to the giant, occasionally spooked by his shadow. "What if golems existed? What if Clara controls a small army of slave golems? Imagine it: we enter the home, and we're bombarded by a horde of humans made from other humans. Two heads. Six arms. Faces on their bellies."

"Stop it."

"They overwhelm us. Image that. They're piling onto us so heavy and thick, we can't breathe—we can only smell the rotting of the corpses they used to form the monsters."

"Stop." Fred covered his ears and closed his eyes. "How did I get sucked into doing this?"

While Fred distracted himself, Alina bolted to the front door and rang the doorbell three times in quick succession. She exhaled and backed away a step, glancing over her shoulder.

Fred hurried to her. As he approached, the front door opened, hooking Alina's attention forward.

Armando Lopez stood framed in the center with a confused look on his face. "Hello. Can I help you?"

"Hi," Fred and Alina said in harmony.

Alina glared at the bearish man, but he didn't hesitate to seize control of the conversation. "We're hoping to speak with Armando Lopez."

"That's me."

"This is my daughter, Alina." Fred placed a giant hand on Alina's small shoulder.

Alina etched a big, fake grin over her face, though she mostly felt annoyance toward Fred. "Hi."

"She's about to start her junior year of high school. She had a little summer assignment for her AP History class."

That was the exact reason Alina wished Fred would shut his oversized mouth—he sucked at creating a false narrative. Too many unnecessary details, not enough persuading truths. The best lies come wrapped in beautiful, bow-topped truths.

Alina butted into the conversation, hoping to take over before Fred led them to a point of no return. "Do you mind if I ask you a few questions, Mr. Lopez?"

"How could I possibly help with an AP History assignment?" Mr. Lopez asked.

Alina bit her tongue to prevent herself from verbally ripping Fred into pieces.

In her second of hesitation, the oaf answered. "The class is creating a memorial for all the students who died before they could graduate."

That makes no sense, Alina thought. How would that relate to AP History? Why even say that? He could have said an extracurricular newspaper class wanted to remember previous students. Simple. Believable. Not AP History, which had nothing to do with anything.

"I'm not sure I understand the assignment?" Armando asked. "Why would you need to ask me questions for a memorial?"

"We're working with the school newspaper," Alina said. "Each remembered person will have a Remembrance Page—that's what we're calling it. The school paper will publish the Remembrance Page, and we'll create a summarized version to place beside the student's name on the memorial wall." Alina's skin crawled. She felt dirty to use Maria, Armando's dead daughter, as an excuse to enter his home. Why had Fred created such a horrendous story?

"I see," Armando said, scratching his neck. He cleared his throat and glanced behind him, into the darkness of his home. After a second, he turned back to Alina and Fred. "Of course. Please, come in." He stepped aside and gestured for them to enter the house.

Wrong Address. Saturday, July 22nd. 1501hrs.

"Round Table Pizza," Detective Wilson answered my call. "We're currently out of pepperoni, pineapple, and mushrooms. How can I help you?"

I shoved his playfulness aside, not feeling too light-hearted with Maya playing the vigilante. "Do you have someone stationed outside Chase's house?"

"That's an affirmative, Captain."

"Are you the person stationed outside of Chase's house?"

"Bingo was his name-o. How did you know?"

"You only get this chipper when you're excited, and you're only excited when there's a possibility of violence." Had Maya entered the house already? Had Wilson observed her go into the Lion's Den? Was that what had him dancing on Cloud-9? "You plan on inflicting violence."

"I'm going to rip his head off his shoulders and bounce it off the sidewalk like a basketball."

"So you saw Maya, then?"

"Who?"

Had Wilson and Maya ever met? I wasn't sure, but I didn't think so. "A thirty-year-old woman."

"Aggressively attractive?"

I hesitated, slightly embarrassed to admit it, though I wasn't sure why. Maybe I didn't enjoy degrading Maya to a physical caricature with Wilson. Either way, I paused for a beat before saying, "Yes."

"Unfortunately, the only woman I've seen looks like a toe left in the water for too long—pale and wrinkly. My guess, she's about thirty, though."

I scratched the back of my neck and cracked a knuckle. How had Wilson missed Maya? "You're sure you haven't seen her?" I asked. "Average height and weight." I cringed to describe Maya as average. She was anything but. "Afro."

"It's in my nature to never miss an attractive woman, especially an attractive woman with any kind of afro. I would've seen her and offered to help her in any way possible."

Why hadn't Wilson noticed Maya? I stared at the popcorn ceiling in my office, listening to my heart attempt to crash through my skull.

"August, you there?" Wilson asked.

"I'm thinking," I said.

"Don't think too hard. I'd hate for you to get a hernia."

Maya had shared her location with me. I tapped the speakerphone icon, scrolled to Maya's text messages, and found the address she had sent me. I read it to Wilson.

"What's that?" he asked.

"That's where you're at, right?"

"That's across town from where I'm at. Fifteen minutes away from me. Why?"

My heart thundered between my ears, deafening me, driving away all coherent thought beyond one repeating question. Who had the wrong address, Maya or Wilson? Who had the wrong address?

"I have to go," I said.

"Everything okay?"

"I'm going to text you that address, and you need to send a unit there."

No hesitations, no questions. Wilson said, "Will do, buckaroo." He had his faults, but he was reliable and there when I, or anyone—even those who despised him and the badge and all it stood for—needed him. That counted for something.

I hung up the phone, copy-pasted the location into a message, and sent it to Wilson. The destination Maya had shared was only seven minutes from my office. Five minutes if I ran through a few stop signs and ignored the speed limit.

I flew out the office door, dialing Evan as I rushed down the stairs.

"Hello," he answered.

"Where you at?"

"In Davis, working."

"It's a Saturday."

"What are you doing?"

I grimaced. "Working."

"On a Saturday? What's wrong with you?"

I didn't have time to play along. "Have you heard from Maya recently?"

"Not for a few hours. Why?"

"I needed to tell her something, and I thought she might be with you. If you hear from her, have her call me."

"Okie-dokie."

I arrived at the Honda and patted my pockets in search of the keys. Nowhere. They popped into my head, though, clear as the summer day, sitting atop my desk back in the office. I cursed and sprinted back up the stairs, my body numb.

BLUD. Saturday, July 22nd. 1503hrs.

Despite the overbearing heat outside, the vampire's house was dark and cold, and it stank like something unspeakable. Maya wrinkled her nose in disgust. Behind her, the front door clicked shut. The deadbolt twisted into place, sealing her into this mausoleum.

Maya wheeled around, her entire being buzzing with nerves—excitement mixed with fear. The interior darkness limited her vision. She saw overarching details—silhouettes and angles—but not color and texture.

Chase's face was nothing more than a shadowed smear.

An ache formed in the back of Maya's throat, and a sour taste filled her mouth. She thought she might vomit.

"Do you have a phone I can use?" Maya asked, trying to keep her composure.

"Do you know who I am?" The vampire spoke as if his innards burned a fire and smoke escaped through the chimney of his throat and mouth.

"No." Maya spoke as if her voice didn't exist. She stared at the locked front door.

Where was the cop watching Chase's house? August should have warned the officer.

Chase Richards broke into a full-bellied laugh.

"Should I know who you are?" Maya asked.

"No, no, no. I'm sorry. You woke me from my sleep, and I'm a little delirious. My phone is on the kitchen counter." He gestured to an archway. "You can use it while I use the restroom."

Maya padded into the kitchen, and Chase split in the opposite direction, vanishing around the corner. His cell phone charged on the kitchen counter, as he had said.

Maya freed her cell phone from her back pocket with a trembling hand, and she called August.

"Maya!" He barked into the phone. "Are you okay?"

"Did you tell the police that I'm in here?"

"You're at the wrong address."

"What do you mean?" Maya asked, turning to the archway and staring into the empty darkness beyond.

"I don't know what address you're at, but it's not the address the police have."

"I'm in his house," Maya said, keeping her voice low. "It's him."

"You're in his house?" August asked. "You're sure?"

"Positive"

"Get out of there. Now."

"I can't."

"You can't, or you won't? What do you mean?"

"Send someone over here."

"And what, Maya? They can't break the door down unless they suspect a crime is happening."

"Tell them a crime is happening."

August remained silent for a second. "Get out of his house."

"It's not his house. It's his mother's house."

"It doesn't make a difference."

Footsteps sounded from the darkness, heading toward the kitchen.

"Send someone, quickly." Maya hung up the phone and returned it to her back pocket. She snatched Chase's phone from the charger and clicked it on just as he entered the kitchen. "It needs a password," Maya said, turning to the vampire.

"Blood," he said, cackling like a loon. "B-L-U-D." He produced a machete from behind his back and grinned something malicious.

Maya reacted as if stuck in sludge—fear the sludge that held her glued in place.

Choices Saturday, July 22nd. 1503hrs.

ALINA AND FRED SAT at the nook table. The afternoon sun shined through a window over the sink, staining the countertops bright. A family portrait hung on the wall behind Alina. It showed Armando, Clara, and Maria huddled together and grinning.

Fred studied the picture with no motive other than passing the time. Alina had taken charge of the conversation, asking questions off the top of her head as if from a pre-generated list. Fred couldn't help but feel impressed with her improvising.

When a lull in the questioning presented itself, Fred jumped on it. He cleared his throat, drawing Armando's attention to him. "Do you mind if I use your restroom?"

Armando's face twitched, and he hesitated, but after a second, he nodded. "Down the hallway to your right."

Fred nodded and splashed a carefree grin across his face. He padded toward the bathroom, leaving Alina alone with a potential—probable—murderer. They had row-sham-bowed, the best of seven, to see who stayed with Armando and who explored the house.

If Alina went in search of Jackson, she could face five golems controlled by Clara, along with Clara. If Fred split away, that left Alina alone with Armando. There wasn't really any ideal situation.

Actually, there was. They should have stayed at the office and drew up another, more sound plan. Fred had actually presented that idea to Alina.

"We don't have the time," she had said, "to collect evidence and present it to the police, wait for them to act. That could take weeks or months. Jackson can't wait that long. He needs us now. Glacia needs us now."

"There has to be an alternate method than putting you in danger," Fred said.

Alina snickered. "Oh, ye of institutionalized patriarchy. Don't worry about me."

"That's not possible." Fred tapped the desktop with his fingertip. "What about Jake?"

"What about Jake?"

"He's almost through with the police academy. He's much more equipped to handle this job than you."

"Why? Because he's a dude?"

"Because he's trained for this," Fred said.

"Nope. We can't put all his hard work, his future career, and his family in jeopardy. Jake doesn't go. Neither does Daphne. Don't even utter your wife's name."

"What about Evan? He can handle himself."

"He's in Davis for the next week, working on some bird research."

"Davis is only twenty minutes away. He can swing by after work for an hour and help me out."

Alina crossed her arms and spoke in a tone that dared Fred to refute her. "I'm doing it."

"Think about it. You're a liability. I can't leave you alone with Armando. I can't allow you to search the house by yourself."

"I can handle myself."

"You're a girl."

Alina's face shifted into a caricature of pure anger. "Fredrick Norville Rogers. I know you didn't say that." She inhaled, winding herself up to unleash a violent lecture.

"That's not what I meant," Fred said, hurrying to defend himself before Alina started.

"What did you mean, then?"

"You're a sixteen-year-old girl." It had sounded more convincing in his head.

Alina furrowed her brow.

"I'm not saying it right."

"All you're saying is that I'm a girl."

"I know what I'm saying, but it's not right."

"No, it's not right."

"I mean, it's not what I mean."

"What do you mean? That if I was a sixteen-year-old boy, you wouldn't mind me tagging along and putting myself in danger?"

"You're twisting up my intentions."

"But I'm not wrong, am I?"

"No," Fred said, lowering his gaze and staring at the floor, embarrassed by himself. "You're not wrong. It's just, I wouldn't ever forgive myself if something happened to you."

"I'll be fine. Trust me. August wouldn't have hired me full time if he didn't think I could take care of myself in the field."

"Wait... what?" Fred dug into his pocket and removed a bag of roasted walnuts. "August hired you full-time? Since when?"

"A few days ago." Alina shrugged. "The paperwork hasn't gone through yet... but he's going to pay me."

"He's not even paying me."

"You do nothing but cost a fortune in food and snacks." She stared directly at his walnuts. "Besides, go to him about it. It's not my job to console you. It's my job to solve supernatural cases, such as this golem case."

Fred quickly concluded he couldn't defeat Alina in an argument, and August would most likely take her side. So, they had to settle their debate.

Alina would distract Armando while Fred explored the home. Fred rationalized the decision, believing that at least, while left alone with Armando, she only had one person to worry about instead of six or more.

Fred now snaked his way through the house, opening every door and peaking into each room. He noticed nothing beyond the usual—beds, dressers, toilets, a desk.

Alina mentioned Armando had renovated the house. She also slapped the Google Maps printouts onto Fred's desk and forced him to study them against the original floor plan, which she had got from the county. Mentally, Fred ran through what he remembered of the images.

The garage.

They had altered the garage, making it bigger.

Fred returned to the kitchen. Alina and Armando continued their chat. He cleared his throat, interrupting them. "I realized I forgot my cell phone in the car. I'll be right back." Without waiting for a response, he walked as confidently as possible to the front door.

He hated every second of opening doors and exploring dark hallways and never knowing what the next turn might bring. If a paid position meant performing more field work, Fred would settle for his volunteer position. It's not like he needed the money, anyway.

Once he closed the front door, Fred paused and stared blankly across the street. His heart raced, and a cold sweat formed on his back, grabbed his shirt, glued it to his skin. A sickening realization settled over him.

He hadn't entered the bathroom, let alone flushed a toilet or washed his hands. Worse, he and Alina had taken an Uber to Armando's house.

What if Armando noticed that? Weren't criminals always on high alert? Didn't they have a sixth, a seventh, about fishy situations? Would Armando have noticed a toilet not flushing? Would he have noticed they didn't have a car out front?

Fred swallowed back his concern, knowing he had no other course but to continue forward. This was their one shot.

"It's like football," he mumbled. "Miss a tackle, keep playing. Keep playing."

Fred circled the garage, searching for an exterior door. He found one after hopping the gate and landing in the side yard.

Two choices.

Storm into the house and rough up Armando until he shared viable information. What if they were wrong, though? What if Armando had nothing to do with anything?

Kick down the door and trust Alina could handle the fallout.

Fred carried an imposing physique. He had played professional football for almost a decade, and though he had taken an office role and loved to snack endlessly, his explosive strength hadn't faded.

The door nearly blew off the hinges.

"Good luck," Fred said, trusting Alina to take care of herself.

The Safety. Saturday, July 22nd. 1507hrs.

A SHARP CRACK FROM the garage silenced Alina mid-question. She held her breath for a second and studied Armando's response to the sudden noise. His head darted upward, like a meerkat standing at attention.

Before too many wayward thoughts could cross his mind, Alina had to diffuse the situation. "What was that?" she asked, curious herself what Fred had done.

"I don't know." Armando rose to his feet, magnetized to the source of the crash.

"It sounded bad, didn't it?"

"I don't know." Armando moved three steps toward the garage. He stopped and glanced over his shoulder at Alina, questions cutting across his eyes. "Who are you?"

"A student doing a report?"

"He's not your dad, is he?"

"Who are you to say that? I'm adopted. So what? I can call him my dad. He raised me, and he's the only dad I've ever known."

Armando frowned and moved away from the garage, toward the front door.

Alina remained seated, leaned over, and grabbed her backpack. In it, she had stowed the gun from Maya's room. Maya didn't know she had stashed it. Fred didn't know. Hopefully, Armando didn't know, either.

"Your dad's not outside." Armando stood near the window, pulling down a blind and peeking out. "Neither is his car."

"We parked a few houses up the street," Alina said, having the excuse ready after Fred had misspoken. "The navigation led three houses past your place."

"Where is he?" Armando asked.

Alina stood from her chair and raised the gun. She advanced toward Armando, holding her breath with each small, careful step.

He turned toward her, and his hands shot into the air. "Wow. Hey. What are you doing?"

Alina pointed to the couch with the gun. "Sit down." Her voice squeaked out of her tight lips, barely escaping her mouth. The gun seemed to anchor her breath deep in her torso.

"Let's talk." Armando faded toward the couch. "What's going on?"

"Sit down." Her hands trembled, and the gun felt heavy, but she kept it aimed at his chest.

"You ever shoot one of those?"

"Do you want to risk that? Sit down."

After another few heartbeats, Armando nodded and fell back onto the couch. He stared at Alina with pure hate and fury.

"Take out your phone," Alina said.

"Will you shoot me if I don't?"

Tears stung Alina's eyes and bile rose to her mouth, but she fought them both back into her system. She had grown accustomed to holding in her pain. "Where's Jackson Armstead?"

"Who?"

"You know the name of the boy responsible for your daughter's death. Now tell me where he is."

"How would I know?"

Alina licked her lips. "Where's your wife?"

"I don't know."

Alina needed to call the cops, or August, but she wouldn't risk removing a hand from the gun to grab her phone. Both hands on the gun. She knew that much. *Keep both hands on the gun.*

"Is it even loaded?" Armando asked.

"There's one way we find out," Alina said. "I won't shoot you in cold blood, but if you come at me and I feel threatened, I won't hesitate to pull the trigger."

"In my house? You're a stranger shooting me in my house? How do you think that will go with the police?"

"I'm fine with whatever consequences I face, as long as we stop your little horror shop operation."

"What exactly do you think we're doing here?"

"Kidnapping young men and women and recreating your dead daughter."

Armando bit his lip and nodded. "Where's your dad?"

"Where's Jackson Armstead?"

"They took her from us!" Armando screamed, losing his poise. "They should sacrifice themselves to give her back to us."

Armando, quick for his age and build, lunged from his couch at Alina.

She reacted and pulled the trigger. It didn't click and fire. The trigger barely budged back at all.

Alina had left on the safety.

Armando's full weight bore into her, and he slammed her hard to the ground.

Golem Attack.
Saturday, July 22nd. 1507hrs.

Fred came to another locked door, this one at the far end of the garage. He kicked it free. Who needed a key when you had the kick of a horse?

A half-dozen steps led down a dark tunnel, which plummeted thirty feet beneath the ground.

Fred used the flashlight on his phone to guide his way. The blue light orbed outward, battling the pervading darkness around him. At the bottom of the stairs stood another door, also locked, but also a regular door.

So long as the Lopez's hadn't installed thick security doors, Fred could continue to punt each one open.

Including the two in the garage and the one at the bottom of the stairwell, Fred had splintered seven doors in total. His foot throbbed with a dull ache, and his heel spit pain whenever he put his weight on it.

As he ventured deeper and deeper, the tunnel became cruder and cruder, like something from a medieval horror movie. Wooden beams supported the hallway from collapsing, and occasionally, a spattering of dust snowed to the ground for no reason other than to nearly incite a claustrophobic, hyperventilating attack.

Fred abhorred the dark, but he feared, maybe more than monsters and heights, tight spaces. He was a big man, and navigating through the narrow, dark passageways made him more than uneasy, especially with the looming threat that his destination would have monsters waiting for him.

All three of his fears now piled into one terrible adventure.

Maybe he wouldn't ask August for a raise, but he would ask for a lifetime supply of free lunches and snacks.

He kicked the eighth door open, and he entered a blindingly bright room.

Fred squinted, allowing his eyes to adjust to the sudden light. A blurry display presented itself. As his vision cleared, he saw Clara Lopez, beautiful and terrifying all at once. Flanking her stood two golems, one far more crude than the other, which appeared nearly identical to Maria Lopez. A third golem kneeled atop a prone woman, pulling her face upward. Jackson Armstead leaned over, hands on his knees, losing his last meal.

As Fred crashed into the room, every eye—all twelve of them—settled on him.

Not knowing what to say or do, Fred provided an arced, shoulder-to-shoulder wave. "Sorry to interrupt. I was looking for the cafeteria, but this place is a dungeon. Do you know if I'm close?"

"Kill him!" Clara screeched.

The three golems acted on command like obedient dogs. Their footsteps scurried toward Fred like something from a nightmare, accompanied by a harsh wheezing.

Throughout his career of playing football, Fred had his fair share of scuffles. Competition, especially physical competition, called on violent individuals, or at least individuals unafraid to back down from a fight. Fred could hold his own against the most dominant athletes in the world.

With golems, though, Fred lost any semblance of sanity and calm.

As a golem straggled toward him, Fred reacted aggressively, mostly out of blind fear. He closed his eyes and threw a wild hook, connecting with the creature's jaw.

It dropped like a bag of sand thrown from a cliff.

A current of lightning-white pain shot up Fred's arm. He might have broken his thumb or wrist on impact.

A second golem—half Fred's size—slammed into Fred's searing-hot arm. Pain exploded up to his shoulder, and bile filled his mouth. He dropped to his knees, gripping his inflamed wrist.

"Enough!" Clara's piercing voice echoing throughout the chamber.

The golem looming over Fred backed away, and Clara came into clear view. She held a syringe in one hand, which she handed to the golem beside her. In her other hand, she wielded a menacing scalpel.

"Who are you?" Clara asked.

Fred's attention flicked beyond the woman to Jackson. He worked on the prone young lady's restraints. "What kind of sick, depraved experiment is this?" Fred asked.

"You shouldn't be here."

"I shouldn't," Fred said, full-heartedly agreeing. "My list of fears is pretty extensive, but dark, cramped dungeons, ravenous monsters, evil scientists, and dead bodies top my list. We're hitting the holy grail here, and I'm not enjoying a second of it."

"Well, things will only get worse from here."

Fred nodded, not doubting her threat. "There's a lot I'm afraid of. I was afraid of getting hurt as a kid, but my mom forced me to play football. She must have seen something special in me. Or she wanted a couple of hours with me out of the house every day. Either way, she had me confront my fears head on. Did you know I'm on the ballot for making the NFL Hall of Fame? How's that for a comeback story?"

Fred channeled Alina's spirit, knowing he had to keep talking, keep stalling. He had to keep Clara and her golems occupied. He licked his lips.

"My wife, who's incredible and so gosh-darn sexy it's not healthy for me, also pushes me to overcome my fears. She made me take this job. Said it would be good for me. Again, like my mom, I think she wanted me out of the house."

Clara pointed at Fred. "I'm tired of listening to him."

The golem holding the syringe stepped toward Fred.

"Wait!" Fred held his good hand before the creature, palm out, gesturing for it to stop. "You'll want to hear the end."

The Maria golem moved closer to Fred.

Fred inhaled and spoke quickly before it reached him, injected him with whatever poison Maria had loaded into the vial, and tore him to shreds. "My amazing wife is on the phone right now. FaceTime. She's screen recording everything. She has also notified the police. They're on their way. Probably close, if not here already."

"Then there's no reason you should live," Clara said.

"I thought you might say that," Fred said. He licked his lips. His well of creativity had dried, and he no longer had a tactic to stall. He could fight, but with his dominant hand broken, Fred doubted he would last long against two golems and Clara. Fred's head tilted to the side as a realization struck him.

There were three golems, and he had knocked out one already, leaving two. Only one harassed him, though. Where had the other gone?

Fred scanned the scene, and he saw the Maria clone sneaking up behind Clara with a surgical saw. The golem grabbed the woman's hair and pulled back, setting the serrated blade against her taut throat. Fred closed his eyes to what happened next, but he heard liquid splash against the floor, a terrible gargling, and the heavy thunk of a body landing on stone.

He slowly opened his eyes, not wanting to witness the horror laid before him.

The Maria clone held a remote control with four buttons, her finger on the uppermost one. She looked at Jackson and worked her lips into a soft smirk.

Jackson helped the young woman to her feet.

"This dial," Maria said in a man's voice, referring to the dial on the side of the control, "allows me to select which creation to shock." The golem glanced over at the cruder version of Maria and pressed down the button.

At first, nothing happened, then the golem convulsed. Blood leaked from its eyes and ears and nose and mouth, and it fell to the ground in a violent spasm.

The golem with the remote twisted the dial. She looked at the golem Fred had knocked unconscious, and she repeated the murder.

Jackson stared at her with wide, tearful eyes. "Don't do it, Ashton," he said. "They'll accept you. They will. Please, don't do it."

"Thank you," Ashton said, "for freeing me." He twisted the dial on the side of the control and pressed the button.

Jackson screamed. Fred winced and turned away.

Vampire Slayer. Saturday, July 22nd. 1507hrs.

I IMMEDIATELY SAW MAYA'S car parked across the street from the address she had shared. I pulled into the driveway, parking beside the white van, and I didn't bother to turn off my car or close the driver's door.

I sprinted to the front door. It was open, splintered, as if someone had broken it. Without caring to consider that development, focused purely on Maya, I pushed open the door.

The stench from the house bombarded my senses. I swallowed disgust, pushing forward to find Maya.

Despite the late afternoon sun, the boarded windows and shutters and blackout curtains pitched the interior into a gray darkness. I could make out forms and figures, but nothing more.

I breathed, focused on calming my nerves. I had to remain poised. Slow is smooth. Smooth is fast.

With careful, purposeful steps, I moved through the house. I first came into the kitchen and found nothing. I explored further, shouldering open each door I came to. I opened the door furthest down the hallway.

A bedroom lay behind it. A canopied bed stood in the center of the room, the drapes pulled tightly shut all around it.

I slowly inhaled and entered.

As I cleared the threshold, the door to the ensuite bathroom flew open, and a figure lunged at me, crashing into me.

Like rolling with a punch, I didn't push against his charge, but used his momentum to blunt the impact. I fell, rolled with him, and pinned myself over his body.

Without thinking, because that's how fights often go (instinct, reflex, impulse), I grabbed his collar and pulled him upward as I drove downward and head-butted him. A resounded crack split through the room.

The man groaned and went limp.

"Stop," Maya said. "August, get off of him."

I wanted to drop my elbow onto his face and break his nose or jaw, but I restrained myself. I glanced over my shoulder and saw Maya appear from the bathroom. She had her phone out, the flashlight on. The beam illuminated my attacker's face, showcasing Vermont Wendsdale. He had a nasty gash across his forehead, and blood masked his face.

I backed away from him and stood, turned to Maya. "What's going on?"

"That man saved me."

"Him?" I asked. "How?"

"Chase was going to feast on me, and he appeared from nowhere and saved my life."

I fixed my attention on the self-proclaimed vampire slayer. "Why did he attack me?"

"We heard you come in, and he didn't know if the vampire had allies."

"Other vampires," Wendsdale said. He grunted as he worked to a seated position. "Sometimes they work in pairs."

I cracked a knuckle. "Where's Chase?"

Wendsdale chuckled. "I already told you, Mr. Watson, I came to this God-forsaken city to kill the monster and save innocent lives, seeing that you're incapable of doing so. It seems you should thank me for my service."

"The bed," Maya said. She hugged herself.

I glanced at the closed canopy draped over the bed, walked over to it, and pulled it open.

Back at Home.
Sunday, July 23rd.
1431hrs.

FRED HAD HIS BROKEN wrist. His right wrist, too, which made for an entertaining time watching him doing anything at all with his left hand. He sat on the living room floor across from me, next to Daphne, with his right hand resting on her thigh.

"You should have seen me," he said, a smile wide as the Grand Canyon on his face. "I dropped that golem with one hit."

"Were your eyes closed?" Alina asked. She had a bruise on her face where Armando had struck her, but she shined with a brilliant, unmatched confidence.

"No," Fred said. "My eyes weren't closed."

I had heard Fred's rehashing already, and his story fell on the tragic side of outcomes. Not only had Clara died, but three of her golem experiments. Jackson had survived, as had the young woman Clara wished for him to murder. The police arrested Armando. He sat in a jail cell, awaiting his hearing with a few on-call guards to make sure he didn't escape their custody.

I hadn't heard Alina's side of the story yet. The police had interviewed us through most of the night. We were witness to five total deaths, after all. They needed to document our involvement in the golem and vampire cases. When they finally released us, we went our separate ways. I'm not sure if anyone had the energy to rehash our experiences.

Alina went back to Maya's and slept until the early afternoon.

"What about you?" I faced Alina, curious about her bruise and how she had escaped from Armando. "Are you okay?"

Alina rubbed the back of her head, where a goose egg had formed. "Armando charged toward me." She paused and looked at me. "I was so scared, and I pulled the trigger."

My stomach sank. Though Armando hadn't suffered a gunshot wound, I knew the weight of having to pull the trigger.

"The safety was on," Alina said. "But I pulled the trigger. What if I had killed him?"

"You didn't," Maya said. She sat on the floor, leaning her head on Evan's shoulder.

"But I pulled the trigger. Intention matters, too, doesn't it? I intended to kill him."

"You intended to protect yourself," I said. "That's all. Not only did you protect yourself, you saved Jackson Armstead's life. You saved that young woman's life." The police refused to share her name with us. "They're alive because of you."

"He tackled me," Alina said. "My head smacked against the hardwood floor, and a searing flash cut across my vision. I thought I was going to die. Desperate, I lashed out. I was terrified and desperate—no romanticism or heroism there. It was as good as closing my eyes and swinging, getting lucky and connecting with his chin." She stared wide-eyed at Fred.

"What? I didn't close my eyes," Fred said.

"You can't convince me otherwise." Alina giggled. "Anyway, I slammed the butt of the gun into his face. He ripped it from my grip, turned it around, and shoved the barrel against my cheek." Alina touched the bruise on her face. "That's when it happened."

Stefan, one of Vermont Wendsdale's cronies, had burst into the living room and surprised Armando with knuckledusters to the temple. He dropped unconscious.

Apparently, according to Wendsdale, he ordered Stefan to follow Alina, and Arthur (another of his henchmen) followed Maya. Wendsdale tailed me. Arthur phoned Wendsdale about Maya arriving at a boarded-up house alone. Wendsdale abandoned stalking me and raced to Maya, antsy to slay the vampire. Stefan hadn't called Wendsdale, but had acted of his own will after witnessing Armando spear Alina to the ground.

"Have you spoken to Jackson or Cecilia?" Alina asked.

"No." I doubted I ever would. What would I say to them? I would have Fred invoice Cecilia, but I didn't need to speak to her. That was their business, not mine. My business was solving the case and securing a meeting with Quinn.

"What about the vampire?" Fred asked.

My body went frigid, and I glanced at Maya.

She snuggled tighter against Evan, and a pang of jealousy shot through my heart. "He suffered a physical disorder known as Gunther's disease, and a mental disorder known as Renfield's syndrome. He believed, because of his bodily disorders, that he needed blood to live."

I cracked a knuckle. "Did you ever figure out the address dilemma?"

Maya nodded. "The police went to the address on his driver's license. I'm not sure if that was his personal address, his father's address, his childhood address... I don't know yet. I went to the address his mother provided when she signed him into a mental health facility during his teenage years. I didn't know another address existed."

"How did it happen?" Fred asked. "How did he die?"

"Pierced through the heart." Maya chuckled. "Accidental, ironically enough. He had a machete, and when he and Wendsdale wrestled, the vampire fell right on the blade."

"So we'll never know if he was an actual vampire or not," Alina said, glancing at Fred. "They could still exist."

"Well, Wilson got the collar and is a local hero right now," I said. "He deserved it, too, after the mess Madden left for him."

"He wasn't a vampire," Fred said.

"You know that for sure?" Alina asked.

Fred bit his lip and glanced at me, as if begging me to disprove Alina's suggestion.

I ignored him and looked at Maya, though I spoke to the group. "They found his mom's bloodless corpse in the house, lying in a bed. Autopsy hasn't come back, but they're guessing she's been there for over a year, at least."

"And Wendsdale?" Alina asked.

"Gone," I said, thinking back to the moment. I had opened the drapes canopying the bed, and I saw Chase lying facedown in blood-soaked sheets and the machete's tip rising from his back. Muffled footsteps moved from the bedroom. I closed my eyes and allowed Wendsdale to leave.

Silence reigned for a few seconds. Bagley barked as he and Gerald played on the other side of the living room, outside of our powwow. We all had a lot on our minds, I'm sure—I did—but nothing to say.

Alina broke the spell. "I'm going to a magic show with my dad tomorrow."

"What?" Maya asked, bolting upright off Evan's shoulder. "Why?"

"He asked me to. I said no at first, but after what we've gone through—what I went through... I don't know. I feel like I should go."

"A magic show?" Fred asked.

"I used to really love magic," Alina said. "I knew a few tricks, too. That's another reason I want to go. He doesn't know me anymore, but he's trying. He asked me to go, knowing I might still enjoy it. I think that means something, right?"

"I think so," I said.

Time went on, and the afternoon turned into evening.

Daphne busied herself in the kitchen, preparing a celebratory dinner. The rest of us remained in the living room, hanging out and enjoying each other's company.

Wilson called, and I excused myself and walked to the back patio. "Congratulations, Mr. Big Shot Detective."

He chuckled. "I owe you all the credit."

"Funny, it didn't seem like that when you had a dozen microphones in front of your face."

"Yeah, well, you know how it goes. People need confidence in their police force, not their fringe investigators."

"Yeah, yeah. What's going on?"

Wilson cleared his throat. "They're gone."

I scrunched my face. "What do you mean?"

"Armando Lopez and Jackson Armstead."

I reached out and grabbed the wall for support. "What do you mean?"

"Not at home. Not at the hospital. Not in jail. Vanished, like all the other people connected to your cases."

"How is that possible?"

"I think you should tell me."

My phone chirped as another call came in. I pulled it away from my ear. Unknown Caller. "Wilson," I said. "I have to go."

"August, what do you know about this? Let me help you. If you're in trouble, let me help you. If you have something to do with this, tell me now."

I hung up on him and switched the line. "I solved the cases. When and where?"

"Tomorrow night. 2300hrs. The Old Town parking lot."

Disappearing Act. Monday, July 24th. 1847hrs.

ALINA RODE IN THE passenger seat of her father's beat-up old Chevrolet truck. He had owned it before she was born, and he would until it sputtered out and died on him. The familiar stench of acrid cigarette smoke, dust, and fart absorbed into the upholstery strangely calmed her. She felt like a little girl again, blind to the dangers of the world. Everything she saw was bright and beautiful, most of all her father.

He would never hurt her. He would never become ugly.

Except innocence is a fragile thing, and it takes little to shatter the illusion.

It was more than her father driving his stinky, cracked-windshield, dirty truck, though. It was the promise of their destination. A magic show.

Stephen, when he had a few spare dollars after purchasing the necessities—booze, pills, girls—always took Alina to magic shows. They would laugh at the corny jokes and ooh and ahh at the unexplainable feats. On the drive home, Alina would pepper her dad with questions, mostly pertaining to, "How did he do that?"

He always offered the same single-worded, simple response. *Magic.*

Stephen gripped the steering wheel hard now, hard enough to whiten his knuckles. He clenched his jaw, and his entire face seemed to smash into a single wrinkle.

Alina wondered what had him stressed, but she didn't ask. Her mind filled in the blanks—a dangerous exercise for an imaginative teenager, to allow her suspicions to paint the picture.

Stephen wanted custody of his daughter, for whatever reason, considering he had never cared to care for her before. This outing may well prove his only chance at making a decent impression, at securing a wedge into the battle between him and Wanda.

Alina predicted his stress hinged on absolving all his wrongs in one outing.

Stephen turned into the marina's parking lot on the Sacramento River. The magic show took place in a riverboat. They walked up the boat's ramp.

A few dozen people already had cocktails and appetizers, and they sat at tables surrounding the stage. Their conversations rose like a colony of bees.

According to the itinerary, the riverboat departed at 1900hrs; they served dinner around 1930hrs, and the magician stepped onto the stage shortly thereafter.

Alina and her father found their assigned table. Stephen pulled the chair for his daughter, and she took a seat. Six other people circled the table. An elderly couple dressed for a ball thrown by J. Gatsby, not a riverboat magic show, and a family of four—a middle-aged mother and father (both attractive) and their two kids—the boy eight or nine, the girl Alina's age.

"Evening," Stephen said as he scooted his chair nearer to the table and unfolded the cloth napkin onto his lap.

The elderly man smiled and nodded at Stephen, then he leaned to the side and whispered something to his wife, never removing his reptilian eyes from Alina.

She suddenly wanted nothing more than to leave and return to Maya and her mom. Call it a sixth sense or instinct, but Alina felt nervous about drifting to the middle of the river, stuck on the riverboat with her father and four dozen strangers.

"You okay?" Stephen asked, placing his hand on her wrist.

Alina flinched, startled by her father's voice and touch. She had zoned out, losing herself in thought. "I think I want to go home," she said.

He licked his lips. "Was it something I did?"

"No."

"Why do you want to go home?"

She couldn't explain it. How did she say something felt wrong? How did she say the world no longer seemed bright and beautiful? How did she say life had stripped away her innocence, and the single answer—magic—had lost its charm and power?

"I don't feel comfortable."

"Is it me?"

Maybe, Alina thought. "No. It's... I'm too old for magic shows. Magic isn't real."

They couldn't go home, though. Alina knew it as well as her father. The riverboat had departed a minute or two ago, signaling their departure with a loud blast of its horn. Maybe that's why she felt so nervous. She drifted away with no support other than her father. Her unreliable, unsupportive father.

"I thought you would like this," Stephen said.

"I need to use the bathroom." Alina jolted from her chair and sprinted to the women's restroom.

She locked herself in a stall and sat on the toilet with her pants on, breathing through a wave of sobs. Once she had herself under control, she removed her phone and scrolled to August's (not her mom's and not Maya's) contact.

Riverboat on the American River. She paused and fluttered her eyes, pushing back tears. *For a magic show. With my dad. I'm...*

She stopped typing and stared at the ceiling. She almost erased the message, put her phone in her pocket, and returned to the table. Instead, she typed the last word.

Scared.

Sent.

Alina remained in the restroom for a few more minutes, thinking of how the entire situation felt so strange, like one of those horror movies where there's a few esteemed guests invited to a dinner party, but the dinner party is nothing more than a trap.

"You're paranoid," Alina said. She spoke aloud to get out of her head and ground herself in reality. "You've seen too many scary movies. You've solved too many scary cases. Your dad has wronged you too many times. It's a terrible combination, and it's all working against you. That's it." She inhaled, exhaled by saying, "That's it," on repeat until her nerves settled.

Alina returned to the dinner table and sat beside her father. She smiled at him. "I'm sorry."

"Are you okay?"

Her eyes drifted around the table. The old man and his waxy-skinned wife stared at Alina with predatory eyes. The children at the table were silent and statuesque. They stared at Alina, as did the parents.

Alina shied her eyes away and peered at the stage where the magician would perform his act.

"You okay?" Stephen asked again.

Alina nodded.

They ate dinner (steak, potatoes, and grilled vegetables, all prepared to perfection). Dessert was even better. As much as Alina enjoyed the food, she thought Daphne could have improved every dish.

The thought of Daphne stenciled a smile across Alina's face. Daphne and her incredible food, married to Fred, August's oldest friend. August had changed Alina's life. He had given her a family, an actual family who cared for her and loved her.

Why had she entertained this adventure with her father when she could have stayed at home and hung out with her actual family?

As they finished their dessert, the magician made his way onto the stage. He was a short, pudgy man wearing an ill-fitting tuxedo and a top hat. As he made center stage, he bowed to the crowd.

"Hello, hello, hello!" He said, each successive hello getting louder. "I'm Iniduoh, or Houdini backwards. I'm not an escape artist like the master. Instead, I've mastered the art, the magic, of disappearance." He snapped a finger. "But that's not all I do. For example." The man performed a series of simple tricks. He pulled flowers from his sleeve and a never-ending string of handkerchiefs from his pocket, and he executed a few card tricks.

He directed the first part of his act at the children in the audience. With their big, mesmerized eyes, they would turn to their parents after every trick.

Alina remembered when she used to look at her father with that same expression.

"How did he do it?"

The parents, excited to see their kids excited, also bought into the show. "Magic."

They kept the illusion alive. Why not? What did it hurt?

Everything.

Illusions are nothing but complicated lies.

After forty-five minutes, Iniduoh scanned the crowd. "It's time for my last trick. I need help, though. Do I see anyone who might like to volunteer?"

Arms shot into the air, waving with anticipation.

The magician narrowed his eyes and scrunched his mouth as if contemplating who to choose. After a few seconds, he pointed at Alina. "What's your name?"

"Not volunteering," Alina said.

"Quite a specific and unique name."

The crowd chuckled.

"Alina," Stephen said, answering the magician's question.

"Ah, Alina. That's a beautiful name. Do you care to volunteer?"

"I care not to."

Stephen cleared his throat, leaned in, and whispered to his daughter. "What are you doing? He's asking you to volunteer."

"And I refused. You volunteer."

Stephen's familiar fury filled his eyes. "You're going up on that stage."

"Will you drag me up there, because I'm not walking up there?"

"Alina, do what I say."

She shrugged. "No."

"Alina, I brought you all the way out here, tipped the magician to select you. Now go up there."

Alina chuckled, realizing why her father was so insistent. She looked across the table at the other girl about her age. "She has her hand up. Why can't she head up there and have her fun?"

Every person in the room stared at Alina and her father. Her skin burned, and she wanted to dart away and return home. She didn't want to stand in front of the crowd. Not that crowd, with their wet, hungry eyes.

"Alina," the magician said. "You care to help me?"

Stephen stared at his daughter with wide, scared eyes. "Please, Alina. Do it for me."

Alina snickered, and a smile stuck to her face. She couldn't have shaken it off if she tried. "For you? Sure. Why not, Daddy-O. Let me do it for you, the same way you've always done so much for me." Alina leaned back in her chair and crossed her arms. "By doing absolutely nothing."

The magician, probably having exhausted the worth of Stephen's tip, shifted his gaze to the other girl sitting at Alina's table. "What about you, young lady? What's your name?"

She rose from her chair with a shy smile and said, "Samantha."

"Well, Sammy—may I call you Sammy?"

"That's what everyone calls me."

"Perfect, head on up here."

Samantha ambled toward the stage, and the crowd applauded her bravery. Once on the stage, the magician directed her to a coffin, which stood on its end.

"Now, as you can see," he said, raising his voice for the audience to hear him, "there's no trick door. Sammy, do you mind trying to open the back of the coffin?"

She pushed on the bottom panel, but it didn't budge.

"Is there a door there?"

"No," she said.

"I don't know Sammy," the magician said. "I've never met her in my life. She has no reason to lie on my behalf." He turned to her. "Could you step inside the coffin for me?"

Sammy followed his instruction, moving as if walking on the bottom of the ocean floor. She stepped into the coffin.

Iniduoh faced the crowd. "You see how narrow-backed the space is? There's no room for a false door to hide her. Is that right, Sammy?"

The coffin appeared cramped—almost unnaturally cramped, as if the magician had stuffed a smaller coffin into a normal-sized coffin, like a nest of Russian dolls. "That's right," Sammy said.

"Well, there you have it, ladies and gentlemen. No gimmicks. Just plain... magic." Iniduoh grabbed the open lid. "You ready, Sammy?"

"Yes," she said.

Iniduoh closed the lid.

Alina bit her nails until she tasted blood.

After a handful of seconds, Iniduoh dragged the lid open.

As promised, Samantha had vanished.

The crowd hooted and applauded. Iniduoh closed the lid once more, spoke a few nonsensical words, and slid it open again. Much to his and the audience's surprise, Samantha hadn't returned to the coffin. The magician tried again, and again, but Samantha had vanished.

The Meeting. Monday, July 24th. 2300hrs.

I arrived at the parking garage early, about an hour early, and I patrolled the vicinity for anything suspicious, for anything that might signal me to Quinn. I preferred to confront him on my terms, not his, but my attempt to earn the upper hand proved futile.

The hour of surveillance passed with nothing fruitful occurring.

I parked, stepped from my car, and leaned against the trunk. I held my phone in my hand, waiting for it to ring as I scoured the low-lit garage for anyone approaching.

Right on time, a windowless van—one nearly identical to Chase Richards' van—pulled up and stopped in the middle of the ramp directly before me. Feet touched the ground on the driver's side, opposite from where I waited. A second later, the man who referred to himself as Daniel Quinn rounded the hood. He paused a few feet away from me, wearing a maniacal smile across his chiseled, handsome face.

"August Watson," he said. "We finally meet again."

The End

More Books by Alex Gates

Dorian Miller, a private detective specializing in the supernatural, investigates a blackmail conspiracy involving the daughter of one of Sacramento's elite families who partook in a satanic ritual.

But the simple assignment soon turns un-deadly.

Zombies and golems rise around the city. The corpses of vampires are found slaughtered in a horrific manner. And rumors warn that a

Revenant—the spirit of a dead Necromancer summoned back to this world—stands behind all the mayhem.

How much longer can Dorian run from Death before it catches up to him?

Once struggling to make rent, Skylar must now use her budding magic to save the world...

As a child of abuse, Skylar Neveah knows desperation and terror from first-hand experience. But nothing in her past prepared her for a date ending with her getting sacrificed to a fallen angel. By blind luck and a touch of magic, Skylar escaped with her life. To do so, she murdered two wealthy, influential men.

On the run from the police and the supernatural world, a man approaches Skylar. He offers her refuge at a secret university for humans like her with magical powers. She hesitantly accepts his offer. But her problems aren't solved... far from it.

A cosmic war has kicked off. Somehow, Skylar landed in the middle of it. And the fallen angel has fixed his attention on her. He will stop at nothing to see her killed. Will Skylar stop running, learn to control her magic, and fight back?

Other Books by Steve Higgs

The paranormal? It's all nonsense but proving it might just get them all killed.

When a master vampire starts killing people in his hometown, paranormal investigator, Tempest Michaels, takes it personally ...... and soon a race against time turns into a battle for his life. He doesn't believe in the paranormal but has a steady stream of clients with cases too weird for the police to bother with.

Mostly it's all nonsense, but when a third victim turns up with bite marks in her lifeless throat, can he really dismiss the possibility that this time the monster is real?

Joined by an ex-army buddy, a disillusioned cop, his friends from the pub, his dogs, and his mother (why are there no grandchildren, Tempest), our paranormal investigator is going to stop the murders if it kills him ...... but when his probing draws the creature's attention, his family and friends become the hunted.

Today's tasks:

1. Escape from underground cell

2. Recruit snarky d-bag werewolf to help

3. Invade demon realm and rescue a girl

For wizard detective, Otto Schneider, magic has always kept him out of trouble. Now it's working in reverse ...... and he's just started the fight of his life. There's an ancient secret buried in the Earth's past and he just uncovered it.

UNDEAD DREAD

Magical beings once ruled over us until their betrayed leader made a death curse with his final breath. Banished from the realm of man for over four thousand years, the curse is weakening, and these beings, these ... demons, are coming back to rule the Earth once more.

They are powerful, immortal, and unstoppable, but they don't know everything.

They left some of their magic behind and their return has sparked an awakening.

Heroes will rise ...

Free Books and More

Want to know where all the books came from? How Steve Higgs writes and what his life is like? Want some FREE books in your inbox? Sign up to the author's newsletter to get sneak peaks, exclusive give-aways, behind the scenes content, and more. Plus, you'll be notified of Fan Pricing events when they occur and get exclusive offers from other authors because all writers are automatically friends.

Click the link below or copy it carefully into your browser to sign up for FREE.

https://mailchi.mp/fd47a6eb4ae5/patricialist

Want to follow me on Facebook?

Join me on Facebook by clicking the link below or by copying the link into your browser.

https://www.facebook.com/groups/1151907108277718

More Books By Steve Higgs

Blue Moon Investigations
Paranormal Nonsense
The Phantom of Barker Mill
Amanda Harper Paranormal Detective
The Klowns of Kent
Dead Pirates of Cawsand
In the Doodoo With Voodoo
The Witches of East Malling
Crop Circles, Cows and Crazy Aliens
Whispers in the Rigging
Bloodlust Blonde – a short story
Paws of the Yeti
Under a Blue Moon – A Paranormal
Detective Origin Story
Night Work
Lord Hale's Monster
The Herne Bay Howlers
Undead Incorporated
The Ghoul of Christmas Past
The Sandman
Jailhouse Golem
Shadow in the Mine
Ghost Writer

Felicity Philips Investigates
To Love and to Perish
Tying the Noose
Aisle Kill Him
A Dress to Die For
Wedding Ceremony Woes

Patricia Fisher Cruise Mysteries
The Missing Sapphire of Zangrabar
The Kidnapped Bride
The Director's Cut
The Couple in Cabin 2124
Doctor Death
Murder on the Dancefloor
Mission for the Maharaja
A Sleuth and her Dachshund in Athens
The Maltese Parrot
No Place Like Home

Patricia Fisher Mystery Adventures
What Sam Knew
Solstice Goat
Recipe for Murder
A Banshee and a Bookshop
Diamonds, Dinner Jackets, and Death
Frozen Vengeance
Mug Shot
The Godmother
Murder is an Artform
Wonderful Weddings and Deadly
Divorces
Dangerous Creatures

Patricia Fisher: Ship's Detective Series
The Ship's Detective
Fitness Can Kill
Death by Pirates
First Dig Two Graves

Albert Smith Culinary Capers
Pork Pie Pandemonium
Bakewell Tart Bludgeoning
Stilton Slaughter
Bedfordshire Clanger Calamity
Death of a Yorkshire Pudding
Cumberland Sausage Shocker
Arbroath Smokie Slaying
Dundee Cake Dispatch
Lancashire Hotpot Peril
Blackpool Rock Bloodshed
Kent Coast Oyster Obliteration
Eton Mess Massacre
Cornish Pasty Conspiracy

Realm of False Gods
Untethered magic
Unleashed Magic
Early Shift
Damaged but Powerful
Demon Bound
Familiar Territory
The Armour of God
Live and Die by Magic
Terrible Secrets

About the Authors

Alex and Steve met online through their mutual love of urban fantasy. Both established writers with their own successful series, they chose to collaborate on a spin-off of Steve's Blue Moon Investigation stories.

They duo hope to meet in person one day when pandemics and other global dramas allow, but one of them will need to cross the Atlantic first. Until then, they will continue to churn out thrilling fantasy tales.

Read on and enjoy.

www.ingramcontent.com/pod-product-compliance
Lightning Source LLC
Chambersburg PA
CBHW070338170726
48291CB00001B/97